BORN
BARRON

BORN BARRON

CRYSTAL C. KANE

Designed by Susan Turner

Cover image: YAY Media AS / Alamy Stock Photo

Library of Congress Control Number: 2021915279
ISBN: 978-1-951568-16-0

SMALL
BATCH
BOOKS

493 SOUTH PLEASANT STREET

AMHERST, MASSACHUSETTS 01002

413.230.3943

SMALLBATCHBOOKS.COM

To all the fabulous weirdies of my life, who have taught me to listen,
laugh, travel, talk to strangers, eat cake for no reason,
drink champagne because there's always something to celebrate, and
to never judge because we all have something in common.
Finding it is the fun of this crazy life.

And for Lily, who comes from a long line of independent women.
My only goal is to raise you to be happy, brave, and kind.
Always honey over vinegar!

CONTENTS

Pajama Coma

I wake up from the feeling of being burned. Goose bumps litter my skin, every tiny one prickling in pain. My heart is beating uncontrollably fast and I don't know how to slow it. I reach for my chest, and my fingers follow the waves of a sopping wet shirt that moves up and down with each rapid breath.

I use both hands to peel the shirt from my throat, but it sticks with my own sweat made glue. I weakly rip and yank at the neckline until it reaches my cleavage. The fresh air and newly exposed skin marry, and in this moment, the painful little pinpricks and burning sensation cease.

The inflamed bumps of skin smooth over and absorb back inside my body like a turtle retreating into its shell. I take a deep, full breath and then another, and another, grateful for the power of fresh air.

Feeling freed from the fiery, sauna-like suffocation, I worry less about the still-throbbing discomfort and more about my where-abouts. My head is pounding so badly, only one eye opens to see. I push fingers into the cushions, raising my head in hopes the body will follow, but dizziness overcomes me and I fall backward into a slump of misshapen pillows. I close an eye and try to kick the scorching hot covers off my legs. The couch and still-present achi-ness triumph and I lie back, giving in to its squishy defeat.

Just as I come to terms with the hell I am feeling, a new hurdle arises as I hear a loud futzing of noises around me. It's a throbbing echo of opening and closing of drawers and clanging of dishes. I want to scream at the inconvenience of so many sounds, but instead I curl into my damp shirt, pulling and twisting at the collar in frustration. I internally blame this person for the additional mis-ery that they're causing but realize that most of what I'm feeling is, no doubt, self-inflicted.

"Jake?" I call out, pondering a guess that it's a familiar and not a stranger. No one answers. I call again, but my voice is high and streaky. Sounding unattractive and severely dehydrated, I recoil back to the safety of the couch and my shirt. Thoroughly annoyed by the now-reminiscent noises and lack of response, I let a minute or two pass and call for him again. I wonder if he can hear me or if it's only the hush of morning air coming from my mouth?

Everything hurts, from my hair to my toes, and the energy exerted to call for reassurance is causing more frustration than fruition. Just as I am about to give up for good and fall back into the quicksand of cushions, an outline appears. Jake. My husband. He's approaching with caution, slowly and methodically, as if I were an injured cub. I flinch at his presence; I'm still in extreme pain and worry he might try to touch me.

He sits down on the far edge of the couch, a safe distance away, and I lie there, waiting for him to speak. His voice is soft and paternal.

"How are you feeling?"

I can't help but squint from the light and stinging pain. I try to show interest and even make direct eye contact, but it's blurry and uncomfortable. He doesn't seem to notice my efforts and, seemingly concerned, dives into conversation whether I'm connected or not.

"You gave me one serious scare! What the hell happened to you?"

Huh? I wonder to myself. I can't recollect either. I lie and listen to all of his questions, but his nervous tone and awkward pauses force me to respond.

Just as I am about to approach the English language for the third time this morning and defend my current state with the little strength I have, he throws me off guard and hands me a familiar mug. Suddenly, any doubts of my whereabouts or worries of last night's indignities vanish like a fart. An equal mixture of sadness and relief come over me as I realize that I'm home, inside our tiny apartment, and not somewhere else, anywhere else. I hug the safety of the pillow and reacquaint myself with the sparsely filled walls and floors, furnished by tag sale and thrift store finds from the fancy side of town. The tips of my fingers twirl around the chipped Williams Sonoma cup as I move my lips to the opposing side, avoiding the exposed ceramic shard. I dig my hot toes into a crease of the fuzzy, shit-colored couch and settle in for what will be a long, disciplinary talk. We've been through this drill before.

The haze is clearing, and my first thought is, Where are my pills? Jake continues to blabber on, but I've stopped listening. My attention is on the floor, where I scan across the room and under the table for my purse. Jake unknowingly blocks the view with his wide, round shoulders, waiting for me to respond to all of his inquiries.

I wish he would stop talking. His voice is a constant reminder of our crappy life inside this little box we call home. We've lived within these walls ever since I left my past life and our town hall marriage was officiated. I did the best I could at decorating, always riding on the coattails of the Richies and their ever-changing style, their decorators constantly searching for new tastes and what's hip and pricey—and sometimes damn ugly. All that turnover leaves high-end secondhand merch for people like me. I am more than happy to have last year's name-brand hand-me-downs. Unlike those of my childhood, they would always be clean and appreciated. Looking around, I'm reminded that no matter what designer names I fill this place with, it's only a silk blanket over a damp diaper. The desperation to be something we're not oozes from the apartment's pores.

I thank the lumpy, second- or third-hand Ethan Allen couch cushions for holding me up as I peek around Jake's slumped frame to locate my purse. He won't move without prompting, so I take an oversized gulp from the smooth side of the cream-colored Christmas cup and purposely begin to choke. As predicted, his lumbering body moves to whack me in the back, and I hack a few cheap coughs. Feeling satisfied that he's stopped the fit, he jumps at the chance to fill my cup with more water.

As he walks away, I shiver in pain, feeling both hot and cold at the same time. My entire body tears with sweat, and the coughing fit has made every fiber of my being dance to the tune of agony. I can barely stand another second of sickness, and just as I am about to scream defeat, I see a light at the end of the miserable tunnel in which I live. My purse is in view. Pills! The only thing that can end my suffering is an arm's length away. The oversized, floppy sack is wedged between the coffee table and the mismatched recliner. I reach hard and with every ounce of strength inside me try and grab the strap, but the blanket is tangled between my legs, causing me to fall over myself and land hard on the floor. I don't care how much the fall hurts or how many new bruises I've earned because I'm finally in reach. The search for my favorite amber-colored bottle of swallowable secrets is over. I pull apart the purse's magnetic snap opening and feel around, but nothing cylindrical surfaces.

My frustrated fingers carefully molest the sides, bottom, and top of the purse but they aren't inside. Jake is heading back, full mug in hand. Panic overtakes me as he enters my space. What the fuck, where could they be? I need to find them to feel better, and Jake won't leave me alone.

He reaches out his hand to help me back on the couch, never asking why I'm on the floor, and continues with yesterday's news. I can barely hear him because my swirling brain is consumed by thoughts of my lost medication and where it could be.

"When I got home from my shift last night, I found you passed out on the couch with *The Golden Girls* blasting on the television. I tried to wake you, but you didn't budge, so I covered you up and went to bed. I didn't think it was a big deal, but when I woke up this morning and realized you never came in, I was kind of worried. Oh, and the freaking cell phone kept going off in the middle of the night, but I was too wiped to answer."

He moves closer to me, feeling confident to come forward, and with his kind eyes and their long lashes continues the famous Jake inquisition.

"Are you alright? What happened to you? You're seriously scaring me, Shane. This isn't the first time I couldn't wake you for bed. Is it work? Are you that tired? What's going on? Just tell me."

As the worried words exit his mouth, I begin the internal process of piecing the forgotten night's puzzle back together. Poor Jake. He really doesn't know anything about me, but his concerning ways are a cute type of pathetic chivalry and are appreciated.

The Night Before: Puzzle Pieces and Pills

The shift at the bar last night was miserable. Some of my older and now surprisingly successful friends from high school came in for a visit, forcing me to serve them like the bar wench I am. Who knew trashy was the new trendy?

Melissa, a lonely and ugly Puritan in high school, strutted in like a modern-day slut sporting a tie-dyed miniskirt and a well-dressed man, whom she constantly referred to as her fiancé. He was over-the-top obnoxious, ordering the sticky-with-dust, top-shelf liquor for their Manhattans and Tom Collinses and flashing fifties like a low-level coke dealer. Not having any clue how to make their snazzy-named cocktails, I threw a bunch of alcohol into a glass with ice, shook it, and finished with a lime or fluorescent pink cherry for garnish. The regulars got a kick out of watching my fake concoctions come to life and laughed when I changed the recipe each time. The eventually very drunk group from my past didn't seem to mind, and if they did, they never said a word about it. Dumb shits.

I chuckled to myself each time Melissa's increasingly idiotic and buzzed fiancé stared at my breasts. Whenever she was pre-occupied or chatting with girlfriends, he went all staring contest with my boobs. Bending down to get cocktail ice was a lot more fun than usual, knowing that she hadn't a clue her scumbag pre-hubby was getting hard from watching me. Poor thing had no idea she'd end up like every other sad housewife in the Richies club. I assume she was just happy to be out of her house and, for the first time in her adult life, around a guy with a little bit of money. Just like me, she was born white trash and fell for the first guy who took her away from our hometown. The only difference is that she was smart enough to pick a man with some cash.

After hours of ordering ridiculous drinks and loud behavior, I pretended to care with goodbye hugs and cheek kisses as they left, trashed and laughing out the door.

As soon as they were gone, I went to the back room and wiped my imploding tears with rough, brown paper towels. Their success and happiness were equal to my pathetic life and what I've made of it. I hated them for being able to go out just to have fun.

The night dragged on and I continued to work, but I couldn't stop thinking about them. My mind raced with a mixture of sadness, regret, and nostalgia, reminiscing about the past five years since high school. I came to the conclusion that being born to fail isn't as disappointing when you actually do, and I moved on.

My favorite regulars helped me close up, with our usual routine of checking knobs and switches, rechecking locked doors, and finally waving goodbye with reciprocal "goodnights" slurred back to me.

I crushed two pills between my molars and swallowed some old water from a half-empty bottle that was rolling around the front seat of my car. I made the ten-minute trek home, where another monotonous night awaited me, stripping off my smoke-drenched clothes at the door and falling asleep on the couch, only to be awoken by Jake when his shifts were either beginning or ending. Rewarding myself for having had such a terrible evening of feeling sorry for myself, I took two more of the Tic Tac–shaped pain reducers when I got to the apartment. I always feel better about life when I'm not feeling it at all.

As routine would have it, I found myself lying on the lumpy brown couch in a euphoric and slightly-happier-about-life haze, flicking through the channels until I must have dozed off.

Still III

I'm not listening to anything Jake is saying. Scanning the rest of the room for pills is my only priority. I need to find them, swallow them, and end this misery I'm feeling without them inside me. Where the hell could they be? A growing fear that I've lost them is settling in, and I prickle in pain from anxiety. Thoughts of begging my doctor for an early refill or an unnecessary emergency visit for phantom pains rush through my head as viable options. I push on the scratchy cushions for support and stand up without falling to begin a more serious search. I'm successfully upright but feeling soggy and downright sick. I need to find the snowcapped bottle of my sweet little meds so I can feel well. The rest of the world can wait.

I stagger toward our bedroom but Jake stops me, catching his hand on my arm. He won't stop until he gets the answer he wants to hear. His begging eyes and tight grip force me to confront his inevitable questions. I casually wipe the sweat from my hairline into my bangs and tell Jake *my* recollection of last night—not the real one, but the one he wants to hear.

"I'm really okay, I just want to get to the bathroom." His eyes squint with frustration. I continue the charade to appease his annoying worry. "When I was at work, I felt sick, like a cold or something, so when I got home, I took some of that cough medicine your mom gave you and I must have fallen asleep. I'm sorry I never made it to bed. That gross green stuff must've knocked me out."

"Jesus, Shane, that shit has been in there since we moved here. You're lucky you didn't die or something. I meant to throw that crap away a couple years ago. God, I'm wicked sorry, Shane."

I go on to explain just how sick I feel and tug at my sweat-drenched jammies as proof. He hooks my clammy moist arm around his and leads me to the closet-size bathroom and starts the shower. I'm perfectly fine with his stupid guilt and this liquid green lie if it means he'll leave me alone so I can find my fucking pills.

I peel sticky clothes from my skin, climb inside the shallow tub, and close the pink-mildew-covered curtain. The hot water stings but it hurts too much to cry.

"Are we okay?"

What the bejeebers is he talking about now? I thought the run of the water meant he was satisfied and the talk was over. He's still silently standing outside the tub, and I open my mouth to beg for privacy, when I spot a glossy gold luster peeking out from underneath the folded green towel we use for our mat. I've found them! Joy overcomes me and I speak cheerfully and upbeat. "Jake, I'm already feeling better. I just need some privacy, please."

The door closes. I smile outwardly at the win and climb halfway over the blue porcelain tub and pick up the bottle as water pours to the floor. I step back inside the tub and place two lovely little pills in my damp palm. I chew them both with the hot water that's pouring down my face and lick the residue from my hand. Immediate relief rains over me, knowing that all of my miserable symptoms will soon disappear.

In only a few minutes or so the magic beans will take effect and Jake can talk about whatever the hell he pleases. Come on first minute, I am counting on you. As I daydream about how good I will soon feel, Jake knocks on the door. I swallow hot water and answer with a gargled "What's up?"

"Nothing. I just want to make sure you're okay. I don't want to leave knowing that you're sick. I'm worried, that's all."

Jake is a notorious hoverer. I am not.

He's mellow in nature and hates any type of conflict. His favorite line (which nauseates me) is "I'm a lover not a fighter," and he enjoys discussing every single detail of an issue until he's taken it apart into microscopic pieces and put it back together. I prefer to steamroll over things and keep the monotony plugging along. I do appreciate knowing he will never lash out or be anything but kind to me. A shrink would probably say this is the reason I married a mere stranger the first chance I got. I know one thing for sure, I don't want to end up like my mother. An emotional shell of a woman destroyed by a man she could never have.

"May I finish my shower and change? I'll be out in a minute. Please, Jake?" I beg like a whiny toddler for a few minutes of space. The crushed pills are taking effect with the accuracy of a Swiss watch. My head clears, the prickles disappear, and a lovely lightheadedness takes over my thoughts. I step onto the soaking wet mat and cover my bottle and body with a robe. I see Jake's feet away in the kitchen so I shut the door to our bedroom, hiding the bottle inside a box of tampons inside my dresser. Soon I will match the purse to the pills and they will be back together where they belong.

Choking on Truth and Brown Bread

I hook a nude bra, slip on a long B-concert T-shirt, and pull on a white thong and a pair of striped leggings. A welcome addition of Fancy Ladies' hand-me-downs. Feeling an infinite amount better, I walk into our open living room–kitchen combo and insincerely thank Jake for curing all my ailments by turning on a faucet. "Thanks, Jakey, that shower really helped. I feel so much better."

I grab the mug he's already filled with coffee and sit on the far arm of the couch, letting one leg hang off the side so I don't appear too comfortable, in hopes of avoiding more conversation. A snarly glance from growling eyes proves he knows all my tricks. Despite my somewhat clever physical objection to long talks, he dives headfirst into our relationship issues.

"Shaney, I can tell you're not happy. You've been sick a lot lately, and I don't know if you're just exhausted or . . . what's going on? I know you don't like it here, but I really do, and I have no plans to move. This is our home. Yeah, it's not a mansion, but it's our place, and when you finish school and things get easier for us, it will get better, I promise. I'm truly sorry I can't afford to buy you all the material stuff you dream about, but that's not *our* life. We aren't rich and never will be! You can watch all the goddamn television shows, study the overpriced smut magazines, and buy name-brand, overpriced shit we can't afford, but at the end of the day you aren't that girl. Considering where you came from, you should be happy with what we have. I don't know why you think you're better than this? This is the life we've built together, so start fucking accepting it!"

He escalates from nice to angry and catches his rising tone.

He knows the last thing he said pushed it too far, and I'm fine letting him feel badly. I wonder if he's picking a fight because he's truly sick of my shit or if it's the guilt he's feeling about leaving for two weeks. I've inadvertently lifted an eyebrow and can see by the expression on his face that he's noticed. It's a stupid tell that I am utterly annoyed.

"I'm sorry, I shouldn't have said that. I want you to have everything. I really do. But Shaney, we aren't from that kind of family, neither of us are. I don't want you to want for anything, and it kills me that I can't give you more. I'm sorry I'm not enough for you, but you need to realize that what we have is as good as it gets. Please, please be happy with the way things are. If you can just do that for me, then I promise I will always love you and work hard. Fuck, I'll take on three more jobs if that will make you happy. Just tell me what to do to make you happy."

He breathes deeply, and I see his dark lashes start to shine like onyx paint, so I let it go. I've never seen him cry before. All he wants to do is love me and take care of us the best he knows how. The same way his father did for his mother, the same way lots of regular families do.

"So this is where we start, from the bottom like everyone else, okay, sweetie? For now we've got to eat our fair share of brown bread, like my dad always said." A tear hovers in the corner of his eye. I can't look at him. My throat constricts as I try to swallow my own tears. I need the salty little droplets absorbed back inside me. I can't be defeated; he cannot be right. I won't let him convince me of what I already know is true—we are destined for nothing, we are poor, we will struggle for everything, and no matter how much we work to escape this rented shithole, it will always be home. We are two regular kids from the wrong side of the tracks playing house in a rundown shack.

"We've been together long enough that you should know this by now, and it should make you want to work harder. I know it makes me want to work harder. Let's both take on a few more hours at work, and I know you're going to ace your finals and be a college graduate soon. We are doing it, Shaney, and we will make it. You'll see, there are good things in the future for us."

He sounds like a father giving a half-ass speech to a naive teen daughter. I know the thought of a happy future is cute and all, but reality set in a long time ago that this is my life, present and future (though admittedly not nearly as bad as the past). The salty buggers prevail and ski-jump three and four at a time off my cheeks. I curse the tears for betraying my face. I am so angry at everything, but mostly at knowing that deep down he's right and that my destiny is set. Truth be told, it has been since I was born.

"Work harder? Are you fucking serious, Jake? You're going on vacation!"

I try and listen to his pathetic response, but my brain defies all that he's saying. He's vomiting words, and I can feel myself getting more and more frustrated. I am not prepared for a shit-show with Jake. He's pushing harder than usual, and now I'm the meek one. The more he talks the less I do. It's a twisted punishment for slightly overdosing on the couch, and the constant echo from his monotone voice talking over and over about the same stupid things makes me want to crush another couple white ones between my teeth.

Jake and I can both work for a thousand years, twenty-four hours a day, and still be apartment-bound for eternity. I am well aware, and he is too, that we will never experience our adult years with privilege like the überwealthy who live across town. This is what makes his fantastical words so fucking obnoxious. We will never have a dishwasher, beautiful paintings littering long walls, patios to entertain, or laundry machines inside. I've witnessed luxury and prestige beyond any magazine's pages or lifestyle show and even for a glimpse of my childhood felt like I was part of it. I have dreamed over and over to be back in my old friend's mansion surrounded by her silky clothes, velvety furniture, hallways that lead to more hallways, heated pools, and massive grounds for us to run and run. I pinch my wrist to stop myself. If I drift back to those memories, I will never come out of them. I know what followed, and that's why I am here now. I need to live in the now, within my means, and exactly how I deserve. This is my birthright and the punishment for what I've done.

I try to start listening again and nod my head in agreement to not have this unwinnable argument keep going. Normally I'd pull on the gloves for a good ol' boxing match of words to settle our unmatched souls but today I'm not up for the fight. His words are aggressive, hurtful, and truthful to the core. I'm done listening. Why didn't he leave me on the couch? I could still be dreaming in my opiate-induced, sweaty pajama coma.

I grab a pillow and place it over my belly, squeezing it so hard it hurts, and tuck my face into my knees. I must remain agreeable or he'll never go on this trip. Despite my jealous feelings about who deserves the break more, I definitely need one from him.

History of Jake and Me: I Hate the Word "Meals"

Jake and I got married on my eighteenth birthday. It was immediately after high school, when every normal teenager was procuring a family job or heading to community college. As far back as I can remember, I was planning an escape from my mother's house, and on July 16 of that year, I left forever. The couple of years before that had been the worst in my life, and I was dying to leave the place where everyone knew who I was and what I had done.

There wasn't any kind of job waiting for a girl with my reputation, and college was a knee-slapping joke, so I opted for folding laundry and cooking meals (damn, I hate that word *meals*), thinking that escape was an immediate trajectory to happiness.

Jake and I met at an out-of-town house party when my

promiscuous and literally lovable friend left me for some guy she'd spent the night locking legs and lips with. As cliché as an '80s movie, he sat down next to the lonely girl on the couch and waited while my friend finished. He made me laugh, and the time passed quickly. After a few hours of genuine giggles and exchanging light stories and numbers, we realized she had left with the dude. It wasn't unlike Lizzie to ghost with a guy, so when Jake offered me a somewhat sober ride, I took it. He was nice and didn't question me when I asked him to drop me off on the side of the street, a block from my house. He was from another town, a nicer one that I had heard of but never been to, roughly an hour away. That night I thanked the always-burnt-out streetlights and crescent moon for a near-black sky, because he had no idea the slum he was pulling into.

We talked every night about all kinds of things, but never did he question my home life. Either intuitively or because someone warned him, he avoided the topic like a plague of rats. The one-hour distance between towns and his having grown up with a whole different kind of childhood kept rumors of me, Shane Lacy, at enough distance. With love as his motive and time as mine, we saw each other daily over a few weeks' time. He spent every saved dime to afford our apartment, and when he handed me the keys, the freedom felt like an orgasm between my fingers. Within a month, and with massive objection from his parents, we had moved in together and got married.

It was a lackluster courthouse ceremony that only we knew about. He wore a white shirt, and at the last minute, looking down his chest, I realized he wasn't wearing (nor owned) a tie, so I borrowed a sharpie from the old lady clerk. The cotton head shook her head and sighed in disgust as I drew a tie down the V of his shirt. Compared to me he looked a little silly, but terrifically handsome. A formal dress was out of the question, so I took one of his long white tees, tied it to the side with a hair scrunchie, and voilà,

I was a bride. We looked absolutely ridiculous waiting next to the other fiancés, but in that moment we felt great. He accepted me, didn't know anything about my past, and promised to take care of me. I trusted in his genuineness and naively assumed everything else would fall into place.

Five long years later, I've learned a few things, like: Marry for money the first time, so you can afford love the second. If I ever were to have a daughter (hopefully we won't because we can't afford one), that would be my first teachable lesson.

The truth is, now that all this time has passed, I hate what's happened to us. I hate what's happened to me. I don't want to feel this way, and while I can't imagine anything better than where we are, the truth is real. I can't stand folding another one of Jake's collar-stained white tees or cooking another fucking crescent roll potpie in a muffin pan. This is my life, and Jake is right—neither of us came from *that* kind of family. He came from a different type of crazy, but the stable kind with two parents and a house where a family ate dinner that his mother would serve on a doily-laid table each night. They had pizza and Chinese nights, company for holidays, and made pie crust from scratch. His mother is an obsessive-compulsive housewife who thinks it's still the 1960s. Her hairdo, clothes, and vinyl-covered couches all match. She waits on Jake's father like a nanny, never sitting down in hopes of his needing something. His father is a stern man who can't stand the thought of Jake with me because he thinks I work too much, talk too much, think too much, and am definitely not "ladylike" or equipped to take care of his son. Jake's parents only understand traditional husband-and-wife roles, so neither of them visit because they can't understand us. If I knew something about traditional roles maybe I'd try one out, but all that I've learned comes from television, and last I knew, their generation's shows have all been canceled.

My background is not as straightforward as Jake's. The catastrophe of my home life with my mother, Agnes, was borderline asylum-worthy. I'm not even sure it deserves the word "family," more like birth mom, kid, and a bunch of made-up celebrity fathers she would make me call "dad." She was—and as far as I know still is—a reckless neurotic who thrives on living in the past. Real life, not the one she likes to confuse it for, consisted of her daughter dodging her creepy boyfriends and keeping the authorities just comfortable enough not to take her away. Turning the stove off when she passed out drunk, being driven around for days and nights on end without a destination, missing huge chunks of the school year, and having teachers leave food in my locker so I could eat . . . these plus a multitude of other insane and odd behaviors are what made up childhood normalcy.

She fucked up my entire world from the day I was born until the day I escaped, and I cannot help but desire more than I had. The narcissist in me believes I deserve it. I've been a witness to and participant in more bad shit in my littler years that I feel like God finally owes me. And having seen firsthand how the one-percenters live, I want it to be my turn. Sometimes our marriage stings so badly, I just need to forget, because I know who I am and where I came from, and I don't need a fucking reminder. Unlike my mother, there will be no special past to fret over.

Here I am five years later, after escaping the Agnes-run penitentiary we called home, and not much has changed. The only difference between the past reality and my current one is it's a whole lot cleaner and a lot more structured.

Stop Talking, or I'll Run Out of Pills

I'm lost inside my own planet of alien thoughts of adolescent hell and have slumped down to a complete fold, squeezing the pillow so tight my knuckles hurt. I look at Jake, who, to my surprise, is staring with distraught, guilty eyes, seemingly realizing the extent of his previous and most vicious of words. I spear my head back between my knees as Olympic-skier tears fly down my cheeks, and I distractedly count them as they hit the floor. Jake's bulky presence hovers over me. With tear thirteen, I see his shadow as he moves to gently kiss my buried forehead. Clumsily he misses as I flinch, and his lips tap the top of my unkempt hair.

"I'm sorry, I shouldn't have said that."

Which part, I wonder? Do you mean all of it, asshole? I rise from the crouched position, pleased that I feel physically better despite the contradictory puffy, red evidence all over my face. I place the mug with a swirl of leftover coffee into the sink and spot a bowl of cereal, the milk carton, and a spoon on the bar. Jake must have set it up when I was showering. I pretend not to notice and rinse my salty eyes under the kitchen sink, drink from the faucet, and wipe my face on my shirt. I sit down on the one wobbly stool, glance at the milk carton that expired yesterday, and smell it for good conscience. It barely passes the test, but I pour it into the bowl anyway and at the same time give up, give in, and start another day.

About twenty or thirty minutes have passed since I broke down, and Jake is ready to talk . . . again.

"Shaney, I'm going to ask again. How are you feeling?"

I wave a hand to show my mouth is full of little wheat shapes and sugary charms. He's going to have to wait a little longer for me to open up. And I'm going to need more pills to get through this morning.

He's in his work uniform and looks cute—handsome, even— but much older than when we got married. Our long hours and poor habits are taking a toll on both of us. I feel badly because Jake truly believes he is doing everything right and because of that, I have no other choice than to give in. Jake is getting ready for his other job at a local casket factory. It completely freaks me out that he's inside one of those old buildings undoubtedly haunted by angry, claustrophobic ghosts who by their choice would've chosen cremation. Thankfully, Jake doesn't think about that kind of

thing and is willing to work pretty much anywhere, unlike one
of my many white-trash neighbors whose girlfriend works three
jobs so he doesn't have to. The wiry-looking bastard sits on the
couch all day playing video games and jerking his tiny weenie to
online porn waiting for a settlement check to arrive. Stupid fucker
scammed his mobster boss, a pizza parlor owner, saying he dropped
a hundred-pound sack of flour down a flight of stairs at work, but
really he flipped his four-wheeler. I wonder if that girl will ever
figure it out. She is just as nasty as he is, going to work all day and
night while he bangs another neighbor, taking turns between their
filthy abodes.

Our apartment walls must be made from the thinnest material
allowed for building. Sometimes I wonder if there's anything separating them besides cardboard, chipped plaster, and lead paint. It's
horrible, noisy, and, sadly, feels like home all at the same time.

We May Be Poor but I Ain't Gonna Sound like It

I finally respond and his drooped face rises up. "Thank you, Jake. I
am well, very well indeed."

He's not even fazed by my sarcasm anymore. It makes me feel
sort of sad.

I have always made an effort to speak in a proper fashion even
when I'm joking around. We may be poor as rocks and she as crazy
as a loon, but my mother always taught me to never look or sound
it. I remember like it was yesterday, her smacking me at the deli
counter when I ordered a half pound of cheap bologna, and she
yelled at me, "Again! Say it again!" Screaming and shaking her
head at the waiting customers. "It's *may* I, Shane. Now do it again.
I didn't raise a hooligan."

The counter staff thought she was nuts. They didn't know the
difference between "can I" and "may I." It was all just bologna
baloney to them.

She believed that studying etiquette books was a better education than actual school. Looking back, that's probably why I missed most of my junior and senior years and she had to pull a Mrs. Forrest Gump with scruffy, balding Principal Schmitz. She was fixated on language and poise to an obsessive degree, taking me out of school to study everything she thought she knew about being classy. It was all a ruse, pretending it was for me and how to become a proper young lady. I never complained about leaving school early for another nutty lesson, but I knew all this ridiculous training was for her, hoping she would impress the man she missed and longed for. I was a pawn in training, all so she could hone her own skills and impress a man who would never return and never really want her. I didn't have the heart to tell her that no matter how hard she tried, she'd always be a townie. All the training in the world wouldn't change who we are.

Rubbing Sticks and Dicks Together

Jake waits for the perfect time to bring up the topic he's been dying to discuss all morning, like a patient hunter waiting for his prey. It's right after he's heard me say I'm fine, but before he heads out the door. It only took a couple of hellish hours of drawn-out bullshit conversations and some nasty withdrawal symptoms to get here. He's calculated and has my attention.

"Remember, I have the fishing and hunting trip coming up tomorrow, and I'll need to get all my stuff ready. Shane, I think it's a good thing, and it will give us a little break"—he cracks a smile; he has a terrific half smile—"and you can start that paper for your writing class. You have to do that, Shaney. Time is running out. I want my girl bringing home an A-plus."

I hear him loud and clear. More of that fatherly, condescending crap. At least I assume those are the types of things a nagging dad would say.

Jake is ecstatic talking about the annual fishing and hunting trip and is shaking the floor with his bouncing knee, making some of the prints shake and knock against the thin walls. A
fly swatter—or fist—pounds against the wall from the other side
and nearly knocks one to the floor. Fucking neighbors, fucking
cardboard.

The trip's roster includes his father, younger brother, and some
high school buddies whom he's kept in touch with. These are the
boys who didn't make it to college either; let's say they *settled*,
mostly for hometown sweethearts and screaming babies, and this
is their big escape for the year. Jake's dad has been trying to keep
this tradition with his boys and their former Boy Scout troop alive
since they were peanuts. There are only a few of the original pack
left, but no one seems to care as long as they keep it going.

Last spring, for the first time in his life, Jake missed the outing
because we couldn't afford for him to take the extra time off. It's
another check on the list of "Why Walter and Priscilla Hate Me."

Jake moped around for a couple of months after that but
then snapped into planning mode, saving and working like crazy,
determined he would never miss another trip no matter what it
took. In a year's time, he's managed to work enough overtime to
scrape up enough loot to make the outing and cover our joint bills
while he's gone—and he's about to explode into break dance with
excitement.

He looks to the rattling print on the wall and puts his elbow on
his knee to stop it from shaking. The quiver in his lip tells me he's
going to go over his plans for the millionth time and most likely ask
for some sort of favor. Words shake out of his mouth.

"Can you get everything ready for me? I have to head to work,
and I won't have time to fix it the way you do. Please, Shaney,
please. I am so excited. I will miss you like crazy, but I haven't seen
these guys in forever."

I nod my head and he leans in to kiss the top of it.

Camping, hunting, stick rubbing and all that other crap bore me to death. It's nasty and dirty, and it takes me three extra times through the washer (and a lot of extra quarters) to get the testosterone of all those species out of his clothes.

He is right about one thing, though. With Jake being away it will give me the time I need to work on the essay for school that I've been dreading. I am trying like hell to get through it and finally obtain an associate's degree. It's not the bachelor's or master's I'd love to have, but community college is good for one thing: poor chicks like me who married too young and stupidly thought their husbands would provide it all.

Writing class is miserably hard for me because I lack the creativity that the teachers are looking for. Math and science stuff comes a lot more naturally. I think I use the left brain more than the right, or something like that, but mostly I'm not a writer or an artist, and I can barely spell, either. All the rules I'm supposed to know just to reference more things in order to reference those is more time-consuming than learning a second language. I'm convinced there are just some things in life I don't need to know—nor do I care to.

Having put it off for two years, I have to complete and pass a six-credit writing-intensive class to get my liberal arts degree. I dislike the class almost as much as the lunatic teaching it. The professor is just plain weird. He's eerie looking, with wild boar hair and wacky mannerisms. One time in class he wrote "AND WE FUCK THEM" on the chalkboard for all of us to respond to. He broke the chalk by writing with such force and then squished the broken piece on the ground like a cigarette into a thousand baby chalks with his hippie sandal. I didn't raise my hand that day because whatever it meant, I knew I was guilty. I wonder if you *can* fuck indifference?

Professor Looney Tunes requires a long-term project that makes up our entire grade for the class and is due at the end of the semester. I am fairly certain we get some kind of credit for showing up to the Wednesday night classes, which I go to on my only night off from work, but I can't take the chance of losing any part of the grade. I have a near-perfect GPA, for the first time ever in my life. I barely passed high school with a C-minus average (and likely wouldn't have passed at all without my mother's sexual promiscuity and persuasion). So I really don't want this guy to fuck up what I've done on my own.

He is berserk and barely approachable. During class, when he's not off on a tangent talking about God knows what, he takes a moment to emphasize the importance of this one assignment, so I know it's a really big deal. We mostly talk as a class about off-putting phrases that he says or writes on the board, and we occasionally watch clips of old flicks that no one understands. Then, like clockwork, we spend the last hour in a circle jerk discussing our thoughts about the whacked shit we just witnessed. All of this wasted time and complete nonsense, he says, is "prep work to lube our minds for the end-all paper."

The groovy thing is, we can write about practically anything. If half the class wasn't from my high school and didn't already know my history, then I would probably write about how much I hate how my life turned out. But then again, they probably would, too.

Michelle Cross is a perfect example of one of the many who moved out this way after high school. Skank-ugly, as I affectionately refer to her, would go squealing to Jake, psyched to expose my unhappiness for him. She is a revolting redhead who blew him in a Taco Bell bathroom at least ten years ago and loves to tell me about it over and over with all the details. She recently spotted my husband while he was picking me up after class one night and galloped over to him so fast that she tripped over her own knobby knees and almost took him out in the process. The overzealous ginger jumped higher than I've ever seen a human leap and wrapped her stringy, pasty-white legs clear around his torso. I ignored the entire scene while others gaped in disgust, like watching a dog with diarrhea, and climbed into the passenger's side of his truck and turned on the radio. When he finally peeled her off of him and joined me in the vehicle, he feverishly tried to explain what happened and how he knew her, but it was obvious to us both that I really didn't care.

I think about Skank-ugly and how no one ever taught her the appropriateness of when to give a blow job. My mother always said unless it's for forever or for money—or for forever money—then don't do them, period. I laugh internally about the embarrassment Jake feels about her and wonder if I should write the paper about sluts? I would have plenty of references, and it would make Jake squirm when I read it to him.

Either way, I need to get crackin'. Jake leaves tomorrow and not having him watch my every move is exactly what I need to get this done. No meals next week for this girl! I might be more excited than he is.

Cheap Life, Expensive Past

Jake left for work and I covered the morning shift at the bar.

After my shift I scramble to the grocery store before I have to go back to work for the night shift. I need to cram in making snacks and packing coolers of breakfast treats for Jake and his camping cohort before they leave tomorrow. With only an hour to spare, I am running ragged to get all the supplies I need so I can make everything in the morning.

Everyone from his group brings something, and Jake's contribution for the trip's feast is more like what I can whip up for him. I don't mind that much because I know the sooner I get it all prepared, the sooner he will be packed and gone for two weeks. Jake in his own right deserves the break, we both do. Even though it's technically Jake's trip, it's really a vacation for both of us. Selfishly,

I think I need it more, but he thinks it's business as usual for us. It does piss me off a bit, because we've never actually taken a vacation together. I've never even had one. A few years ago we tried to go away, even coordinating the same day off work, but by the time we added up how much it would cost in gas, food, and a hotel, we stayed home, watched *Sixteen Candles*, and stuffed our faces with popcorn and soda. I guess that was our honeymoon.

I arrive at the grocery store and my car stalls just as I pull into the space. This isn't anything new. If Hope isn't overheating or the hood isn't smoking, then she's stalling or hiccupping over the pavement. I've nicknamed her for the optimistic superstition that I *hope* she will make it from point A to point B without failing me. I'm often begging out loud to her, "Hope, don't die . . . Hope, don't crash . . . Hope, please get us out of this sketchy neighborhood."

So far she's lived up to her namesake, but she's just another reminder of the poverty high wire we balance on.

Luckily, Jake and I have our own vehicles. One of his friends shares a car with his girlfriend and, almost all the time, leaves poor Jess stranded at home with three bratty, snot-nosed kids, while he's fucking around doing God knows what with everything that has a hole.

Hope is throwing a tantrum and I debate dropping her off at Don's—a friend of Jake's who's a whiz with cars—but remember he'll be on the trip, too. If I see Jake tonight, I'll ask him to leave me the truck just in case she finally fails me.

I grab the first grocery cart I see, toss my purse inside, and hit the aisles as fast as I can in search of the cheapest grub money can buy. We are always tight when it's just Jake and I eating, but it's even worse when I'm buying for all his fat buddies. I thumb through the cash I made at the bar today, and although it was slow, someone I didn't recognize left me a $10 bill on top of the courteous 20 percent, which will help out a lot.

I pick up two of the cheapest cartons of eggs I can find, big ugly white ones. Not the cage-free ones I'd love to buy. These guys could care less about where the chickens live. I hustle to the next aisle, skipping over the pricey brands on the middle shelves in a blur and grabbing from the less-expensive no-names on the bottom.

I add four boxes of muffin and sweetbread mixes and a whole bunch of fatty bacon, ham, and more plump pig carcass to the cart. The meat is putting the camping budget over the top, so I'm only buying frozen and anything prepackaged. The bread aisle offers up four loaves of white Wonder, and I finish the list with a quick jaunt to the cold aisle for the largest, cheapest gallon of orange-colored juice I can find.

If I didn't get free meals at the bar most nights, this is better food than I eat. It's doubtful they'll even notice the shit I grabbed when everyone combines their shares.

I reach the register and recognize one of the cashiers and keep my head down, opting for a different but busier lane. I can't remember her name, and when I look up at her to jog my memory, she smiles wide. I hesitantly veer my cart into her line and wait behind another customer. I want to hurry things along and avoid any awkward conversation, but the woman in front of me is one of those nutty coupon people. She has taken over the entire stopped conveyor belt, spreading fifty or sixty neatly cut savings certificates, arguing and handing each one to the familiar girl. I make eye contact again and shrug to see if I should change lanes, but she puts up her finger up for me to wait. I roll my eyes and she laughs, a sweet, young-sounding giggle. I remember her now, she's from high school. Why do so many people move out here? Yeah, it's a little bit nicer of a dump than where we grew up, but it's still a shithole. The adorable girl has a short, blond bob and crystal-blue eyes. She is naturally pretty, and it makes me feel bad that someone so cute is a cashier, but looking at her you'd never know she's anything but thrilled with her job. She has a joyful face and childish laugh but I wish better things for her. I wish it for all of us from that dreadful place. Instead, she's waiting on crazies same as I do, except the alcohol she sells is corked, pricier, and takes coupons.

Coupon Cuckoo is taking her sweet time. I glance at the assorted boxes of chewing gum and junk candy, debating if a pack is a worthy purchase. I study the different fruity flavors, listening to Cuckoo talk aimlessly about the different sizes of yogurt cups, and I notice something disturbing in the corner of my eye on the newspaper rack. I turn to read the full headline, but I don't believe it. This is not one of those typical one-liners about Brad and Angie or another Kardashian pregnancy. I *know* these people. This is *my* past, the life I thought was done. Now it's as fresh as flowers and splattered across the front page of nearly every paper, all neatly tucked inside the wire racks that curve around every checkout lane. I gulp hard, speed-reading all of the different front pages and covers. The largest newspapers in the country, all the gossip tabloids, and local papers mix together like a can of nuts, each with some variation of the same thing.

"William Barron dies in prison—the conspiracy behind his life and death," "Billionaire Barron DEAD," "Bill Barron's death, scandal, and secrets from prison insider," "Barron's prison sentence: Who really sent him there, and were there more victims?" "Unknown woman peeled from Barron's cell."

People magazine dedicates a quarter of its cover to the famous family: "Barron dies hours after visit from strange woman: daughter Simone isn't talking."

His face is everywhere, staring back at me with those unforgettable Barron eyes. I have a sudden urge to vomit. My belly feels like a thousand knitting needles, and buckling over is the only way to release them. I can feel the cereal from this morning churning up my esophagus as the cute schoolmate interrupts my impending throw up with a cheerful "Hello." Coupon Cuckoo walks away and the girl fingers me forward. "Shane, hi, how are you?"

I shake my head, looking around for a place to vomit. Without saying another word, she scans the items I've robotically placed on the belt. I hold my mouth with one hand and with the other grab the local paper that shows a picture of Simone next to her late father. I place it facedown, hiding the headlines, but by the droop of her face, she's already seen it.

The once joyful clerk put two and two together and recognizes the severity of the situation, printed in permanent black ink, and my direct connection to the Barrons. She hands me the bag of groceries, and with eyes facing down toward the conveyor, says, "Take care, Shane."

Ten minutes ago, she treated me like the lost bestie that she couldn't wait to reconnect with, but after reading a few printed words she barely bids me goodbye. I walk away with the weight of a thousand grocery bags hanging off my shoulder. I can overhear her and the bag boy gossiping a little too loudly. I think the whole store is pointing at me. I hit the edge of the glass door and throw up into a waste can outside.

I shuffle to my car like a mental patient on an overdose of Thorazine, unconcerned with my surroundings. A car beeps and I stop to stare and move out of their way. Startled by my inability to focus, I climb inside my own car, tossing the two bags of groceries in the back seat. I look in the rearview mirror at a pale and scared complexion. There is a look of death upon my face. I shall read the paper in private and not in the parking lot.

I buckle the passenger-side belt and stick the newspaper between the straps for safekeeping. I pull it tight so it won't move, but Simone's beautiful face peeks from behind the strap. She's even more gorgeous in mourning. I reposition the paper so only the articles about an underground gambling ring and a wheelchair that was made for a cat are showing.

I turn the ignition over, give her gas, and on the third try Hope starts up like the beast she is. My hands are shaky, my head is dizzy, my mouth tastes of puke, and I'm eager to get out of here. I throw her in reverse without looking, and a woman starts screaming bloody murder. I slam on the brakes as hard as they'll allow. I look behind me to see a small child attached to the hand of the woman, who's shouting profanities, flailing her free hand about. I mouth to her "I'm sorry," but she flips me off.

I obsess over the folded black-and-white pages tucked under the belt, constantly checking to make sure they haven't shifted or moved position like a mother driving home a newborn baby.

The words within this paper and the story behind it aren't of innocent humans. It's poison, and like a moth to a flame I can't stay away. I know it's only a matter of time before I have to unbuckle and face the fire and all that I've caused.

I check the time, which has officially stopped until this exact moment, and reality slaps me in the head. I have twenty minutes to get home, unload, and get back for my night shift at the bar. I make a difficult but conscious decision to read the newspaper after work, when I'll have the time to concentrate and can examine every word.

I jiggle the key in the lock and open the apartment door, paper tucked under my armpit like a delicate vase, when the most hideous ringtone blasts from the counter. I don't have time to answer, but I check to see who is calling. "DON'T EVER ANSWER" appears on the screen. I know this contact well, because I put it in myself. It's my mother. I hit "ignore," and the sound stops, but the illumination it leaves behind disturbs me: "14 missed calls," all from "DON'T EVER ANSWER." I can only assume she's seen the paper and is an emotional wreck, hoping to drag me into her downward spiral of madness. I can't deal with her now, or ever.

The entire bubble in which I've been hiding is collapsing all around me. It will all be here to face the second I get home from work. I thought it was behind me, but here it is, five years later, a fresh, bloody wound. I debate calling out of work, but that will only cause more stress. Fuckety, fuck, fuck! Magic Genie, please send me a plane. North Korea could work.

I compose myself with deep breaths and a little white pill. I throw the groceries, bags and all, into the fridge and freshen the Show Orchid lipstick from MAC (a major splurge) and walk out the door. Before closing it, I loosen the grip of the newspaper I've been carrying without realizing it, and it falls between the frayed carpet and door's threshold. My arm collapses at my side, sore from squeezing.

I try hard not to, but can't help and look down. Thankfully, it's only partial headlines about other worldly problems, nothing that's connected to me. I thank my white, cramped arm for creasing the truth away. Shaking the blood back into my right side, I run to Hope, where she's surprisingly not stolen and still running.

Peeps, Creeps, and Regular Ol' Weirdos

I arrive back at work and barely set my purse down when I spot Dave leaning against the pool table. He's my boss, an old, worn-out rich kid whose parents gave him this bar for a hobby, and he's chatting up some young blonde. He walks over and without so much as a hello whispers, "Card her." Then, in a regular voice, he explains all about this trash bucket he's been hooking up with, knowing I don't care. The stupid gist is they slept together last night and she's shown up uninvited, hoping for round two. He's used to girls understanding the phrase "one-night" in the "stand" part of sex and thinks two nights are just too long. Somehow, Dave's STD-laden problems are my problems. He's a stupid nasty fuck and should have asked how old she was before slipping it in, never mind serving her his cheap beer. She probably slept over in his basement fuck nest, an office with a stained, sheet-less mattress in a tiny corner room downstairs. I've only gone into it once to grab a tardy check from his desk, and the raunchy smell alone had me running for the stairs. I feel like vomiting for the umpteenth time today just thinking about it.

He's already drunk and annoyingly aggressive. "Shane, fucking card her."

"I literally just walked in the door and don't have time to run interference on another one of your shitty decisions."

He walks away because he knows I'll take care of it, like I always do. Before I go to work cleaning up Dave's mess, I pour tall drafts for two of my regulars, giggling to myself as I eavesdrop on their nonsensical banter.

The Vet looks even sadder than usual. He has deeply wrinkled skin similar to a sun-soaked farmer, and it droops and sags around his unhappy face. He's been coming here for as long as the doors have been open, and before that, another neighborhood bar and probably another one before that. Over my time here, I've been lucky enough to learn little bits about him. A tiny tease of history seeps out from time to time by the younger local gossips and, on one drunken occasion, from him. He spent the formidable part of his teens in Vietnam, arriving at only sixteen years old after his father forged the documents and forced him to join the war "because he wasn't making him any money in school." Upon his return, as a grown but still immature man, he did hard, manual labor earning a living as an ironworker. He dedicated his second postwar life to his new wife and daughter. With a second baby on the way, he picked up as many hours as the foreman would allow, plus any odd jobs as a carpenter or anything else that came along. He worked constantly to provide for his family in a way *his* father hadn't. It's the time he spent away from his young family that haunts him and is how I see him now. He was working the night shift when he lost them all to a house fire.

Some of the old-timers say he was so tired, he left the stove on, others say he tried to cut the unborn baby from his dead wife's belly, while some admit he never made it back in time. I pass the house, about a block away, every day on my way to and from work. It's been at least forty years, and it's still charred black on the slate roof and around some of the windows, while half of the home is burnt to oblivion. He continues to live there and will most likely die here or there. Over the years the city's peppered the house with condemned stickers and constant threats to bulldoze, but as of yet, no one has the heart to do it.

He's interesting and extraordinary for so many reasons, but notably for his uncanny intelligence. I assume the immeasurable loss that he still feels has made him study like a priest or that he was born this brilliant. I've never seen him with a book, but he speaks multiple languages, can solve a Rubik's Cube in less than ten seconds, and can outtalk any politician who would be brave enough to face him. A long time ago, before I knew better, I asked him why he wasted his time here when he could be saving the world or running for president. He told me this is the only place that his mind doesn't run wild. I assume the alcohol and illiterate company contribute to the purposeful daze.

Now, I understand the need to shut my brain down, so I will take his advice and let this place do its job. I enjoy having him and some of my other regulars around, and I'm happy to assist in easing their pain. Today especially, they are my distraction. Normally, I am theirs, a barkeep therapist with only one prescription to give—alcohol.

The Vet isn't always sweet, though. Most days I have to keep him from smacking the doctor off his seat or yelling at him absurdly about things none of us are smart enough to understand. Ye Old Doc, affectionately nicknamed Ye Ol, is another drunk who is as old as dirt. He's an accomplished PhD in the field of mathematics and, as far as I know, has absolutely no reason to be here. He has a family, a beautiful new home in a fancy development, and a job at the university. However, I have heard that he's a son of a bitch to have as a teacher and barely passes anyone. The strange thing is, when he's here, he's joyful and spends all of his free time on the raggedy barstool next to the Vet. I adore watching these two in action, fighting like two lovable cocks. They are the odd couple in the circus freak show. Both are strange in their own ways but also equally human in their search for companionship. Their affection for each other is as strange as it is true. They are equal parts sadness and genius, and I adore them both.

I pour a bowl full of free nuts for Ye Ol and walk steadily over to two-too-many-nights blondie. I'm not feeling very confident today, so I'm probably coming across more bitchy than sweet, and she can tell. When I reach her chair at a corner table, her eyes scan the room for Dave, but he isn't here, having snuck off into the kitchen. "I need some identification, please."

She says I should talk to the owner, who knows her well, and that I need to find him to explain. She ushers me off with the back of her hand.

I try and compose myself before I completely lose it and say, "That's so funny, because every single girl who comes in this bar looking for Dave tells me that he knows them well. But you know what, today I don't really care if you're first cousins or engaged to the guy, you either show me an ID or leave."

My one eyebrow must have risen high, because her lips frown and she mutters something snide under her breath that I can't make out. My bitchy goes from first gear to full-on fifth, and now I, too, am scanning the room for Dave. This naive little slut is not *my* problem.

She concedes under my evil glare and wonky eyebrow. Under the circumstances, I probably would, too. She sucks the straw of her cocktail hard until I hear nothing but the gurgle of ice and backwash, finishing the drink in seconds flat. She looks around the room one last time and gets up and walks out.

I watch the door close behind her bubble ass and march into the kitchen, where I find my asshole boss cracking up with the fry cook, Eddie. If I didn't actually like Eddie, I would lose it on him, too. I have zero respect for the owner, and today may be the day I could actually go dive-bar-postal and totally lose my shit!

Eddie realizes how angry I am and immediately stops laughing. He changes the subject, asking if there are any new orders, or if I'm hungry.

Dave knows I'm mad as hell and walks away, inevitably to scout new pussy either here or at a strip club. I can't be mad at Eddie. It's not his fault for being dragged into Dave's House of Raunch.

Forty-five minutes or so go by, so I assume Dave has passed out in his office or is gone for the night. It's a good thing because I really don't care to babysit his bad decisions. I'm too busy cleaning up a spilled rum and coke and breaking up an argument between the Vet and some hood rat-looking kid. Eddie bends to the floor with a clean, moist rag to clean up the rest of the sticky mess of rum and soda. When I stand up to let him finish for me, I see a bowl of homemade soup and crackers in the shape of a smiley face left on the counter. He makes the most amazing soups and is a wizard with my bad moods. I'm not sure why he wastes his talents driving this far to work at a dive and deal with total nonsense, but he's so nice to me.

Eddie is a good kid—young, maybe nineteen or so, and still lives in the neighborhood I grew up in with my mother. It may explain why he hasn't moved on from a fry cook and me from a bartender or my second job as a part-time jewelry store sales chick. There is something special about Eddie. He is sincere, kind, and his soul is older than his teen years. I always feel safe around him, and for some crazy reason he holds me on a pedestal. He knows about my reputation back home and has never passed judgment on me or spoken a word about it. For that, I appreciate him very much. Today of all days, he could have easily brought it up.

About a year ago, some local schmucks were playing pool in the back room and thought it would be funny to grab me, put their hands over my mouth, and carry me horizontally, tossing me in the back seat of a running car. It was a packed night and no one cared to notice or hear the commotion of my kicking and muffled screams. The off-duty cop whose attention I tried to get didn't budge from his Busch Light or Newport cigarettes. I am still not sure how, but Eddie knew I was missing and, like a goofy super-hero, sprang into action.

He came barreling out of the kitchen, pushed through the ignorant crowd, and grabbed my legs from the men putting me in the car. I was so scared, I let him carry me over his shoulders. After dropping me safely in the kitchen, he walked back to the barstool where the cop sat smoking and drinking and hit him in the jaw. The valiant Super Eddie almost got arrested and beat up by everyone who witnessed the punch. It turned out that the cop was actually on duty when it happened, so thanks to his being dirty, we all kept our jobs.

That night changed my perception of Eddie. He isn't just the guy I give food orders to; he is a trusted friend, and those are hard to come by. I like knowing he's there, behind the scenes, the way chefs are supposed to be. He makes me feel secure, and since that night, I've never done a shift without him.

The rest of the evening drags by. At midnight or so I swallow two more of my sweet oval pills to keep me going. The unusually quiet grumblings of Ye Ol and the Vet are almost calm enough for me to sleep. There is only an hour to go before closing, so I start cleaning and ask for last call. I'm hoping to nudge these boys out a few minutes early, but they're ignoring my blatant hints, so I go to the ladies' room.

I squat to pee and walk to the sink, and while washing my hands I'm confronted by Dave's two-too-many blondie from this afternoon.

"Get out. I am not in the mood for your shit." Seriously, what is wrong with Dave? I am not covering for him again. He makes his own bed with these chicks and now, like a big boy, he can lie in his DNA hazmat mess of a bed. I'm pissed because I get to clean up spilled beer and cigarettes for *his* bar while he fools around and has fun. Dave rounds the corner just as we're exiting the bathroom and I snottily tell her to leave, but he interrupts me by grabbing her arm and swinging her into him, kissing her lips. I give up and walk away, shaking my hand in the "whatever Dave wave."

The shift is officially over. I triple-check the locks, plugs, outlets, knobs, and anything else I may have left on or open. I blame my mother for the obsessive paranoia that I feel about being unsafe. Three times as a child, I came home to fire trucks in the driveway when my mother left lit cigarettes on the couch or hot dogs cooking on the stove without a pan after she'd passed out drunk. I can't help but feel nervous.

After the fourth check, I'm satisfied the bar is safe, but like a drunk angel, Ye Ol double-checks them again and we leave the bar together.

Eddie, the Vet, and Ye Ol almost always walk me out. Occasionally, we have some regulars join us amigos who know our routine, but tonight it's the regular foursome. They used to poke fun at my OCD ways, but now they're just as crazy about checking everything as I am. They even blame me for their doing it at home now, except for the Vet—he never says a word about the subject.

The routine is always the same. They bicker the whole way to the parking lot. Ye Ol always offers the Vet a ride home and he always declines, knowing there's nowhere to squeeze him in, even if he did say yes. Ye Ol gets annoyed by the Vet's stubbornness and climbs into his 1976 model 2002 BMW, cranks open the wind-up sunroof, flips off the Vet, and squeals his tires as he peels out. Tonight isn't any different, with the Vet shouting that he's a Communist as *The White Album* blasts from the stereo. The car itself could be straight off of a 1960s album cover. The tiniest square of glass makes up the windshield, and the view is barely visible from inside or outside the car. You can only see the top of Ye Ol's bald head through the collection of stuff he hoards inside. Every square inch, including the back window, is filled floor to ceiling with piles of paperwork, research, boxes, and even a few stuffed animals, which are always pigs or frogs. On his extra drunk nights, ephemera flies straight from the roof and litters the parking lot. Eddie and I always pick up the loose papers, saving them for the next night he rolls in.

The Vet walks home. I've never seen him in a car or take a ride, even when he's stumbling. He has a cane in hand, and every single night that we're all together he smacks the back of his friend's BMW right before the middle finger flies from the sunroof. Ye Ol doesn't hear or see anything over all the music and junk, and probably wouldn't care anyhow.

I want to believe their kindness and loyalty are the reasons they walk me out night after night, but the sad truth is, they need me to physically leave before they actually will. Either way, I am grateful.

Eddie and I collectively drive off with a queen's wave to one another, each headed to our own special hells we call home.

It's 2:00 a.m. when I arrive at my apartment to find the door stuck. I'm pushing so hard, I nearly fall face-first into the peephole, only to then trip over the newspaper I'd dropped before. It's crumpled from being wedged between the doorjamb and carpet and creased in half from the hold I had on it before heading to work. I pull it unstuck, ripping the want ads and funnies on accident.

For a brief few hours at work, my mind drifted from the inky hell that's been waiting for me. Everything I've escaped and tried to forget over the past five years is forcibly branded back inside my brain. I feel sick knowing it's been waiting, like a patient killer, for me to come home and read it.

I strip off my smoke-filled clothes and walk baby naked to the bathroom. The scent of moist Marlboro air fills the shower stall as I step inside. When my feet hit the fiberglass floor, tears flood my eyes. The day's events, plus years of hurt and shame, have finally caught up with me. Beads of water envelop me until I crouch down and curl into a fetal position. Time passes, the water gets cold, but I can't move. Goose bumps and shaking from the cold finally force me out. I pull on my frog pajamas, crunch a pill, and lie down on our lumpy used mattress. Jake will be at work until at least 7:00 a.m., so I have plenty of time to read the Barron article, again and again and again.

I Can Do Mundane All by Myself

A kiss on my forehead startles me awake. I reflexively sit straight up, feel like I have the flu, and fall right back down. Where are my pills, I wonder? I need the entire bottle to face today. The newspaper is strewn all over the floor on my side of the bed. I've been sleeping on a damp, tear-stained pillow. It's a familiar feeling to have awoken to salty smears on my cheeks and bed with notably pink, puffy eyes.

I whisper "hi" to Jake and groggily ask him for a glass of water. He doesn't mention the paper, either because he knows the hurt it will cause or because he just doesn't get it. He walks away and I reach into the nightstand and pull a pill into the gum of my cheek. He returns with water and it makes for an easy swallow.

Every morning, I wake with the same physical achiness, but in twenty or thirty minutes my sweet little oval cure dissolves and I feel well all over again. It doesn't fix the psychological hangover I'm feeling from last night's read, but it will do the trick to get me out of bed.

Jake changes and climbs into bed, tired after his night shift. I get up to start working on packing food for his trip. He sleeps like a corpse, so I cook freely without concern of noise or commotion waking him up. We both work so much, coming and going at all hours, so it's common practice for us to pass like strangers. I wonder if it helps us or hurts us, living together yet separately?

Sometimes I fantasize about winning the lottery and imagine Jake and I living it up on a tropical island somewhere. At the same time, that sounds like freedom, so I don't think Jake would be there. I try like hell to keep the love alive in my head, *hoping* my heart will follow. I cannot have married in vein! Until yesterday, the last five years with Jake have been quiet and uneventful, without a peep from my past.

I stir muffin mixes with water and eggs and place the tins into the oven, which heats only on the left side, making baking tricky. I should have done this yesterday, but I didn't have time, and mentally I wasn't able to think about anything except Simone and Mr. Barron. I still can't. I grab trash bags, Ziplocs, and plastic wrap and start getting everything packed while the muffins bake. I work at Stein's Jewels at 10:30 this morning and then I'll have to rush to get ready for the night shift at the bar. The boys head out this evening, so it's imperative that I get this processed food cooked, wrapped, and in the cooler.

The scent of artificial blueberries fills the apartment air. I pop another sweet pill and roll up five more for later inside a paper towel and stick them in an interior pocket of my purse. They give me the perfect mix of energy and fuzziness that I need to get through the workday.

While the last batch of muffins cook, I pack my clothes for the transformation from jewelry store salesgirl to bartender. I try not to disturb Jake, but the dresser drawer sticks, and my loud "FUCK-ING STUPID THING" wakes him. He rolls over in bed toward me and says with a sleepy voice, "Hey, your mom called again."

"What the hell? When?" I ask. My face must be changing colors, and the wonky brow is definitely up, because now he looks more awake and more upset than me. My heart races and I can feel the saliva drying up in my mouth. "What did she say?" I press him hard because I need to know what he knows and what they both said. She is extremely manipulative, and I have to be careful that he's not going to eat her apple and fall into one of her fairy-tale spells. Jake has no idea what she's capable of.

He met her one time, and it was by accident. It was a couple months after I'd left home, and Jake and I were newly married. She spotted us shopping at Target, near our new apartment. It was an awkward thirty-second introduction followed by skidding feet and an abandoned cart as I ran out the automatic doors. Jake chased after me, but I could hear him in the distance apologizing to her as he tried to catch up.

That was almost five years ago, and until the phone call yesterday, neither of us have seen or heard from her since. Once in a while someone I know will say she's asked about Jake or me, but since there isn't much to tell, I assume people say that we're working—a lot.

Keeping the past and present separate takes constant energy on my part, and with her somewhere nearby, it makes it almost impossible. Jake wants everyone to be happy, but he has no fucking clue.

She was once a strikingly beautiful woman who is now wrinkled and tarnished with age and regret.

He feels badly and likes to encourage me to connect with her.

"She didn't say anything. She sounded really upset and asked if I would please have you call her. She was begging me to tell you."

I snap at him, "So you answered the phone? Why would you do that? I don't understand what you were thinking? You know what the caller ID says. It literally reads 'DON'T EVER ANSWER.' How much simpler can I make it? Stay out of it, Jake, you don't understand any of it and you had no right!"

I am freaking out, and he doesn't know what to do. I'm not sure anyone else can set me off the way my mother can, and Jake's quickly finding that out.

Jake and I share a cell phone because we can't afford two, and this is the only number programmed to never answer. I thought saving her contact as "DON'T EVER ANSWER" was as subtle as a sledgehammer and he wouldn't pick up the freaking phone.

Jake is up now and is pacing, his face angry and confused like he did something horribly wrong, like run over a person or kill a puppy. In my eyes, it's just as bad. His voice rises as he tries to defend himself.

"Shane, listen to me, I didn't know it was your mother. The number was different than the one you programmed. I'd never seen it before. There was no caller ID for me to follow instructions from. I am so sorry, I didn't know it was her, I swear to God, Shane!" His face has turned from self-protective to sincere and I believe his pleas are true. I circle the couch, trying to calm my racing heart and heightened nerves. Every time I round the corner of its brown arm, I see the phone's outline on the bar. It's an eerily still object staring back at me like a ticking time bomb. The mere existence of an object inside my house that is directly connected to my mother is enough for me to implode. I want it—and her—gone, out of my house and out of my life. I'm too afraid to touch it for fear it might ring or redial, so I ask Jake to put it in a drawer.

My mind is running wild and I have no idea what to do next. As it is, I am barely able to handle the amount of schoolwork, work-work, and the babysitting of Jake's departure. Now I need to make more room in my already-confused brain to fit thoughts of my mother, the Barrons, and the entire clusterfuck that is my life.

I take a deep breath, and upon the exhale whisper to Jake,

"Okay, I know you need me to get everything ready. Let me finish putting everything in the cooler." Jake doesn't move or say a thing.

I go to the bathroom, inhaling and exhaling deep breaths, trying to relax myself, but my hands keep shaking and my heart is beating ferociously. I feel dizzy and weak, and I'm afraid an attack of my senses is coming on like the ones I used to have. I flush the toilet to muffle the sounds of blowing my nose and then rinse my eyes with water from the faucet. I stare into the mirror, mindfully talking to the girl standing in front of it—blurry eyes, white as a hotel sheet, shaky—and tell her that I'm a grown-up, not a child. I tell me that I have the power, not my mother. I made the changes in my life to be nowhere near her, and she can't just call whenever she wants and send my emotions into a fucking tailspin. I repeat the mantra, "I am a grown-up, I am a grown-up, I am a grown-up." I can't stop staring at the mirror, and all I see is a scared, tired-looking teenager who left a very bad situation only a short five years ago. The emotional hold she has on me hasn't skipped a day. The repetition of words is calming, and I take one last inhale and exhale as I exit the bathroom.

Jake is oblivious to the bathroom breakdown and assumes I was peeing. I am not fazed by his ignorance and start filling little plastic baggies with artificial goodies and blue-collar food. He is staring at me from the bedroom and it looks endearing, but I'm growing frustrated with him because I need help and he's just freaking staring. He walks into the kitchen, taking the items I've pre-wrapped and placing them inside the cooler. My face and mood are lifted with his gesture of assistance, and like that the fight is over and we are back to normal.

"Did you get any crickets for Andrew?"

Shit, I completely forgot. When in the world will I squeeze that in? Andrew is our White's tree frog that he bought me as a wedding present. We didn't have money for anything at all, never mind a honeymoon. Since we met, I had talked about my dream trip and that it would be to Australia. He knew even back then that there is no way we will ever make it. Instead and very Jake-like, he creatively and thoughtfully surprised me with the most oddly adorable presents I've ever received.

On our wedding night when we got back to our apartment, I found a rectangular wrapped present on our coffee table. Inside was a ten-gallon cage holding a little blue lagoon filled with a half inch of water, green felt carpet, a long piece of driftwood, and the tiniest, smiling green frog stuck to the side of the glass. Inside there was a tiny, handmade wooden sign glued to the cage's floor that read: "Welcome to Australia!" He had joked about how cool it would have been for us to keep a kangaroo in the apartment, but said this little guy was more our style, and he was right.

Andrew is like our kid and, luckily, the type of child we can afford to feed.

"No, I forgot, but I will get them at some point. Don't worry about it, I'll take care of the little guy while you're away. Can you finish up, because I need to leave for Stein's?"

Jake looks at the clock. It's 9:45 a.m. and I need to be there for 10:30. Patti, one of the managers, is opening, which frees up an extra half hour this morning because I don't have to pull the jewelry from the safe for display. She's great to work for and super lenient, but my presence is still expected when the doors open.

I look at Jake, who's still staring at the clock. After a long pause, he notices me and looks back. At that moment, we both realize that we won't see each other for almost two weeks, and even though he doesn't leave until later, I have to work and I'll miss seeing him leave. I'll miss him a lot, but I know the break is good for us. It will also allow me to get a bunch of schoolwork done, beginning with choosing a topic to write about.

I grab my bag stuffed with the change of clothes and shoes for later and drop it next to the door. Jake meets me there, and when I turn around to say goodbye, he swings his arms around me, holding on tight, and burrows his head onto the shelf of my breasts. He raises his head and taps my lips with his. He whispers goodbye, showing his adorable half smile, and I almost start to cry.

Normally, I'm fairly emotionless, but the last couple of days have taken their toll, and now they're nearly impossible to hide. Jake and I don't spend a lot of time together, but we've never spent much time apart, either. This trip is longer than usual, but he's been waiting two years for it, and he's earned it, literally. Deep down, I'm very jealous that *he* gets to escape the monotony of work and our pathetic home life, but I don't think that's ever occurred to him.

We hug and he kisses me on the forehead. Like a trained puppy, I bend my neck for him to reach my head. We both say I love you and he says, "Bye, sweets, I'll call you from my dad's phone or from one of the guys'. It will be once we get settled, so don't worry if you don't hear from me right away. Be careful, and call my mother if you need anything at all. She knows you're alone and can come in a flat second if you do."

In my head my eyes are rolling because we both know there's no way in hell I would ever call Jake's mom. I don't even know why he mentioned it, unless he's feeling guilty for leaving. If an apocalypse hit and jellyfish were falling from the sky and I had a choice to call either of our female creators for help, I think I'd toss the phone out the window and take death. I politely but sarcastically say, "Thank you."

As I close the door behind me, the oven beeps. Oh good, the last set of muffins are done. No more making *meals* this week, baby! I really hate that word.

Richie Bitches, I Wish I Was One

It's a normal day of work at the jewelry store; customers come in and out. Wealthy white women exchange their lavish gifts from Valentine's Day for ones they like better. All while I listen to their bleeding hearts, telling me how badly they feel for returning the gorgeous gems in the first place. I recognize the jewelry they're bringing back by their husbands who picked it out. A few flirt with Patti and I during the peak holidays, hoping to get a discount when they can, or sweet-talk us with tips so we don't snitch when we wrap their wives and mistresses different presents, color-coding the bows. Patti and I are from similar backgrounds—poor as shit—and eat up the attention from rich businessmen. We both know the decorative gold and diamond pieces aren't destined for our fingers, but it's still fun to play. I don't even own a wedding ring, never mind a custom-made piece especially for me just because it's Cupid's day.

Jake didn't have enough money to buy a ring. Any hopes of inheriting a dead aunt's treasured antique was out of the question, since none of our parents have siblings. Instead, he proposed with an origami frog, indicative of the live honeymoon present that was about to come. It was cute that a guy like Jake, sort of a "guys' guy," took the time to learn the ancient craft in hopes of my saying yes. That little paper frog, faded from the sun, still sits on the windowsill next to our bed. Back then, we were silly in love, or at least he was, and it didn't matter that my engagement ring was made from craft paper or my honeymoon present had slimy, green skin. Jake was a reminder of everything new and, most importantly, everything old that I had left behind. Meeting him was fun and exciting because all he wanted to do was get to know me. He didn't care or ask about my past or ask why I was running so fast from home; he only cared that I wanted to be with him for the rest of our lives. At the time, this made him as innocent and charming as a virgin prince.

I married into Jake, like marrying into money, but the opposite. The *idea* of him, and his physicality as a human, made for an easy excuse to leave. The reality set in that when I said "I do" in that white tee five years ago, I got exactly what was promised: a new start. If only someone, like a mother, had warned me that young love fades, and the euphoric feelings we once had would last only a year or maybe two, then maybe I could have chalked it up to teenage escape and be doing something better with my life.

Hearing "It just isn't my style. . . ." from another Richie who is returning a $4,000 pendant doesn't exactly bring out my guilty senses. I wonder if these women thought the husbands they married would bring them happiness or if their husbands thought that this jewelry would bring their wives happiness or are we all just fucking disappointed?

I'll never know because I was hired to smile, model my neck, wrist, and fingers, and give a pretend shit about their first world problems. While the Richies are returning Earth's precious rarities for store credit, my husband is heading off to hunt innocent animals so we'll have food in our freezer. Today is going to be an annoying shift full of spoiled complainers, unappreciative bitches, and fake grins.

Chirpin' and Slurpin'

A quick stop between jobs and I walk inside the bar, Andrew's crickets in hand. I can't leave them in the car to die from suffocation, or any other cricket-related death, so they've come to work with me. Dave puts his hand up in protest when he sees me carrying the little critters toward the back room. I explain in the nicest possible way that my frog needs them for food. I wish I could put my hand up in protest every time he drags in a new chirpin' slut.

"I know, I know. I didn't have any other time to get them because the pet store will be closed when I leave and he hasn't eaten in days."

He stares at the clear plastic bubble of hopping bugs and snickers. "Why don't you have your supercool husband get your wedding present its own food."

I don't even know how he remembered me telling him that.

His pickled brain doesn't even know the names of his employees, but he spouts off a memory about my wedding from five years ago like a fucking prodigy. Eddie sees us talking and casually comes out of the kitchen to supervise. He's wearing an apron and his hair is tousled like he's just had sex, and without saying a word he takes the moving bag of amphibious food from my hand and walks away. His assertiveness is new and attractive, especially in such a younger man. Dave is bored talking about the bugs and walks away, pointing at me and winking. I'm sure he's put worse in his mouth.

I put my purse away in the back room, a simple action that's the virtual time clock stating that my shift has begun. I grab a bottle of whiskey and a shot glass and stop in front of Ernie, who is sitting alone at the very end of the bar. It's my job to know when someone needs a drink, and I think he might. His left cheek is on the bar and he has a blank stare on the side of his face that's visible. I think he's about thirty or so, but this place and its cheap liquid poisons have a way of aging people like presidents.

Several years ago, he lost his baby daughter in a drowning accident. Every single customer in this place has a story and a thirst to forget. Night after night, people like Ernie feeling sorry for themselves and their lives drown in sadness and regret until I tell them it's time to go home. A simple shot of Jack placed in view makes his eye smile and he sits up, cheek splotchy from lying on it so long. I crouch to meet his short stature and whisper, "It's on the house, Ernie. Our secret!"

I can relate to Ernie and most of the sad men and women who walk through these doors every day. I do what I can to make my customers as comfortable as possible for the time they are with me. They may not ever be happy, but I like helping them forget. We all need a pick-me-up, and while some like liquid, I prefer a tiny little oblong solid. We really aren't that different, the regulars and me. We're all poor and sad, trying to forget that we're poor and sad.

The rest of the night meanders on. The Vet is here and he's

yelling loudly at Ernie to pass the nuts, but after two long shifts of bullshitting with people, I'm too tired to intervene. Just then someone yells over the Vet, "This goddamn hellhole needs to be shut down! I'm gonna call the health inspector tomorrow. It will fail everything. All I can hear is goddamn bugs chirping. Shaney, what the hell is wrong with this place? You deserve better than this dive. There's fuckin' buggies crawlin' up in this joint, I can hear 'em. I can feel 'em." He scratches himself, and others do, too.

I giggle, shaking my head in agreement, and wipe down the bar. I go in the back and check on the chirpers, who are causing the ruckus. Andrew's dinner is getting feisty, sliding up and down the clear plastic bag. "Don't worry, guys, I'll be done soon and get you in a proper home—well, sort of—but I promise it will be better than in there. You'll meet Andrew soon, too, and I am really sorry he's going to eat you, but he's otherwise a really sweet boy." I hear feet behind me and I turn and look to see Eddie, who has just overheard me talking to the crickets. He laughs, puts a hand on my shoulder, and goes back about his business.

Like every other night, it starts and ends the same. I begin the shuffle around the bar, asking everyone for last call. I have to ask three or four times before anyone takes me seriously. I pour and refill each customer's glass, then do the cleanup and restocking part and get ready to go. Dave left early on, and Eddie has to go for some family phone call he didn't want to talk about, but I overhear him ask the Vet to walk me out at closing.

I am the only one left who works here, and since I'm hitting the umpteenth hour of straight work, the regulars can tell I'm tapped and ready to go and begin their slow descent toward the door. Ye Ol must be working late at the college or maybe stayed home for once because I haven't seen him all night. The Vet stays by my side as we check all the knobs, buttons, outlets, and plugs, assuring each other they're all off. The other regulars walk out like picnic ants in a line, and after I turn the lock for the night, Ernie triple-checks it to be sure. He pulls a couple of times on the door to show me it's truly locked, confirming with a friendly wink. I smile and wish everyone a great night. I walk with the Vet to my car, Andrew's meal hidden inside my purse. Once we reach my car, he turns away, beginning his nightly stumble home, but stops to yell, "Fucking bugs, Shane! I can even hear them outside. I'm switching establishments."

I shout back with laughter in my voice, "No, you're not. I'll see you tomorrow!"

He ignores me and sways side to side, using his cane for support.

I climb inside Hope and place my purse on the passenger seat and say to the bugs, "You guys caused a lot of trouble tonight. Soon we'll be home and I'll get you out of this plastic trap."

Batshit Beauty

It's after midnight when I arrive at my apartment's parking lot, and after a circle around I see that Jake has taken his truck. "Shit, shit, shit" runs through my mind like pellets. I had completely forgotten to tell him about Hope's issues. Luckily, she's been a good girl today, but what I really need is for her to keep going for a couple more weeks and then she can fail all she wants. When Jake gets back from the trip, I'll bring her to Don's. Hope won't let me down, I think, that's why her name's Hope; she knows better than to leave me stranded. I park her in a safe spot and make the trek through the sketchy parking lot to my apartment.

Inside I strip smoky clothes from my body and walk to Andrew's cage, naked as a reptile. I look behind me at the closed blinds, knowing I can't wait until after my routine of shower and pills, because my little green guy is hungry. I rip a tiny air hole in the plastic and pour a couple crickets into his cage. Two hops until

Andrew gobbles them both up. He pushes the second one's leg into his mouth with his tiny gecko-like fingers. I take the survivors and drop them inside their own little cage with a toilet paper roll to hide inside. I add a slice of apple that's starting to turn and a crumpled piece of wet paper towel for drinking. I know they're frog bait, but we all gotta eat.

It's nearly 2:00 a.m. when I finally sit down to turn the television on. Tomorrow evening I don't have to work. It's the only day of the week my jack-off boss allows me to go to class instead of work. I told him it's the law and the dumb fuck believed me. I can't wait to see what obscenely offensive thing the professor has written on the chalkboard this time. I assume he won't break habit this week and it will be the same insane jargon. I have never thought anyone was actually insane, except for my mother, but this guy takes the cake. The last few weeks he's scribbled quotes such as: "Stepmothers and babies, breast milk for Daddy's growth," "Asparagus, the one honest fruit," or some variation of the many classics in the months prior: "Death by salivation" or "Tickling time bombs." The guy is absolutely, positively nuts, but he offers the six-credit course I need to graduate so I do what I'm told.

I swallow a pill and look for the TV clicker, finding it tucked under the blanket, which when touched, lights up like a firecracker. The dark room is illuminated by a fuzzy screen. It's the freaking cell phone wrapped inside the blanket and I'm too afraid to touch it, but I need it out from underneath me. I know who it is, so this calls for a second pill, which I pop in my mouth while leering at the screen as I carefully pull it from the covers. "Shane, 911! CALL ME! Rob."

Are you fucking serious? I put the light-filled bomb down next to me, gulp down the pill, and think about what to do. Despite my better judgement, reading 911 on a screen evokes a sense of emergency and leaves me feeling confused. I can do one of two things: Ignore it completely or call and face the insanity.

The clock is closing in on 3:00 a.m., so the time he texted has me curious and, if I'm being honest with myself, slightly concerned. With a shaky hand and pounding heart, I pick up the phone and dial.

Rob sounds scared when he answers. I don't hear my mother in the background and wonder if he's calling me in secret? He goes on to explain how poorly she's doing and that he could really use my help. I listen to his plea but only say one word at the end of the conversation, and that's "goodbye."

I call Stein's at exactly 3:46 a.m. I leave a nasally, semi-convincing message about my sudden illness, explaining that I can't open the store tomorrow and how sorry I am. I send a follow-up text to Patti, hoping it doesn't wake her. I bet she'll think I've been up all night sick as a dog, furthering my story of sudden death. Hopefully she won't be too mad since I was covering for another girl anyhow. Wednesdays are my study days, not workdays, but I never turn down the opportunity to make extra bank.

I haven't slept in two days, but there's an urge to get to my mother. She is like the sides of a magnet and I am unable to resist her push and pull no matter how hard I try.

I mow down an unpacked muffin I'd saved for myself, throw on some sweats from the dirty laundry pile, grab the whole bottle of pills, and stuff everything into my purse. It's 5:00 a.m. and the lot is still dark and scary. I walk to Hope just as a neighbor I recognize from a couple complexes down is walking away from his car. When I pass it, I can see that it's scraped to shit on the driver's side, and he nods when he sees me staring. It looks like there are scratches on his face, but I can't tell for sure in this light. I hear a baby crying, and he looks at me again and then turns around. He forgot a child in the car. I wonder if it's hurt, too? Not my problem, keep moving, Shane, I think. I have my own problems, one big baby named Agnes. My thoughts are a jungle, and I'm trying to untangle the strangling vines that are my mother. She is suffocating me and I haven't even left this god-forsaken parking lot.

I arrive in my once-forgotten hometown about 7:00 a.m. Hitting the early morning traffic from the city slowed me, but I arrive just in time to see the sun glow over my old house. Getting in and out of here is the only mission at hand. I haven't been here in almost six years, and the feeling I get just as I am about take the turn into the driveway is one of regret.

I graduated from high school, barely survived the Barron scandal, and drove as fast as I could away from here and into Jake's arms. Everything I believed in and trusted turned out to be wrong. In the real world, post-Agnes, I learned what was up was down and vice versa. This entire town is the Alice in Wonderland of my life and I am Alice, a naive young girl who caused all the hysteria and ran like a little white rabbit from one hole to another.

I am shocked and slightly disappointed that Hope made it the entire trip without incident or, more appropriately, an excuse. I park in the driveway behind a red hatchback Subaru. I am surprised to see it, because my mother always made fun of them, calling the brand Lesbaru. She claimed only lesbians drove them, probably because the only lesbian she ever knew, Diane, drove one. I'm hoping that's Rob's reason for the urgent call. It's to tell me she's come out of the closet and the car's the proof.

The house is in poor—almost condemnable—condition, even worse than I remember. It's light peach in color, with green moss growing over the roof and, below that, gutters that are unhinged and dangling. The right side of the house features a scrawny butterfly bush without flowers barely camouflaging a huge white propane tank, a comical attempt at landscaping. My eyes peruse the rest of the exterior, and memories flood my insides with nausea and nerves. I see the same cracked bedroom window still has a hole where the mosquitoes would enter and eat me alive at night. I used to sleep with a layer of bug spray, but it didn't keep them from buzzing in my ears or biting my face. The hole is covered with black duct tape, and I question why she didn't do that when I was sleeping there?

Waiting and not wanting to exit the car, thinking about all the idiosyncrasies of childhood has my stomach churning. I can't believe how bad the house looks. Apparently having a male companion to help keep it up hasn't proved to be helpful at all. Rob the Blob has lived up to his name and is as useless to my mother as he is enormous.

I take several deep breaths, open my purse, place an oval treat on my tongue, crush it, and swallow hard without water. I am nervous. I walk to the front door but trip on one of many gravel craters that make up the driveway. I fall, grabbing the rusted side of the Subaru, which causes more harm than help. I bend to wipe bits of tar from two newly skinned knees, only to see the driver's seat has a newspaper with Mr. Barron's face across the front.

It is confirmed. I know without any doubt and with complete certainty why I'm actually here. I need to get out, now.

I hear a fire alarm blasting and people laughing. There is a lot of commotion, but it certainly doesn't sound like panic, more like a party. What the fuck? This isn't an emergency. A part of me wishes the house were on fire and I am the emergency, here to watch it burn. This house is the only constant thing that my mother has held on to; no matter how disgusting, she'll never let this piece of shit go. A paid-for hushy present for being a good fuck to a powerful man who she can never forget.

Standing at the front door, thinking of how aloof Rob was on the phone, I have no idea what I'm about to walk into, especially so early in the morning. He made it clear in derogatory and rather condescending terms that ". . . it's an emergency worthy of a visit to see your estranged mother, Shane." I knock. No one answers. I knock again and still nothing, just laughter and the sounds of a blasting alarm. I knock louder and more aggressively because this is becoming ridiculous and annoying. I shout, "Hello, hello!" I even scream "Publishers Clearing House," knowing her constant desire for money, but no one answers the door. The alarm that I've now deemed to be a smoke detector continues to blast and mixes with muffled voices. I laugh to myself, surprised that my mother even owns a smoke detector. I don't ever remember that noise as child, and had she remembered to cook for me, it most definitely would have gone off, a lot.

I give up on the traditional means of an invited visitor and jiggle the front door handle. It's so loose that I have to cradle the bottom half as it nearly falls off in my hand. I walk inside. I've entered the mother of all twilight zones.

The fire alarm is ten times louder than outside. I cover my ears from the raw beeping. Rob is sitting in an oversized recliner, oblivious to what's going on around him. He is the perfect homage to his nickname, Rob the Blob, a grown man who literally doesn't move for anything, even the fucking fire alarm. He is fiddling with some sort of wooden object, a puzzle perhaps, but that would take intellect. A small child is walking steadily by with a book on her head and my mother walks next to her. She waves a hand towel in the air nowhere near the alarm. I am a spectator to absolute insanity, and no one in this little ranch has noticed me.

I can tell that my mother is in one of her *states*. In the short time since this treachery began, I'm feeling the realization that I am exactly where I need to be.

"Mother, Mother, hello?" I don't shout because the scene is chaotic enough. Finally, after five or six more increasingly high-pitched "hellos," bright green eyes look up to me. I can see my mother's lips moving as the child walks, hand guiding the book along just above her head. It looks like a half-ass attempt at runway Reiki. The child's stare and mine are unlocked when her piercing green eyes move with her head and the book falls, hitting the carpet with a cushioned smack, sending dust and hair flying.

The odd child does nothing to alert my mother of my presence, all the while the beeping has temporarily taken my hearing. I take it upon myself to grab a stained towel that's lying on a fake wood stand next to an overflowing ashtray and wave it hastily below the beeping alarm, as dirt, fuzz, smoke, and bits of birdseed fly wildly all around me. The alarm stops, and silence emerges. The additional flying debris was not in vain. Beautiful emerald-colored eyes attached to this unattractive child's face watch my every move.

"Mother, who is this kid?" She ignores me, seemingly more surprised that the noise has stopped than by my presence.

"Hi, Shaney bug, how are you? I didn't see you there. What are you doing visiting us this morning? Are you hungry?"

Rob looks up from his wooden puzzle, finally noticing me, too. The silence seems to confuse everyone, and they are all looking at me like the uninvited alien.

"Oh, hi, Shane, I didn't see you there. Everything is fine, ya know, but good seeing ya anyhow. Did your mother ask if you're hungry?"

Why are they asking me if I want something inevitably burnt to eat? I decline. I can only imagine how long the alarm was ringing before I arrived. Meanwhile, no one has checked the stove or looked to see what might still be burning.

Rob makes a loud grunting noise when he rises from the chair and waddles to the kitchen. I haven't seen him in many years, much longer than my mother. He's gained at least one hundred pounds, if not more, adding to his already obese frame. Rob is a tall man, but you can't tell because his girth is now the same as his height. Patti likes to call it "puffy," but this is way more than puff. He's enormous. A pregnant man belly filled with sextuplets of junk food and laziness. His tattooed body parts are stretched taught, including his ballooned hands with the letters F-U-C-K-Y-O-U imprinted across seven of his nine fingers. I have no idea what happened to the missing one.

Rob and my mother met at a pawnshop where she worked for a small period of time. He would bring in junk for her to appraise as an excuse to ask her out. At first, he seemed like an okay dude, taking her out to dinner and treating her like a lady. My impression of him dramatically changed after a few weeks of their dating and his insistence on moving into his apartment. She left. I was stuck here in this peach pit during the tail end of my senior year of high school with four stray dogs, a handful of breeding goldfish, a nasty mean cat, and a bunny that pooped everywhere and chewed everything. Two kindhearted teachers took pity on me, taking turns making me dinners and leaving them in my locker. My mother found out and was furious. She said I didn't need their help, but it saved me and the animals from starvation and from social services hauling me out. High school came to an end, graduation commenced, and I ran as fast as I could from this place and all its ridiculous responsibilities. As witness to it now, I made the poor assumption that with me far away, the Blob and my mother would move back in and he'd help keep it maintained. Standing here today, looking around, it appears he has done about as much for this house as he has his body.

I feel sick inside as I peruse the filth that's all around me. I look at each person in the room. Rob the Blob's body is large, but his face and hair have weathered and aged twenty or thirty years. I give credit to the plumes of smoke that constantly fill the house from multiple lit cigarettes at a time. My mother doesn't seem to notice or care what Rob's become. Rob the Blob is just another mouth to fill and brings to light her obsessive tendency to force-feed absolutely anything that walks through the door. This includes the many bugs, mice, amphibians, or any assortment of humans and animals that would take the food she unwrapped and put on a plate or in a bowl for them to eat from. Growing up in our filthy abode with no money meant lots of shared crumbs between all of us critters.

The past floods back to me like a wave of giant, plastic-wrapped tuna casseroles, and all I want to do is bolt for the door. I hold my ground and squeeze my heels into the shit-stained carpet, determined to get a good look at my mother and figure out why I'm here, besides the glaringly obvious. She's been gone from reality for as long as I've known her, and I'm not sure what makes her tick anymore. The only exception to her insanity is the memory of her young life and the absolute Vixen she once was.

I feel badly staring, but they look like a funny cartoon family featuring my mother as Olive Oyl and Rob as Hamburger Man. Their appearance reminds me of one of the few things he said on the phone: "She's back to her old self. She's not eating again." Nothing he said prepared me for the sight in front of me.

She is shockingly thin, grotesque by any culture's standard. Once known only for her beauty, never her pedigree, she was tall and striking in her prime and had the reputation to prove it. I don't know anything about my grandparents or their ancestry because she left home at such a young age, which feels embarrassingly similar. I only heard bits and pieces of stories when she felt like divulging, and all of them are about the trash bag family we come from. I believe the lack of provenance drove my mother completely mad because no matter how hard she tried or how beautiful she was, she couldn't convince any man that she was worthy enough to marry. Today, she's a bony structure, and it looks like she's carrying a loaded diaper in her pants from the bagginess of her behind. A tan bra strap hangs loosely on the middle of her right arm where a biceps should be, dangling like a piece of yarn, as her hunched shoulder blades glide back and forth. She's a malnourished skeleton, ugly, sick, without any trace of soul in her eyes, and barely reminiscent of a human being. She is nothing like the dusty pictures on display. Her cheeks and eye sockets sink inward, and every bone that makes up her face has caved in like a dug hole. The black sundress she's wearing is barely held up by bony clavicles that were once shoulders. The cotton fabric hangs off of her bones and thinly stretched skin. I can only assume by looking at her that she hasn't eaten in months. The sight of her is almost unbearable to view, like a National Geographic exposé on Ethiopia's lack of food. It's sad to see her illness thrive like a parasite again.

Ironically, pictures of her posing as a strikingly gorgeous woman hang in the hall like trophies from a past life. Her face is barely visible under the screen of smoke and dust that covers the frames, but I've seen what's underneath and it's breathtaking. If the glass frames were cleaned even with one swipe of Windex, her gorgeous mug would appear, giving a young Grace Kelly or Elizabeth Taylor a run for their money.

I want to murder Rob the big, fat fucking blob for not calling me sooner.

My mind races with abandonment. I left almost six years ago, and at that time she was nuts as usual but in a physically healthy state. Even the time Jake and I saw her at Target, she looked normal in stature and even a little curvy.

What did I do? How did this happen? I feel horrible. Waves of emotion come over me as I fail to hold back the tears. Seeing her brings my entire childhood back into focus. It reminds me of all the crazy nutritional regiments she would make us try together and the lengths she would go to try and stay skinny and beautiful.

In sixth grade, the school nurse called protective services on my mother. The cupcake diet she put us on had me falling asleep at my desk. They assumed I was abused or caught mono or something. In ninth grade, a nosy teacher made an unannounced visit to our little peach shack because I kept a jar of peanut butter with a spoon in my locker. That time, it was my mom's newest fad food—nutty protein—not to mention Jif was all we could afford. Lunch money was a luxury and not one I was afforded. My mother was convinced that giant food companies were giving schools the scrapings from the factory floor and remarketing it to taste better when you bought it from the store. She insisted it was part of a larger conspiracy to get kids hooked on junk food. Either way, sometimes I ate like a queen at my friends' or like a third-world peasant at home. It's obvious that my mother isn't doing either, because she isn't eating at all.

My stare alters from the horror of my mother's figure to the ugly little girl as she moves to a plastic picnic table in the far corner of the living room, just past the Blob's chair, and starts to color. I move in to watch her more closely, but the texture of the tabletop makes everything she colors bumpy and it's ruining the picture. The poor child, whomever she is, deserves more than a piece of plastic junk to play on. In her defense, it is the only thing not covered in dust, dirt, feces, or cigarettes.

I need fresh air, so I open a window to allow oxygen to flow and alleviate the scent of smoke and oven scorch. My mother stops me with two flailing hands in protest like ten strands of spaghetti in the wind. "No, Shane, not that one. I'll open the back door, but not the front, okay, sweetheart?" My mother has a way of talking that makes everyone listen and abide, no matter how nuts it sounds. I raise my eyebrow in question, but she ignores it and opens the broken slider to the deck. I feel the house breathe in the fresh air and exhale out a hacking yogic breath.

"May I use the bathroom?"

"Yes, of course, sweetie pie, you know where it is." She points in case I forgot. I walk down the narrow hall, passing up close to the dusty frames picturing her posing as the striking woman she once was in front of her old workplace on the Barrons' estate grounds. I get chills thinking of the deceased spread all over the papers.

The wood floors that have never been swept make balls of hair and fuzz dance and swirl around my feet, so I shake my leg to keep them from sticking. I can't believe how disgusting the house still is. It infuriates me, further fueling the ill feelings I have toward Rob. How dare he live for free inside the only goddamn thing my mom owns and not lift a fucking finger?

I walk inside the bathroom, close the door, pull duct tape from the latch on the swelled-shut window, and inhale, gorging on fresh, clean air. I choose to squat over the toilet, which is half sunk into a yellow, vinyl-covered floor, making it a gamble for anyone over my mother's weight to sit on it without falling through the floor. I wonder if Rob craps and pees himself to avoid falling through to the basement doom. Shit, there's no toilet paper. Realizing this midstream, I peer around for something to use—paper towels, coffee filters, anything at all. Nothing but a black-stained tub and a burgundy towel that looks crunchy from overuse. I peek into the vanity from the angle I'm crouched in, contorting my waist, and reach for the toilet paper I see through the missing door. I take the old roll off and go to place the new one on and watch in slow motion as it slips from my fingers and rolls behind the latrine. Gross, gross, gross! I twist again, trying not to drip everywhere, to reach the lost roll. I reach for it behind the exposed plumbing and quickly pull back my hand. Jesus Christ, a fucking tarantula! I move my hand faster this time and grasp the white tissue with a flick of my wrist and the arachnid scatters under a wild mushroom growing next to the white porcelain base. I take off the first few layers that have touched the fungus and are covered in dusty little bits. I wipe, flush, and finally get up. I take a few more deep breaths of clean air, wash my hands with a hairy, yellowed bar of soap, and walk back out to face the asylum.

"Mother, there's a freaking huge spider in the bathroom. I thought it was going to bite my hand."

"Oh, Shaney bug, that's just sweet old Henry. Don't worry about him, he has plenty to eat in there."

"Yeah, a goddamn wild mushroom feast."

"What, sweetheart?" There is a slight weakness in her voice, so I leave it alone.

"Never mind, it's not important."

I walk up to my mother and ask her if we can talk privately. She peers at the strange little girl, who is still drawing jagged art, and shuffles toward her.

"Mother!" I say it sternly to get her attention.

"Okay, okay. What's up, pumpkin pie?"

She walks and I follow. Being behind her is like walking in the shadow of a moving corpse, every bone from her head to her toes creaking like a biology room skeleton. The bones shift and the skin follows in a rhythmic fashion, gliding and touching, in and out, in and out, like a perfectly wound watch. I still can't believe what she's become, and I don't know where I should start.

"Mother, Rob called me and said you weren't doing great. He said you were on one of your diets, but it doesn't look like you've dieted at all?" I pause, because I can't help tearing up, causing my voice to crack. "You're just not eating anything?"

"Shaney, I am fine, never better. In fact, I feel pure, clean, and wonderful. I'm drinking water from Poland Spring and it's working great. I will pick up some more today, if that makes you happy? How long are you staying? I am so glad you are here. There is so much to do and talk about. Goodness, it's going to be great having you."

There is excitement in her voice, and it reminds me of the infamous happy mania days. I feel a touch of guilt telling her the truth. "I only came for today. I have to work tomorrow. I skipped class today to come and see you. Truthfully, I don't understand what is going on? Who is that kid? Please tell me you didn't have some freak miracle baby with Rob?"

Deep down I need to know what's been happening here; the house is a dump, Rob's gigantic, and there's an orphan hanging around the living room. Just as she opens her mouth, Rob calls from the other room. "Aggie, Aggie, I need you."

Lazy fucker, can't even get out of his chair to politely interrupt us. Instead, he has to yell through the whole little house. I follow the bony structure from the bedroom back to the living room.

Holy shit. I freeze. I feel faint. I'm going to collapse. How much can one person take? Was this planned?

Goddess From the Past

"Hello, Shane," she whispers. I can't answer. I'm thoroughly confused. The weird girl automatically rises from the table, as if she has done it a thousand times before, packs various items into a marker-stained designer backpack, and stands erect next to the leg of Simone Barron.

Unlike my mother's current state, Simone is absolutely stunning, always has been. Drop-dead gorgeous with long, blond hair, naturally bouncy curls, and eyes the shape of almonds and color of blueberries. She stands there in perfect posture, wearing a navy blue dress with a cherry red belt and nude wedge heels, Chanel or Dior, I am sure. I haven't seen Simone since I left and, unlike my mother, certainly never expected to ever again. What I can't fathom is, why is she here? This is my house, not hers. She has a huge one; an entire estate to call home, with pools and caretakers and guesthouses. Why the hell is she slumming it in my hood? Simone grew up on the fancy side of town—incredibly fancy, actually. She is one of the wealthiest people I have ever known or even heard of. The Barron money makes A-list celebrities look ghetto poor. She was born with a silver spoon while I ate with a plastic one. Her father, William, was supremely wealthy, and Simone is his only daughter.

As children we played together while my mother worked for Mr. Barron, cleaning or attending to him, and for a short while we lived in a guesthouse. She was extraordinarily sensitive to my situation and always made sure to share anything and everything material with me. My time with her shone a pin-sized light into the other side and allowed me to look and act like her from a very young age. High-end clothing, purses, and makeup were forever strewn all over her master bedroom and mine for the taking. I used to wonder if I was some sort of charity case her family felt badly for, but our friendship stood strong even after my mother's employment ceased. I don't know what happened with Mr. Barron, but next thing I knew, we were moving into a peach-colored shithole on the bad side of town, and fears of losing my best friend were real.

Thankfully, my mother let me sleep over in exchange for feeding her gossip about Mr. Barron's personal life. This allowed me to visit and stay with Simone as often as I wanted. I remember her housekeeper taking loads of laundry from me to wash while I was there. As children, growing up side by side, though on opposite sides of the wall, we didn't realize how immeasurably different we were. The older we got, the more apparent our separate paths became. From the time I met her, Simone always had a driver to and from her school or anywhere she needed to go, and during the week she practiced cello, took equestrian lessons, and learned how to speak French. I walked to the bus stop, not wanting a ride even if my mother offered one, because she drove a rusted, black hand-me-down truck with a white No Fear sticker splattered across the rear windshield—not exactly a magnet for popularity. When summer came, Simone would leave for various camps, taking a private jet, and I would play in the dirt. When we were really little, it was to Maine, then later to the South of France to practice her French and perfect her sailing. I would play in the woods or at the park with other kids, trying to avoid the alleys littered with used needles and tiny baggies. But no matter how different our upbringings were, we had always remained friends. When she left for her trips, I would write to wherever she went and wait patiently for the responding letters to arrive. She would tell me about her adventures, the boys she met and made out with, how her counselor hit on her, and when she lost her virginity. I would tell her about the strays (people and animals) my mother took in and pretend I wasn't working two summer jobs to keep food, booze, and cigarettes for my mother on the table. My mother would host many men in our house, and staying out of their way was the key to our messy little fucked-up home. I never told Simone the hell I endured while she was away. I wanted to protect her from such horror and preferred her to see my mother the way she liked to, as sweet, pretty, manic Aggie who adored anything and everything *Barron*. Though it drove me insane and she had no idea how I lived, I never told her the truth about any of it. And no matter what, her entering this house was an absolute NO. She thought everything about my mother was funny and said she liked being around her. I never understood why. When I asked her about it, she said that being trained to be something you're not wears on you, and when she was with us, she felt free to have fun and be normal. It was funny, because being with her allowed me to be something I wasn't, too. We were the oil and water of status, but when we were together we made the perfect dressing of a facade.

Everything changed six years ago. Now she stands before me, a goddess from the past. But what is she doing here? And what is my mother doing with that ugly little kid? Could this unattractive little being belong to Simone? Holy shit, could she actually have a kid? And why are they here, why now? It's truly a disgusting place, not appropriate for a Barron heir, or really anyone who gives a shit about her child. There must be a nanny—or several, like she'd grown up with. My mind is spinning with assumptions. It doesn't make sense to bring a loved child to a house of filth and nuttiness. I can only imagine the reprimand her father would give if he were alive to see this. He may possibly have killed my mother just for letting them in, and with her desperation for his attention, she would have welcomed the knife.

I have lived through Simone's pseudo-family, and her nannies were like real moms to me. My favorite au pair was Julia, who spoke Spanish to us. She always played like a child, being silly and whatnot, making us giggle out of control. When we were about ten years old, she was teaching us how to make flan in the maid's kitchen when Simone's father walked in. He was so infuriated by the idea of Simone learning to cook that he fired Julia instantly. He told Simone, while Julia watched, that "cooking is for workers, slaves, and immigrants, so knock it off! That's not a lady's position. You either, Shane, knock it off!" He threw the flan in the trash and walked out. I cried hysterically, but Simone seemed unfazed and just ignored me. The next day a new nanny arrived. It was like she'd been pre-ordered and came in with the morning mail. After that, we never played with the help, just amongst ourselves, and only checked in for snacks and, for me, a ride home. I followed along like an adopted dog, not wanting to make waves, although I knew his actions were cruel and, more importantly, hurt Simone. We were kids and didn't know we were part of a caste system, but I recognized that we were different. If Simone did, too, she never let on. She never had to see me go without anything, at least at her house, because whatever I yearned for—food, clothes, toys, etc.—I would get, since she always shared everything with me. I was allowed to live in the shadow of her excess and play pretend. I was the second princess in her fairy-tale life and wanted to be like her, but most of all, I loved her dearly.

Six years ago my loyalty payment to her was paid in full, and in exchange, our fates were altered forever. I never thought I would see her again.

"What the fuck! Are you kidding me? Why is she here? How could you?"

Simone ignores my verbal protests and calmly talks over me. "How long are you staying?"

I can barely edge out words from the nervous frothing of my mouth, when I make eye contact and am hooked. She has me in her snare, and I know I'll fail trying to escape. Her eyes don't move from mine. I answer but try looking away. "I am going home, now!"

She doesn't flinch and is feeling me out. "Why home?"

"I, uh, just came to visit. I was just walking out the door and then I saw . . . it doesn't matter. Nice to see you people, goodbye everyone."

I didn't expect her calm composure and can't compete, plus those fucking eyes. Two sets now, and I can barely hold it together. I am sad, hurt, infuriated. I had written so many letters pleading for forgiveness and called over and over for two years straight, until her number finally changed. Emotionally, I gave up on her, and on my mother, too. They were my past. I feel a sudden urge to bolt for the door, but I can't move. I'm frozen. How dare they gang up on me! I am only here because Rob the Blob asked for my help, and that wolf-crying fatso hasn't even moved from his chair.

I want to talk about her father, give condolences, but I have no idea how to go about it. The lame "I'm so sorry" won't cut it. Instead, I get the Simone look, with those familiar, piercing eyes. I just saw them in a three-foot-tall munchkin and here they are again. I can feel my pulse pounding, and the crease in my brows is causing an instantaneous headache. I need to mellow, calm myself down, and get out of here. I can't deal with all the confusion of this very moment. Nothing makes sense, and they're all staring at me, all reminders of the past. The cigarette smoke and burning stove smell is still in the air. I feel sick, dizzy, my stomach is queasy. I'm going to vomit.

Escape Is My Only Out

I wake up on top of a musty, sour-scented bedspread. My body aches all over, and it hurts to move. I look around without moving my head or budging my body from the horizontal position I'm lying in. I see a cluttered nightstand with a metal ashtray and a filthy, cream-colored lamp with a thick layer of dust on top of it. I can just make out the old pictures of my young mother. I turn on my side for better viewing, and a moist cloth falls from my fore-head. Trying to move only makes me feel worse. There must be at least a dozen frames, mounted crooked on the walls and covered in smoke film, dust, and animal hair. I don't recognize some of them, but then again, I block out a lot of this place. A couple pic-tures have both Simone and I as little tykes, and I recognize us in front of the Barrons' grounds. It must have been when we lived in the guesthouse? I can't remember when it was, and the pain from my aching body is making it hard to concentrate. The pictures of Simone and I, adorable and innocent, don't stand out, but the beauty of my young mother does. Her eyes were vibrant and alive, not the sunken holes I saw today. She looked happy, beautiful and smiling. Her hair was long, her figure trim but with curves, and her entire body radiated with glee. A single photograph of her para-lyzing beauty might have won her the cover of *Time* magazine. A modern-day Marilyn Monroe. I try to remember her like that but I can't. I lie here wondering what happened to her and how she could have changed so much. I blame myself for all that was wrong with her and how much worse she has gotten. The guilt floods me like an overflowing bathtub. I need to get up and never look back.

First, though, I must figure out why I'm lying in a dark room on top of a smelly comforter. I look behind and all around me to find my bearings so I can head for the door, when I notice the moon's illuminating glow coming through the curtains. Fuck, it's dark out? The next steps need to be tactical, as I want to sneak out of this house without rousing anyone. I need to make as little noise as possible, but it's rather dark and hard to see. I move to get up and notice wet spots on the mattress where a flat sheet should be. I am drenched in sweat. Oh no, not again. At that moment, I realize I don't just want them, I need them. Where is my purse and where are my pills? I left it in the car because I was only planning to stay for a few minutes, but I must have passed out? Fuckety, fuck, fuck, how am I going to pull this off? I need to sneak out of the room, find my keys, make it to the car, chew my pills as I slam Hope into drive, and speed as fast as I can from this trap. I sit up and use the moon's light to find the door, walking like a zombie, and follow the sound of television.

"Hey there, Shaney bug, how are you feeling?"

Are you fucking serious? Was she waiting outside the door for me? Goddamn this tiny house, I can't escape its eight hundred square feet of nonsense. "I need to get my purse." It's all I can think about, and I don't have time or the desire to engage in fake small talk. I grab my keys from the table next to the front door, shake the accumulating hair and dust off of them, and walk barefoot to my car. The hard pebbles and broken tar hurt my feet. I get in the car, find my purse on the floor of the front seat, open the bottle, grab my favorite oval treat, and chomp it into crushed pieces in my mouth. I take a swig of leftover water from the drive down, close the door, foregoing my shoes inside, and hit skin to pedal. I throw Hope in reverse, and as I straighten her out and head left from the driveway, I see a bony structure in the rearview mirror running after my car. I slam the brakes as she grazes her hand on the taillight. I roll down my window. My mother is panting from breathlessness, holding the edge of the glass window to stand.

"Mother, I need to go!"

"No." It comes out as barely a word and she tries again. "No, Shaney, no."

"Mom, I need to go home, I have responsibilities. I need to go."

She is catching her breath and a full sentence follows. "Please, please don't leave. I need you, Shaney bug. There's so much going on here, and I'm sure you've heard about darling Bill. Please, just stay for a bit."

I look down at my naked feet and then back at my mother's sickening state and choose to give in. "Yes, I have. Let me back up."

We walk inside together. An enormous chunk of time is missing, along with Simone and the child. My mother acts as if everything is normal and asks if I want some grape juice. I look at Rob, who hasn't moved from his chair and has an even larger pile of dishes and crinkly bags of junk next to him. I wonder if he is consuming everything my mother isn't, like a conjoined fetus that feeds off its sibling? As my mother hands me the purple drink in a glass that's crusted around the rim with something yellow, she says, "Honey bug, you passed out. What is going on with you? Should I be worried? Where's your husband?"

Here we are, back to mother and daughter roles, and I feel inclined to answer. "Jake is camping with his dad and his friends. What do you mean I passed out?"

She ignores my question and presses on. "Oh, wowee, Jake goes camping? I didn't know that about him. I hope he's not hunting—you know how I feel about animals. He better not be a hunter. I didn't raise my little bug to marry a mammal killer."

I have never fainted before, but being with her after all this time, I understand why my mind and body shut down. It's a brilliant defense mechanism, and I'd like to do it again.

"Mom, I really need to go. Do you know where my shoes are?"

"No way, absolutely not! Shane, you are not leaving this house. You cannot drive at night. I won't let you. Tell her, Rob. Tell Shane she isn't leaving."

We both look at him. He's nodded off and doesn't even know what she's talking about but utters something anyhow. "Yep. Bad idea."

What the fuck? This is a crazy house and I am their newest patient. I ask for my shoes again, and my mother, faster than a cheetah, jaunts to the front door and blocks it with her bitty frame. It takes everything in my power to stop from laughing uncontrollably. I can move her aside with the flick of a finger, but she's mistaken herself for a mighty bear. A very fucked-up mama bear. The phone rings.

"Don't you move, young lady, do you hear me? I am going to answer it, but you cannot leave, don't move."

What does she think I'm going to do, run away like a defiant teenager? Been there done that. I stand still and her eyes watch me as she walks backward to the phone, still glaring as she greets the caller.

"Oh hi. . . . Yeah, she is. . . . Yes, she's feeling better."

I mouth, "Who is it?" But she waves her hand fanatically to stop me from talking, all the while keeping her eyes locked on mine.

"She wants to go, but I have her right here and I'm having her stay the night. . . . No, that's silly, I have it all set. . . . Okay, okay, I will let her know. Bye now . . . uh huh, bye-bye."

She hangs up the phone and answers me.

"That was Simone, she is coming over to get you. She wants to take you to get a bite to eat. She's concerned. This is good for you two, I know how much she misses you."

I am more than furious. "Mom, what the fuck? Are you kidding me? I called her for—"

She marches at me with pounding feet and growls in a low voice, "Listen here, Shane Catherine, don't you dare take that tone with me, and don't even think of using that language in this house. You are the one who left, and you are the one who caused all of this, and if you want to blame someone or be mad at someone, you better look straight in the mirror. Do you hear what your mother is saying to you? Do you have any idea what I'm going through?"

My breathing labors, and I feel ill again. The disgust and odor of the house and my mother's truths are too much to bear. Tears flood from my eyes, followed by mouth sweats. I am a pathetic child all over again. She sees my crying face and slaps me across the cheek. I want to hit her back, slam her to the floor, kick her for all the pain, but I can't, she's still my mother. My eyes blurry with salt water, I run to the bathroom and close the door.

My back slides down the vanity, and on the way down I grab a towel, creating a semi-clean barrier from the floor for me to sit on. I sob into cupped hands, my nose running as saliva and mucus puddle between my fingers. She's right, I caused this and I ran from everyone. I can't take this stress. I have never been able to handle anything, and she knows it, it's her favorite weapon. My mother has always used her vindictive ways against me, knowing I'm a soft pawn. She knows that when it comes to her and Simone, I fold under pressure, and the brilliant bitch is using them both to hold me hostage.

When I was a young girl and would sleep at Simone's all weekend, I'd return to the wreckage of an unfit mother who'd let loose and was loose the entire time I was gone. I was constantly picking up her empty bottles of liquor or sweeping piles of powder into the trash. Eventually, I would get to my breaking point and snap. With the little bit of motherly instinct she carries inside, she would know when I'd had enough. Despite how destitute we were, she always found a way to use the public school's therapists to her advantage, managing to get extra sessions or convincing them to take her frantic phone calls. She would make up stories of how I saw visions or heard voices, and right away, I'm a schizophrenic and they're shipping me off to the funny farm for a couple weeks of state-funded rehab. By the fourth stay in seven years, the nuthouse caught on that we didn't have money for copays and declined any more of the pseudo-vacations. They were a business, and we were the shoplifters, unable to pay for their services. My mother convinced me it was okay because it was a nice trip that insurance could pay for and that I should enjoy everything it offered. She liked to compare it to an all-inclusive vacation, the kind we would see commercials about. Looking back at my unfathomably fucked-up childhood, I realize how insane she actually is. I would enter the hospital as a fairly normal tween, forced to escape daily life with *her*, and *bam*, two weeks later I'd exit with an eating disorder or afraid of water or wanting to light shit on fire—the dysfunctions were endless. I would become immersed in the home of diagnosed crazies and start to become one. I swapped one nut case for another, and actual disorders were born where there hadn't been any. It was like entering the school nurse's office with a sprained thumb and leaving with a broken leg.

When I'd get home and seemingly assimilated back into school, where she told the teachers lies about the fanciful trips we were on, I was in actuality trying to undo all that I'd seen. The last time I went was around Halloween, and Simone had been away for a program abroad. Thankfully, she doesn't know about any of the visits, a secret I will hold till my grave. My mother came to the ward drunk, seven days after Halloween, carrying grocery bags filled with costumes and makeup for all the kids to celebrate and dress up. The wacky friends I'd made were thrilled for a chance to be someone they weren't, but the staff recognized a real nutjob when they saw one and stopped the chaos before it ensued. My mother freaked, grabbed my hand, threw the bags of goodies down the hall while calling everyone Nazis, and made me run for the car. It was the last hospital she made me go to.

By the time I was seventeen, a senior in high school and almost legally allowed to make my own decisions, I did everything I was supposed to do to please my mother and keep her calm. She was declining into one of her states, so I did whatever I could to help and make her proud, including graduating high school and helping financially by getting a second job. I was too old and knew better than to go back to the hospital, so when I graduated high school, my options to escape had considerably narrowed.

I met a guy named Jake who was nice to me and knew nothing of my past with my mother or the Barrons and was exactly what I needed when I needed it. The timing was right, so I moved out, married him, and never looked back. Until now.

I'm stuck on the bathroom floor, bawling my eyes out with

nothing but fungus, spiders, and an occasional jumping flea for company. This is why I don't come here, because it's enough to make anyone want to go to the loony bin, and this time I have decent insurance.

I need to follow my routine, which for the past five-plus years has kept all of this at bay. My job now is to work and be a good wife to Jake. The plain and simple keeps me sane. My brain floods with regrets, and I can't stop from weeping harder and harder. A door knock echoes inside the bathroom.

"Shaney, open up, it's me, Smoney." Why is she being so nice? I haven't called her Smoney since we were kids. I don't deserve any kindness, not after what I've done, even though I did it for her.

"No, I need to go. I need to go home." My words jump around as I talk through hiccupped breathing.

"Open the door, Shane. Please, let me take you out. I really want to talk."

I can hear my mother in the background coaching her. "Please, Shane!"

I sit on the floor and take deep breaths, feeling my belly rise and lower as I inhale and exhale. Simone's stern voice breaks the meditative rhythm.

"Shane, listen. You owe this to me. Please come out, I need to see you."

I feel like a shamed child and want to curl up in a ball on this dirty floor and cry forever. I will let my body melt into the sinking linoleum, eventually becoming part of it, and then a new turf of mushrooms will form.

She speaks again, this time sweet and breathy. "Shaney, please. I am here. I am waiting for you." This fucking girl has always had a hold over me. It's incredibly frustrating that no matter what I do, I cannot escape Simone Barron. There's a part of me that wants so badly to open the door and face her, but I can't find the strength to do it.

"Shane, I need the bathroom, can you hurry up? I gotta piss like a bloated racehorse." Are you kidding me? Rob finally gets off his ass, and it's to interrupt me? I feel like laughing like a hyena at the absurdity of it all, but mostly I don't want to hide anymore. I feel drained and completely worn out, torn down from hair to feet. I stand up, brushing myself off, and glance at the puffy eyes staring back in the mirror, wondering how the hell I got here. Oh yeah, fucking Rob the Blob. I slowly turn the knob and Rob pushes past me without even looking and nearly takes me out with his giant belly. The whizzing of his pee quiets my mother's encouraging words. "Go, honey bug. Go with Simone and have some fun."

I notice the kid is back. It's embarrassing to cry in front of a child, but this odd duck doesn't seem to care about anything. I smile at her, and she stares at me without blinking or saying a word.

"Shane, say hi to Vienne." My mother formally introduces us. "Look, Vivi, this is Shane. Shane is my little girl. Your mommy and my Shane are going to play together."

Upon introduction, the girl breaks our stare and walks away to the bumpy table to draw. I don't have the gumption or energy to get into that conversation yet. All I can think is, what a freakishly weird and unattractive kid. I cannot believe Simone has an ugly child. Nothing makes sense anymore.

Ritzy Richie

I grab my purse, slip on the sneakers that are now appropriately placed next to the door, and walk out behind Simone. The fresh air feels so good. A large weight has been lifted as I leave the house, but an even bigger one is about to take me to dinner. I have no idea what I am doing; I am basically an exhausted monkey following the circus trainer. There is no more energy in me. I know driving home without falling asleep isn't possible, so I succumb to Simone.

I get inside the passenger's side of the dark-colored, two-door BMW, and interior lights show off baby butt–soft, cherry red leather. I buckle up and wait for Simone to provide direction and set the night's tone. She backs up perfectly, avoiding Hope through an extremely tight squeeze with foreign-car precision and turns left. Where are we going? And why am I leaving looking like this? I'm too nervous and downright exhausted to ask. I am allowing my former best friend-slash-enemy to lead the way without so much as a question to where we may be headed. We've been driving for six minutes exactly, which I know because I've been staring into the clock the whole time. Simone finally speaks. "How are you feeling, Shane?"

She pauses, waiting for me to answer, but I'm not ready to.

"I promise to take you somewhere good, and everything will be okay."

Boy, I must be a mess. Why else is she being so kind? The paranoia sets in, and I am beginning to think I should've hugged my mother before this possibly permanent goodbye. Is this what happens when you get murdered, a smooth drive in a fancy car, only to have your face bashed in by a frenemy? I need to talk. It will keep me awake and maybe alive a little longer. I can barely say anything without a sleepy drag to my voice, but I try anyhow.

"Simone, I want to tell you how deeply—"

She stops me. "For my loss?"

I feel stupid. "Um, yeah. I am sorry, everyone is probably saying that to you, and when I say it, it probably bothers you even more than anyone else. But I mean it, I really do."

She doesn't speak for a minute, or ten, and then with a whisper under her breath says, "Shane, I don't want to hear that right now. I just want to hang out with my old friend and have a nice night. Can we do that? No heavy shit, okay? I know I'm dealing with a lot, enough for both of us, plus you seem to be dealing with some serious things yourself. So let's just stop. We will discuss it another time." She sounds so sad. I gulp with guilt because I know the conversation about Mr. Barron is inevitable and, secondly, why will there be another time?

"Simone, let me just say one thing, please." I am going to crap myself, I'm so nervous, and my sleepy voice cracks.

"Okay, shoot, but nothing serious, okay?"

I watch her lips as she speaks and see a brief smile appear and just as quickly fade away. My God, she is beautiful, how could I have for even a moment almost forgotten. Her beauty is ridiculous. What did she do right in a past life to be born both gorgeous and rich?

"Okay, okay, I promise, geez Louise." I make a tiny high-pitched giggle on accident. It's the first time I've laughed all day, and it feels so good to let go. I'm a little less worried and starting to feel safe, but in my heart I know we aren't even close to getting started.

She begins to crack up, almost like we used to. "No one, and I mean *no one*, says geez Louise. Only you, Shane Lacy." I can tell she's trying to keep it together like a trained Barroness, but within minutes together, the weight slides off her shoulders and we're both laughing like idiots. "You are such a crackerjack, seriously, who says that stuff?"

"Um, are you joking? Who says crackerjack?"

She starts laughing again. "You do, that's why I said it."

We are giggling like schoolgirls, and she turns on music to keep our vibe going. The Harman Kardon stereo blasts out the latest songs and we sit silent until a good one comes on. Just as we are both about to sing our hearts out to Katy Perry like teenagers, I see an illuminated sign, The Ritz-Carlton. The car veers right past it, and she drives to a parking lot in the back.

"A hotel? What are we doing here?"

Simone laughs and says, "Come with me. I told you we are going to have fun tonight."

I grab my purse, and before I can comprehend anything else,

I'm looking for water to take a pill. I keep thinking how intuitive it was to have brought the whole bottle and not just a few wrapped in paper towel, stuffed in the side of my purse like I usually do. We walk up to the revolving doors, only to be distracted by the shouting voices of more Richies from their BMWs and Range Rovers. One of them is a girl much younger than us who hits a post, distracted by the come-hither guys. She starts yelling at the bellhop, though he's concerned for the hotel, not her; he's already fingering maintenance to come fix the damage. I cannot even imagine such a scene at my complex. If some loser rams their piece of shit 1990s Cadillac into the side of my building, a few bricks would fall out and a lady from the top floor would swear and throw an egg. I laugh at the pure absurdity of it. I don't usually see cars like this at home, unless I go to the fancy side of town, but even those aren't like the ones these teens are driving.

I walk behind Simone, and when the bellman catches notice of her, he literally drops a customer's bag to open the door for us.

"Good evening, Ms. Barron, so lovely to see you tonight."

"Thanks, Mr. Ryan." Simone keeps walking without introducing me to the fine-looking worker, and I scurry to keep up with her. My eyes are distracted by the extreme wealth and gold decor. I glance forward, and she's thirty steps ahead. I jog to catch up, and as I come up beside her she smirks. "God, Shane, have you been living under a rock?"

I don't dare respond, as the truth of my life since leaving could lead to a fit of laughter or further the possibly approaching murderous plot. Aren't people killed inside hotel suites all the time? It's easier for the maids to clean it up, I suppose. My brain is running wildly since we are in her territory, not the somewhat safe confines of Aggie's nuthouse. I cling to her like a suckerfish to a nurse shark, and soon we are standing in front of an elevator. This is at least the fifth or sixth bellman who I'm starting to think are assigned to Ms. Barron and are watching her every move. This tall, goober-looking guy does more than gawk at her, he presses a button. I thank him, but he doesn't pay attention; I am no one. He places a special key pulled from a zipped pocket on his uniform into a secret keyhole behind the emergency stop button. I watch the numbers rise to the highest floor shown on the board of numbers, but the elevator keeps going. It comes to a smooth, hydraulic stop and I get out behind Simone, but not before thanking the goober again. He is more interested in staring at Simone's backside than to "you're welcome" this nobody, so I block his view with my imperfect and shorter body. I look back to see him still staring, so I say with immature jealousy, "Why don't you take a picture? Seriously, it's icky." He furiously hits the button with his bony, bent finger, and the metal doors close, but not before one last glance.

Simone breaks the silence as she laughs and says with a smile, "I have to see that creep all the time. He knows where I live, ya know."

She lives here? I feel stupid and look at my feet. She pulls a key from her purse—an actual key, not the plastic hotel kind—and slides it in the lock, a smooth fit. We walk in and the scene is surreal, majestic even. It's brand-new and strikingly familiar all at the same time, but in a different way than the Barron estate. The scent of fresh lilies overwhelms me, and I spot them in at least three of the exposed rooms. The aroma makes me happy as I think of Simone's nannies picking them from the garden and arranging them in vases around her room. I inhale deeply and Simone takes notice.

"Don't fresh flowers make everything better?"

I agree with a nod of my head and keep peering around without being too nosy. A fleeting thought comes over me. I hope these flowers aren't because of her father's passing? Upon closer inspection, I decide they aren't, and my mind moves on. The rooms alone are eight or ten times the size of our entire apartment. I had no idea hotels could be this big. Actually, I've never stayed in a hotel, but from what the movies show, I thought they were smaller, closer to the size of my apartment. I stand still, staring at the perfect decorations and bright whites that surround us. Coming from my mother's smoke-stained dump, I feel almost too unclean to enter such a place.

"Come on in. Get comfortable. I need something to drink." Simone walks to an oversized fridge and grabs two large blue glass containers that read "Saratoga." I examine the bottle when she hands it to me, thinking it will fizz up when I open it, but it doesn't. I pause when she takes a swig directly from the narrowed opening. I've never seen her drink straight from the bottle before. Those kinds of tasteless manners would get a smack in both our homesteads. I take the bottle and walk to my purse, near the suite's door, where my jaw is still resting from when I first walked in. I undo the zipper and pull a pill from the bottle, then swallow it whole with a delicious gulp of fresh spring water.

"What do you have there? Are you taking something?" The sharpness in Simone's voice is direct. How does she know? No one ever notices.

"Nothing, I just need it for my headache." She seems annoyed that I'm lying and flips her hair back. I don't think she's used to people fibbing.

"Shane, you never take medicine."

Boy, she really doesn't know me anymore. "It's just Tylenol. No worries, I'm fine. My head hurts from earlier." She is somewhat convinced and walks away into what could be a bedroom or who knows, maybe another wing? I take the opportunity to explore the suite's entirety. I cannot believe she hasn't changed a bit and there are still clothes and shoes thrown all over the floor. It's exactly like when we were kids walking into her side of the mansion. I step over mounds of piled laundry, tiptoeing around it, but cannot avoid stepping on a random sleeve or inside-out skirt. Once I get through the initial mountain of textiles, I look up to see there are three large bedrooms, one of which has kids clothes with tags on the dresser, toys still in packages, and a made-up bed with a princess coverlet. I cannot help but shout, because the absurdity of the penthouse's size is overwhelming. "This place is fucking amazing!"

She yells back, and it echoes from another room. "Thanks, it works for now, at least until everything gets straightened out." She pauses, then starts again, but more excitable this time. "But honestly, Shane, I don't want to think about that now. You know why?"

This must be when a movie crew jumps out and makes fun of me for falling for her antics all over again. "Um, no."

"Because I have an idea! That's why!"

Okay, so no cameras. Then this must be when she tells me how she'll be dismembering my body and having Ryan and the other houseboys discard the remains for her. Just as I was feeling my body relax, it's as tense as a steel post and I'm terrified to hear more.

"How about we get all dressed up, go out, and have a good time?"

Um, okay, not what I expected. I like this idea much better. I need to stop being so nervous. She sounds happy, and her voice is silly and gleeful. I want to oblige her, but I can hardly imagine myself worthy of being in this part of town, and I look and feel like pure exhaustion. She walks out of what is presumably her personal master bedroom, because from a distance I can see that the cascades of clothing are higher there than anywhere else. We make eye contact and I point at my frame, gesturing up and down, showing her with my hand and frowning face how shitty my appearance is. "Look at me! I don't have anything to wear. I have been crying all day and I'm exhausted and ugly. I came here to see my mother, because Rob the fucking Blob called frantically and told me it was urgent, not because I want to be here, no offense. I mean not here in this hotel, but you know what I mean, um, back here. Fuck, I need to stop talking. I'm sorry, Simone."

Barely paying attention to anything I'm saying, she answers my plea to leave with casual kindness. "No worries, I got ya covered. I think we're still the same size, and I have plenty to choose from, even underwear . . . if you use that kind of thing." She giggles, exposing a glimpse of her textbook straight teeth.

"Simone, I am so tired, please, I have to work tomorrow." She looks annoyed and gives me the infamous blue Barron eyes. A second or two passes and I start to give in, cowering under their magical power. Ignoring my protests, she goes about gathering towels, soap, and a razor.

"Here, take a shower, you'll feel better, and I'll find you something fabulous to wear. You can have anything you want, and we'll go out and forget all about this shitty, shitty day."

One eyebrow rises in my last attempt at objection, but she laughs it off. I snatch the soft towels, smelly soap, and packaged razor, which I am grateful for, and walk to the one bedroom without expensive stuff thrown everywhere. "May I use the shower in here?" From my small tour, it seems that each bedroom has its own bathroom, and this one looks to be used the least.

"Yeah, totally. Take whatever you want, just get ready!"

I close the door, locking it just in case, and run the water full blast before climbing into a hot, hot shower. The floral soap's aroma fills the stall, creating what I envision as a spa-like experience. I cannot believe this is happening. Jake would be shocked if he knew I came back home to see my mother, never mind all this. I can only imagine his state if he knew I was at a hotel. It would most definitely raise some husbandly questions. I step onto the warm floor and a velvety-looking rug. I reach in to shut the faucet off, but it somehow knows and stops automatically. I feel one thousand times better and wrap my hair and body in the most luxurious, heavenly scented towels. These are the most perfect swabs of supersoft fabric to dab dew from my lady parts. All the towels I have ever used are so scratchy and crusty from not having a dryer to fluff them or from running out of detergent and using dish soap that I'm more used to pain, and the drying off is just a bonus. Who knew such a fabric existed, and not just reserved for the kings and queens of Monaco? I don't feel worthy, like I'm somehow making the towels dirty. Selfishly, not knowing when this will end, I snuggle one of them into my nose, inhaling and letting it touch the tip of my tongue. If skin could talk, my epidermis would thank me.

I walk out barefoot to find Simone standing tall in a lacy green thong and matching bra. She was always much more sexually open and definitely more comfortable with her elongated curves than I am. Her body is magnificent, perky, taut, and exceptionally smooth in appearance. I stop and pretend like I'm not as creepy as the elevator guy and that my weird stare is only admiration of her Victoria's Secret model self. "Do you have any cream or makeup I can use?" Deep down I want to compliment such a showcase of beauty and perfection, but seeing her like this just makes me feel worse. Her beauty is a religion, and there are a lot of followers.

"Of course, whatever you need. Carte blanche to anything, just take it. I told you, only fun. No bullshit tonight. Like old times, Sugar Shane."

My mouth and heart simultaneously smile at the playful childhood nickname. It's extremely endearing and I swallow it up whole. I nervously walk inside her bedroom and over the peaks and valleys of clothes that lead to an even larger bathroom. Standing on an even bigger, softer mat, I eye at least twenty or thirty bottles of Chanel makeup, lotions, powders, and perfumes. Some are upright, others tilted and spilled all over the marble, leaving a snail trail of expensive mud. I treasure the tube of MAC lipstick that I splurged on just for me, which cost almost an entire night of tips at the bar. But here, there is at least a few thousand dollars in creams and shadows, cast out like yesterday's trash. I really have no idea what her life is like, but exactly like when we were kids, she seems happy to share, and I graciously receive. "Are you sure I can choose anything?"

"Yes, absolutely. You already know that. Do I need to come in there and pick for you?"

"I have no idea where we're going?" Hoping for an answer but never receiving one, a strange sense of calm comes over me knowing I'm not planning anything. I don't have to work or make dinner or pick up after anyone. It's an incredibly freeing feeling. I yell to Simone from inside her closet, "Please give me a clue to what we're doing so I know what to wear?"

"Just put your damn makeup on and let the outfit decide for us," she says. A bohemian idea, and I love every part of the adventure it allows for. I don't think I have had this much fun in years, and so far it's only been a few hours. I need to remind myself not to get too comfortable and keep up a guard with Simone. I have no idea what her motive is for forgiveness, but letting go comes so easy, for both of us it seems. I inspect the packed closet carefully, choosing the most elegant and simple dress I can find. It's strapless, black in color, with detailed beadwork around the hem. I look at the tag on the back, Yves Saint Laurent. I slip it on and pull it up toward my chest. Simone walks in, giddy with anticipation, and grabs a fistful of material, zipping it up to the base of my neck. She stands back and screams with delight. "Oh my goodness, you look amazing, what an awesome choice, I love it! I had forgotten all about that one, so freaking cute!" I take a quick peek in the mirror, happy with its simplicity, and catch a glimpse of what she's slipped on over her green lingerie. It's an elegant, cream-colored, and tightly tailored shirt that tucks perfectly into a lengthy pencil skirt that barely covers her knees. The seams of material highlight every twist and turn that make up her body. She doesn't even look in the mirror. "Ready?"

We begin walking out for the night when I reach down to grab my purse. I don't have any presentable shoes. Normally, I wear the same thing every day, so this has never happened. The dirty sneakers that I wore here lie ripped and worn by the door. Oh my goodness, this is awful. Doubt casts its black shadow over me, and I am suddenly reminded how inferior I truly am. I look absolutely

ridiculous. Who am I to think that I can jump back in with Simone, play dress up, and pretend like everything's perfect?

She immediately notices my change in affect. It's like watching
a light bulb turn on above her perfect head. She looks down at my
pathetic shoes and says, "Who cares, throw 'em on. You know you
will rock them!" She starts laughing. "I know you have those dwarf
feet and won't fit into any of mine, so I'll get my own."

I find the jab at my little feet endearing; it's something she's
always found hilarious. She walks back toward me carrying a pair
of hot pink Nikes. Without another word, she pulls on the neon
sneaks and closes the door behind us. I look absurdly ridiculous
but feel beautiful inside and out. Confidence is creeping back
inside me. Simone has a fabulous way of doing this. The ups and
downs of emotion are common with her presence, but I still stand
up straight, absorbing every single moment. We enter the elevator
that's oddly waiting and are politely greeted by a different bellman.
We both start laughing uncontrollably when we catch ourselves
staring in the elevator's mirror at each other's feet. I can't help but
call it like it is. "We look like crazy people, ready to run from a
fashion show."

Before she can respond or laugh some more, the man speaks
into a microphone hidden inside his collar. "Car for Ms. Barron,
two-minute arrival. She has a guest. I will need two, repeat two."

Two what, I wonder. He looks like secret service talking into
his shirt, calling for the motorcade to come around front. Maybe
it's two armored cars?

We exit, and every door is opened at least twenty feet before
we enter through it. Two men are waiting outside, one on each
side of the midnight blue Beamer, here to open those doors. I
thank my personal valet and hop in the passenger's side, wondering if I should tip them? After driving and giggling for a bit, we
finally arrive in front of a brick building with thick velvet curtains
separating the sidewalk from the entryway. Someone must have

seen us pull up, because the curtains open like magic and Simone thanks yet another serviceperson with a wink. She moves around me, approaching an older man who immediately recognizes Simone and escorts us to a table, where our seats are pulled out and, simultaneously, drinks are delivered. "This is the 1588, it's their specialty. I hope you like it?"

I take a whiff. Not recognizing the aroma, I sip cautiously, still considering that murderous revenge could be on the horizon. Instead, a butter-smooth taste of orange and cinnamon touches my lips. "Whoa, this is insane." It takes me a moment to nail down the different flavors, and without sounding too stupid I offer a guess. "It tastes like a ridiculously smooth scotch or bourbon but with a hint of orange and something else, but I can't pinpoint it, maybe cinnamon or cloves?"

Simone cracks a smile, looking amused, and answers playfully, "What are you, some kind of bartender or something?"

My shoulders slump, realizing again that I don't belong here. I answer honestly and with a whisper. "Yeah."

"Oh my gosh, seriously? I am so sorry."

I'm annoyed by her apology. What did she think I would become, a fucking doctor? "Don't be sorry. It's what I am." I sit quietly, gathering the gusto to speak again. "I'm working on school, too. It's only part-time, but I have one project left and then I'm done. It's just my associate's, though."

She tries to make me feel better about my accomplishments and says, "Look, Shaney, I haven't done much either. I was forced to attend Harvard, which I did, but I hated freezing-cold Boston. I left and did a year abroad in France. Plus, it was so good to get away."

I wasn't surprised but pretended to be. "Oh, did you go to the South of France, like you used to for sailing?"

"Holy shit, you remember that? Yes, actually, I did. I stayed in Antibes with some friends on their boat and attended school in

Nice. Wow, good memory, Shane. I always felt bad when I would leave for the summers and you were stuck at home. I used to beg my dad to let me bring you, but he said Agnes wouldn't allow it."

I am shocked and not sure if I should believe her. "Are you kidding me, my mother wouldn't allow it? I didn't know that. That woman is beyond nuts, seriously. I would have died to go with you. Remember all the letters we would write and the hilarious pretend dating service books I would send?"

She bursts into a cackle, so hard and loud a couple people sitting at the bar look over to see what's so funny. "I remember those, they were the best. I think I still have some. You used to cut out people from magazines and make matching profiles about how great they'd be to date. One of my favorites was the one who talked on and on about eating pussy, remember? Contact me at www.icecreampussy.net. The guy looked like an African warrior or something, but boy he liked his pussy." She's cracking up again, and envisioning those silly scrapbooks made from leftover gossip magazines my mother would read has me laughing, too. "Okay, so tell me more. You're bartending and going to school. What else? I know you got married, what's that like?"

This amazing and delicious drink is relaxing me both in mind and body, and I'm opening up. Feeling she won't judge me, I let my guts spill out all over the antique wood floor. The night and drinks pour on, as do the confessions of a pathetic life. I tell her all about the potpies and the way I hate the word *meals*. I talk about working for the schmuck Dave who screws anything that has a vagina and my job at Stein's jewelry store, and it turns out she knows the owner's son. The drinks are so good and she has always been such an amazing listener, I keep going on and on, careful not to say anything too serious, her rules. I talk more about how much I hate the stupid apartment that we live in and about Andrew, my live wedding present, and how we rely on my tips for grocery money. I continue on about how all Jake and I do is work and come and go during the night without much of a relationship, never mind a marriage. She listens attentively, taking it all in and never looking bored or disappointed. Everything I pour, she soaks in, so I keep going, because what do I have to lose? I tell her how frustrated I am with my mother and Rob's situation, and when I drift into guilt about her and Mr. Barron, she stops me cold.

"Listen to me, none of that."

I feel dumb telling the richest girl in the world about my poor problems. It's like a mouse complaining to the lion about its size. I don't want her to feel badly for me, but I am so used to being on the other side of the counter listening, it's so nice to let go. This is the only cathartic release I've had since leaving, and it's funny I had to come all the way back for it to happen. She halts my verbal vomiting by saying, "Your mom isn't eating again."

"Yeah, I can tell she's emaciated." She has done this on and off since I was young, going through all her phases of dieting with me along for the ride. Simone is well aware of her issues and knows food is always a trigger for her, no matter how it comes out.

"No, it's different. This time she isn't eating at all. She only drinks Poland Spring water and is afraid of all other beverages or foods."

I feel myself sobering up. "What do you mean, afraid?"

Simone is dead serious and I can see by her almost-full glass that she's not been keeping up with my drinking. "I mean she thinks she's allergic to everything. Every type of food she freaks out about and refuses to try. She won't even chew gum. She flat-out refuses and will not take a bite of anything. She's been like this for a while, and then all of a sudden it's taken a drastic turn. Before cutting out everything, she had a list of safe foods that only under some sort of supervision would she even attempt to eat. You know how much I adore Aggie, I even sent her to a doctor friend for help, but nothing is working. He did the safe foods list, which was working, but now it's just Poland Spring water, nothing else. She thinks she is allergic to everything."

My brain is racing like a hamster on a wheel, trying to wrap my mind around my mother's health problems and getting all the intel from Simone, of all people. "That must be why Rob called me. I thought it was about your dad. . . . I'm sorry. . . . He didn't say much on the phone, only that I needed to see her and that it was an emergency. When I got to the house, I could tell she wasn't eating, but I just assumed she was stressed or something."

"Shane, I asked him to call you."

"What the hell, Simone, you know I can't deal with this. I don't want to be a part of her insanity. I left it behind when I left this fucking place after ruining everyone's life. Between my mother and your father, I can't even." I see her eyes change. "Can't you just leave it alone! She's my mother and she's a fucking nut. You know this." I am so mad, and apparently drunk, that everything I say is coming out louder than I mean. A very well-dressed man walks over, bends down while gripping his tie, and whispers in Simone's ear.

"Let's go, Sugar Shane. They have a car for us out front."

"NO, I don't want to go. Who is this guy anyhow, why does he decide when I leave? I want to find out why the hell I'm here, and you won't let me talk about anything. Like that mute kid, who's apparently your daughter? Why was my mother watching her? Dammit Simone, you know how messed up I came out, who the hell would let her take care of another innocent victim and twist them all crazy, too? Seriously Simone, you wouldn't have anything to do with me for years and then all of a sudden your father dies and I am ushered here under false pretenses. This is really fucked-up." I've lost my cool and I've crossed a very big line. I gulp hard and tears come barreling down my face. Her fierce blue eyes are now fiery red with anger. I need to stop talking, stop shouting, too. I realize that I am creating a scene, and this is certainly not prep school etiquette, especially on her turf. She speaks to me through her teeth, just as my mother did earlier.

"C'mon, we are leaving, and you better get in the car before you say any more than you already have."

I look down to see her hand on my arm and feel one of her rings digging into my skin. I pull it away, compose myself, smile outwardly, and agree. I stumble a little out of the oversized chairs, but she and the well-dressed man escort me outside and into a town car. I am a sloppy mess. Fuck me. "Simone, where's your car? Where are you taking me?" Drunk panic starts to set in.

"Don't worry about it, they'll get it to me later. We're going to the hotel. Cocktails and cars don't mix."

~~~~~~~

Tylenol Delivered on a Sterling Silver Tray Is Weird

I wake up feeling like a freight train hit my head at full speed and then double rolled over onto my stomach. I am spinning and it feels eerily similar to waking up on the couch a few days ago. I know the cure, it's just a matter of finding those sweet little medical candies. I look around, adjusting positions to try and view my purse. I nearly fall off the bed because it's up so high and the covers are slippery. I deliberately slide off the edge, taking advantage of gravity and the silky sheets. The second thing I do is figure out where I am. I'm in the hotel suite, sleeping in the guest bedroom that no one was using.

I walk around hunched over, looking and calling for Simone, but she's nowhere. I call her again as I pull a pill from my newly found purse and chew it up. I need something stronger for this headache, like Tylenol, and more sleep. I'm uncomfortable in this gigantic place without Simone and feel oh so crappy.

Oh fuckety, fuck, fuck, I am supposed to be at work. What the hell am I doing here? I had no expectations to ever stay this long and need to call Patti, immediately. I am not there to open. What the hell time is it? My mind is racing and hurting, racing, hurting. I look around for the time, anywhere, cable box, walls, but nothing. This fancy-ass place has everything, but it's like a casino with its hidden clocks. I grab a blue bottle from the fridge and see a green glimmer from the stove that reads 9:07. Holy shit, I'm supposed to be at the store for 10:00 a.m. sharp. I grab my cell but it's dead, and frantically look for the hotel's phone. I pick one up and without dialing, an operator asks what Ms. Barron needs. I pretend to be her, asking the lady to connect me to Stein's Jewels. While I'm on hold, the door key wiggles and in walks Simone, cool and collected, carrying two brown bags in one hand and a tray of coffee in the other.

"Oh my gosh, let me help you. I'm calling work. I can't believe I forgot. I'm coming."

She ignores me and puts everything on a round piece of furniture holding the largest display of lilies. "Shane, hang up."

"Simone, I am calling work, just one second."

She looks at me with a quirky, matter-of-fact smile. "Yeah, I know. I already called Gershon. You're all set."

"What? Who's Gershon?" Patti answers the phone just as I am grasping what Simone is trying to tell me. "Hi, it's Shane. I'm so incredibly sorry, Patti, but I feel so sick. I know I was supposed—"

Simone giggles and Patti interrupts. "Hey girl, no worries, you are all set. I got a call last night from the owner and he said you would be on vacation and not coming in. But you're sick? What's wrong, honey?"

I'm dumbfounded. "Oh, um, okay, that's weird. Thank you,

Patti, I am really sorry. Please call me if you need anything, you know I don't mind coming in. . . . No, I guess I'm not sick. I mean, I don't feel great right this second, but . . ."

Patti sounds as confused as I do. "Well, either way, have fun and feel better. You need a break, sweetheart, so take it. When you get back, I can't wait to hear all about how you know the owner and got him to call out for you. I have been here ten years and have never even seen the guy. Oh, gotta go, FedEx is knocking at the door. Bye, honey."

I say goodbye too, still dumbfounded, but the phone clicks, so I hang up.

"I told you last night, I know the son, Gershon Stein. He and I did some of the same summer camps and we've been in touch here and there over the years. It's really no big deal, he didn't mind doing me a favor. It doesn't hurt that I think my dad's spent half a fortune buying jewels from him, for one chick or another."

I am starstruck all over again by both Simone's natural beauty and her ability to pull clout from absolutely anywhere.

"Holy shit, Simone. Thank you so much. This is crazy. I was freaking out when I woke up and you weren't here, and I thought I was going to lose my job. I barely had any idea where I was and I feel like total shit. Thank God Jake is out of town for a couple weeks or he'd kill me. Now I just need to call the bar, or do you know Dave the fucker, too?"

She smiles and takes a tiny sip of coffee, pursing her lips at the temperature. "No, I don't. You can do that one yourself."

I cannot imagine a way that I can get myself together, then drive the two-plus hours with traffic and make it to the bar tonight. I have never called out before, so hopefully he won't be too mad? "I don't think anyone will be in for a few hours, so I'll do it in a little bit, but right now, I need coffee!"

"I got us some food and coffee. I figured you wouldn't be up for going to get breakfast, and honestly, the room service isn't great.

I've been thinking about getting a chef, but then I get busy and forget."

I smile at her with my dirty teeth and bad breath from last night. "Thank you, I really appreciate it. I've been trying to piece together last night, but my head keeps pounding. Do you have any Tylenol? Also, I don't know if you want to hear this, but I feel really bad, like I was a total ass. If I was, I am so sorry, Simone. Truly, I am. It's weird, I work in a bar, but I almost never drink. I don't know what my problem is, but I'm assuming I was a total shitshow. I am just so, so, so sorry for whatever I did."

She looks away, annoyed by my ignorance, and picks up her coffee, hiding her face behind the cup. I can only see what she wants me to see from behind the cardboard shield.

"Shane, you apologized at least one thousand times last night. It's really okay. We are good." Her sincerity is shining through as real, but I have no idea how or why? I don't remember much of it, but I'm fairly certain that I was a shitshow and made a fool out of both of us. She peekaboos out from behind her coffee, laughing, and says, "I just don't think I will ever wear that YSL dress again."

My stomach drops. "Oh my gosh, that masterpiece, what did I do to it?"

She smiles. "You really don't remember?" I shake my head no. "You threw up all over it. No worries, Shane. It wasn't a favorite, and even if it was, who cares, it's just a dress. A stylist sent it over, and I told you, I had forgotten all about it. It's at the dry cleaner's if you want to keep it. They will fix it. Trust me, I'm sure they've seen worse."

I feel a pit in my belly, and the ulcers that formed yesterday are having baby ulcers, and I run to the nearest bathroom. I finish vomiting my brains out, and as if on cue, Simone grabs Tylenol from a silver tray that the bellman has brought up.

"I am so, so, so sorry, Simone. I'm such an idiot and really fucked everything up. I'm going to grab my stuff and try to make my bar shift tonight."

Simone walks to me confidently and puts her hand on my shoulder. I look into her flawless face as she hands me three over-the-counter oval pills and says in a sweet voice, "First of all, you are fine. Nothing is wrong. Just feel better—take the Tylenol, drink some coffee, and go lie down. You are welcome to stay for as long as you like. I love that you're here. It feels like old times."

I think she's still drunk, acting like this is a good time. I want to take her advice, but first I need to call Dirty Dave and tell him I'm wicked sick. He throws a tantrum, but I remind him that I've never called out. He hangs up and we're good. I'm off the hook.

Under the Cuff

When I awake and nearly fall out of the goddamn giraffe bed, the clock reads 2:00 p.m. exactly. I walk out to an empty living room. I drink more clean, cold water and plug in my still-dead phone to charge. I am feeling a hundred thousand times better than before but still need to take one of my pills to keep the good going. There's a note on the counter. I don't need to pick it up to read it; Simone's writing has always been huge, with every word in capital letters. "WENT TO MY DAD'S HOUSE TO DEAL WITH SOME THINGS, WILL BE BACK LATER. DON'T LEAVE! I HAVE SOMETHING PLANNED! ~SMONEY." Where did she think I could go? I don't even know the address of where I am, and my car is still at my mother's house.

The rest of the day flies by with time spent lounging in a robe on the couch, taking in the cable channels, and then another hour playing around in the bathroom with different soaps and perfumes. These towels should be framed and reveled at like museum art. They are so fucking great. Such texture.

Around 6:00 p.m., Simone enters the suite and startles me while I'm mouth deep, munching on some chips that I'd found.

"Don't eat that, we're going out to dinner. And those are Vivi's. I would never eat that fattening crap."

I want to spit the mouthful of potato and oil mush into a napkin, feeling gross for eating it in front of her. "Dinner?"

Her eyes are wide open and excited. "Yes, dinner. It's a surprise and so is the company. Just get ready, you'll like it. Same drill. Pick anything you want. Something nice is a good idea."

I am in a daze thinking about the past twenty-four hours. Time flies with Simone Barron. I get ready as requested, and like *Groundhog Day*, we head out again. The bellman calls in his earpiece for Simone's car and two door-opener people. She is like a walking muse, admired by every passing man and woman, and then there's me, in sneakers. Once we are in the car, I reach for the radio dial and a big smile comes across her face. "Oh, I almost forgot, I got these for you." She reaches behind the passenger's seat and pulls out a large red box that reads "Salvatore Ferragamo" across the top. I delicately flip open the top, revealing the cutest strappy wedge sandals, with multicolored soles and golden straps, that I have ever seen. I look at the box again, and it reads size 5. How the hell could she have known these would match my outfit so perfectly? What an amazing gift. I love them so much, but I would prefer to exchange them for the money I'm missing out on by not working.

"Holy smokes, Simone! Are you serious? Is this because my sneaks are so embarrassing?"

She laughs. "Yes, it's exactly because of that reason, nothing else. No, I just can't have us going out in sneakers again. What will people say? Do they fit your freakishly small feet?" Even she knows how silly we looked last night and starts laughing. I giggle with a high-pitched, nervous cackle, and that makes us both laugh harder. I sit back, allowing this feeling of being next to her sink in. For the second night in a row, I am leaving the evening's itinerary in Simone's hands, and with the fear of murder on a far horizon,

I'm excited for yet another adventure. I strap the shoes around my feet and ankles, a perfect and surprisingly sturdy fit.

We drive toward downtown and pull directly in front of a bank. "I'll be right back, just move the car if anyone comes." Simone jumps out and I wait, watching the rearview mirrors just in case the police want to ticket us. A few minutes pass, and with Simone still in the bank, I take in our surroundings. It's been so many years since I've seen this part of town. I can barely see through the bank's tinted glass to where Simone is talking to someone, but not a teller. More people come and go through the double doors and I sit patiently waiting. I play with fancy controls, but too afraid to mess anything up, I stop fidgeting. I look up to check the mirrors again for the elusive cops, and in their place see a very well-dressed man running away from the bank. I crack my window to hear his shouting. Oh my goodness, maybe it's a bank robbery and that's what's taking so long. I am nervous for Simone's well-being and not sure what to do. I wonder if I should hit the "SOS" button I observed earlier on the interior roof of the car.

The man has something in his hand and is yelling for another man to stop. A black man with tattered jeans, a dark green shirt, and flip-flops turns around, easefully takes a brown bag from the banker, and keeps walking. The well-dressed banker seems relieved to have caught his attention and turns around, heading back in the direction of the bank. What the hell is going on? What kind of lending institution chases people? This is the opposite of a robbery, the bank is actually giving money instead of taking it—forcefully, too! I watch carefully and my brain swarms with ideas. The now evidently homeless man stops, opening the bag to examine its contents. He has on a Boston Red Sox baseball cap, with hints of salt and pepper strands peeking out, and looks maybe fifty or sixty years old. He walks with an odd confidence, not a shuffle, like I would expect of a homeless man, but upright and with a careful stride. He pulls out two sandwiches from the mysterious brown bag, holding one between his teeth and the other between his knees while he carefully folds the brown paper bag, still thick with something, and places it in his pocket. That's nice, he doesn't litter, I think. I hate assholes who litter.

I keep checking the mirrors to see if Simone is coming so I can tell her all about it, but just then I notice a huge and scary-looking, unleashed dog come out of nowhere and sit directly beside the homeless guy, as if he's on lookout waiting for his master, knowing a meal is on its way. Where in the world did this dog come from? The man hands the dog the sandwich from between his knees and the dog swallows it in a couple of monstrous gulps. The enormity of the canine is intimidating, and if I had to guess, it's some sort of pit bull and tiger wolf mix. His coat appears to be gray, but it's littered with big white slashes or scars all over his head and body. One of his ears is either missing or bent over, I can't really tell. Either way, this dog is menacing. I giggle to myself as people just about trip over themselves into oncoming traffic to avoid being on the same side of the street as the well-mannered dog. He is sitting perfectly still next to the man, who's eating the other sandwich in the middle of the sidewalk. I've stopped taking mental notes that this is some sort of reverse robbery, because it appears that this is simple, kind generosity from the bank and nothing else.

I'm squinting my eyes, trying to see more of the scenario and piece it together, when Simone jumps in the car and throws it in drive. I'm strangely excited that we are driving right past them, and as we get closer, I watch as the two walk in perfect harmony together, neither faster than the other, and with the full width of the sidewalk to do so as more people move aside to avoid them. I arc my neck to see just a little bit more, but her speeding car is no match for this guy and his dog. "Did you see that?"

"See what?"

"When you were in the bank and I was just sitting here waiting, the strangest stuff kept happening. First, some guy from the bank comes flying out of the building chasing this homeless dude, that guy and his dog that we just passed, and then gives him a brown bag, which I thought was odd, but then the guy opens the bag and there were sandwiches inside."

Simone doesn't seem amused or interested. "Cool, maybe they're doing some kind of charity thing, who knows?"

"I don't know, maybe. But then this dog comes out of nowhere and is all mangled and messed-up looking and people keep swerving away from them, but the dog is so well trained, he stays perfectly still next to the guy without a leash or anything. Well, it seemed strange when I was watching the whole thing unfold, but you could be right, just another wacky day in the city."

We keep driving, and although I can't get the image of them out of my head, I think less and less about it the farther away we get. Just as I'm about to break and ask where we are going, knowing she would just call it a surprise, we pull up. Holy shit, I think I hear Robin Leach narrating *Lifestyles of the Rich and Famous* in my head. Soon I'll wake up and realize this is one big dream. We've arrived and it's a castle, not like Simone's compound, but a real antique-looking fairy-tale castle. We must be somewhere in the country because I've never seen anything like this outside of a Disney flick. Its aged steps are forged like a twenty-layer cake, one incredible architectural feat after another—and this is just the front. I look at Simone's face, and it lights up like a Christmas tree when she sees my amazement. It appears that she actually receives joy from my utter wonderment at what has always been all around her. I am surrounded by the Richies, and their lavish wealth is apparent from the ear-to-ear smile on my face. From the car to the castle's peak to the multitudes of bellmen and waiters, I think I have literally gone to heaven. This entire experience has been one big bowl of ice cream, and I intend to lick the dish clean.

Simone hands one of the valet men her keys and asks him to

fill it up and have it washed. He nods in agreement. "As you wish, Ms. Barron."

We begin to walk up the marble layers, and I stop to take it all in. Simone stops too, looking at me weird for freezing on the castle's steps. I smile and barely eke out a "thank you" from my nervous lips. She is the most stunning woman in the world, and her luscious body in that incredible dress could double for a real-life Jessica Rabbit. I take a deep breath, look down at my new shoes, and shake my head, waiting to wake from a dream. Simone hooks my arm around hers and we continue the walk up the tapered stairs to the largest, most ornately carved door I've ever seen—built for real-life giants.

Once inside, I am speechless. The architecture, delectable scents, and beauty of something so old but so well kept makes me want to cry. I count three fireplaces, all burning real wood, and that's only from the first few feet inside. Almost immediately upon entering, we are approached by two extremely attractive gentlemen. They take turns hugging and kissing Simone on each of her rosy cheeks. Then in sync they turn to me. I am already so incredibly nervous. I don't know if they work here or are friends of hers, but I'm starstruck. I try to calm my shaking hand when the more gorgeous one reaches for it and kisses it like a prince. The other just smiles and locks arms with Simone, breathing in a whiff of her blond hair. I am married and feeling extremely uncomfortable. Suddenly, all I can think of is Jake. I'm feeling like this is one big setup, and I've never been around another man in such an intimate setting since marrying Jake. If he could see me this very moment, he'd probably aim his rifle in my direction.

"Shane Lacy, this is Martin James." The tall, blond man with distinct masculine features and wearing a turquoise silk tie turns to me and smiles, and I close my eyes as he kisses both of my cheeks. I stand still like a statue. Then we repeat the process with the ridiculously hot guy who's got me flustered and anxious. There's something about his look, a seductive sweetness, and my instincts are telling me to PUHA (pick up and haul ass) out of here! "Shane Catherine Lacy, this is Sebastian Kane." His smile is both sweet and sensual at the same time. His teeth are pearl white and nearly perfect except for two slightly crooked front canines that stick out the tiniest little bit. It reminds me of the actress Patricia Arquette or Vera Farmiga. He is about the same height as Martin, at least six feet or more. I cannot think of a man as tall as these two, except maybe the deceased Mr. Barron. He isn't wearing a tie, and the top button on his white collared shirt is undone. I already spotted his green and gold cuff links when he pecked my hand, but their glamorous design is more evident as he buttons his suit coat and we enter the main room. "Shall we?"

I'm so worried that I will trip and fall or say the wrong thing. I can barely walk in my new shoes, so I try taking deep, subtle breaths, hoping the present company doesn't notice. I don't belong here, Jake has been right all along, this is not who I am and I need to face it. I can't handle these people, this lifestyle. It's all too much. My dreams are literally coming true—living, looking, and eating like the Richies—but I'm crumbling under the pressure. These are adult, grown men, not like the boys I dated or married. They probably run major companies or are doctors and have explored the Seven Wonders of the World. What will I talk to them about? How will I converse? I haven't been anywhere, and certainly don't know anything about politics or how to speak in another language. I have never even crossed state lines, except one time to buy beer on a Sunday during high school. I own a frog from Australia, I can talk about him, but that leads to Jake, so I better not. My mind is racing. Geez Louise, there's a giant fucking chess board and a piano in here. If a harpist starts strumming classical music, I'll slip off my painful new shoes and run barefoot all the way home. I have no idea what to do or why I'm here. I want to help the waitstaff or make customers drinks. That's what I know, that's my comfort zone. I am so thankful my mother isn't here to witness her only child's behavior cracking under the pressure. She would scold me for not having absorbed the etiquette books she made me study and balance on my head. I never thought I would actually need them. It was fantasy fun so we could both pretend I wasn't born and raised in poverty. It was make believe, never to come to fruition. What the hell is Simone thinking, bringing me here on what feels like a date? I need to get her alone, apart from these male Gods.

We are escorted into a private room in the rear of the fortress. There's yet another wood-burning fireplace engulfed by carved white marble and long drapes that hang from oversized windows that curve around the circular room. Even the wood floors follow the curved walls with inlaid designs in fancy light and dark contrasting colors. There's a bouquet of green and white lilies inside a crystal vase with a silver base placed in the exact middle of the table that we're seated at. Two waiters enter the room, one carrying a bottle of champagne, the other shadowing in case a bubble drips, or who knows what. The darker-skinned server bends down, meeting me at eye level, pours the clear fizz into my glass, and stands upright, catching a driblet with a white scarf cleverly wrapped around the bottle's neck. The other man reaches for it with a second white sash but isn't fast enough. The room is dimly lit, but I catch a corner of the label, which reads Krug 1988. I have no idea what that means, since I've never had champagne. We don't have it at the bar, and Jake and I celebrated our wedding with craft beer that his uncle made. I look at staring eyes with confusion, hoping my eyebrow hasn't risen, because no one else has champagne in their glass. I don't want to start drinking before everyone else, especially after last night's fiasco. Why are we just sitting here? Martin finally speaks. "Have a taste, tell us if you like it."

My legs quiver beneath the table and I nervously speak. "Me? Um, what are we celebrating?"

Everyone starts laughing, except the waiter, who stands utterly still like a guard at the unknown soldier's grave. He's making me even more nervous, and then Sebastian speaks directly to me. His voice is gentle and caring. "We want your opinion. If you don't like it, they will take it away, it's as simple as that. Just close your eyes and taste. Take your time and pretend no one is here. Let the bubbles meet your buds."

I submit to the pressure and trust everything this outsider is saying, even though my brain is screaming stranger danger, stranger danger! I pick up the glass and, knowing he might make me, close my eyes and take a healthy sip of the drink. It's magnificent, crisp with fruity flavors, tastes like edible flowers, and I would love to have more. "Wow, that's delicious."

Everyone claps like it's my birthday, so I smile, but am silently mortified that everyone's celebration was held up by my dim-witted knowledge of champagne etiquette.

The entire meal consists of lots of large plates with tiny amounts of food on each one. We keep eating, course after course after course. At one point, and I am not sure when, they serve sherbet to us. I thought that it was weird to add lemon ice cream in between our meals, so I looked at Simone for help. Instead, Sebastian took the opportunity to explain each item to me with a sweet-tempered whisper in my ear. "To cleanse your palette . . . to freshen your hands . . . to sip during dessert . . ." Every single awkward moment is erased with his patient words. I feel completely out of place, but the only one who makes a point of noticing is Martin. Everyone else is kind and understanding, including the staff. This makes me feel closer to and more trusting of Sebastian as the night goes on. His mannerisms are calculated, confident, and above all, truly thoughtful. He is extremely handsome in a seductive way and for some reason is overly sensitive and tuned in to just me. I can feel myself blushing, and thoughts of Jake's bullets or arrows shooting through my chest fade with every sip of that luscious champagne.

Martin rubs me the wrong way and speaks poorly to the staff, who are just trying to satisfy his every whim. I want to stand up for their rights and demand respect as a fellow server myself, but I am too afraid. He comes across like a pompous ass, and it annoys me that Simone is spending her time enamored by him. She deserves so much better than some rich asshole who isn't very nice to anyone, including me.

Besides the minimal disrespectful interruptions by Martin toward the staff, the conversations flow easily. Martin runs a software company that he started at age thirteen or fourteen as some sort of child prodigy and has bought and sold other companies along the way, making more and more money. Sebastian does something involving imports, but I didn't really understand it well. Honestly, it sounds shady, the way he skated around his involvement in many different businesses. The types of companies he owns or is a part of are something you might see in a mobster movie and has me suspicious. He lights up when he talks about ships, saying that he has spent most of his life traveling or living on or among them. Simone speaks only at appropriate times, when the men stop, and shares her experiences sailing on the Mediterranean in France. Sebastian and Martin share similar stories but don't wait for me to share mine. They know I don't have any.

"So how do you two know each other?" I feel it's fair to ask the two men how they came to be friends since I was brought here unannounced to share time with them in this intimate setting. As Martin is about to answer, another wealthy passerby peers into an open slit in the velvet curtain separating our round room from the main room, presumably to see what famous people are behind it. I smile at him. I cannot believe I'm among this type of crowd. I only wish someone here would recognize me and confirm whether this is real or a dream. I feel like a princess in a real-life castle, though my feet don't agree, damn beautiful shoes are rough on the soles.

Martin turns to the man and in a condescending voice says,

"Excuse you, we are trying to enjoy a private reception here and really don't need your déclassé manners interfering in our evening." Flustered and probably frightened, the peeping man closes the curtain and stomps away.

My goodness, the poor guy could be the Russian president for all I know—this place could certainly host such a crowd. Martin looks back to us to continue the conversation, as if his snide remarks to the stranger had never happened, and begins to answer my question. "My company did some work for one of Sebastian's companies, and then we ran into each other a few times at various dinners, awards, etcetera. Plus, it turns out we have a mutual friend and some similar interests."

Sebastian turns and, with quiet poise, puts his finger up, and an olive-skinned lady immediately halts, just about tripping over the carpet, and enters the circular room. In what sounds like perfectly spoken Spanish, he orders something, then comes back to the conversation. "Excuse me, please continue, Martin." Remembering the topic, Sebastian laughs with a dark, breathy laugh and says, "Yes, we do. We have shared many experiences together."

I don't like where this is going and see a side to Sebastian that makes me feel uneasy. I get shivers all over, and for the thousandth time wonder what I'm doing here. I feel so uncomfortable and try to distract myself with more nervous talk and not let my mind wander anymore. "Tsavorite garnets?"

"What?"

Everyone looks at me. "Oh, I'm sorry. I was just admiring your cuff links. Most men don't wear them, and I have always liked the way they look. Are they tsavorites? I apologize. It was rude of me to interrupt." He looks shocked, and for the first time tonight Sebastian isn't in perfect form. He appears taken aback. By me? I wonder. He composes himself and speaks with a half smile and in what looks like direct admiration of me.

"Yes, they are. I am very impressed, Miss Shane."

Simone starts cracking up. "No, silly, it's not Miss, it's Sugar. Sugar Shane."

I must be turning four shades of rouge because only Simone calls me that, and generally not while surrounded by wealthy strangers. I tilt my head down and Sebastian reaches over, placing his index finger under my chin, lifting it ever so slightly. What I can't believe is that I let him. "Hey, that's incredible. Your knowing what kind of stones these are, it's extraordinary. No one has ever been able to tell. For that matter, no one has ever asked. Bravo to you, Sugar." He snickers and I laugh a little, too.

"Thank you."

Just as the awkward moment passes, the pretty olive-skinned lady comes back in carrying gorgeous little sugared jellies in beautiful bright colors. Sebastian says a few more words in Spanish and touches her arm. She seems flattered and then looks to me and scatters. I guess he makes all women feel special. I am a little annoyed, but quickly realize how ridiculous that is. We each choose a couple delectable treats, and the flavors pour from their sugary shells like ripe fruit. The mango is unbelievable, sweet and juicy like the real fruit, and makes for a perfect ending to this strange but wonderful dinner. I have never eaten in this setting or foods as unique as the ones I had tonight. Between all the different pairings of cocktails and champagne, I am feeling quite giddy.

Just as we're about to say goodbye and thank the men for a lovely evening, a gentleman wearing a tux approaches our table and says something to Sebastian. I am barely listening because Martin is telling a funny story about Simone, and I'm distracted by his enthusiasm. Sebastian answers the man in Italian, I think? It's not Spanish. Actually, I have no idea. Sounds funny is all. He then turns to all of us and says, "Are you ready?" Just like that, Martin sums up the story in a few speedy words and we all rise from the table. I wonder where the bill is? Do all rich people have a running tab at restaurants so they can come and go as they please,

not to be bothered with such things as money? My menu didn't
have any prices, so I can only imagine that it's free or some sort of
secret society Richie tab? Any guess would only be speculation,
and either way, it doesn't seem to be of concern to anyone, not
even the house. Dave would cut off my arm if he caught me not
charging a customer for their flat yellow beer.

Simone excuses us both to the ladies' room, and we walk from
our secluded round room, past the rest of the diners while they
stare. I look to the floor in flattered embarrassment as we make our
way through the grand room. Simone, perfectly poised, grabs my
hand to escort me down the beautifully ornate wooden staircase to
a door marked "Powder Area~Ladies Only." The room is huge and
smells of fresh flowers and rosemary. The bathroom's toiletries,
L'Occitane soaps, lotions, and makeup, are piled neatly for the use
of the guests. There are even small samples in a basket lined in
antique linen, with a variety of more perfumes and salves. Simone
laughs when I grab a handful and slip them in my purse. I also take
full advantage of the free deodorant, as the alcohol has me feeling
warm all over, and put that in my purse, too. I'm afraid to admit to
myself how much Sebastian has me flustered and convince myself
it's the fancy drinking. I'm more nervous around him than anyone.
Only when Simone's father or the nannies yelled at us did I feel
this way, but that was punishment, not wooing, if that's what this
is? I cannot think of another person as confident as these two men.
I wonder if it's because I work so much and for so long that I
haven't taken the time to notice people? This particular man has
me on edge and thinking more and more about Jake. I still haven't
heard from him, and briefly wonder if they've eaten all the food
I sent? Or are they living off the land like cavemen? My mind is
wandering, grasping on to anything and everything in order to be
less nervous about going back upstairs. I can hear a faint tinkle
after Simone enters a gigantic bathroom and I take my bottle of
pills out of my purse to chew a fresh one, but its clanging about

makes entirely too much noise, so I run the water as a pathetic disguise. I swallow quickly without drinking, and the taste of broken pieces is bitter and awful. I gargle with mouthwash like a truck driver to rid the bad taste from my mouth. The thoughts of home diminish to a mere droplet when we reach the top of the stairs and find Sebastian and Martin patiently waiting.

Sebastian says in a cutesy tone, "Come on, ladies, we have a surprise for you. Something fun." He sounds a lot like Simone; it's a never-ending birthday with these two. I can't imagine anything else topping this night, and I reluctantly and curiously follow as we walk down a long hallway, escorted by an Italian-speaking (I think?) man in a tuxedo. We reach the end, where he opens a twenty- or thirty-foot-tall carved door similar to the front door. The warm air outside fills our lungs. The Italian reaches into a prepared basket and hands both men a flashlight. I am thoroughly confused and feel a sudden wave of panic. I wonder if this is some sort of revenge from Simone and these are my killers, posing as wealthy business-slash-hit men? At least the last meal was stupendous. I am internally laughing nervously when Sebastian grabs my hand and says, "Come on. Let's play hide-and-go-seek."

Is he serious? Every single scared nerve ending in my body takes a little nap and I giggle nervously in agreement. Simone doesn't flinch and is excited about the idea. Simone and Martin run off into the night, flickers of white bouncing from their flashlight and illuminating their path. I am warming up to the idea of fun rather than imminent murder and looking forward to a childhood game. Here I am on the grounds of a castle, having eaten the best food in the world, with two handsome strangers and my former best friend, and now we get to run around like kids. These still may be my last breaths of air, but damn, they've been good ones. I can't stop giggling nervously, and a sharp cackle escapes. Sebastian smiles and says, "Let's have some fun, life is way too short to be so serious." Who is this guy and where did he come from? I never let loose, because my life doesn't allow for it, but this fun reminds me of the crazy times Simone and I used to have. I haven't done anything silly in years. I'm an adult and have always been one, even as a child.

Sebastian bends down and pulls his shoes and socks off. I happily follow his lead since these things are killing my feet. He can tell I'm anxious to leave them here, and telling me it's okay, he grabs them from my clenched fingers and waves down someone far away to take them. Why do I trust this guy? He grabs my hand and we run barefoot onto a lush carpet of grass in search of our friends. We stop at a tree not too far away and count to twenty out loud, so they can hear us. I am overwhelmed by endorphins as we take off again, running through the grounds looking for evidence of a flashing light.

I peer back over my shoulder at the mansion in the distance and can faintly see diners standing at the windows, probably mortified that an escaped prisoner is loose on the grounds. Nope, it's just us playing like children, and I'm in love with every second of it. I feel free—no work, no responsibility, just loose. We stop by a row of trees, and Sebastian, never letting go of my hand, puts a finger to his lips and we tiptoe together like Elmer Fudd hunting wabbits. I think I hear them too, but maybe it's just a squirrel? I can't help but giggle, and he whispers, "We have to find them, let's go look by the pool." I don't say another word and follow his every move, taking it just as seriously as he is. Actually, I don't want to find them, because that means the clock will have struck twelve and Cinderella's night will be over, and it will be back to reality. Unfortunately, I don't own a glass slipper, just a new pair of very painful Salvatore Ferragamos, and I am not leaving even one behind.

"Ha, we got you!" Sebastian and I turn the corner and we've found them. They are under a cabana near the closed pool, clothes strewn about—Simone's doing I am sure—and are openly having sex. We both start laughing at our horned-up friends who admit defeat with all their hands up in the air. Almost in sync they both say, "You win," like it was ever a contest. With Simone missionary on Martin, she asks Sebastian if he'll take me back to the Ritz.

"Of course, it would be my pleasure."

"Bye Simone, I will see you soon?" I don't know what the girl code for safety is in this situation, as they aren't strangers to her and she never seems threatened or scared. I walk away, to be escorted back to her own hotel palace.

We walk for around ten minutes, finally reaching our shoes, which are now placed in a to-go bag, with slippers perfectly set beside them. How did they know? I reach down to grab the bag, but Sebastian assertively grabs both pairs of shoes. We shuffle back with a nursing home stride to the front door, where I had met him only a few hours before. An elderly couple, him in a three-piece suit and her in a beaded gown, look us up and down in disgust. I notice our dirty, grass-covered feet smothered in posh, white slippers and apologize with a dip of my head.

Truth or Dare

Just then, the valet hands Sebastian his key and in exchange he turns over the flashlight. He escorts me down the marble staircase, even though I'm still uncomfortable allowing his hand to touch mine, and out to a running car. It's dark, but the logo looks like a jagged king's crown or King Triton's spear from The Little Mermaid. Go figure, a car made for a king. It's another two-door, with dark-blue leather interior, which I like very much. I sink at least two feet deep into the seat, which could easily double as a fancy airline recliner meant to put me to sleep.

"Buckle up, Sugar."

I do as I'm told. The roar of the engine takes us away from the mansion and the safety of my friend.

We talk in the car, chitchat mostly about small things, and I ask

Sebastian what languages he was speaking back at the restaurant.

"Spanish and Italian. Do you know what I said?"

I laugh at the absurdity of the question. "No, not at all. I wish I did. But honestly, I never had the opportunity." He makes me feel shameful.

"Everyone should at least know how to say hello and converse a little in every single language, that way you can be anywhere in the world and still make a friend." I can't believe a man like this gives a shit about making new friends; he can buy as many as he wants. "I'll teach you."

His confidence is alluring. "Me? I am terrible. I tried to learn French when Simone would come back from her trips, but I could never follow. When we were kids I wanted it to be our secret language but I couldn't figure it out, so she ended up speaking to her other friends in French and me in English. How did you learn so many?" I look to him to answer, and for the first time I really absorb the beauty of his almond eyes, which are intently staring at the road. He has a natural eyeliner surrounding and under his eyes, and dark, frown-shaped eyebrows. His brown hair is tousled with zero effort to look sexy. Everything about him seems to come naturally.

He replies, "Not so many, I guess they just come easy once you learn the first few. My mother is from Spain and my father is American. I was born in South America but then lived a good period of my life in Johannesburg. We traveled quite a bit for my father's company, so I suppose I just sort of picked more of them up. Of course, my mother spoke Spanish to me, but my father was the one who taught me to make the effort to learn others. He said it would help with business when I got older." This guy is too much. I want to study him like a good book. "Enough about me, tell me about you, Miss Sugar Shane?"

"Oh my goodness, I can't believe Simone said that, it's so embarrassing."

He says kindly, "I like it. You are sweet, it makes sense."

I am utterly thankful for the car's dark interior and dim light of the crescent moon so he can't see my ridiculously flushed skin.

"How about another game?"

I can't believe this guy and his games. He is so full of life and adventure, something as foreign to me as all those other languages. "Really, another? Okay?" I am hesitant to agree, but when he speaks his voice is playful and teasing like a toddler.

"Let's play truth or dare."

"You're not serious?"

"Yeah, come on, you could use some fun, I can tell."

He has a weird spell over me, and I can't say no to him. "Okay, I think. I mean, I can't believe I'll agree to this, but only if I can go first? And we need to have some rules?"

Surprisingly, he seems genuinely intrigued. "Sure, of course. You choose and I will play along."

I respond quickly, so as to not leave too much time to think this through. I need to be precise and cover myself, as well as the vows I took with Jake. I think quickly. This has the potential to get uncomfortable very quickly. "Okay. Here are the rules. First, nothing too dangerous, you're driving. The second is, you cannot move on until the other person has completed their truth or dare. Third, you must alternate between truth and dare. And finally, the truth questions must be answered using only one word."

He doesn't flinch, taking in everything I say seriously. "I accept those rules."

I can't help but laugh to break the tension. Now I am the silly one. "Great, I accept them, too. May I go first?"

"Yes, please, Shane, it's in your hands."

"It's a truth question: Are you married or dating anyone or do you have children?"

He answers quickly. "No. Now it's my turn. Truth: Did you have a good time tonight?"

"Yes." Doesn't he know this? You would literally have to be blind, deaf, and retarded not to have enjoyed every second of this evening. My turn. "Dare: I dare you to pull up to the next traffic light and blow kisses at whoever is in the car, man, woman, family, it doesn't matter."

He continues with seriousness but I can see the smile in his eyes. We drive about a minute when we hit our first red light. It's a convertible packed with teenybopper girls. They all look very young, and I am kicking myself for having thought up such a ridiculously dumb dare, especially with this gorgeous guy. I think God is punishing me. He looks at me for approval and I nod my head to play along, so he puts down his window and blows cheesy kisses at the girls. Their car starts screaming and cheering. The blond passenger flashes her boobs, which are huge and bursting out of a hot pink bra. I can't help but laugh, what are the odds? He laughs too, and looks back at me to move on. "Dare: I dare you to show me your favorite toy."

"What do you mean? I don't understand, like Legos or Barbies or something?"

He chuckles. "No, your favorite toy for yourself."

The question finally clicks and my comfort level crashes and burns. How am I going to get out of this? "Oh. Oh gosh, I know what you mean now. Um, I don't know." I am mortified and feel anxious, my heart is pounding and my palms are sweating. I'm not prepared for this. Wherever this game is going, maybe it's time to stop.

"How do you not know?"

It's the fucking Spanish Inquisition and I have no idea how to answer. "I am being honest. I don't know, because I've never tried one." Nervously, I continue talking. "I know Simone likes them, and some other friends have talked about it, but I've never had one or used one or whatever. You know what I mean." Why in the world did I mention Simone, it's none of his business. I'm so nervous that I'm spouting whatever jibber-jabber comes to mind. I'm such a fool. "Okay, well, since I can't show you that dare, let's move on. It's truth for you now, isn't it?"

"No, no, no, you don't get off that easy, we are going to figure this out."

Why does this guy have such power over me, a male Simone? He is barely persuasive, and without putting up much of a verbal fight, I succumb to the game. He reaches across me, opening the glove box and pulling out his iPad, and I recoil back into the seat. He notices that I'm uneasy, and it seems to bother him that I look uncomfortable. "Can you type 'adult toys' into the map for me?"

"Oh my goodness, seriously?"

"Your rules, Shane. We can't move on until the previous one is completed. I'm just following them."

I go ahead and type, all the while wondering what in the world I'm doing. Jake has only been gone a couple of days, and here I am in a car with a complete stranger searching online for porn stores. "It says there's one in 2.1 miles from here. It's called Leg Up."

"Okay, sounds good. You don't get a truth until this dare is complete. So we have to go."

"What if I want the game to end?" I feel defiant talking back to him. We drive in silence for the 2.1 excruciatingly long miles, and there it is, plain as day, lit up on the left-hand side. I'm a little surprised to see how not-too-slutty it looks from the outside. There isn't any graffiti on the building or policemen arresting pedophiles, but I'm still a nervous wreck.

He can sense how worried I've become, and before reaching for the car's handle, he looks directly at me and says, "Are you okay? Do you want to stop the game?"

I swallow hard and take a deep breath. "Nope. I'm okay. Let's do this."

He continues to stare at me and says, "Okay then. Dare: Find your favorite toy!"

We both start laughing at the irony of the situation and get out of the car with swagger and confidence, still wearing our mansion slippers. I accidentally slam the door and apologize, but he doesn't even acknowledge it. At this point, I realize it's a Maserati, dark blue in color just like the interior. We enter the store, and the inside of Leg Up is surprisingly classy, in a freaky-deaky sex shop kind of way. An attractive woman approaches us, offering her assistance. Sebastian speaks for both of us and says we need to look and will ask if we desire her assistance. I wonder if he's being clever by using the word desire? He is about as subtle as a sledgehammer, and it feels like he has more tricks up his sleeve, almost a little too confident for my liking. The woman walks away, and seeing how pretty she is makes me feel more out of place. Why is he here with me? He could be with this hot sex kitten who actually knows and probably treasures her favorite toy.

I peruse the room as Sebastian stands back, always watching me from a distance. I look back a couple times only to find him staring back. There is a wall of gorgeous glass dildos; the colors are lovely and they look like pieces of art or paperweights, or expensive drug paraphernalia. I feel their texture to see if they're really glass and they are, but I'm too afraid it would break inside me if I ever had the courage to try. I move on to another corner of the store, where every imaginable object in existence that could be used to whip, beat, scorn, or violate is on full display. Since brutal rape isn't my type of thing, I veer left. I come upon the mother lode, an entire wall dedicated to ladies' vibrators. There must be a hundred different kinds. Some are huge, others tiny, and all in different colors and shapes. Weird shapes, nothing like any penis I've seen. I make eye contact with the pretty lady who's also been watching me, and her long legs with her body attached walk toward me.

"Do you like something here?" She turns a few on, and with her hand on mine makes me touch the large vibrating shafts and feel the little beads twirl around and around. The interaction must have risen my wonky brow because Sebastian notices my apparent anxiety and tells her we are fine. She walks away, recognizing some other sex-crazed weirdo.

I speak softly to Sebastian, barely audible, telling him I want something small. He places his hand in the middle of my back and rubs softly. My eyes land on a vibrator very small in girth and length. It isn't at all special in comparison to the others. It's lavender in color and doesn't have the twirling things or pokey stuff like the others. It does, however, have a slight curved tip, much like a circumcised penis, and only one speed and button: On. It's also the least expensive of the sex gizmos, but I feel pleased with its obscurity.

"Your favorite?"

"Um, I think so?" I hand it to him, but he grabs my hand and pulls me into him. He is a lot taller and bigger, so his arms spread over me like eagle wings. A fateful mistake, I let him kiss me. It's soft, sensual, and sweet, with his lips barely parting mine, and I can only feel the very tip of his tongue pressed into mine. He pushes against me, into the sex paraphernalia and the rest of the vibrators on display, and they poke my back, falling from the hooks. I giggle and he softly pulls away, never taking his eyes off mine. I am so flustered and utterly attracted to him, I want to try my new favorite toy right now on the floor. I have no idea what I'll do with it, but I need something inside me. The kiss is giving me shivers all over, and my vagina's wet and numb with excitement. My whole body is on an endorphin high, and all five senses are heightened to capacity. Sebastian looks surprised to be as taken aback as I am and walks the lavender-colored package to the register while I wait, ashamed, at the rear exit. I overhear him apologizing for the mess, pointing to the slew of fallen vibrators, and thanking them for their help. They seem obliged by the extra cash he throws on the counter, and we walk out together, shuffling in our slippers to the car.

I can't speak. I'm overwhelmed by the entire evening and feel an urgency to jog down the freeway and get some of this energy out of my system. He drives a few minutes until the beautiful Ritz Carlton sign is in front of us. I'm so happy to see it and, starting to come down from my high, thankful we are out of that store and that nothing else happened. I barely let the car stop before I jump out, toy bag in hand. My slipper falls off, but I arrange my foot back in, grab my shoes, and in speed language thank him for the night and run to the door. The valet people watch the entire incident and automatically open the door and wish me a pleasant evening. I don't look back. I've cheated on Jake, and moving ahead is the only option. If I don't keep going, everything else in my life will be compared to this. An amazing man who took my breath away. I cannot compare the two men. In fact, I need to escape the entire scene, or the past five years with my husband will be worth nothing. An entire marriage reduced to a blurb of young love, chastised by the cheating gold digger, Shane the whore. Every single amazing experience I've enjoyed over the past couple days has been nothing short of magic. I've been living like the Richies, and the truth is, I can't handle it. The food too rich, the men too generous, the friend too beautiful, and lastly, my mother, too fucking crazy. Tomorrow morning, homebound. For good!

Two Sebastians!

Upon entering the spectacular suite, I'm reminded of everything I'm not, and the gluttonous leech I've become. I brush my teeth and shower, imagining washing away every molecule of Sebastian from my mind and body. I check the clock and it's almost midnight. Simone isn't home, so I pop a pill and climb into the luxurious bed that I don't deserve for the final evening of my pathetic fake life. Just as I feel myself drifting asleep, the cell rings. I don't want to deal with it, because it's probably Simone trying to get me to come out for a nightcap and I am comfy cozy in the nicest bed I will ever sleep in. I glance over curiously to confirm my suspicion. Fuck, it's

Jake calling. I debate voice mail, but he'd assume I'm working and call the bar next.

"Hi." I answer sleepily, trying to cover my tracks in case I slip up.

"Hi, are you sleeping? I was just about to go to bed, too, but how are you, can you talk?" He sounds excited to hear my voice and I try to follow with the same enthusiasm.

"I'm good and awake now. I'm glad you called. What's going on, how's the camping trip going?"

"We are set up and it's been a bit slow on the hunting front, but we're going to try again tomorrow. The food you sent was a hit, actually it's all gone. Wait, why are you sleeping? You're not at work?"

I take a deep breath, which usually makes him leave me alone, and say, "Well, it's been crazy and I will fill you in when you get home. You won't believe this, but I am out by my mother's."

"What? Wait, did you say you're with your mom?"

I continue on, hoping to plow right through tonight's adventure and bring the focus to my fucked-up family. "Rob, ya know that guy she's with, he called me and said it was an emergency. You should see her, Jake. She is so skinny, it's disgusting." I go on and on, nervously sputtering on about Rob the Blob and Olive Oyl and Hamburger Man and a bunch of other nonsense, hoping to confuse the both of us.

"Wait, stop. So you are with your mom now? Holy shit, Shane."

I can tell he's been drinking, too. Busch Light or some watered-down crap I assume, nothing compared to the fancy schmancy cocktails that I consumed, but I won't dare mention them. "I know, there's a lot to tell, I'm just really tired. Call me when you can and try to get us something good. Whatever you catch will keep us stocked with food for a while and save us a bunch of money."

"Okay, Shane, I will, sweetie." He is slurring his words a bit and I can hear men's voices in the background calling for him.

"Oh, and please try and be nice to them?"

"What? How am I supposed to do that?"

"Ya know, before they die. I don't know how you can be nice. Just make sure they don't suffer, okay? Please. Promise me, okay?"

He laughs and says, " Okay, I will do my best. No suffering, got it. Love you and I will call you again when I get to the next stop, hopefully tomorrow or the next day. Oh, and tell your mom I said hello."

"I'm going to pretend I didn't hear that. Talk to you soon and love you, too."

Phew . . . a deep feeling of relief falls over my entire self, and I promise God and every dead relative and pet that I will never do anything like this again. It felt good talking to Jake, and shortly after hanging up, I must have drifted off.

I wake up suddenly when the song "Hotel California" screeches through the room. It's my ringtone for unknown numbers, so I don't answer. I picked a song I liked because listening to its lyrics until it hits voice mail takes awhile, and the Eagles turned out to be the perfect strangers' ringtone. For curiosity's sake and because of how late it is, I look at the phone, but no number appears. There's nothing, not even letters, just a blank screen, which is freaking me out, so I let the song play on until it stops. I wonder if Simone is calling since I don't have her number? If she needs me, I want to be there for her. If it rings again, I will answer. I check the voice mail to be sure, but there's "no new messages," so I fall back onto the pillow and doze off again. I'm awoken from a lightly sleeping state by a loud bing, a text message, I think? Why is the universe fighting my sleep? All I want to do is forget about tonight, wake up in the morning, say thanks, and drive home to my real home, the one I belong in. I roll over several times, dramatically, like I'm rolling down a hill, and reach across the enormous bed, pulling the corner of the phone toward me. I wipe my eyes as the dark room is illuminated by the bright screen.

Are you up?

Not an hour earlier, I said my prayers and asked every dead person plus God for forgiveness for all my sins. I am not sure the point of responding to whoever's texting me, because I'm done for the night.

It bings again.

Guess not.

No shit, Sherlock, that's why I didn't respond. This yahoo is annoying.

A third bing sounds.

I didn't see that you got into your room safely, so I wanted to be sure you were okay? Bonne nuit (i.e., goodnight. Your first French lesson.) SK.

Oh my goodness, it's Sebastian, how did he get my number? I look at the oversized chair in the corner of the room where I'd thrown my new toy and then back at the phone. What the fuck do I do now? I decide to respond politely and end this once and for all.

I am fine. Thank you. Goodnight, i.e., English.

Bing, it rings again.

Can you talk?

Why?

Because it's your turn.

Is he serious? The phone rings and the screen's blank, apparently Sebastian's calling card. "Hello." I try and sound sleepy.

Sebastian sounds drowsy, too, but in a sexy, raspy way. I imagine him lying around in boxers, engulfed by silk sheets, marble floors, and a bed twice as big as this. "Hi, did you get in okay?"

"Yep." I don't want to fuel this fire, so I try hard to keep it short, so we can end this silly charade.

He continues. "Are you okay? I am under strict orders to make sure you are kept safe and well. Plus to have some fun." He laughs. His fucking ridiculous adorableness has me giving in and answering every question.

"Thank you for my, um, present and for everything else tonight, too. I never expected any of it and I had a lot of fun, so your orders are complete."

"Speaking of presents, did you like yours?"

I really don't want to answer. This guy makes my heart palpitate, and I know giving in to his requests will only lead to more naughtiness, but I can't help myself. "Um, sure. It's fine. Seriously, Sebastian, I really don't do that sort of thing, but thanks for it anyway. If it's okay with you, I will probably give it to Simone."

I can tell by a slight grunt that he moved his body, probably sitting up in a more attentive manner. I think I've piqued his interest, frustrating him, perhaps? I really need to stop and keep my mouth shut. "No, it's for you! Don't you dare give it to Simone."

I play along. "Dare, huh? Is that your turn?"

He seems unfazed by my joke. "Please, Shane, do me a favor. Go get it, open the package, and tell me about it."

My skin prickles. I need a pill. "Are you serious? This is embarrassing. You saw it, what's to tell?"

"For my turn, which is not the dare, by the way. Instead, I want to know about your favorite toy. Tell me about it?"

I had sex with other guys before meeting Jake, but they were all pretty plain about it. We never did anything but the normal stuff.

Jake and I haven't done much of anything in the past year or so, plain or otherwise. You need time for that.

"Are you there?"

"Yes, I'm here. Sorry, I was just thinking." I can't play fantasy Shane sober, I might as well go to hell feeling good and with a white med in my mouth. I get up and instead of reaching for the toy, pull out my little container and swallow two pills, washing them down with cool water from the blue bottle.

"Sugar, it sounds like you're up. Do you have it?"

I make the trek across the room and pull it from the bag, opening the package with an obvious and loud tear. "It's smooth, slender, and kind of squishy feeling. Oh, and purple."

"Will you try it out for me?"

How do I respond to such an obscene and perverted request? This guy has some nerve . . . . But on the other hand, his confidence and power make me cower under his soft-spoken words. My brain's telling me to run, but my body wants to stay and find out what all the hype's about. A combination of nervousness and fear, turns out, is a big bowl of Spanish flies to me and I can't resist. "May I just be honest?" I take a deep breath and exaggerate the exhale for dramatization and to sound a bit more scared than I am. I don't have anything to lose, and since I don't need to ever see him again, why the hell not be completely truthful? Unless he's recording me or this is some sick practical joke, which I don't think it is, I will follow along and tomorrow drive home for good.

"Always!" He is serious about this.

"Okay. Honestly, I don't know what to do. I don't ever touch myself or really anything like that, well not inside anyhow. Plus, I need to wash my hands and this thing, too. I like everything clean. I don't even know if it's waterproof?"

He starts laughing a deep, funny type of laugh. He's finding genuine humor in my honesty. He's still cracking up and finally composes himself after I jokingly say, "Ahem."

He speaks up in a sexy tone while remaining the fun guy from this evening. "Okay, why don't you go wash your hands and your toy. Yes, I bet it's waterproof . . . because, ahem, if you think about it, it kind of has to be. Then bring it back to bed with you. Go."

For some insane reason I get up and follow his exact directions and settle back under the covers, detached purple penis in hand.

"The next part is very important."

"Okay?"

"I dare you to follow directions."

"Wait, isn't it truth time?" I giggle and prepare for the worst, ignoring my silly plea to follow our game's rules.

"Reach under your blankets and pull your pants off. Put them on the floor. Now go back under the covers and pull your panties down, not completely off, but so that they are looped around one ankle. Then grab your new toy—"

"Wait, if I am going to do this, then I don't like the word *toy*, it freaks me out."

"Okay then, let's name it. First, did you follow my instructions thus far?"

"Yes, I followed them exactly. I don't need to name it. I could call it purple divorce?" He doesn't appreciate my humor and stops talking. A minute passes, and I say, "Hello?"

He responds, "Are you ready?"

"I think so."

"How about Sebastian?" He laughs as the words leave his mouth, knowing how ridiculous it sounds.

"Yes, Sebastian makes a great name for a vibrator. Seriously, though, this is as close as the human Sebastian will get to his purple brother."

He ignores me. "Are you and Sebastian ready?"

"Um, I guess?"

"Now make sure your panties are dangling around your ankle, then take that same leg and make a triangle and open the other leg. Is your leg wide and are the panties tangled around your foot?"

I answer hesitantly and truthfully. "Yes."

"Good. Now I want you to take Sebastian and hold him on the very tip of your clit."

My breathing is soft, and I'm terrified, awaiting the next instruction.

"Now turn him on."

I concede to move ahead with a soft, breathy, "Okay."

"Now hold him there and reach with your right hand below Sebastian but not quite inside and tell me if it's wet?"

It is indeed starting to feel moist and warm. "Yeah," I whisper.

"Now move your finger around but not inside, doing what feels comfortable. Then pull some of that beautiful, natural lubricant up to your clit and swirl it around using Sebastian as your fingers." He waits to hear me respond. "Are you okay?"

"Yes" barely ekes out from my lips.

Without hesitation, the next step is given in a direct manner. "Now take Sebastian and move him down to where your finger was and hold him there. Then rub your clit with it while pulling more and more sweet wetness from inside you and up to your clit. Now slowly let Sebastian inside you, keeping your finger on your clit while he eases, slowly, inside you."

I am letting myself go, relaxing around the purple softness and its small girth, breathing heavier and heavier, allowing the vibrations to stimulate inside me. I pull the purple pleasure machine from halfway inside me, deliberately stopping at the opening of my vagina. I'm finding my own ways to extreme satisfaction, not awaiting the next move by either Sebastian. I start moving Sebastian from my clit and switching fingers with it and then vice versa, taking turns to see which feels better. I cannot believe how this feels. My back and legs automatically arch, melding into the silky covers, and I can't help spreading them apart, breaking the triangle. I feel a need to get this deeper inside and let the opening swallow it whole. My clit fights my vagina for attention and keeps my fingers slippery and wet while I keep exploring the fully engorged form.

"Shane, talk to me."

I can hear Sebastian's gravelly voice in the distance. I have let the phone fall from my ear and it's tucked between my loose hair and the fold of a pillow. "Hold on a sec." My voice is barely audible. Every word is short and breathy. I squeeze the tip of Sebastian inside using a Kegel to keep it in place while I move my right hand to my clit and grab the rogue phone with my left. "Sorry. My fingers are so wet, the phone must have slipped."

"The phone is wet? That is so fucking sexy, Shane, you have no idea what you are doing to me!"

I've never heard him swear, and it strangely turns me on, reinforcing what I'm already feeling. The forcefulness of his voice makes me slow my pace, allowing him to catch up with my last moves.

"May I keep going?" I'm literally asking permission to orgasm, which is what I assume will happen if I let this keep going? Sex has always felt pretty good, but nothing like this.

"Wait. I want you to do something else for me." I listen distractedly. "Shane, listen closely. Control your breathing." His voice softens and he sounds more endearing, really caring about what's happening inside me. "I adore the sounds of your short breaths, but I would prefer you feel a true orgasm."

True? What is he talking about? If there's more than this, I may lose my hearing. I can barely take the constant vibration against my clit, I am beyond overstimulated, and my breathing is heavier and heavier with every single instruction.

"Control it, Shane!" His stern voice startles me. "Now, when you feel like you're going to climax, hold your breath. Find the spot and keep rubbing your beautiful soaked fingers all over your clit and hold your breath until you come."

What is he talking about, why would I do this?

"Shane, only do it for a few seconds right before you come. Have you found your perfect spot?"

I don't answer because I am back on track and it's becoming more and more intense. I move my heels around the mattress, pushing harder as my legs widen. I concentrate hard and take long, deep breaths, rubbing my clit with my fingers while the purple machine buzzes at the tip of my opening.

"Get ready, and hold."

I am beginning to go deaf, my ears are ringing from all the sensations, my hand is engulfed in warm, wet fluid, and my vagina is accepting everything I do to it.

"Shane, tell me what you're doing. Are you going to finish?"

"I am taking Sebastian and holding him with my muscles while he vibrates and with my fingers swirling and rubbing my clit over and over with the wetness coming from inside me."

"You are making me crazy."

I ignore him because this has become about me. I reach my middle and index fingers around the warm, wet lubrication around my clitoris and rub furiously, holding in one deep breath until I can't hear the phone. Sebastian is holding strong between my legs so I keep rubbing, harder and harder, fingers slipping about. I don't take another breath, and it feels like I may pass out, I'm so light-headed. The oxygen is disappearing from my brain and reappearing inside my engorged clitoris. I rub faster and faster, when the most ridiculous euphoria takes over my entire body and I screech, "Aaaaaaaahhhhhh!"

I let out the biggest gasp of trapped air into the phone with smaller catch-up breaths coming through my nostrils. My vagina pulses like a heartbeat as the interior walls move in and out, tightening around the vibrating machine. I am dizzy and can't see anything. I recognize this fuzzy high from my pills, and only when I've taken way too many, but it's never this good. I reach down and pull the vibrator out from inside me, only to hear his sultry voice.

"So . . . is Sebastian your favorite toy?"

An enormous wave of guilt floods every part of my being and I feel horrible about myself and want to die. I just experienced the highest high and now the lowest low. A literal orgasm with vaginal tears for enjoying too much pleasure. Now that the feeling is gone, my brain is catching up to my body, and I feel sick about what just happened. "I'm sorry, I need to go." I don't hear anything on the phone. "Sebastian? Hello?" Is no one there? I say his name three more times but nothing, so I hang up. I wipe the sheet between my legs, absorbing the excess moisture and leaving a wet spot resembling a wading duck. I get up and put my underwear back on, only to find an even bigger soaked spot, this one more boring in shape. Despite the circumstances and how it was achieved, insane is the only thing I can say about what just happened. Now it's time to forget, sleep, and move on, leaving the purple cheater behind. I cannot handle the lifestyle of these seductively beautiful people, their obscene ways, and ridiculously erotic orgasms. I thought I could handle it, but it's too much. I belong in Jake's world. I want our shitty little apartment.

~~~~~~~

Mute Rider and Sandwich Chasers

In the morning, I wake, and the first thing I see is Sebastian, the purple cheater, on the dresser next to the bed. I was so out of it last night, I don't even remember what I did with it PIO—post–insane orgasm. The lost oxygen must have taken a toll on my brain because I've never been high from sex before, only pills. I get up to get a drink of water and see there's a note stuck to my door from Simone. "Hey there, Sugar Shane! You're sleeping so I am leaving to deal with estate stuff. Make yourself at home. —Smoney."

I wonder when she got in? Holy shit, she probably saw the sex toy just sitting there. Ick! I look at the clock, 7:48 a.m. I jump in the shower and then gather my things to leave. I wrap my wet hair in a loose ponytail, pull on the same dirty clothes and sneakers without socks from a few days ago, and scribble a quick note to Simone. "Thanks for everything, Simone!"

The elevator opens and the bellman offers his long arm to take my purse but I decline. White must have come over my face because the bellman looks at me strangely. "Are you okay?"

"Um, I don't know. I don't have my car here. Do you think I may be able to get a ride somewhere?"

Without flinching from what would otherwise be an annoying request at any other hotel, he answers, "Yes, of course, Miss Shane."

How does everyone know my name and number? I follow him to the door, and right before exiting the lobby, I pull out the bag from the sex store with Sebastian inside and toss the purple cheater in the trash. I stand in front of the town car, but they block my entry and open the back door. I've almost forgotten where I am, trying to grab a shotgun seat like I'm in high school. I oblige with an embarrassing "thank you" and announce my childhood address to the driver.

We arrive a short while later, and when I try to open my own door, he runs from the driver's side to catch the handle before I fully exit. I can hear my mother from the driveway and purposefully raise an eyebrow, and the man smiles. I thank him and pull the few dollars I have left in my purse, apologizing profusely for the crappy tip. I walk to the door, and the closer I get, I realize she's yelling at Rob. "Stand still, stand still, I need to look at it."

I knock on the door, and like a couple days ago, no one answers. I knock louder, jiggling the handle, but it's locked. I hear Rob telling my mother the phone's ringing, but she tells him he's crazy. "You're losing it, the phone's not ringing. I think the metal got in your brain."

I knock again, louder this time, assuming the looney tunes inside will recognize a "bang-bang" on the door over the "bring-bring" of a telephone, but they don't. I can still hear arguing, but they must have moved rooms, as the topic isn't clear. A fiddling from the door's inside handle allows it to creep open, and the mysterious little girl is standing there. My goodness, she is not adorable. Her eyes are ferocious in color and shape, but the rest of her is plain-Jane. I feel bad thinking that way about a child, but with Simone as her mother, she should be a knockout, even as a toddler. Her hair is blond, stringy, and uneven, her lips are thin, and her little body is bony and awkwardly shaped. Her father must not be much of a looker, which is surprising considering Simone's impeccable taste. But manners are manners, and she did open the door for me. "Good morning, Vienne." She remains quiet and still as she stares up at me. I shake my head at the utter weirdness of her silence.

Just then, my mother comes running from the bathroom. She looks like a flying skeleton darting through the filthy hallway with bits of dust and hairballs tumbling through the air. "Oh my gosh, Shane, thank goodness you're here! Rob burned himself putting Pop-Tarts in the microwave."

"What? How? They go in the toaster. . . ."

"Yes, I know that sweetie, he left the wrapper on and it exploded or something. I don't know, but his hand is all messed up. I think he needs a doctor."

Just as I begin to speak, Rob comes from the bathroom with a disfigured hand hidden by bundles and bundles of toilet paper. It's comical, and I can't help but giggle at the absurdity of yet another nutty situation at my mother's house. He looks like a badly bandaged mummy with a hand at least six times the normal size, thick with white paper and Dora the Explorer Band-Aids holding it all together. For goodness' sake, this is one more thing for my mother to fret over and make him even lazier.

"Shane, sweetie, can you watch Vivi? I don't want her stuck at the hospital with us, it could be hours."

"Mom, what the hell? I came to get my car so I can go home,

not watch this kid." I point my finger at the odd-looking mute standing by my side, and instead of being offended she reaches her finger up to mine and makes a "bzzzzzz" sound. This is the first sound I've ever heard her make.

"Shane, please, please help me. She will be so bored."

I give in, and when my mother isn't looking, I smile at Vivi.

"Oh, thank you, thank you. Rob, get your shoes on. Oh my gosh, Rob, honey, I need to do your shoes. Don't move, I'll do it for you."

She sounds even more frantic, while Rob walks around aimlessly in circles with his arm frozen in the air, like the entire limb is affected. Rob the Blob is the biggest pussy around, how can she stand him?

"It will all be okay. Call me if you need anything at all, we won't be too long. Well, I don't think we will." She grabs Rob's other arm and walks him out like he's limping and blind. She closes the door and about thirty seconds later bursts back through, yelling at me like I'm not standing right there. "Shaney, Shaney, I almost forgot, I really, really need a check deposited before noon. I have to get it there. I don't want to bounce anything—the fees are so expensive. Can you drop it off for me? It's on the counter." She bolts out the open door, leaving me alone with the check, the house, and the weird kid.

I grab the check and tell Vivi to get her shoes on because we need to deposit this for Aggie. She follows along like a loyal pup and I start the car. I slam her into reverse, but when I look back, Vivi's not there. I put Hope in park, get out of the car, and walk around to the back passenger side door, where she's standing. I ask her what's wrong, but she doesn't answer. "Vivi, I can't help you if you don't talk to me. What do you want me to do?" I look inside the window, wondering why she won't get in. I see there's some miscellaneous crap sprawled along the back seat. I open the door to move it, and she pushes past me, climbing onto the mess and buckling herself into the seat. Little spoiled shit needed me to open the door for her.

Damn car starts to rumble when I put it back in reverse. "C'mon, Hope, c'mon," I plead with the old girl. "Hope, don't make me beg, please work." She bucks a bit but we drive off with the radio blasting. I look in the rearview mirror to check on the quiet passenger. Her eyes stare back at me but then to the window, never allowing eye contact for more than a few seconds. I keep shaking my head, thinking this is the strangest child I've ever met. No wonder Simone leaves her all the time. They have nothing to talk about.

"Okay, we're here. Are you ready?" We've arrived at the same bank that Simone brought me to—the only branch in the area that I know of, which thankfully matches my mother's deposit slip. "Will you come in with me? Sometimes, banks have lollipops. I'm sure they'll give you one." I get out of the car and wait for her to exit. The silent princess doesn't move. I walk over to her door and open it wide, and she unbuckles and comes out with ease.

We enter the lobby, and with it approaching noontime, the line is longer than expected. I take the time to examine the check, but I don't recognize the name in the upper left corner and it's made out to Rob. Maybe he sold something or did some work? It's doubtful, but I don't care, as long as he's helping my mother. The line starts to move, but there's at least a dozen more people ahead. Vivi follows at my side. An antique-sounding bell rings, meaning another customer has walked in, and all the bored customers, including Vivi and me, look to the door. Oh my goodness, it's the homeless guy from the other day. He's back, and this time I can see him up close. He's wearing the Red Sox hat and stands tall, looking straight ahead, never paying attention to the customers staring at him. I try not to stare either but watch an elderly lady step out of line, obviously offended by his presence in the bank. I move ahead in line, overhearing a confident and deep voice ushering people along. It's the same well-dressed man who talked to Simone and chased this

guy down the street. He finishes some light banter with the customers and approaches the homeless guy, whispering something.
They both enter a room, but it's out of the public's viewing. Maybe
he's here to pick up lunch? This is so interesting, and my affinity to
stare is noticed when someone taps my shoulder to move forward.
I finally, after a long wait, meet the teller and ask her to deposit
the check for my mother, the whole while checking back to see if
the homeless guy has come from the back room. I ask her if they
still give out lollipops and she asks what flavor I would like. "Oh,
thanks, it's not for me." Knowing Vivi won't answer, I ask if I can
show her the colors and let her choose. The teller kindly obliges
and hands me a glass jar packed with suckers. I turn around to
show Vivi but she's gone. "Vivi? Vivi?"

"Excuse me, is everything okay?"

"No, I can't find her. I need to find her!"

"Um, your daughter, ma'am? I didn't see her, sorry. What does
she look like?"

I shout louder so the people in line can hear me. "Vivi, please!
Vivi, answer me!" There's only silence, except for gossip and gasps
from the awaiting customers. My heart is racing. I am panicking,
because even if she does hear me, she won't respond. The most I
have ever heard from her mouth is a buzzing sound, and that came
from a finger. What am I going to do? How many Barrons' lives
will I ruin? Every single moment from when we stepped into the
bank is running through my mind, but I can't remember the last
instance I saw her. I run around the lobby, yelling, "Vivi! Please,
Vivi, answer me. Just talk this one time, please."

Everyone looks around but keeps moving forward, like an
assembly line of herded cattle, to the waiting tellers. They ignore
the pleas of a citizen in need while they wait their turns. I run
out the glass doors, looking left and then right. I see her. She's
halfway down the block, standing next to the homeless man's
gigantic dog. Her standing height is the same as the dog's sitting

height, so her face is directly across from his ferocious teeth, ideal placement to maul a child. I run like a track star to Vivi, but when I reach her she looks at me without expression. She keeps stroking the dog's head and playing with the cropped ear that's half missing. I finally come within a foot of her and the dog, approaching with caution. I don't want to startle the dog, plus I can barely catch my breath from running as fast as I ever have. My heart is beating out of my chest, and my heart is audibly pounding.

"Vivi, hi." I put my hand out, and neither human nor canine acknowledge me. In fact, Vivi starts tracing her index finger over the dog's many scars, past his head and around his eyes and snout. Passersby stare in awe, and one lady tries to grab Vivi's hand, but she pulls away and moves in closer. I bend down on the sidewalk to reach her level, realizing the dog is not tied and probably hasn't gotten his sandwich.

"Okay, sweetheart, I need you to come with me. Just walk away and leave the doggie. I can get you a lollipop." She doesn't move. Just as I am planning a scheme of scooping her up and running for our lives, I hear an angry voice.

"Have your child move away from him."

I look back and see the homeless man, paper bag in hand. "Um, I am so sorry, she won't move. Neither of them will." I try to verbally plea with her again. "Vivi, this man owns the doggie. We need to give him back." She looks up at both of us, then sits flat on the pavement and wraps both her hands around his thick, stocky body and says, "Good."

"Holy shit, you talked! I am so proud of you, great job!" I'm overjoyed to hear her first word, or whatever it is, but the man's not amused.

"Yes, he's good, but let him go and leave him be."

"Good." She says it again, and kisses the dog on top of his head. They both stand up, and he licks her all over her face, slobbering everywhere. All I can remember is a doctor telling me that dogs always bite where they've licked, and I try to grab her again, but she pulls back like I'm the danger. "Good." She says it a third time and walks toward me.

The disgruntled homeless guy is overtly annoyed by us. "Are we done now?"

"Geesh, I'm sorry, I was in the bank and looked down and she was gone. She was out here with your dog, who isn't even on a leash." I'm getting angry now. Who the hell is he to be annoyed by a child?

"Whatever, lady. Keep your kid on a leash." He walks away, and the dog rises up to receive his sandwich while the man folds the brown bag, again filled with something else, and tucks it in his pocket.

Vivi doesn't say another word. I bribe her with McDonald's to pry more words out of her, but she doesn't speak a syllable. I have to guess what she likes, even asking her to tell me what's "good," but she doesn't answer. So I go with chicken nuggets, assuming all kids like those, and she indeed seems to.

We drive back to my mother's, and thankfully when I pull into the rocky driveway, her car is there. I am relieved that I can rid myself of yet another fucked-up experience and go home. I get out of the car, and once again, Vivi waits for me to open her door. I explain to her that no one does that for me, but that doesn't seem to interest her. I open her door and she reaches out her scrawny little index finger, waiting for me to do the same. Then she pushes them together, makes the "bzzzzzz" sound again, and pulls them apart. I laugh, but she doesn't even crack a smile and heads for the front door. This little girl is freaking odd.

"Oh, hi there. How is everything?" I call out. I can see Rob is back in his chair, reclined to its maximum position, his mammoth stomach sticking out like a hump of hay in an old painting. He has a thick pile of sugary and salty snacks to choose from. I wonder if

my mother secretly knows he's diabetic and is slowly and intentionally trying to kill him. My mother shrinks and he continues
to grow; they're the ultimate tumor of relationships. How poetic:
Both are dying, but from different food disorders. I walk into the
kitchen and see a carrying case on the floor, the kind for cats with
air holes all over. I bend down to see inside and then screech with
fear as I nearly get my eyes pecked out by a wild bird. "Mom, what
the fuck? This thing is evil."

"First of all, stop that language."

"Sorry, just what the hell is that?"

"Oh, sweetie, that's Mouse, our new pet chicken. Rob and I
were coming home from the hospital, and for almost the entire
ride we were stuck behind a truck that was filled with a bunch of
metal crates. All of a sudden the truck slammed on its brakes for
a red light, and one of the containers came sliding out the tailgate
and landed on the pavement in front of us. I beeped like crazy, so
the guy got out of his truck and threw the fallen container onto the
back. At the next light the same thing happened, and before he
could throw the poor thing back on the truck's bed, I grabbed the
cage and put him in the back seat. I wanted to call the police, but
Rob thought I would get shot or something. Whatever. His name is
Mouse, and he's the sweetest thing."

"Mom, it's a chicken or a rooster or something. What are you
going to do with it?"

"Oh, I don't know. For now I'm going to set him up in the house
so he can walk around until he feels better and then I will let him
go at the park."

I can't imagine the insanity of letting what is most likely a fighting cock wander around my childhood home, pecking the already
stained carpet for crumbs and leftover food. I look at Vivi, who is
now drawing a picture of the bird at the bumpy table. I feel intense
guilt for leaving her here, fearing she may end up like me some day.
I barely know the bizarre little thing, but we're "bzzzzzzing" friends,

and this place is a nuthouse.

"Mom, can I talk to you in the other room for a second?"

"Yes, you may talk to me."

I sigh and walk behind her bony structure and back down the hall. We enter her bedroom, and I step over heaps of dirty clothes and close the door behind me. "Is Vivi okay? She doesn't talk, and then today I finally heard her say something and it was to a dog. Or about a dog, I am not really sure. She's just odd. Is she okay?"

"Oh really, she talked? What kind of dog?"

"Mother, that's not the point, she just seems slow or something? Doesn't Simone have nannies for her?"

"Oh, I am so proud of her, I need to fix her a grilled cheese." She starts to open the door, and rather than argue about the miniature mute stranger, I follow behind and let another crazy subject be. God help that poor thing, but she isn't my problem to worry about, and I'm sure she has plenty of help and money available. I just don't understand why Simone's not using it on her?

My mother thanks me for visiting and says she hopes to see me more, but seems preoccupied making food for Mouse and Vivi, talking to them both in the same high-pitched voice. "Who wants a grilled cheese, who wants one?"

I wave to Rob, who is now snoring loudly, and say goodbye to Vivi, who extends her finger. I laugh, thinking of her as a mini Drew Barrymore mimicking ET in the movie. I walk over to buzz her one last time and she reciprocates, but then turns back to her chicken drawing. I whisper in her ear and tell her she's really "good."

Bar Family, Meet Prince Charming

I drive home without stopping, and with so many things running through my head, the ride flies by and I reach the apartment quickly. It feels like weeks, even though only a few days have passed.

"Are you serious?" I say aloud, wondering what white trash

neighbor bought this? My usual parking space is blocked by a running black Mustang with a deep throaty sound, shiny chrome wheels, and black tinted windows. I pull into another space close by when my nasty neighbor whom I share walls with comes out hollering. "Shaney girl, hey hey, girly friend, look my man got his settlement, we fuckin' livin' good, girl."

I wave and yell "congratulations" and her man winks at me, nodding his head toward the passenger side. She mouths something to him, stupid jealous girl, and jumps inside the rumbling GT, which peels out with absurdity onto the main road. Wait until the Italians catch up to him, I hear their cars are much faster.

I walk into my apartment, and it's exactly how I left it, but it also feels so different, tiny, like home should be. I sprint to Andrew's cage, worried about him since I've never left him for so long. His water is filthy, with five long, pellet-shaped poops, and I worry how hungry and thirsty he must be. I check the cricket container and there's one survivor still hopping around. I clean his cage, fill the lagoon with fresh water, and feed him the remaining cricket, which he gobbles up in one quick move. I spend the remainder of my time gathering laundry and doing the few dishes in the sink. Then I take another shower, rinsing the final heebie-jeebies from my clothes that I've worn, and then worn again. It's no comparison to the shower at the Ritz, but it's comfortable and feels normal. The water trickles down my body and I fantasize about Sebastian's voice, rubbing soap around my clit while I practice holding my breath. I gasp aloud when I hear yelling from outside the locked bathroom door. I was so turned on and pushing the time to hold my breath, and now there's a knock. My heart is beating wildly. I've always had a strange, longstanding fear of being abducted or killed in the shower, and it's coming to fruition, holy fuck. I am scared shitless. I rinse off fast, leaving the water running to fake them out, and wrap my drenched self in a crusty, dry towel as quietly as possible. The shouting and yelling starts up again, but it's not coming from inside my apartment. Phew. My blood pressure drops a few points, and I tiptoe to the front door and peer through the peephole to see the shouting is from two really big men pounding on my neighbor's door. Too bad they just skidded off in their new hot rod. I shut the shower off, quickly get dressed, pop a pill, and wait for silence. Once they are gone, I leave for my shift at the bar.

I arrive at work to an obscene amount of people asking questions about where I was and what happened to me, and I spend a majority of the shift confirming rumors that aren't true. I start the evening with one loud speech, saying that I was visiting an old friend and am back for good. "Now show me how much you missed me with extra tips." Everyone laughs, moving on to their regular nonsensical jibber-jabber.

I go back to the kitchen to hand Eddie the food orders and he quizzes me on my whereabouts. "Did you being gone have something to do with Simone Barron's dad dying?" He knew about us because it was almost never that a poor public school kid would be seen with an extremely rich kid, and I didn't make any new friends because of it.

"No. Please, Eddie, I don't want anything getting back to Jake, so can we just leave it alone?" I give him a serious look and he matches my stare but folds when I bite my lip and raise a wonky brow, showing nervousness. "Honestly, my mother is sick, but I don't need the whole town knowing about it."

"Oh shit, okay, sorry, Shane."

"Here are the orders, you-know-who wants french fries on his soup. I know it's gross, but can you do it?"

"No problem, Shane. If you need anything, you know I am always here." He grabs my hand and I allow him to hold it, but within a few seconds he lets go and takes the handwritten orders from my other hand.

An hour or so later I am no longer the topic of interest, and the bar has concurrently, as a group, moved on to other things. My favorite to listen to is the constant verbal war between the Vet and Ye Ol. They are having their own little debate, duking it out over the possibility of a woman ever being president, but the Vet thinks it's crazy.

"My wife could have been president," Ye Ol says.

"The fact that she's a wife makes her incapable for the job," the Vet spouts back.

At one point, I intervene because it feels a little heated—and personal, as a woman. They agree that they're out of line and switch to Roswell and alien conspiracies, with various barstool regulars piping in about the latest flashing light they've seen or tinfoil hats they keep "just in case, to block the rays." I pour more drinks and collect tips with grateful thank-yous, and I feel good, like I'm back home where I belong. This is my family.

Like a psychic, Eddie reads me like a book, carrying out a plate of piping hot chicken wings, with extra carrots and celery with ranch dressing. I thank him with my eyes and he smiles back with his. I check in that everyone is all set and sit in the back, where the slanted pool table sits unused, devouring the messy wings. I walk around front to grab more napkins and nearly choke on the un-swallowed chicken still in my mouth. My heart is literally going to explode. I can't believe what I am seeing. Sebastian.

I immediately think about what I must look like. I'm wearing tight green jeans with a black shirt that has paint stains from when we moved into the apartment and a cut in the neckline, giving way to my small cleavage. My hair is messily thrown on top of my head, and hot sauce is smeared orange over my lips. It is not the princess look I had going when that imaginary night at the castle took place. After driving all this way and seeing me like this, he must be turning around. I watch to see if he runs for the door, jumps in his sports car, and gets the hell out of this shithole before they strip his tires.

I sprint for the back room looking everywhere for napkins, but only finding paper towels, I smear with vengeance the food from my face. I am in utter panic mode and need to get to a mirror to put on some Show Orchid lipstick and fix whatever I can as fast as I can.

When I walk back out, two of Dave's bored cronies are chatting him up, but he seems unfazed. He looks different, too. He is wearing loose-fitting, dark-colored jeans, some sort of sneaker-shoe hybrid, a polo-style shirt, and hair tousled and messy, like an imaginary top was down on a convertible. I try to be as cool and collected as someone in a shocked state can be, heart beating a mile a minute, and look down the bar at my regulars. I can't hold out any longer and glance his way, and he stares at me like he's been waiting years for me to notice him. The slightest smile comes straight from his eyes, and I can barely see the edge of one of his crooked canines. Dave's two young girls see him looking at me and one says, "Oh, you want something, just tell her, she'll get it."

I remind myself to card those little hoes later. I'm frozen in time watching him, and he's watching me, but what I don't see is that everyone else is watching, too. We both break cover and I speak first. "What can I get you?"

His white teeth show a bit more, and the girls are drooling in anticipation, waiting to see what he orders. "They don't have much here, just shitty beer," one of them says. "I know a better place if ya want? We can show you."

He speaks clearly and with poise, looking straight at me, although his words are directed at them. "No. I am fine, thank you. I believe they have exactly what I am looking for."

I'm amused. "Something on tap, perhaps?"

"Yes, that sounds perfect."

Our connection is broken when Ye Ol says, "Shaney, sweetie, get my friend a drink." He's pointing at the Vet, who is obviously inebriated and doesn't need anything else except water and a ride home. "Let's get some shots over here, he was in a war, ya know."

I giggle and shake my head, as everyone in the entire town knows he was in the war, never mind the same old crew of regulars. "You don't say. Okay, Ye Ol, what kind of shots would you like?"

Sebastian pipes up with childlike curiosity. "I would love a shot, too. I will take the bill for these fine veterans." I don't have the heart to tell Sebastian that only one of them is a vet, but who cares, as blue-collar people they all served something or someone in some way.

"Hell yeah, my man, oo-rah America" comes from the Vet's belligerent mouth.

I pour twelve Fireballs, and when one of the stupid girls tries to grab one, I whack her hand with a plastic straw and tell the two chickies we ran out of liquor.

"She's a bitch," I overhear one of them say to Sebastian, but the swearing doesn't seem to get either of them any extra attention.

"I am here for something, and it's not you or the drinks." Sebastian's words are so fucking sexy, I can picture the wet duck print I made on the sheets only a day ago.

"Whatever," the bleached blond one says in the most Valley girl of accents.

I take this opportunity to ask for their IDs, and not seeing Dave anywhere, they head for the door, empty-handed and alone.

All of us take a shot, and for the umpteenth time toast the Vet's career with shouts and cheers. It is a proud moment for all, but the shiniest eyes in the room come from Ye Ol, who adores that grumpy old alcoholic. I pick up the empty glasses and reach for Sebastian's, but before I can get to it, he grabs my arm. This allows his sleeve to rise up, and I can see just the slightest bit of ink. Does he have a tattoo? This man gets more and more curious. How can a successful, multilingual, international businessman be tatted up? Either way, I can't believe how well he's fitting in with our silly little crowd, lowering his standards in every way to be here with us.

He doesn't seem bothered one bit by the mix of old, young, crazy, and trashy in the room. I even overhear him speaking Spanish to my favorite Puerto Rican regular, Jorge, who only ever speaks a few words, usually "Heineken, gracias." I feel extremely stupid that I am so proud of my little corner bar and that this man I barely know from the highest echelon of class is sitting on a ripped barstool, buying cheap shots for all the intoxicated patrons. I want to cry and shoo him away, because he doesn't belong here any more than I belong in a castle with him.

Eddie is calling for me, so I head to the back kitchen. "Are you done with the wings? Do you want something else?"

"No, thank you, Eddie. Sorry, I got busy."

"Yeah, I noticed. Who's the rich kid buying everyone shots?"

I laugh it off, playing like I have no idea who he is. "Oh, not sure, but everyone seems to love him."

"Yeah, because he's buying everyone shots."

I walk out to check on my mysterious visitor, but he's gone. I look around cautiously, in case he can see me searching for him, but he doesn't return. I walk to where his seat was, but he's paid and left. Who can blame him? I feel a pit in my stomach, knowing he probably felt the same way I did when I was in his territory, and our caste system made him realize it was time to end this. I pick up the cash to pay the tab and put the money in the drawer. There are two twenty-dollar bills, a five, and three ones for all the Fireball shots. He was right on for price, and now I realize I never even poured him a beer. Then, underneath all the money, there are one-hundred-dollar bills. My hand is shaking as I thumb through the sticky bills, five in all. Holy shit, why would he leave me a five-hundred-dollar tip? He must really feel bad for me. I didn't realize how obvious I was, but it must be the clothes, or who knows, maybe I'm a charity tax write-off for these Richie fucks. I turn my back to the drinking crowd and look more closely at the money, thinking for some reason there might be clues—Sebastian is a curious dude. I was right, and smile as I read them to myself. The first bill says "For," then the next bills read, in order, "your" "time" "with" "Sebastian." A different word spelled out in marker on each of the bills, five words equaling five hundred dollars. Oh my fucking word, my heart is pounding, my palms sweaty and shaking. I fold the five bills and push them deep into my jeans pocket, ignoring the fact that there's word porn written all over Franklin's dead head. I want so badly to rip them into a thousand pieces, or give them to a homeless person, but I need the money so badly. I feel ill in my stomach, like I'm going to throw up. Does he think I'm a hooker? What the fuck did Simone tell him about me? I close the register and go back to work, grabbing and filling empty glasses, feeling completely woozy and anxious. My whole body is pounding, and I am oozing with nervous energy. Every free moment for the rest of the shift, I think about him and the money and why he would have written those particular words and then afterward walked out? I have a million questions for him, like why is he paying me and why does he keep disappearing or dropping calls and how does he know my number or where I work? Is this how Richie guys work? First they make you feel spectacular, then track you down, pay you for your time with them, and when they've had enough they up and leave? I sneak another shot to calm my nerves, but the cinnamon flavor is reminding me of him, everything is, even in Dave's shitty bar.

The night comes to an end and I get all my stragglers to either close up with me or leave like normal. Ye Ol checks the door like he always does, and I watch him carefully drive away, knowing he would because I switched him to seltzer hours ago. The radio blasts from his Beamer way down the street, and the Vet begins his trek to his charred house. I drive away, waving to the uninterested regulars, thankful this night is over.

When I get home, I undress at the door, bag my icky clothes for laundry day, and walk directly to the shower to get the sticky liquor and smoke smell off of my skin. I would like to throw away all my clothes, along with the fancy Ferragamo shoes and the money in my pocket, plus everything else that reminds me of Sebastian, but I don't. I curl up on the couch after a long, emotionally freaky night, pop two pills between my teeth, and reach to turn on the television when the phone rings.

"Hi, Jake!"

"Hey there, sweets, you sound happy."

"Oh, I had a good night at the bar for once, that's all. I was really worried after missing a couple days, but everyone was extra generous, so it all worked out. I should be able to pay the electric bill, too. Well at least the past-due part."

"That's awesome. You did miss those days, so I'm glad you are making up for it."

Asshole, but he's right.

"How did everything with your mother go? Did you survive?"

"Oh yeah, it's fine. So much weird shit happened, but I am over it and back home and back to normal, our normal. Oh, I almost forgot. The crazy neighbor must have gotten his settlement money, because he has a flashy new car, a Mustang I think, and then a bunch of creepy-looking guys showed up, banging on the door."

"Jesus, Shane! Stay the fuck away from them. Don't even answer the door. Do you want me to have someone come over and check on you? My mom can if you want, and she can bring you food."

"You're joking, right? Anyhow, I'm totally fine. Andrew and I are just chilling and he's got a wicked right hook with crickets, so I can only imagine his little green pod fingers against a mobster. Tell me more about your trip. Are you all settled in? Where are you now?"

His tone relaxes when I make a dumb joke and switch the attention to him.

"Oh yeah, it's great! My dad got a buck today, not huge but a good-sized one. But mostly we've been fishing and eating most of what we catch. It feels so great to wake up and not go to that fucking factory or anywhere else to work. I've been thinking, and you're right, Shane, we need better than this. When I get home, we will talk about how we can save for a house or do whatever you want. I will even help you look for jobs when you're done with school or whatever you want. I love you, sweets, and I need you to know that."

"Thanks, Jake, I love you, too. That means a lot. Well, go have some fun, for the both of us. I'm good here and I'll try to get a head start on that fancy house you're dreaming of."

He chuckles loudly and I can tell he's drinking. We hang up and I drink one of Jake's watery beers, falling asleep to the soothing voice of Mariska Hargitay on *SVU*.

~~~~~~~

Truth and a Tryst

In the morning, I wake up, prep for the shift at Stein's, and pack clothes for my bar shift. Arriving at Stein's, I jiggle my key, but the front door is already open and Patti is frantically waving me in.

"Seriously, girl. Tell me everything, I'm dying here. Whoever called out for you came straight from the top. What kind of secrets are you holding from me?"

I chuckle at her excitement this early in the morning and over someone like me. "Honestly, I have no idea. I just spent some time with my mother and saw one of my old friends. Nothing that juicy to tell."

"Whatever, I know you'll tell me eventually, and I'll be waiting. You can't hold on to these goods without spilling them to someone, and I know you're holding something back. I can tell, Shaney."

I smile, reiterating that there's nothing fun to tell. My stomach is sick trying to put all of the strange events behind me, never mind hack them up for Patti's gossip wheel. I keep thinking about the castle and my crazy mother, having left Simone with a note, and that bizarro kid. Sebastian is taking up an entirely different section of my anxious brain, and even a fleeting thought of him puts me on edge. I spend all my free time chewing pills, breathing deeply through the panic, and ignoring Patti's winks, as if that will open me right up like a pickle jar. The busier parts of my shift are spent filling orders and taking in repair jobs, and when I'm doing that I get to hear about all the bad sex Patti's having with her new boyfriend. The thought of sex reminds me of the purple cheater, and the infidelity illness waves over me all over again.

It's quarter to five and I'm ready to leave when Patti's boss, a.k.a. our big boss, Samantha, asks, "Can you stay a while longer? We're really slammed here."

"I'm working the night shift at the bar, but let me give them a call and see if they mind if I come in late."

"Okay, we'll try to get you out of here by six or seven at the latest. Thanks, Shane."

Where are the favors from the higher-ups when I need them? I'm missing Simone and all the perks that come with her. But the extra money is helpful and will hopefully keep my mind thinking of anything besides Sebastian. I call Dave and tell him they need me at Stein's awhile longer.

"Jesus, Shane, it's a fucking Saturday, are you kidding me? The place is already filling up."

"It's just for a couple hours, can't you get Eddie to help?"

"You know what, Shane, just don't bother coming in. I'll deal with it myself."

What is wrong with him? Some girl must not have put out and now he's hard up and taking it out on everyone else. Whatever, I'll get paid overtime here to make up for it, and maybe even get home a couple hours early.

When I leave Stein's around seven o'clock, Hope starts with a grumble plus a new rattling sound, but she's good enough to get me to the pet store for crickets and home to the couch. Around eight I finally lie down on the lumpy cushions, stuff my face full of Cheetos and cheap beer, and fall asleep in front of the television. I'm abruptly awakened by hard pounding on my door. Holy shit, this is fucked, and the threat of mobsters outside is real.

I rise up from an impaired sleep, wide-awake with panic, and tiptoe to the door, fearing a creak in the carpet that might alert them. Our apartment is so small and open, with only two picture windows, both near the door, and I question whether I should peer out, but I'm too afraid they'll be looking back at me.

Knock, knock, knock. It's even louder this time, and so are the beats from my chest. Holy fuck. Okay, Shane, you can do this. Just answer the door and tell them you know nothing about him or his crackerjack girlfriend. I grab the knob, and at the same time the door swings wide open and I scream, scaring myself. To my shock, Simone is standing there with tears flowing from her puffy eyes. I can't think of a time when she ever looked truly upset. I don't think I could have even imagined it. "Oh my gosh, are you okay?"

"No, I need to talk to you. Now."

I don't want to allow her in so she can see how grown-up Shane lives. At my mother's house I have an excuse, but here I am, twenty-three years old, living in a one-bedroom, one-bath shoebox in a very shitty and fairly dangerous complex.

"I'm coming in, Shane. I need you."

She pushes past me and goes straight to the couch like she's been here a thousand times. "What's going on? Hold on one second. Let me get you some tissues. Do you want something to drink?"

"Yeah, sure, thank you. Something strong."

I walk to the bathroom realizing I'm in full bedtime gear: frog pajama bottoms, a silky tank without a bra, hair on top of my head, and no makeup. What a sight, but she doesn't seem fazed by any-thing right now. I pass her a fistful of toilet paper on my way to the kitchen in search of something strong. I find an old bottle of bottom-shelf vodka in the back of the cabinet, holding it up for approval, and she nods "yes." I pour it over generic orange juice and ice, handing her a glass first and keeping a second for myself. She takes a sip and, for the first time since busting through the door, laughs her sweet laugh.

"Jesus, Shane, this shit is disgusting. What kind of bartender are you?"

I laugh, too. "Hey, you're at my house now, that shit is caviar!" We both know it's more than awful going down but clink glasses and toast to "disgusting shit." Not a minute more is wasted before she tells me why she's here, though deep down I already know. I've been dreading this moment since I saw the newspaper with her family plastered all over it only a few days earlier.

"I need to tell you about things. I need to get it all off of my chest. But before I start, how do you like Sebastian? He is such a sweetheart, did he take good care of you?"

I am a bit shocked that she's asking about him, but it makes sense since I ran out of her hotel with only a few quick lines on a note and we hadn't had any time to catch up or gossip. "Yeah, of course, he's super nice, but I'm married. Wait, what do you mean 'take care of me'?"

Her tone quickly went from sobbing to playful inquisitiveness and now to serious business. "Shane, I don't want to go into all of that right now. Can we just talk? I know before I didn't want to, but I really need to." Her voice crackles as a tear begins to swell in her blue eye, and soon crystal-clear tears fall like rain, pouring down her face. I study her beautiful physique that can still shock even when she's sad. Even morose looks good on her. Her hair is pulled back in a loose bun with unkempt wisps of loose, blond curls fram-ing her flushed pink cheeks. She's wearing stylish ripped jeans and a fitted orange tee, probably the kind that costs a couple hundred dollars even though it's just a cotton shirt. I'm a little stunned and maybe even in awe, since I don't recall ever seeing her cry. She's never shown emotion and was raised to always, under any circumstance, look strong and beautiful. I remember Mr. Barron telling her to "never be weak enough to cry," and she wasn't, even when he went to jail or shipped her off to faraway camps, or when she watched nannies who had raised her like moms get fired or she broke up with serious boyfriends. Everything has always rolled off, like her body and soul are made of Rain-X. I'm the one who constantly cries and has had baby ulcers since I could walk. I've always been weak and her so very strong.

I stare at her, waiting until she's ready to talk. She takes several deep breaths through her gloss-stained lips followed by huge gulps of her screwdriver and winces. "Here goes."

"You're freaking me out. Simone, are you alright?"

"Shane, my dear, sweet Shane. I am so, so sorry for what I did to you and what I made you do. You don't understand who you are to me and I just need you to know how sorry I am."

I am completely freaked out listening to her affectionate confession. "Simone, it's fine. I am sorry for what I did. You know I did it for you, right? Please tell me you know that, it was always for you, to help you, never ever to hurt."

Her voice rises and she's serious again. "Yes, of course I do. I fucking know what happened, and for that I am mad with myself but I'm not mad at you. Everything is so messed up. My money is tied up and the attorneys are holding me prisoner. I can't do anything and I feel so trapped. Everyone who thinks they're anyone or were someone to him is coming out of the woodwork, trying to get a share of my father's money, which is what caused this shitshow in the first place, my being fucking greedy. I can't take another fucking second of it, it's my goddamn money, no one else's!"

What does she mean broke and greedy? I went to her suite,

which is incredible, and she drives a fancy-ass car. How strenuous could it be? Her face is angry now and I try to comfort her, but I'm feeling a little strange, too. "That doesn't make any sense. You should have more money now than ever before. Oh shit, I'm sorry I said that, I am so bad with words. I shouldn't have said that, are you okay? Where's the money, like who has it?" She finishes her drink and hands it to me to make another. I look at mine, still full, and politely grab hers like the trained dog I am and go to the kitchen. I find an unused straw and add it to her drink. When I hand her the glass she takes a big sip, and I can already hear her hitting the ice. She makes a funny face trying to get it all down and continues.

"Shane, you don't understand. I didn't think this would happen, I didn't think he would die. He was just supposed to suffer a bit the way he made me suffer. Us suffer. I never should have asked you to lie for me. I was just so scared and a pissed-off teenager and I didn't know what I was doing." The tears start flowing, fast and loose this time. She wipes her face with the used tissues. I go to get more but she protests with her hand and I sit back down.

"Simone, what are you talking about? Back then I thought you were trying to keep your stepsister, Amanda, safe? True or not, I thought you thought he was doing something to her. That's why I lied. I did it for you, Simone. Because I thought you wanted that for Amanda?"

"No, Shane, I didn't give a fuck about that stupid little bitch. The second my dad was in trouble that girl and her gold-digging mother left me to fend for myself. I think she ended up marrying one of my dad's investors. At least they freaking divorced, or she'd be asking for money, too." She laughs aloud in a peculiar way. "You really thought it was for Amanda, didn't you. Oh Sugar, you really are sweet. She was just an excuse. She probably would have loved the attention, that ugly little whore."

I'm stunned. If this wasn't for Amanda, then why did Simone ask me to lie for her?

"Oh? Seriously, then why? I don't understand."

"Come on, Shane, can't you do the math? I was fucking pregnant! I knew he would kill me, hush me, abort the baby, and ship me off somewhere to never be heard from again so I wouldn't ruin the family name. I couldn't let him near my child. I knew what would happen if we both stayed. I couldn't bear to look at him knowing what he'd do to either of us." She is sobbing and keeps talking through the hiccups and tears. "If it's anything like what he did to me, well, I couldn't fucking let him, okay. That's why I needed you to tell the police that he raped you, because I knew they wouldn't believe me, or they would just cover it up. Everyone always covers up everything for him. I swear they still are. They all had something to fucking gain, every fucking last one of them. I couldn't take it anymore. You and Aggie were the only ones who helped me."

"Wait, I need to understand this. What are you saying, Simone? Are you telling me he never touched you or he did?"

She grabs the pillow, holding it over her belly and squeezing with such force, her knuckles are shaking. "I got too old for him, Shane. He liked them little."

I feel sick to my stomach. I wonder if this is why my mother had us move from the guesthouse?

"I knew what he was like and needed to keep him from the baby. Just like I kept him away from others. Well, at least I tried. Remember the nanny, Ruthie, who he fired? It was because she found out what he was doing so he threatened to send her family away, get them deported or some shit. Didn't you know why I never fucking invited you on any trips? It was because I didn't want my perverted fucking father to take from you what he took from me and would have taken from Vienne. I was his favorite. It was all I knew, Shane. Don't judge, do you understand? Don't judge us. But my child, that was mine. Not for him to abuse and fuck up."

She holds out her drink for another refill. I give her a

questioning look—she's drinking awfully fast, even for a regular—
but she shoves the glass in my chest. She continues talking while
I'm in the kitchen.

"I guess I realized that there was no hiding anymore and I
wasn't going to let him fucking punish me for getting ME pregnant. I didn't want her. But I had no choice, especially when I
found out she was a girl. I saw him light up and I hated it. I hated
her for making me feel that way."

I hand her the drink and take a big chug of my own, which
doesn't go down nearly as easily. It takes everything in me to keep
from verping.

"Look, Shane, don't be naive. If I said he was abusing me as
a teenager, they wouldn't question it. I knew he would find out if
I snitched on him, but if it were my friend, well that's honest and
that's an investigation. I knew the board and all the people involved
in his empire would want it silenced and just pay you to be quiet.
But instead for whatever reason, they conspired and put him in
jail, serving their own financial needs I guess. It's not what was
supposed to happen. I honestly don't even know how it happened.
It was awful, and no one will say why it went that far. They were
supposed to pay you with a settlement so you and your mom could
get a nicer house and I could take care of you the way you did for
me. You lied for me. You risked everything. I knew Aggie would
let me and the baby live with you, and there would be more than
enough money for all of us to have ten houses if we wanted. We
had a plan. She knew what to do and helped me so much because
of everything that had happened with them, when she was young."

My stomach is in my throat and I'm not sure I can talk. Our
entire childhood is flashing through her swollen blue eyes and out
her pouty glossed lips. I can see and hear her pain and feel her
desperation to release it. All these years since I left my mother and
my best friend, only to learn he *was* an actual abuser. It was all up
in the air back then and it's so scary to think that like a puppet, I

followed the master and did exactly what Simone asked. "Oh my gosh, Simone, I didn't know. I am so sorry. I didn't know he did that to you. How come you didn't tell me? Seriously, Simone, we could have done something sooner. I could have helped! I didn't know any of this. I was just doing what I thought was right in order to help you. And I don't understand this about my mother? She was obsessed with him."

"You did help! You were the ultimate best friend who exchanged your reputation for my freedom. I'm just sorry it didn't work the way it was supposed to. It was a lot to handle when they put him in prison. Everything folded, and my trust for anyone became tighter and I was fearful of everyone who was trying to fuck with me. Let's just say it hasn't been as easy as I thought it would be with him gone. You are the only normal person in my life. Everyone else acts fake or has money or is after my dad's money. My entire life people have walked on tiptoes around my father because they all had something to gain. You are the only real person in my life, you and Aggie, and I see that now. He had carte blanche to do anything he wanted, including me."

I gulp. "Jesus fucking Christ, Simone. I'm so sorry."

"Listen, when you did that for me, regardless of how it worked out, I knew right then that you were my one true friend, my friend for life, and your mother was going to help us all figure it out. You guys never asked for anything from me. It is so different with you than everyone else. Without you and your mom, I never could have faced him. I take care of Aggie whenever she needs anything, but she never asks. I know she was still seeing him and keeping him informed of me and Vienne. It drove him crazy that the baby and I were with her."

"So my mother knew?"

"Yes, she knew what he was like. That's why her mother quit working for the Barron family and took her away. I couldn't face anything, and she helped me a lot, before and after you left. She also knew what he was capable of, and that's why she supported anything that had to be done with him."

"Wait, are you saying that my grandmother, whom I've never met, worked for your family, too?"

"I don't know, I feel like I am saying way too much. In vino veritas, I guess? I can't believe you don't know any of this? I think something must have happened because your mom came back as an adult to work for my father."

"Wait, hold on. My mother always told me that my grand-mother wanted nothing to do with us because I was some bas-tard child made out of wedlock. But the real reason is because my mother went to work at your house and brought me along?"

"Yes. I think so. I didn't ever meet her either, it was way before us, but your grandmother used to bring your mom to work, too. My father and Aggie are only about ten years apart, but I guess he was like that back then, too? I don't know, I don't want to think about him with anyone, it's too weird."

"Holy shit, I can't believe this. Why the fuck would my mother go back there and bring me?"

"I don't know. She was older and must have thought you were safe because I was with you. Or maybe it was to keep an eye on both of us? I don't really know, we've never discussed it."

"I cannot believe all of this. I didn't know our families knew each other for so long. I can't believe this. My crazy mother chose your father over her own mother? Why would she do that?"

"I think it's that whole rich and powerful thing? I have no idea, Shane. He gets a hold over people and that's it, the handcuffs are clicked."

"Yeah, kind of like Aggie. When I left and married Jake, you were pregnant and all alone and I did that to you, just like my grandmother did to my mother?"

"I guess, but I really don't know the story, just that she worked there and I assume he was doing it then, too? Don't worry, I wasn't alone, I had plenty of care and your mother was good to me, she understood and always listened, no matter what. It was a chaotic time and not good for any of us. Nothing went as planned, nothing. Now he's dead. Again, not planned." With one tear flowing down her face, she barely makes a half smile, trying to lighten the mood, but I'm not nearly ready. She is slurring, but like a good bartender, I keep fueling the fire and put another glass in front of her.

"Why didn't you tell me to stay? I thought you were so mad at me for how it turned out? I was a wreck. I was so upset for so long, worried that I did the wrong thing, worried that you hated me. I was literally a mess and couldn't stand to see what would happen. People found out and blamed me. I was embarrassed and scared, and I'm so sorry Simone. I didn't know. I just wanted to be like you. I would have done anything for you."

"Well, you did do it for me, and I am still in shock even after all this. No offense, Shaney, but you don't exactly handle stuff well. I didn't want you to know. Honestly, I was embarrassed for you to see that side of me. I didn't want your knowing what he did or knowing about the pregnancy to change how you felt and what you knew about me. No one was to ever know that, not even you, so don't ever say anything. Do you understand? You can't say anything to anyone. Vienne is the only thing I have left of my father."

I try to hug her but she moves my incoming arms and keeps talking. "I didn't even want to admit any of it to myself. I even stopped eating, thinking that would keep her from coming. Nothing worked, I was stuck and had to react. So I used you. I knew you and Aggie would do anything for me. The Lacys always do, for the Barrons. I am so sorry. It's generationally fucked-up. Shit, that sounded harsh. Sorry, Sugar it's the truth."

She softly runs her fingers affectionately down the side of my cheek and I can see her red nails out of the corner of my eye. I cannot respond. I am still in shock. I feel like a pawn in the game of Simone. The famous Barron heiress apparently appreciated my crazy mother and me for never using her, just as I learn that she was using me the entire time. I was poor and she was rich and all I have ever wanted was to trade my life for hers. That is, until this very second, when I realize I don't want it anymore. She's sick, he's sick, they are all fucked-up and have dragged me into it. How could they get me involved? Why? I want to call my mother and scream at her for answers. I want the truth, all of it.

Simone gets up and walks to the bathroom. I use the time to wipe my tears, pop a pill, and fill up our glasses again. She comes out looking refreshed and beautiful, although her gleaming blueberry eyes are still puffy. She sits down and stares at me, mouthing "I am so sorry," and her eyes gleam with tears. I collapse like putty into her drunken words. We both pick up our drinks and at the same time and for some strange reason, clink our glasses. "To the truest of friends."

I smile, and we both chug the horrible-tasting screwdriver. "Can I ask you a question?"

"Sure, anything. But I think you know everything now." She laughs.

"Um, the father of Vivi, is it really . . . ?"

"C'mon Shane, eventually it was going to happen. Why do you think Aggie was so willing to help? It was a Barron baby!"

Vodka and orange juice creep up my esophagus and I verp inside my mouth, swallowing it back down with another swig of bitterness. I was expecting everything I've eaten in the last five years to tumble out of me along with my guts all over this fucking couch, but I hold it together. My entire childhood flashes before me, and for the first time it occurs to me how grateful I should be that Simone and my mother, working together, saved me from this horrific man. It could have been me he raped. It really could have been me. I don't know what to do or what to say. It suddenly occurs to me I've lived the last five years out of guilt, marrying a stranger to avoid the confrontation, and it was all to protect myself. I'm a fucking idiot.

"Simone. Oh my gosh, Smoney, I don't know what to do. I don't understand. I cannot believe this. I'm such a fucking asshole. I ran from you. I didn't know what I was doing, I thought I was help-ing because it's what you wanted, and now I know it's what you needed, and I just feel—"

She puts a finger up to her own lips to seal the subject closed. I want to keep talking and crying forever, but her glare won't allow me to continue. We sit for a few minutes on the couch, looking at one another. I get up and walk around nervously and without shame pull a pill from my purse and swallow it in front of her. I've gathered enough nerve to change the subject, and I'm feeling just fucked-up enough to try.

"Did you say you don't have any money? I don't understand, how could that be? I mean, I don't mean it like that, but you know what I mean. I was wondering why you weren't at your family home, but then I just thought maybe because of memories or something, but definitely not this, not because of people controlling it. I had no idea, but then again, I am just a clueless idiot. I wish I could help you, I wish I could offer you something better."

We both laugh at the absurdity as she glances snottily around my apartment.

We begin talking more and more about how much time has passed and about everything we've missed about each other. "Shane, those fucking stupid jokes are what I love the most." We continue to share stories of our pasts as I pour another crappy drink, slurping it down in between girly-pitched giggles. I tell Simone what she means to me and that I am sorry for putting her father in prison, I didn't know there was a plan. I didn't know any of it. I was just trying to make her happy. Except knowing what I do now, I'm not sorry for his early death, but I would never say that.

"I still feel responsible, even though he did this to you. I put him there."

Suddenly our joking is gone, and it's serious time and her tone changes back to what it was when I first saw her. "I told you to, Shane. I did it. I did what I thought was right. I was trying to fix it. It wasn't supposed to happen the way it did, but either way, I kept him away from Vienne, and that's what needed to happen."

Catching her snappy reaction, she reaches over, wrapping her smooth arms around me. I can smell her infamous Chanel perfume and the light scent of lavender deodorant through her shirt. We sit still like that for a moment, embracing each other, until I feel a tear forming in the corner of my eye. She looks up at me and we are face-to-face, staring at each other's sad eyes as she wipes the tear from my cheek. She unleashes her other arm from behind my back and straddles her body over my crossed legs. I undo them under her weight, and she whispers, "You mean everything to me, Shane." She puts her lips to mine and holds them slowly, lifting and separating them with hers. Her hips thrust deeper against mine, and I feel her pelvic bones softly strike above mine. She is completely encased around my waist, digging her knees into the lumpy cushions while bracing her elbows against the back of the couch as she kisses me harder. She tugs on my hair, pulling my neck back and farther into the support of the couch.

I'm both paralyzed and trapped underneath her while our tongues work together, and she moves her hand to my right breast. I kiss deeper, and we both ease ourselves onto the floor. Our legs intertwine, and she moves her mouth down my neck, never unclenching my breast. She works like a lioness, slow and with confidence, slightly tugging my nipple and breathing warm, tiny breaths onto my stomach. After what feels like an eternity of slow torture, she finally reaches the elastic band on my frog pajama bottoms. Her free hand pulls them to my knees, but I push my hands against her small frame in opposition. She whispers into my stomach, "Shhhhhh." I lie back in pure pleasure to Simone's calculated touching as she pulls my underwear and bottoms completely off.

I grab her head and the tethered bun is let free and blond locks tickle the inside of my exposed thighs. I move my neck to see the top of her head and beautiful blond hair caressing my naked legs while she continues to the inside of my thighs. She knows I'm watching, and like the sensual heiress expert that encompasses all that is Simone, she places her middle finger in her mouth, pulling it out with an exaggerated amount of saliva and easing it slowly inside me. My back arches in ecstasy and I try to stop her, but my hands can't find the strength and I fall back. She feels the little bit of opposition, causing her to push and pull her finger in and out with more force. I can barely take the feeling, and my hands clench the carpet beneath me as her tongue deliberately teases the very tip of my clitoris. She swirls her tongue softly, teasing the blood to the top while continuing to push and pull her finger in and out of my dripping wet V-spot. I can't help holding my breath using the lessons learned from purple and live Sebastian. I inhale one deep breath, holding until my heart is racing and pleasure bursts from me, feeling my muscles contract around her fingers and my clit tingle. I exhale a fast, panting breath, screaming, "HOLY SHIT, SIMONE!"

I pant tiny mini-breaths, allowing my lungs to catch up on the lost oxygen. My legs are shaking, trapping Simone's finger inside me. I can't hear or see anything. She leaves her hand, and with the free one grabs a fistful of my hair, touching her lips to mine, allowing me to taste myself for the first time. It's sweet and makes me want her even more. I kiss her harder, grabbing her bottom lip with my teeth. I reach for her jeans to reciprocate whatever this is for the first time in my life, but she slaps my hand. "No! Only for you."

I don't fight her resistance because I'm flat-out exhausted. She gets up and heads fully dressed to the bathroom. I sit up, pulling my pajamas off the floor, and shamefully start to pull them over my still soaking wet bottom. Simone sees me rubbing my panties between my legs, soaking up some of the pleasurable evidence, and laughs. Completely embarrassed, I toss them to the ground and pull the bottoms past my knees to my waist. She sits on the couch, grabbing my hands and pulling me toward her. We both lie together, spooning, my body tucked into the smooth curvature of hers like a matching puzzle piece. She acts like nothing's happened. "What's on TV?"

Is Lesbian Stuff Cheating?

I must have passed out from exhaustion and alcohol because I'm awake on the couch and it's 3:12 a.m. I get up to fetch a cup of water, nearly tripping over my shoes in the process. I crawl into the bed, expecting to find Simone, but she's nowhere to be found. It has been the strangest time, and just like before, she's up and left in the middle of the night. I laugh to myself, thinking of her constant complaints of one-night stands. She used to say, "Stop calling me, what don't you get about one night!"

I hate to think that I'm now grouped in that category, and force myself to think that I'm different than the others—plus, I'm a girl. The guilt is different than it was with Sebastian and the purple cheater, and in my mind I convince myself that lesbianism isn't cheating. Jake would literally shoot me with a bow and arrow like a tracked deer if he knew what I've been up to. I'm grateful for our poverty and the one cell phone we share; it keeps our conversations at a minimum, especially with him away. I climb under my covers, setting the alarm so I'm up in time to open for Stein's in a few hours.

~~~~~~~~

Free to Choose

I wake up to the screaming noise of the clock and bang it to stop, but it falls off the nightstand, still screeching. I need this fucking thing to stop making noise. I need Tylenol! My head is throbbing, and a wave of nausea consumes me. I find my regular pills and add in a few nonprescription ones to start the day, which I'm already dreading.

I open the jewelry store and work at training a new girl so she's ready way before the holidays, our craziest time of the year. She seems really nice, very pretty, and utterly pleased with the extra attention from the male customers.

It's midafternoon and finally time for a break, which I'm desperately in need of. The medicine has worn off, and I need to fill my belly with food and pills to get this sick feeling to stop. I head to our tiny lounge and raid the fridge, having avoided food like the plague just a few hours earlier. There are annoying labels from my coworkers on everything except for Mini Moo's creamers and salad dressings. Patti is a health nut and, lucky for me, left a container of something good for me in the fridge. I know she won't mind, because she's constantly on my case about eating organic produce and protein and other middle-class crap. I heat up the stuffed peppers packed with beans and mow it down with a bottle of half-opened coke. Skylar, my trainee, comes to the back room and stops at the door when she sees me ravenously eating like a rabid wolf. I raise my eyes and wipe my mouth to show her I'm listening. "Um, Miss Shane, sorry to bother you, but there is something I don't know how to do on an order. He's asking specific questions, I'm sorry, I just don't know."

She's meek-sounding with her words, and the businessmen will no doubt eat it up like candy. That is, until her naivety mixes up the orders for a spouse and a mistress. "Okay, just give me a second." Dammit. I'm starving, so I take one more huge bite, put the fork down, fix my face with some Show Orchid lipstick, and pop a stick of gum.

"Oh shit!" I blurt out.

Skylar turns to me in horror. "Um, I don't think we are supposed to say that."

I ignore her idiotic comment and walk directly to the customer, now thankful for the gum. "Hi, may I help you?"

"Yes, please. I am looking for something particular and thought your expertise in stones might help guide me?"

"Okay, what interests you?"

He smirks and says, "In the store?"

"The stones, what kind of stones interest you?" I make sure to emphasize the words, so he knows exactly what I'm referring to.

"Oh yes, of course, I would like something rare, perhaps. I'm not really sure, but it must be unique, unusual, and something I won't find anywhere else." He is toying with me, sexy fucker.

Skylar walks up to us and I allow her to observe. She blindly flirts with the stranger, but her itty-bitty body and cute face don't faze this gentleman. His eyes are intent on me.

"Would you be so kind as to choose it for me?"

I look at him with intensity, and with the same fire he stares back at me. This time, Sebastian is in a full suit, with a tie that has fish swimming in different directions, and hair tossed messily about. I look to his wrists, only to see he isn't wearing cuff links. For some reason, I always picture him with cuff links, even when he's sleeping. "Would you like some cuff links, Mr. . . . ?"

"Kane. Sebastian Kane." He reaches out his hand to shake mine, but I don't reciprocate, so Skylar grabs a hold of his hand, breaking the awkward tension. "Sure, whatever you choose."

"I can choose anything?" Even I am shocked at the looseness of his request, but excited for the freedom. "If you're sure, I have a favorite. They are loose stones, though, and would need to be set into links."

"That's not a problem, there isn't a rush. May I see the favorites?"

Skylar is utterly confused by our interaction and must imagine that every sale is going to be this easy. I head to the back of the store and past the head jeweler, and with a nod he uses his fingerprint and allows me inside the grand safe. I've only seen them once, when I first started working here and a stone dealer was visiting to show off some rarities, and they've never left my memory. They are natural beauty in its entirety, a true marvel outdone only by the Hope Diamond. I envision their turquoise color to be what living on the ocean feels like. I pull the precious Paraiba tourmalines from the shelf. They are cushion cut, weighing at least twelve carats each, but are measured differently than diamonds, so I am not entirely sure how big they are, since these are Mr. Stein's private stash and the wording on the side of the storage case is written in Hebrew. I want to play with Sebastian the way he's been fucking with me, so I'll test his sticker shock.

Before greeting him again, I check my hair and teeth in the

mirror, making sure none of Patti's peppers are stuck, and feeling as satisfied with my look as I can be despite last night and how I feel, I walk back out. I find Skylar hanging over the counter, minuscule breasts popping from her shiny blouse, but Sebastian isn't paying her any mind. He is following my every move from behind the counter, not even listening to her curious questions for him.

"These are Paraiba tourmalines," I tell him. "They are my personal favorite. I've heard the color of these stones resembles the crystal-clear turquoise waters of the Caribbean."

He doesn't even look, never taking his eyes off mine, and says, "They are perfect. Please have them set in a simple setting that will show off these Caribbean rocks; platinum will work fine. Thank you."

Skylar whispers to me, "Doesn't he want to see them? Should I take a deposit, or what do I do?"

I speak directly to Sebastian and answer her questions. "No, it's fine. I believe Mr. Kane will pay for them when he picks them up. And if it's okay with you, I need to check with the owner, but they may be north of forty thousand or so." He doesn't blink at the price. "They should be ready in a week or so." And then, to both Skylar and Sebastian, "We generally get an order from our findings supplier every couple days, and then the jeweler will assemble them for you."

"That works perfectly. Thank you . . . your name again, please?"

Skylar tells him hers, but he never looks at her. "It's Shane. Nice to meet you, Mr. Kane. I believe you will be pleased with our jeweler's creativity."

I don't know where else the conversation could go, so I'm secretly glad to see other customers coming in so I can scoot away from him. Skylar looks anxious that the high-rolling experience is coming to an end and walks away.

"I want to take you out. Tonight." He is definitive in his intentions, and I'm both embarrassed and flattered by the demand.

"Sebastian, you're crazy. I can't tonight, I'm working at the bar."

"No. I will take care of whatever you make."

"That's crazy, you already tipped me so much. I want to give it back, it's too much."

"You earned it, and you deserve more."

I can feel my cheeks blushing, warm pink blood rushing to my face. His broad stature is standing tall over the counter, intimidating my every response.

"Please, let me take you out. Whatever time works? I have something planned for you."

I give in to his kindness like soft goop in his hands. The gesture appears sincere, but my antennae are up. I'm terrified someone might overhear and tell Jake, but then again, who would we know who comes in here? "Okay, fine. I need to go in, but I'll try to get out around ten. Is that too late? How do you want to meet up?"

He isn't the least bit surprised that I wavered and agreed to go with him. "I'll meet you in the Barnes & Noble parking lot and pick you up there."

I shake my head in disbelief but with a flirty vibe. My voice is soft and nervous. "You're crazy, Mr. Kane."

"Simone is with Marty this evening, so it will be just us. Is that agreeable for you?"

I haven't really pictured us alone, and I'm terrified that I will undoubtedly make a fool of myself again with improper manners and etiquette, but my stupid head nods yes. "Okay, I will see you at ten o'clock at the bookstore parking lot. Don't laugh when you see my car!"

He laughs aloud with his deep, throaty voice, and a glimmer of those slightly crooked canines shines through. "I promise I won't. Is it like a Flintstones car or something? Do you use your feet to pedal? Shall I send someone to get you?" He's amusing himself.

"Ha, ha. Her name's Hope. Don't make fun of her or we probably won't make it."

He gives me one more look but sees Skylar coming and, without a word, walks out of the store.

I watch through the store's glass windows as his Maserati drives away.

I realize I'll need more time to change clothes later so I don't reek like cigarette smoke when I see Sebastian. This means I need to escape the bar by 9:00 p.m., race home, and change again. I feel nervous tingles just planning the night in my head.

When I arrive it's slow, so I get busy by filling the fridge with cheap bottles of beer and checking the kegs. Eddie comes from the kitchen to ask if I'm hungry. "No, thank you. I ate at Stein's. Oh, before I forget, I have a ton of homework to catch up on with this paper and I was hoping I could leave at nine. Any chance you can cover me?" Eddie is such a doll, I know he'll say yes to just about any favor I ask.

"No problem, I'll take care of it."

"Thank you so much. I owe you! Is Dave in yet?"

"No, I haven't seen him."

"Wonderful. The later he is, the more sloshed he's bound to be."

We both say "stupid fucker" in sync and laugh as he heads to the kitchen and I go back to the counter. I'm putting away clean glasses when Ye Ol walks in, and I stop what I'm doing to serve him immediately. "So Ye, you're here, but where's our favorite Vet?"

He looks concerned as he glances around but answers in his usual crass manner. "I have no idea where that bastard is. He's not here? And he's definitely not my favorite, you can have that smug fucker."

I shrug my shoulders, tell him they are both my favorites, and hand him the greasy sheet of tonight's specials.

It's almost 7:00 p.m., and Dave hasn't shown up yet. I'm getting nervous for this evening's impending plans, but on the other hand, his not showing may keep me from going to hell. Either way, I can't meet the devil named Sebastian until Dave gives his drunken blessing for Eddie to cover. I keep busy cleaning and filling stock, but still nothing.

Finally, around 8:00 p.m. my skanky boss wanders in drunk with a brunette hanging off his arm. Her overweight body and wrinkled look isn't his usual type, but I don't care as long as he's here.

"Dave, I need to talk."

"Shaney, my sweet little ass, how are you tonight?"

The girl glares at me, but I could care less about his nasty banter. I need him to let me out, and she's not going to stop it. I explain how I need to leave early, that Eddie will cover, and how I've been waiting all night for him.

"You've been waiting all night for meeeeee? Aw, Shaney, who knew? This could be you on my arm."

"Seriously, Dave, I need to leave at nine, I have a ton of homework."

Karen, one of the regular women, yells from the bar, "Jesus, David, let her go. What are you, running a fucking work camp here?"

He agrees, but only if I make shots for him and his "girl," Tawnya.

"Sure, whatever you want," I tell him. Anything to appease his ridiculously unprofessional requests and get me out of this shithole.

Three Hispanic men walk in, very well-dressed; they certainly don't look like our usual crowd. Karen whistles at them with both hands, nearly losing her balance on the barstool that's barely holding her up. I welcome the men with beer, and Eddie makes two orders of potato skins for them. They keep to themselves in the pool room, speaking Spanish the entire time, except when I go to check on them.

The bar gets busier and busier as more regulars stroll in, but not the Vet, whom I'm starting to miss. I cash out Ye Ol as he overexplains that he has papers to grade, but I know it's because after hours of waiting, his friend hasn't shown. I run downstairs to make change from Dave's stash and see the clock reading 9:36 p.m. Oh shit, I'm supposed to be gone by now, but he never came up to relieve me. I knock on the door to the office that doubles as a sex haven for minors and he answers, "What?"

"Dave, you told me I could go, it's 9:36, I really have to leave and Eddie's swamped in the kitchen."

"Fuck, Shane. I'm busy, just finish up."

"Dammit, Dave, I really have to go." He's annoying me something fierce.

"Fine, then get Eddie to cover, I will be up soon."

I run up the stairs, realizing I may barely make it on time, never mind stopping at my house to change. I feel disgusting knowing exactly how I look and smell.

Eddie takes the wad of cash for change and wishes me a good night of studying. Everyone waves and shouts as I walk to my car, but I'm in such a hurry, I only wave back and skip saying goodbye. I check my face in the rearview mirror, fixing my makeup with my sleeve and pulling back my hair.

Little Dinghies and Big Thingies

I fly as fast as Hope will take me, only to round the corner and find Sebastian leaning on a car, some sort of SUV this time, like some kind of movie star. His attire is different, loose and more casual than I've seen before. I raise one eyebrow at the new automobile. "Hi."

He steadily walks to my door, opening it as I go on and on, apologizing for my work clothes and how I smell like cigarettes. He looks puzzled and says, "Shane, you don't need to work anymore tonight, it's only you and me now, no one else."

I look at him, ready to bolt back to the safety of Hope instead of entering the mysterious sport utility vehicle. "That's a weird comment."

He doesn't answer, and I seriously contemplate writing a note to leave on my seat in case I disappear. He holds out his hand, and I nervously climb up high onto the passenger seat. The interior is rugged but classy, with buttery-soft leather seats. I look all around and up to see multiple sunroofs and the stars shining through their dark glass tint. "I use this for work sometimes. Is it okay for you?"

"Are you kidding? Yes, of course, thank you." I am so nervous. I don't look right, feel right, or even smell right. I'm so extremely self-conscious, I want to jump out at the first stoplight and hitch-hike back.

"Thank you for your help today. I wouldn't have been able to choose without your expertise."

"Oh, you're welcome, I guess. I hope you like them. It's extremely unusual to find a perfectly matched pair. They've always been my dream stone, so I'm really happy they're going to someone who appreciates them, too. Plus, they're like the color of water, ya know your thing with boats."

He laughs out loud, a real jolly chuckle. "Yes, my thing with boats."

We drive for a bit, and after only a few minutes, speaking freely comes naturally to both of us. My nervousness is melting away under his caring tone. I tell him about my long friendship with Simone, whom I am a complete wreck over, but fail to mention our lesbian rendezvous or all the other shit that goes along with me. He tells me that he saw Martin earlier in the week and that Simone and him have plans coming up but didn't go into detail what they were. I wonder if she knows, or if it's a surprise like this?

We pull up to a very large and tall gate. A guard in full uniform takes one look at Sebastian and welcomes Mr. Kane in. We drive through the iron gates as they close behind us and continue to the very back of what I can now see is a marina. I can't make out the size or how many boats there are, just shapes and outlines. We park next to a very large one. I put my fingers on the door handle, and like magic a man appears out of nowhere and opens it. I look to Sebastian, but he's already out of the car and talking to someone in another language. What on earth are we doing here?

He walks over to me, grabbing my hand and holding it tight. I walk alongside him, in awe of this beautiful gentleman. I was tending bar at my dive only an hour before, and now I'm here amongst the Richies and their yachts. I feel bad about myself, knowing what I look and smell like, and imagine the marina's workers getting together and cracking jokes about the loser chick that Mr. Kane brought along. I feel sick inside, which is not an unfamiliar feeling these days. I need a pill to space me out.

I imagine seeing the inside of one of these humongous yachts, but I'm mistaken as we arrive at a cute little dinghy that's waiting for us. He smiles at me in the dark, but I can still see the white of his teeth.

"You and that eyebrow, you make me laugh, Shane."

Oh my gosh, I need to sew that thing down.

The man driving the tiny boat ignores the comment as he steers us away from the dock. It's too noisy to talk, and having never been on a boat, I am trying to soak in every possible second. I close my eyes, allowing the salt air to fill my lungs and lightly spray dew over my face. I open my eyes and Sebastian's looking at me, so I explain how tired I am and apologize profusely again for how stupid I look. I think I amuse him and that must be why he keeps inviting me out, for his own personal kicks. I'm starting to think my naivety is a big hit with the Richies! They love to laugh at ignorant poor people—honestly, what could be more fun?

The motor stops and Sebastian takes my hand, guiding me onto a wooden pier. I vaguely hear and see people up above drinking and eating. It occurs to me that we are at a restaurant, duh. I feel ridiculous thinking it would be something more than that, but it's still pretty neat to roll up in a boat, even if it's smaller than Hope.

Sebastian says something to our saltwater driver and we walk up the stairs to an open area. A very pretty girl with perfectly straight black hair, tan skin, and a short skirt approaches Sebastian with a wide smile. He is very polite, and when she looks me up and down in my jeans and striped tank with sneakers, he asks her to give us the menus but her lip curls in dismay. Almost immediately after taking them from her, we are approached by a jovial and overweight man. He hugs Sebastian snuggly, kissing him on the cheek, and he kisses me, too. With an accent he says, "You must be Shane? Anything you need, just think it to your mind and it's done. Done, okay?" He kisses and hugs Sebastian again, slapping his back and speaking a few words I don't understand. I smile, following Sebastian's lead. I can't imagine needing anything else, but the offer is certainly fun to ponder.

We sit down in a corner of the deck that overhangs the ocean below, making it feel like an open-air tree house without the trees. I look around nervously, slightly worried I might see someone I or Jake knows or works with.

Sebastian orders delicious drinks with fun flavors for us to sip. Thankful for the alcohol that's calming my nerves, I slurp the first one down, fast. With every fruity-tasting sip, my body loosens, and soon we're ordering fried pickles and Key lime pie, joking with the table next to ours. They are a fun group, playing some wacky form of charades, and we join in like a couple comfortable with any situation. Sebastian makes friends with everyone, and his charm is infectious to be around. I find myself leaning back in the chair, admiring this stranger who I am truly enamored with. After some time, we shake hands and hug the game players like we're old friends and leave through the back door.

Our adventure as a pretend couple finds us walking past restaurants and storefronts, with me cracking up as I relive the "Jerry Springer" charade, when a guy from the other table fell while jumping up and down like a spring trying to make everyone guess. Sebastian doesn't let me finish reminiscing but suddenly grabs my hands and pushes me, moving my hands up by my shoulders, against the store's exterior brick wall. I'm not hurt but am startled by his force and the mere girth of his body draping over mine. I look up at him and he down at me, slightly nervous about what might happen next.

We stand like this for a few moments as I cower under his wings like a protected egg. I'm nervous and confused as to why I'm here, and my discomfort under him is obvious.

"Kiss her already, kiss her, man!"

I hear shouts from drunken pedestrians across the street, and even though I can't see them, I laugh aloud. He leans in, and with the lightest touch barely grazes my lips with his. My legs quiver under his will, and I wrestle from underneath his arms, briskly walking ahead. He catches up with me within seconds, and it's obvious that my anxiety is real, so he doesn't push further.

We walk as my heart races, and he holds my hand, stepping into an alley. There's trash littered about, and we walk around a sleeping person who is cuddled up against a cement building. Sebastian reaches into his shorts and tucks something into the resting man's hood. I can only imagine it's cash, but it's hard to see and I don't want to ask. I think it's sweet and wonder how much he gave him? The reality is that Jake and I are about one month away from sleeping next to him and having Mr. Kane shove money into our hoods.

Just then, in the corner of my eye, I think I recognize someone and unleash my hand from his. I keep looking back, but the man moves briskly so I race to catch up. Sebastian follows me. "Shane! Shane, stop!" I reach the end of the alley, and we're smack-dab in the center of a white beach. I'm fairly certain it's the homeless guy from the bank, and I want to see him up close. I'm not sure what about him intrigues me, but with Sebastian's wealth, I'm kind of hoping he has a wad of cash to tuck in his clothing, too. I don't see the gigantic dog anywhere, but it did look like the same guy, but I've lost him. Then again, those colorful cocktails have me confused and a little dizzy. Trying to search out a giant pit bull nicknamed "Good" and his homeless owner in the middle of the night probably isn't the wisest idea.

My sneakers sink into the wavering landscape of the sand. When we stop, Sebastian kneels down on one knee and pulls off my shoes, one at a time, and then my socks, folding them in half and putting them to the side. As I look down and see he's already barefoot, he grabs my hand, and before I realize what's happening, we're running as fast as we can into the ocean. I'm smiling ear to ear the whole way to the water until the frigid waves hit my legs. I scream with excitement and he grabs and kisses me. We fall to the waves, and I laugh with our mouths still touching as we hit the wet sand. He pulls me up and I'm trying to hide the fact that I'm freezing, but he already knows and tucks me into his body. I let the size and warmth of his arms envelop me. He holds me as we head toward what appears to be an abandoned sailboat. It's lying far up on the beach, almost in the dunes, tipped over on its side.

Sebastian bends down, reaching underneath the boat's wooden shell, and pulls out a backpack. What the hell?

"There's that curious look again, Shane. Try to relax, because I have something planned for you tonight, but this isn't it. Hmmm, when could it be?"

He seems more amused with himself than I am. He throws the black sack over his shoulder, and we walk together along the coastline, with me shivering and laughing aloud, mostly at the mere fact that I'm buzzed, a little frightened, but so freaking happy. He stops under a skyscraper-sized lifeguard stand and shifts my body like a rag doll into the side of the painted tower and kisses me hard. His aggressive pushing is starting to turn me on instead of freak me out. "You are so fucking sexy," he says. "Do you even realize it? Seriously, Shane."

I don't know how to answer, or maybe it wasn't a question

at all, as no one has ever said that to me. He speaks with assertiveness, and I can picture him as a serious businessman making
multimillion-dollar deals like I order fast food. He takes my hand
and helps me up the makeshift stairs of the lifeguard stand, guiding
me from the steps below. We reach the top, which feels like two
or three stories up from below, and we peer out at the stars, white
sand, and black ocean. The chill from my wet clothes, plus my
fear of heights, makes me uneasy and nervous, and I'm shivering
again. He unzips the backpack, keeping one arm wrapped around
me, and pulls out a lavish, supremely soft blanket and drapes it
around me. The blanket is equal part his scent and the smell of
some kind of flowers or detergent, and the mixture is intoxicating.
He tucks me in like a child and reaches back into his secret pack
for a bottle of red wine and a corkscrew. I wait for a crystal glass
to appear from his clown sack, but to my surprise he hands me
the whole bottle after uncorking it. I take a swig and giggle with
sarcasm. "To taste?"

"Yes, to taste."

I hand it to him and say, "This doesn't feel proper."

"I don't want to be proper tonight, Shane." He is dead serious,
and it's kind of scary.

We swap stories above the ocean, draped in luxurious fabric
on a vacant lifeguard stand, drinking who-knows-how-expensive
red wine while waves crash below. I can't imagine a more romantic
moment in my life. I try to relax and savor everything that's happening, even if the few faithful sensors in my brain are screaming
"No!"

He opens up about his childhood, and I talk about mine, and
the more we drink, the more I tell. Even with the small amounts I
share, he seems more drawn to me with every word. I start to feel
myself getting emotional, and a tear clouds over my eye when I
speak about leaving my mother and Simone and how they really
were and are my true rocks in life. I tell him how I married the first

man that resembled a new start and never looked back, until this
week, and that I have no idea what I'm doing. He listens intently
and appears utterly sad for me. I don't need his rich-person pity,
but now that I've told him almost everything, he must realize I
don't deserve to be treated like this.

"Now you know all my secrets and the fucked-up childhood I
had and how horrible of a best friend I was. Why would you want
to still sit here with me? I am bad news, Sebastian. I need to go.
I don't deserve this, it's too much." I climb down the ladder, tears
streaming, and with blurry vision fall to the sand.

"Shane, wait, please stop."

I hobble away and shout back like a drunken fool. "Don't you
fucking get it? I'm not a princess. I don't deserve castles or boats or
fancy food. I'm not beautiful or wealthy or anything like Simone or
whatever kind of girl you're used to. I shouldn't be here. I see the
way women look at and fawn over you. Go be with them, please,
be with them. Not here with me!"

I try to run, but the sand is wavy and he's already caught up.
He grabs my shirt from behind to slow me and I fall to the sand.

"I'm fucking filthy, cold, and wet. Please, just leave me alone."
I cry into his embracing arms and he squeezes tighter.

"C'mon, Sugar, let me get you warm. Please, come with me.
Please, Shane. I am begging."

I wipe my face and runny nose in my shirt. I stand up with an
unsteady gait, and with his help walk back to the sidewalk. A man
arrives out of nowhere with yet another unfamiliar car and drives
us back to the gated marina. A different guard waves us in, but I
stay low, nearly lying completely on Sebastian's damp and sandy
lap, embarrassed to even exist.

"I'm so sorry, Sebastian. I don't deserve this, please let me go
home."

He strokes my wet backside, and before I can spend any more
time apologizing for being a cheating drunk, we're at a complete

stop. The driver opens the door for me and I tell him how sorry I am for all the sand on the seats and offer to help clean it up. He doesn't respond or even seem to acknowledge my presence, making me feel worse.

Sebastian holds my hand and escorts me onto the largest boat I've ever seen. It must be the biggest one here since it's down at the end, separate from the others. We walk inside the most beautiful and pristine yacht I could've ever dreamed of. I've never even been inside a camper, never mind a sailing house. It's modern and cozy, sexy, sleek, and warm all at once. I forgot my shoes at the beach in my drunken stupor and feel incredibly stupid walking around with sandy feet all over the shiny floors for as far as I can see.

"Sebastian, I'm a mess. I don't even know where my shoes are?"

He looks down at his own sandy body and back at me, laughing at our two grody bodies. "We both are. But this is where I sleep, so I want to get cleaned up and feel comfortable."

"You live here?"

Before he can answer, another beautiful woman, as if there weren't enough already, appears at the door and Sebastian speaks to her in another language I don't recognize.

She says, "Come with me" and ushers me with a tan slender finger.

Stupidly, I follow like a drowned puppy, looking back at Sebastian, who smiles and nods, allowing me to go ahead without him. From behind I watch her perfect apple ass lift up and down as she struts through the corridors. I'm mortified at my appearance, especially when I catch a glimpse in one of the many shiny beams and poles holding the intricate wood in place. Despite my hideousness, everyone we pass smiles and says hello directly at me as I spread millions of grains of sand through their pristine hallways. I nearly fall into the pretty lady's shelf rump as she stops in front of the most luxurious-looking bathroom. It's even fancier than Simone's master at the Ritz, if that's even possible. I imagine Lady Gaga's bathroom looking something like this, at least from pictures in the

cheap magazines I've splurged on. Perfect, I think, a gleaming marble floor for me to litter with messy grits of quartz that are flaking
off every crevice of my body. The pretty lady, who's just a tiny bit
less mute than Vivi, points to the shower that's oddly centered in
the middle of the room and then again to a hanging bathrobe. The
entire lavatory is glistening white, with fresh flowers and herbs
placed around the surrounding tables. She shuts the door, leaving
me alone, and I'm thrilled for the privacy.

I tiptoe over to the sink, where there's a basket of fluffy towels, pull one out, and throw it to the floor, allowing me to shuffle
freely around the room without further messing it up. There's a
huge circular glass window, but I can only see mini white lights in
the distance. I don't remember leaving the dock, but it's possible,
since everything seems dark and far away. I turn to the rest of the
room, and despite its enormity, I feel comfortable, because it feels
comfortable, almost like a woman lives here.

I undress, dropping my clothes and all the sand with them onto
the towel. I feel funny standing naked inside the shower that's in
the middle of the room and worry that the door isn't locked and
another stranger might walk in at any time. My mind fleets back to
Sebastian, wondering where he's disappeared to. My, what a place
this would be to play hide-and-go-seek. My brain is faltering from
the lingering buzz, and when I'm sober I know I will regret every
second. For the moment, I will enjoy the tranquility of the majestic water I am engulfed in and surrounded by. Inside the cocoon
of marble and steam, warm cotton balls of water rain down from
showerheads galore, and my skin absorbs every drop like a desert
frog. I stand still, afraid to open my eyes, not knowing if anyone
can see me through the exterior glass window or doors I entered
through. I have no idea if the whole ship came to watch or if I'm
imagining it all.

But not a thing in the world matters at this very moment,
because I feel warm and special. For starters, I'm inside an actual

yacht, more like a cruise ship, with the most interesting and curious man who is wealthy beyond imagination and wants to be with me. The friendly man's voice from the restaurant echoes through my head as the scented soaps and fading wine dizzy me. "Just think it and it will be done." I cannot imagine a single thought beyond this very moment of feeling rich, sexy, and extremely free, without a care in the world.

My dreaming ends when I drop a bottle of something onto the floor and the crash startles me. I quickly recover it and finish the shower, turning all the heads off with one handle. My hair drips all over the floor, so I slide back over to the sink and grab more towels to sop up the water. The soft shrugs of fabric hug my hair and the skin directly above my breasts as I look around for toiletries. I drop the towels and grab the robe aptly pointed out by the pretty lady with the great butt and wrap it around my still-damp skin.

The door knocks just as I am putting my hands inside the pockets. I feel a crumpling of paper, and suddenly my world crashes. What if I find another woman's receipt or a note and everything exciting about my mystery man comes to a miserable halt? I pull it from the pocket and clasp it in my hand, afraid to look, and ask the person at the door to please hold on a moment. I carefully open my fingers, and in handwritten calligraphy the words read, "Shane, welcome! Please step to your right for clothes for you to choose from. Mi casa es su casa. SLK."

I answer the door, shoving the note deep inside the pocket, but the beautiful mute looks at my hand as I am doing it. "Hi, I know I didn't say before, but I'm Shane. Nice to meet you. I'm really sorry about all the sand. I tried to keep it in—"

She interrupts me. "I know who you are," she says matter-of-factly. "Please choose from the clothing that has been prepared for you. There is also a basket of items for freshening up, and makeup if you choose. I will come for you when Sebastian requests me to do so. My name is Cecelia."

She walks away and I manage to mutter "thank you," even though she doesn't care. I cautiously enter the right side of the room that I hadn't previously noticed because of the shower walls blocking its view. There are even more walls and furniture with fresh flowers and, in the corner, a huge basket. I have no idea how a boat can be this big but also so cozy.

The Barrons' property was the biggest by far in our area, if not the entire state. The grounds were huge, making the mansion feel smaller, but we all knew how obscene a showplace it was. Simone and I would play all day behind the gates, racing sticks in the stream, swimming in the pools, jumping from one to the other, and never spot a soul unless they were sent to find us. We were forbidden to enter one entire wing. There were quarters for everything, where we ate, played, and even where I could sleep over. The formality confused me, and Simone never wanted to be in there, so we usually played outside, but always within those gated walls. I know now why she made so many excuses for us to play outside or go on an errand with the nanny. I wish she had just told me, because I would have put that bastard in jail sooner. I want to believe that I would have had the gusto back then, but in my heart I know that every rich person I meet intimidates the shit out of me. I'm like my mother in that regard, incredibly weak and powerless around the strong and powerful. A psychologist would say it's because I didn't have a father growing up or because my mother would tell me he was too famous to stick around. She would name off movie stars like lottery numbers and claim their sperm for half my genes. Whoever was the A-lister at the time was deemed "your new daddy." For a while it was Bruce Willis, and then Robert Redford, and when I got older she said it was definitely Van Morrison. It seemed that whoever was a popular actor or musician at the time just happened, by coincidence, to be my biological dad. It made for a bullied childhood, her telling people my father, whom no one had ever seen or met, was rich and famous. Only when they saw me with Simone did the parents actually question if my mother's lies were true.

I was just as surprised as anyone when Rob the Blob moved in, taking reign as my "new daddy," because I couldn't have imagined him famous for anything other than eating. He embarrasses me, and his relationship with my mother is exactly opposite of everything she has ever strived for me to believe. It's like she's finally given up on men, life, and beauty. I'm thankful that Mr. Barron never actually abused me, because I fear my mother would have been proud of landing such a rich man, and I'm not sure I would have had the strength to stop him. I think if I were to peer through my mother's looking glass, she would be proud as hell of where I am right now, despite all the moral consequences it holds. I can hear her voice swirling around my head, "Shaney, dreams do come true, marry for money the first time, so you can afford love the second."

This part of the room is almost all floor-to-ceiling windows overlooking the ocean, but I can only vaguely see the black waves in the lighted room. There's an assortment of clothing hanging in a line, dotted with all kinds of patterns and in different styles. The bench beneath an antique mirror holds a basket filled neatly with underwear and socks, perfectly folded and arranged by color. I walk back and forth, studying each outfit as if I'm the owner of a boutique store and can choose anything I want. I pull down a black dress, and the wooden hanger falls to the floor. I can see now that it's lacy in pattern but long to my knees and feels oddly appropriate. I slip it over my thighs and through my arms to find it's a near-perfect fit. I don't see any shoes, and hearing vacuuming in the distance, I don't want to add to the sand by walking it back through the hallways. I slip on a pair of white lacy undies and sift through the basket, finding a pair of soft cotton slippers.

There's another lovely basket filled to the brim with Dior makeup, organic lotions, and other hygiene products. I pick and

choose each item with the same caution as the outfit, finally settling on brands that look familiar from my experience over the years
in Simone's bathrooms. I am overwhelmed by the opulence around
me, and even brushing my teeth makes me feel improper, like the
toothbrush should be made of silver or something. Finally, fully
dressed and unaware of the next move, I mosey around the room,
checking myself in the mirror and staring out at the night sky.

Someone knocks on the door once and I run to get it, but
Sebastian is already in the room. He looks amazingly casual and
without effort, handsome as fuck. His hair is wet, feet bare, and
he's wearing loose-fitting jeans with an off-white button-down
shirt. He smiles at me and says, "Wow, you look beautiful, I love
those slippers on you!"

I look down at my elegant ensemble and then to the grandma
slippers that are oh so comfy. "Um, thank you, I think they really
make the outfit. Actually, this is incredible and I feel like I'm in a
fairy tale, but I have to be honest." He looks at me inquisitively and
I say, "I'm just really worried about all the sand, I feel terrible—"

He interrupts me. "Shane, don't worry about anything. Wear
them if you'd like or don't, you are free to do anything you want,
and the sand is already cleaned up, so stop worrying about anything but us."

The truth is, the slippers are really nice and I would love to
wear them forever. All I want to do is ask a hundred questions
about where we are, the quiet staff and the friendly ones, the array
of clothing, and what in the world we are doing next.

He grabs my hand, leaving the mess I've made behind, and
we pass several other rooms but are moving too fast to see inside.
We go on like this for at least ten minutes, weaving about the
ship until we reach a table on an outside deck, and he pulls out a
chair for me to sit. The moon is bright and shining, and candles
are illuminating crevices in a purposeful way, leaving some areas
completely visible and others in darkness. I am without words,

taking it all in and absorbing the unreal scene, trying hard not to freak out and jump ship.

"Why are you doing this?" escapes from my lips like a whisper.

Just then, a man appears like a faint shadow, carrying some sort of dish filled with tropical fruits, which he delicately spoons over sorbet in front of us. I dive right in with a heaping mouthful. My mother would have slapped my hand. The flavor is so delectable and sweet, it's as if the fruit was paid to grow. "This is the most wonderful-tasting vanilla and fresh fruit I've ever experienced."

Sebastian gracefully sips water that's garnished with lemon and rosemary as he laughingly admires me licking my spoon to get every last piece of mango. "I'm sorry, but this is ridiculous."

"An experience, huh? I will pass on your review. I am glad you like it."

I take a gulp of the water, and a moment later a shadowy girl offers us a bottle of white wine, but I refuse. "Would you like a pain reliever instead?"

"Um, like Tylenol? Yes, please, but not ibuprofen. I'm allergic."

She rushes off, and Sebastian calls out that he'll take some as well. "Thank you."

"I didn't know you had any allergies, Shane."

"Um, yes. I have a few, but Advil is the most serious. A friend gave it to me in school, and next thing I knew, I must have passed out, and I woke up in the emergency room. That was really nice of her to ask us, especially after the drinks and wine. I'm sure I'll feel better with a little medicine. Also, I am really sorry about—"

"Shane, no more apologizing. You have done nothing wrong. In fact, it has all been right. I am enjoying every second and would like to spend more time with you. Would that be okay?"

I'm baffled and a little freaked out. "Why?"

He looks serious. "Because I like being with you, and I will make it worth your while."

"I'm married, Sebastian."

"Yes, about that. It's a hiccup, I will admit. But I promise to reward you, and whenever you want it to stop, please tell me, and it will cease. In the meantime, let's go for a walk."

His forceful ways win again, and I don't agitate the already awkward conversation. The sweet girl delivers our medicine and we both take it. I yell back "thank you," but Sebastian has moved on, grabbing my hand for the stroll.

"This boat is absurd. Is it a cruise ship or actually a floating island? You can tell me."

He chuckles at my poor attempt at a joke. "I told you, I love the dinghies."

We walk around the yacht, passing three more strangers, and he speaks to a couple of them in other languages. I'm unsure what their jobs are, but I can imagine this being a fairly good gig. As we move about the ship, he tells me about sailing and his true love, a sailboat that he's been restoring for almost ten years that he bought with his father. He learned to sail much like Simone did, but in other areas of the world, and it was something he shared with his father. Thus far, it's the only mention of his dad, so I don't push further, as it seems to be a hard topic for him, though I'm not sure why? I tell him that I've never met mine and joke about how my mother would pretend famous people were my father but that I'm pretty sure he's just some loser she won't admit to.

"When I was little I would get laughed at by all the other kids when I told them my dad was Tom Cruise or Stephen Tyler."

He doesn't find as much amusement in my story and says, "Well, I knew mine and I am sorry to say you aren't missing anything. Moms are where it's at."

I giggle at his silly response, because going any further with the subject is obviously a bad idea.

We reach a closed door, and he uses it as leverage to pull me into him and push our bodies hard against it. The more we kiss, the harder he pushes. I can feel the enormity of his entire self pressed up against me. I feel so bad for what I am doing but also so good inside. As we are kissing he has somehow opened the door and is moving us backward onto the bed. I open my eyes as we hit cushion, seeing it's the size of at least two king mattresses put together. "This is the master."

He lowers me onto the thick ruffles of crisp, soft comforters, and I am immersed in the clean, natural smell of his sexy musk. He lies lightly on top of me and begins to move my dress up onto my hips, slipping and sliding the fabric one inch at a time. He takes his time raising and cinching it until he reaches my belly button. I arch my back into his hands as he works my frame, kissing back and forth between my neck and my tongue the entire time. He breathes heavily into my ear. "I want to pleasure you."

I, myself, am working hard to control my breathing, remembering what he's taught me. My feelings of regret over Jake are torn away with my panties, which he roughly rips from my ankle. His subtle fingers move delicately around my slippery wet clitoris and glide inside me with ease. He moves his mouth to my inner thighs, biting down slightly on the skin, and I contort in pain. He moves his mouth back up, teasing me the entire way with his fingers, and kisses my skin delicately. I rip the pillows from beneath my head and throw them across the room. I don't want anything separating us from each other. He works his mouth to my clit and gently swirls his tongue around and sucks it in, still pulling his fingers in and out. I can feel myself ready to freak and cannot hold it anymore.

Sensing my frustration, he kisses my mouth and I taste the sweetness of my own cum. "You are so fucking hot, do you know that, Shane?" He enters inside me and I wince from the pain, from a penis that's much larger than I'm used to. "Oh my goodness, are you okay?"

He is genuinely scared that he's hurt me, not like the other times when he was intentionally rough. He seems nervous, so I feed off his concern. "Uh, it's okay, please go slow, okay?"

He moves in and out of me with careful and deliberate strides, kissing me and pressing his body softly against mine. I can feel the wetness dripping down my leg, and the pain is completely gone, replaced by intense pleasure. I'm panting heavily as he pushes harder and harder inside, and the rhythm is making me insane. I can feel myself ready to scream as I breathe faster and faster. This is like nothing I have ever felt before.

Suddenly, he covers my mouth forcefully with his hand and my breaths form moisture beads in his palm. I picture the end, a night of bliss only to be fucked to death. I panic that he's going to suffocate me, and my body clenches. My legs wrap around his hips as tight as they will hold, but it's no match for his strength.

"Shhh, it's okay. Just hold your breath. Get ready and hold your breath like you did with Sebastian." He is talking slowly and with conviction, breathing and whispering into my mouth. "Trust me, Shane. Let go and trust me."

He slows the rhythm inside me and I feel myself powerlessly relaxing. I concede yet again to his power and let go. The fear is subsiding and I fall into his groove, my body thanking him with infinite lubrication. He thrusts harder and harder, still kissing my lips, and I hold my breath as I am told. My reward for coming will be life's oxygen. My heart is beating out of control, and the harder he pounds, the more I let go. I take one little breath and hold it again as he penetrates deeply, lifting my legs taut in the air, and I feel dizzy and euphoric, like death is impending, and *bam*, it happens. "Ahhhhhhhh!"

I let go like a balloon with a hole. I feel 100 percent wiped out and can't hear anything. There's a ringing in my ears and a starry sensation of confusion and ecstasy. I let out little breaths and gasp for a minute, consuming every last bit of available air in the room. He stays inside me for a while as I feel my vagina clamping around his still hard penis. The song "Maneater" runs through my head and I can't help but giggle at the silliness of our predicament. He pulls out, and for the first time, I feel it. It's real, I did it, I cheated on Jake and found pure, sick pleasure in the act. I wasn't forced or told to, I did it for myself, for the enjoyment I find in this man and his ridiculous power over me. He is my drug and I am undoubtedly addicted.

I lie on the bed, unable to move. My legs are weak and quivering, so I curl up in the fetal position, covering them with the sheet. Sebastian walks completely naked to his private bath, closing the door behind him. I lie here wondering whether I should put my clothes on or spend the night? I imagine waking up to him and what it must be like to be smothered by his overwhelming body spooning me.

From Fairy Tale to Just a Fuck

I'm awakened by a kiss on my lips and realize I must have dozed off from exhaustion or brain damage. Sunshine beams through the windows, and I keep my eyes closed and smile as his mouth touches mine. I curl back into the covers, expecting him to join me, but am surprised with a knock at the bedroom door. I open my eyes when I don't hear or feel Sebastian. He's not in the room.

"Sebastian?" I call for him, but he doesn't answer. I wrap the sheet around my body and embarrassingly answer the door. There's no privacy in this place.

"Hello, Shane."

Lovely. It's happy face from last night. I look to the room for my missing man, but he's nowhere to be seen. "Um, hi."

"I came to tell you that Sebastian had business to attend to, but

Marco is waiting for you, and when you are ready he will bring you wherever you would like to go. We also have breakfast arranged for you." She hands me an envelope, and I nervously take it from her beautifully manicured hands. I feel like I was just dumped and am trying not to let my nerves show.

"May I have some time to get ready?"

"Yes, of course, whatever you wish. I will be here when you are ready."

I thank her again, closing the door, and sit on the edge of the bed. The entire room looks different in the daytime. It's absolutely beautiful, even more astonishing than I remember. There's an illuminated fish tank covering an entire wall, and I stare at the swimming fish, wondering how I could have missed a twenty-foot or longer tank?

I move the comforter out of my way, uncovering a stain hilariously resembling a dolphin, but quickly move it back. The decoratively engraved envelope is still in my hand, and directing my confusion to the fish, I ask them, "What do you think is inside here, guys?"

The back is embossed with a blue and gold seal, and examining it closely reveals an outline of a fancy sailboat. I open it with care to find a typed note: "Dear Ms. Lacy, Please see the information below regarding your new account at the Royal Coast Bank. Account Number: 622200451. Please visit the branch on Main Street to sign additional papers solidifying our partnership. Sincerely, Sebastian Lincoln Kane." Below the typed words, there's a handwritten note: "Sugar Shane, I would like to extend a permanent invitation to continue our arrangement. I will take care of anything you desire. Adoringly yours, S."

I refold the fancy paper into its creases and stuff it back inside the envelope. What the fuck is this? Our arrangement? I don't understand. I feel like the cheap white trash that I am. What do I do? I cannot cross my legs tight enough to take back what happened last night. I want to scrub myself inside and out with bleach and wire brushes. I glance around the room, looking for my clothes, then see that they're neatly hanging in the bathroom, freshly washed. I slip for no good reason on the marble floor, nearly falling as tears blur my eyesight. I shove my feet into my sneakers, stuff the note into my purse, and run out of the room past the delivery girl. I fly down the hallway, bumping into a man. I apologize, but he stops me with a hand on my shoulder and asks where I'm going.

"Breakfast is this way, Miss Shane."

I pull from his grip. "I don't want breakfast! I want to know how to get out of here, please, please. Where do I go?"

He can see my watering eyes and the pain on my face. "Okay, okay, this way please, Miss Shane. May I get you some water? Or shall I get Sebastian on the line?"

I take several deep breaths and follow him down another corridor. Nothing looks familiar, and I wonder how many fucking levels this place has. We finally reach fresh air, and I wipe my soaked eyes on the edge of my shirt. There is a man standing near an SUV whom I believe to be Marco. "Can you take me to my car, please?"

"Yes, of course, Miss Shane." He opens the car door, and I slump down into the seat, placing my face in my hands and squeezing my legs together.

"Do you have any water and tissues?"

"Yes, of course, Miss Shane." He passes them both back to me. I have overslept and not taken a pill since last night and am feeling the effects of withdrawal. I pull the bottle from my purse and chew a white pill into powder in my mouth, almost gagging on the bitter taste.

"I don't mean to interfere, but Mr. Kane told me to take care of you, and I am unsure that I'm succeeding. Is there anything I can do for you?"

"Yes, tell him to please leave me alone. No, actually don't tell him anything. Nothing, please, just leave it alone and don't say anything. I don't know, I just need to think. . . ."

My cell phone starts ringing. "I'm sorry, can you just not say anything?" My eyes are still blurry and I'm so shaken up, I pick up the phone and answer without thinking. "Hello?"

"Shane, it's Rob, where are you?"

"Seriously, Rob, what now? Whatever it is, I can't help."

"No, Shane, don't hang up. Aggie's in the hospital."

"What! Where? What do you mean? For what?"

He sounds out of breath as he ekes out the words. "She just collapsed. I called 911 and they took her by ambulance. She's at the hospital."

I stop listening and hang up the phone. In my distressed state the worst comes to mind. "Excuse me, Marco, can you please take me to the hospital? My mother was apparently just admitted."

"Yes, of course, Miss Shane. Whatever you wish."

We drive for over an hour, finally reaching the front entrance of the hospital, and I jump out, waving "thank you" to Sebastian's manservant as I run to the information desk. I'm immediately escorted to the adjoining emergency room waiting area, where I see Rob and Vivi getting candy from a vending machine. Vivi doesn't even flinch when she sees me, not a smile or hint of recognition. I ignore the weirdness and ask Rob for details. Just then, a doctor walks up and asks if I'm her daughter.

"Yes, I am. Is she okay?"

"Well, that depends. Your mother hasn't eaten in quite some time, months I presume. That isn't her problem, though; it's the dehydration causing her body's organs to shut down. We are working on stabilizing her with fluids and electrolytes. We're moving her to the ICU and will hold her for a couple days until psych can do an eval on her. Does your mother have a history of mental illness or an eating disorder?"

Rob tries to interfere with his wheezing words, but I put my hand up to stop him.

"Yes, she has always fluctuated between diets, but this time it seems it's a fear of food, so she isn't eating at all. She worries too much about overfeeding everyone else"—I glare at Rob—"but I thought she was at least drinking water?"

The doctor looks puzzled. "It doesn't take much to become dehydrated. We believe she may have cibophobia, but right now, treating her dehydration to prevent further damage, especially to her heart, and running blood tests are our priority. She needed to be sedated just to allow us to give her fluids. She told us she was allergic to everything, even water. Honestly, I've never seen anything like it."

Yeah, I think, you don't know my mother. There's nothing like her. "Okay, I understand. Thank you for doing that. She likes Poland Spring water." I look at Rob, but he stands there emotionless, eating his Almond Joy and watching the doctor's lips move. "May I see my mother?"

"Right now, like I said, she is heavily sedated, and she needs to rest. We are keeping her that way until we can get the tests done and some more fluids in her. Then, like I mentioned, she needs to see psych, but if she refuses, there isn't a lot we can do. You can help us by encouraging her to stay."

"Okay, thank you. Just let me know what I can do to help."

"Well, if I were you, I would count on her being here for at least a couple of days. I have already put in orders to move her, but first she'll be in the ICU for a bit."

"Thank you so much."

He hands me his card and walks away. I look to Rob and Vivi, but they both stare blankly back at me. "Okay, so it sounds like all we can do is wait. What the hell, is she really not eating?"

Rob gives me a stupid look, and there's a crumb of chocolate stuck to his lip that I want to slap from his fat face. "Honestly, Shane, she makes my meals and is always running around, so I haven't really noticed. But now that you mention it, I can't really think of the last time I saw her eating anything. Huh. She's always moving around though, so she gets great exercise."

"Seriously? You couldn't be bothered to keep an eye on my only fucking parent? Is all you care about your own snack time?"

He doesn't say anything, so I grab Vivi's hand, which sits limp in mine, and ask, "Vivi, want to go get some food?"

She takes her little hand out of mine and points her index finger at me, smiles, and says, "Bzzzzzz."

I reciprocate with my finger and say, "I'll take that as a yes. Come on, silly girl. Rob, I'm taking Vivi, call me if anything comes up. Oh, I need your car, mine isn't here."

He hands me the keys, and just as we approach the automatic doors, the cell rings. "Hello?"

"Shaney, it's me, Simone. What's up, where are you?"

"I'm at the hospital, my mother collapsed, she's in the ER. Apparently, she wasn't eating or drinking. She's on her way to the ICU, but they want psych to evaluate her. That will be a shit show! It's a freaking mess. I have Vivi with me, I'm taking her to get some breakfast."

"Oh my gosh, are you okay? Is she okay? I'll be there as soon as I can, but I have a big meeting with all the attorneys and board members for my father's estate. It's a fucking headache, I can't even tell you. Please, call me, I will step away if need be. I can send over one of Vienne's nannies, too. Hey, I heard you saw Sebastian?"

"Yeah, about that, I can't see him anymore, and we don't need a nanny right now, I've got her." I raise my voice, which gets Vivi's attention, so I keep walking to the handicap space where the car is parked crookedly. I open the door for Vivi and she climbs in while I stand outside finishing our hurried conversation.

Simone sounds shocked. "What, why?"

I whisper into the phone, "I was at his house last night, and this morning, he gave me fucking instructions for a bank account. I feel like a goddamn prostitute. I'm married, this is nuts."

"Wait, which house?"

"I don't know, a big-ass boat. A yacht. Looked like a freaking cruise ship. Why?"

"Holy shit! Shane, that's a big deal, he must really like you."

"I don't care, NO more Sebastian!" I see the hospital valet staring at me and I realize that I'm yelling.

"Shaney, can't you use the money? Just take it. You earned it, in a way. Oh shit, I hope that didn't come out wrong. I need all the details, but I have to go."

"How are you not fucking shocked? This is insane! I'm married. Whatever, I need to get some breakfast for Vivi, she's in the car and it sounds like we both need to go."

"Okay, I'll call you as soon as I'm done and can come pick her up or send someone."

"It's fine, I've got her, but I need to call into work. Just call me when you're done with your meeting."

"Okay, bye."

"Yep, bye." I've been utterly annoyed by every single conversation since I woke up this morning. I open the driver's-side door and put on a happy face for the sad one sitting in the back seat. "I just need to call my work, okay? I would much rather go out to eat with you than work at the dumb jewelry store."

She nods her head yes, and I smile to encourage the extra communication. If this keeps up, we might be in full sentences by the time she's fifteen or sixteen. I look at the clock and dial Patti at home.

"Hi there, what's up?"

"I am so sorry, Patti, but my mother is in the hospital and I need to call out sick or on family leave or whatever you call it. I'm so sorry, but she's in the ER and I have to be here to help out."

"Seriously, your mom? Are you alright? I mean, is she okay? Whatever, you know what I mean. I've just never heard you mention her, so . . . anyhow, not important. Are you okay?"

"Yes, thank you. I think she will be fine, I hope, but just in case can you cover for me for a couple days? I promise I will make it up to you. Just tell them there is nothing I can do, it's an emergency."

"Okay, sweetheart, no problem, I will take care of it. Don't worry about a thing."

I say "thank you" and go to hang up but stop when I hear Patti still talking. "Sorry, what?"

"Oh nothing, I heard you landed a huge sale with some hot guy? The owner even called to congratulate you, said he's some big shot. Give me the scoop!"

Oh shit, I had forgotten all about Sebastian's cuff links. "Yeah, the guy's an ass and I don't want to deal with him. Can you take it over? I think the order is coming in today or tomorrow. I can't handle any more right now. I have to go, sorry."

I say bye and hang up before she can ask more questions. The thought of anything else to do with him sickens and scares me. My belly fills with anxiety every time he enters my mind, and I squeeze my legs so hard my knees hurt.

Friend, Foe, or Freak

I drive downtown to a little dive down a side street called the Cracked Egg. I look for parking all over, finally scoring a spot a few blocks away. I know the drill and walk around to open the door for Vivi, who is waiting patiently for me to do so. "C'mon, sugarplum, let's get you some pancakes or whatever you want." I think killing her with kindness might engage a reaction, but nothing. We walk along the street and I keep talking, mostly to calm my own nerves, but it's like conversing with myself. All of a sudden, as I'm yammering on, she unclenches my hand and takes off down an alleyway. Fuck, not again.

"Vivi! Vivi, STOP!" I run after her, but she keeps going, through the dirty alley and then under a narrow underpass of a footbridge. I keep calling but I don't see her. "Vivi! Vivi, please answer me, where are you?" My heart is racing. Apparently, I need to keep this unpredictable kid on a leash. I hear water in the distance as I keep running and imagine the worst. I run through the alley, which reminds of the one I went through with Sebastian, and realize I'm on the pier where the old boardwalk used to be. The city is under all sorts of renovations as part of a revitalization project, and everything aboveground is under construction, leaving its history to rot beneath. I walk carefully over the missing boards, staring through the cracks, fearful she's fallen through one of the oodles of death traps. I hop off the pier so I can check underneath. I'm going to die trying to find this little girl, but I continue to shout her name in hopes she will respond.

Up ahead I see a makeshift structure that looks like some sort of shitty camper or tiny house tucked deep under the boardwalk. I wonder if it washed up from the hurricane a few years back? Oh fuck, what if she's in there and can't hear me? We are exposed and the waves crash against the beach and I duck farther and farther under the boardwalk, finally reaching the hidden camper, which barely escapes the water's rising tide by fifteen or twenty feet. I hear a tiny voice inside. My heart pulses and I steady my breath, like I'm trying to catch a wild animal. "Vivi?" No one answers, so I stay completely quiet, and the whispers continue. I look around for a weapon but I have nothing but my own fists. I bend down to bare knees, dragging them through the sand, terrified at what I might find. There's a flap of leather hanging over the camper's entrance, and I realize that this really is an intentional home, not a washed-up piece of scrap crap. My body sweats and my hand is shaking as I reach for the flap to reveal what's behind it.

Vivi is sitting on a heap of pillows with the giant dog she's named Good. "Oh my gosh, you're alive! YOU CAN'T DO THAT! You can't run off, do you understand? Not for Good, not for anything or anyone."

She nods her head yes and repeats his name. "Good."

Her bony little arms are wrapped around his thick, filthy, scarred neck, and she whispers actual words into his ear. I lean in closer to try and hear, but she stops talking. He turns his head and licks her face. She giggles like the little kid she is, and I smile in admiration. My heart slows and I realize that she's no longer in danger, but I still need to get her out of here. I try to usher them both out of the one scary house below the boardwalk by calling the dog with high-pitched, sweet calls. Nothing works, and not knowing his real name, Vivi just looks at me like an idiot and squeezes the dog's neck tighter. I climb from halfway inside to all the way in, reaching for Vivi, but stop in my tracks. I cannot believe my eyes. What the hell? Above the cushions she and Good are seated on— all around, beneath, and to both sides of them—are little brown paper bags. There must be ten thousand brown bags lining every corner, side, floor, and flap of the home. The entire inside of the camper is lined and littered with brown lunch bags. "What the hell?"

Now I'm scared, because this place is creepy and we need to get out of here. I grab Vivi's shirt and pull on her. "C'mon, Vivi, we really need to go, this is someone else's house and we just really need to go, so c'mon, NOW Vivi, I'm not playing around." I try to pull her out the flap of a door, afraid to be here any longer, but she sits firm with the dog as her anchor, not letting go. Suddenly, I hear a man's voice and Good's tail wags hard, hitting the floor with thumping beats.

"What are you doing? Get out of there!" he yells with a deep and angry voice. "Mind your business, get your own goddamn house. My dog will attack you." He moves nearer, but I'm still holding Vivi's shirt and she's holding strong, not letting go. As he comes into focus, I recognize the guy from the bank, Good's owner, the sandwich eater. As he gets closer, I can see the anger in his eyes and I'm incredibly nervous. His strut isn't nearly as sophisticated up close and we need to get out of here.

"Vivi, NOW!" I stand up, allowing only an inch between my head and the ceiling, and grab Vivi beneath her armpits, but Good growls at me. The man climbs inside the hut on his knees and stands up, crowding over us and making the paper shack feel incredibly tiny. "I am so sorry, truly I am, she's my friend's daughter and she loves your dog. I am trying to get her out, I swear. I didn't mean to come in. I am so sorry."

He looks at me, shakes his head, and lures the dog out with some food. Vivi follows directly behind. The brown bag tucked into his pants pocket and the sandwich he just handed the dog confirm that he just came from the bank. Surprisingly, he smiles at Vivi, so she points her little finger out to him, and like he knows exactly what to do, he extends his, too. She says, "Bzzzzzz," and he laughs a deep, jovial chuckle, displaying naturally straight, beautifully white teeth. Not what I expected from an old homeless man. He buzzes her back again, and she pets and kisses the top of Good's head, whispering into his ear one last time. He licks her straight across the mouth and I cringe.

The man bends down to pet the dog as well and thanks Vivi for taking such good care of him while he wasn't home. Vivi fingers the man toward her and he gets closer and closer. She rises up to meet his ear and whispers something to him. I am in utter shock. What is it about these two? He laughs and says, "I'll remember that."

I ask him what she said, but he ignores me. "No, seriously, what did she say? She never talks to me, ever. Please tell me, this is very unusual." He declines. I admire his patience with her, and thank him again—and also secretly for not murdering us. "May I buy you some breakfast or something?"

"No, I'm all set. Just leave. That's what I want. Kids don't belong here."

"Okay, I understand. We just thought you might want something to eat?"

"Why don't you not worry about me and get that sweet little girl some food of her own."

His demeanor changes and, taking the hint, we walk away. Vivi breaks free from my hand and runs back one more time to wrap her arms around the dog. She kisses him on the cheek and he licks her again. All I can think about is her drop-dead gorgeous mom literally falling over dead at the disgustingness of the dog and the scene with the homeless man. If she found out about this, she would completely flip, but luckily, unless she's this guy or a giant dog, I don't need to worry.

We walk for a while, finally reaching the intended restaurant, but there are groups of people waiting outside. Since when is this crappy joint so chic? I push past the waiting parties and flag down a server.

"Sorry, but there's a good thirty- to forty-minute wait. Just put your name down on the paper and we'll call you when a table's ready."

The thought of searching for another parking space and losing Vivi all over again has me scribbling my name. "Okay, thank you, we're just going to take a quick walk, we'll be back soon."

She nods, and Vivi and I walk back past the groups of people again. We stroll farther down the street and along the shops, peering into windows. I continue to narrate the entire time, like there's a ghost at my side. I point out frilly dresses and princess backpacks and even a toy store, offering to take her inside, but her face remains emotionless. Giving up, I say, "We don't want to go too far, so let's see how much longer to get some of their famous pancakes."

When we arrive back at the eatery, the line is nearly gone, and they tell us we only need to wait another minute or so. Almost immediately, we are seated.

"I would love a coffee, please, and do you still make those chocolate-chip coconut pancakes?"

"Um, I think so? I just started and I don't remember seeing that, but I can ask."

"Okay, thanks. I used to come here and that was their big thing. I really want her to try it."

The server looks down at Vivi and says, "What would make you happy, sweetheart? Is there something special you'd like to drink?"

Vivi turns her head from the window, and with the biggest, greenest eyes looks up to the lady and says, "Good."

"Vivi, sweetheart, she means to eat or drink. It's okay, I will order it for you. How about some chocolate milk?"

She winces and doesn't answer. The lady clearly doesn't under-stand and rolls her eyes. "Okay, well then, I will get some of those famous pancakes you speak of, coffee, and some chocolate milk." She walks away, probably to call a crazy hospital from the break room. Joke's on her, because my mother's already there.

"Vivi, sweetie, please talk to me. I know you want to see Good, but he's with his owner. Maybe we can find other doggies to visit. Just tell me what you want to do and we'll do it." I sound more and more like Sebastian, so I rephrase. "Whatever you want to do or say, just point or write it down and I will do my best to understand."

She doesn't budge, continuing to watch the people walking around outside through the glass as I talk. The cell rings, and grate-ful to hear it, I say, "Hold on, sweetheart, I need to see if it's about my mother, or Aggie, or whatever you call her. Hold on, okay?"

The number doesn't show up, so I answer blindly. "Hi, tell me something new?"

"Huh?" It's Jake. "Shaney, you alright?"

"Hi, yes, well, no, not really. I'm back home again. Well, cur-rently out with the daughter of Simone, one of my old friends, because my mother is in the hospital and no one could watch her, I mean a nanny could, but never mind, long story."

"What? Why?"

"I guess she hasn't been eating or is stressed or something, I'm not really sure, all I know is they had to forcefully sedate her, and now they're moving her to the ICU and then psych will evaluate her. Honestly, I am not sure where this could go, especially when they learn she doesn't have insurance. But anyhow, how are you? What's going on?"

He pauses before answering. "I can't believe you're back home again. You hate it there. And who's this kid and why does she need a nanny?"

"Yeah, I know, it's just been nuts since you left. I'll fill you in when you get back, but don't worry, I'm still working and paying the bills and everything is sort of fine. That big bill from when you got hurt at work came in, and I have no idea how we are going to deal with it. Remember when your insurance hadn't kicked in yet with the new job? Plus car insurance is due next month and they already sent a letter about canceling it unless we pay it in full this time. Oh, and that damn credit card, the one you bought the stupid TV on, they sent a collection letter. I'm sorry, I shouldn't be telling you all this while you're away. Just have fun and get home safe."

He interrupts the pity party and says in a soft voice, "One more week, sweets, and I will be there to help. Just do what you're doing and we'll figure it out like we always do."

Jesus, the fucking guilt and stress are getting to me. I need to get off the phone before I tell him everything. "Okay, see you soon, be safe and call when you can. Sorry, I'm at a restaurant and they are bringing stuff now."

"Seriously, Shane? You're eating out after everything you just told me?"

"Jake, what am I supposed to do? I have to eat. I'll make it up in tips, don't worry."

"Fine, I will see you in a week. Work on your paper and pick up some hours when you can. We need the money."

"Yep, I know. Okay. Love you."

We hang up, and putting down the cell is like dropping a thousand-pound dumbbell on the table. I take a few deep breaths, and our food arrives just in time.

To my amusement, Vivi eats every last bit of her pancakes and even sips the chocolate milk. The pancakes are as good as I remember, and I tell her how her mom and I used to sneak out and come here when we were really young. "Your mom had a really nice nanny. Her name was Esmerelda, and she would bring us here whenever I slept over. It was my favorite."

She doesn't seem amused, even about stories with Simone in them. When the check comes, I reach in my purse to give her the cash and see the envelope from this morning. The shiny blue and gold seal flickers like a star from the darkness inside my purse. I feel sick to my stomach and crumple it back up, flipping it over and burying it under other debris. I pay the bill but only have enough for a small tip and apologize to the girl, who just rolls her eyes, knowing by looking at me that I am just another broke customer. I wish she knew whose daughter this is and that Vivi alone could buy the whole city and eat chocolate-chip coconut pancakes and gold-coated bacon every day if she wanted to.

We walk out and I hold Vivi's hand tight, just in case Good is lurking about and she decides to dart across traffic in hopes of seeing her furry friend. We walk back to the car a different way than we came, and I talk the whole way without so much as a sneeze from her. We approach the corner with the bank where I lost Vivi. I stand there, staring at its front doors and then back into the depth of my messy pocketbook. "Vivi, what should I do, pull out the envelope and look at it or throw it away?" She points to the trash can. I start laughing. "You are right, I should do that, but I think I need to know what this is about. Oh, and they have lollipops in there, remember from last time?"

She follows me in and I recognize the man who is always nicely dressed. He smiles when he sees us. His facial cue is a comforting omen that I am doing the right thing. I invite myself over to his desk, where Vivi sits down in the empty chair.

"May I help you?" His question is directed at the little girl, and to spare us from more eye rolling, I quickly answer. "Yes, please, sir. It's kind of private though."

"Okay, come with me and I will take you to my personal office."

Once we're seated in his office, a lady in a pencil skirt and tucked-in blouse with high heels approaches the man and whispers something in his ear. He waves her off and expresses that he's fine.

"So, how may I help you, Miss . . . ?"

"Oh, sorry, Shane Dell. Or my maiden name is Shane Lacy, if that matters?"

He looks at me in surprise and seems a little uneasy, but I go ahead with my questions. "Um, I have this paper that I think has an account, maybe for me, but I'm not really sure. I know that probably sounds weird, but could you please check for me?"

"Well, before proceeding any further, I will need some identification."

I dig deep in my purse, pulling out my license and the envelope with that shiny blue reminder emblem, and hand them both to the man. He looks at the front and then the back, carefully opening the envelope, and I remember the private note from Sebastian and snatch it from his hand, nearly impaling my stomach on the corner of his desk. "Ughhh!" I cry out, as he stands nervously in antici-pation of what I might do next. A slightly tubby security guard sees my forcefulness toward the banker through the glass divider and lumbers over in a semi-brisk jog. I quickly try to recover my overreaction.

"Oh my gosh, I am so sorry, it just has something personal inside. Can I just give you the account number, or do you need the whole thing?"

The guard is waved away but remains at the doorway just in case I lose my shit again. I fold the paper in such a way that only the numbers show. The banker seems pleased and puts on his readers but refuses to touch the paper, probably scared I'll slap it out of his hand with a ruler or bite him. I notice he's glancing back and forth to the envelope that I placed on the desk in front of me. "No, Miss Lacy, I am very sorry. Please excuse my intrusiveness before. You must be here for your account with Mr. Kane? He is an excellent customer of ours and I won't need anything else except for you to accept my apology."

Vivi reaches out her finger to the security guard like it's a pretend taser and buzzes the man on his side. He looks down at her and laughs, then leaves for a moment, returning with a purple lollipop and stickers. For once, she looks delighted. I realize why when I see the animals printed on them. I think I need to get her to the zoo if I have any chance of ever having a conversation with her.

"Hold on just a moment and I will get a pass book for you and a paper for you to sign," the manager says.

"A what?" I'm still in shock that I have an account with Sebastian, but before I can ask more questions, he's already walked away. When he comes back he hands me a blue book the size of a tiny journal with gold embossing and the bank's logo of a whale on the front. "What's this?"

He smiles at my naivety. "Miss Lacy, this is your account. It will keep track of your balance, deposits, and withdrawals. Mr. Kane asked that we do it this way for you, so you can take out money as you wish. There was a deposit made early this morning, so whatever you need is there." He proceeds to open the booklet to the second page, where in black ink a beginning balance of $5,000.00 is clearly typed. I hand it back like it's covered in fleas.

"This isn't right, I don't have that kind of money. I don't think this is correct. Can you just take it back, please? There's a mistake, I know there is."

"No, Miss Lacy, this is your money. No one else is on the account. Only you are named, so no, I cannot take it back. I would be happy to keep the book here if you wish? I also need you to sign acceptance for the account. Please see here." He points to a piece of paper with numbers and "sign here" stickers.

I'm getting frustrated. "I don't want the stupid book, okay? Take it. Yes, please keep the damn thing." I throw the book on the desk, leaving it and the unsigned paper, and grab Vivi, who in turn drops her stickers and starts crying. I turn back and scoop them up, along with the envelope, and run both of us to the car.

I fumble for the keys, and before I can start the engine my eyes well up and tears are streaming down my face. The road is blurred with water and I can't help sobbing uncontrollably. It's all taking a toll on me. First it's my mother, and then the reunion with Simone, and now Sebastian causing me to prostitute myself is what's breaking this apparent hooker's back. I can't stop hysterically crying, forgetting about the miniature person in the back of the car who is neither deaf nor blind. I feel little kicks—*one-two, one-two*—on the back of my seat. I pull over to tell her to stop, and when I do, she looks at me sideways shaking her head. She then pulls her finger from the corner of her eye down to her cheek, stopping there and shaking her head.

"You're right, sweetie pie, no more crying. How are you so smart?"

She nods her head yes. I take some deep breaths and begin thinking about all the events that have unfolded in the past week, and the tears start to stream. *Thump, thump, thump* on the back of my seat.

"Okay, I get it. I'm done, I promise." I start to laugh that a child knows more than me, and I tell her we need to go and visit my mother. I wipe my eyes with the sleeve of my shirt and drive us to the hospital.

When we arrive, I check back in with an ER nurse I recognize, who tells me she's been moved upstairs into the ICU, room 614, and proceeds to give me directions on how to get there and says not to be scared when I see her.

"Why would I be shocked to see her? What's so scary?"

"Your mother has a contusion on her head from when she fell and hit something. I don't know all the details, only that it required stitches, and she is stable now."

An ER nurse who overhears the conversation pulls me aside and away from Vivi, who is intently listening to our every word. "Your mom is really stressed. We're trying to run tests, but she's not letting us get too close. Do you know what could have caused this? I've seen something similar, but she is extreme. Do you have any idea what could have triggered it? It's possible she is having a psychotic break."

"Um, no. We aren't really that close, and I live in another town and honestly just saw her for the first time in a few years. How bad is it?"

"She is showing signs of real agitation and is refusing all foods and medications, telling us she's severely allergic. She has to eat and drink or she will die. We tried sedating her again, but she's refusing all medication, and we can't go against her will. She won't even accept intravenous fluids. She screams at the sight of gloves, bags, anything medical. We just want to help her. She needs hydration. Can you talk some sense into her? And try to find out how long she has been this way? Something must have triggered it. We're still waiting on psych, but in the meantime we are keeping her in the ICU, secure for her own protection."

"Okay, I'll ask. Thanks for telling me."

I walk over to Vivi and kneel down to tell her that Aggie has a bad boo-boo on her head from when she fell and that we might see a big Band-Aid. She doesn't flinch at the news, so I take that as a sign she will be fine, and we head to the room.

Rob is sitting in a chair (big surprise) with an array of snacks on the table. "Hey, Rob, can you take Vivi to grab a drink? I just want to visit with my mother for a sec." As I'm speaking, I give him the car keys, and he moans as he rises from the chair. He and Vivi walk out of the room, presumably to the water fountain or vending machine for more junk food. I pick up a bag of pretzels and take one from the bag.

"Here, Mother, will you have a little bite of food for me?" She looks at me with bloodshot eyes and then at the bag and screams loudly, "Don't you fucking know I'm allergic to pretzels!"

The nurse runs in, ready to shoot her with a needle. I block my mother, who begins to shout. The nurse sighs impolitely and tells her either she stops or gets the drug. My mother looks terrified and starts to cry, turning onto her side.

"Maybe you should go," the nurse snaps.

"Maybe you should get the doctor. Mother, do you want me to leave?"

"No, no, Shaney, I don't. I just don't want that kind of pretzel, okay? No pretzels right now. I need to get home. I don't need them giving me any more shit. I'm allergic. Tell them I'm allergic, Shaney, tell them!" Her tone is weak, and I've never really heard her swear, so I concede by throwing the bag in the trash. The bitchy nurse seems satisfied enough and leaves the room.

"Mother, they keep telling me you aren't eating or drinking. They are really worried about you. I'm really worried about you."

Her mannerisms resume to normal as she switches sides again. "Nothing to worry about, sweetie, I am fine. I just got a little dizzy and fell, no big deal. I'll be home soon and I can get dinner started for Rob and you, too, it will be great and make me so happy."

"Mother, they want to keep you for a few days, so you can sleep and get some fluids. You have to get fluids, even if you don't eat. Please let them give you some water."

Her bloodshot eyes, stitched head, and bony, pale face scold me like a child. "Shane, do you hear me little girl? I am not drinking their tainted water or letting them near me with their dirty syringes." She pauses for a second to think about what either of us will say next. "I will think about drinking Poland Spring water, but that's even questionable. I will try only if you agree to sit with me when I do it?"

"Okay, no problem, I will sit with you when you try, and the good thing is if you have a reaction to the water, we're in a hospital and they can help you right away."

Rob comes back in the room, and before he can get comfortable I ask him to pick up some Poland Spring bottled water for my mother. "Oh, there's water in the vending machine, I'll get it for her."

"No, she wants Poland Spring, you should know this. Please, Rob, you were with her when this happened, and she wants what she wants, so just get it, please." I am losing patience with these grown-up children and getting sick of being the adult.

"Fine, I'll go."

I walk out into the hall with him. "Seriously, Rob. Something is wrong with her. What the hell is going on here?"

"Seriously, Shane? You show up after years of being away and think you can control your mother. I won't put up with it."

"Fuck you, Rob. You don't do anything for her and she waits on you like you're her retarded son."

"Shane, you're a skanky little slut who lied about fucking a billionaire, and when he didn't want you, you suckered your stupid husband into marrying you. You are the reason she's like this, so you can blame yourself. You stress her out."

As he speaks, tiny bits of crumbs stuck to his lips move about, and I scream but hold back from slapping the fat right off his face. "Rob, you piece of shit. What do you do? The house is fucking nasty and you don't help her with money or obviously anything. What the fuck do you do, other than sit around and eat, you fat fucking asshole."

"Shane, I am not doing this with you. I only called you because you're her only child and I thought you could help. If you want to be here with your mother, fine. But I am not going to fight with you. If you want to know, I don't give enough of a shit about you to fight with you, that's how little you mean to me."

My eyes fill with tears and my mouth waters. The last comment hurts the most, and even though I don't care at all about him, I don't hate him. "Goodbye. Please, go. I'll keep Vivi and spend time with my mother, but go away."

"Fine, I will get her the special water and drop it off."

I walk back into her room and into her private bathroom, wiping the corners of each eye, returning with a smile for my mother to see. "So Rob is going to get you some Poland Spring water."

"Oh, that's great news, sweetie. So tell me about what you did today. I heard someone screaming, do you want to see if they're okay? Where's my little Vivi?"

"She's right here." Vivi climbs onto her bed to get a better angle of the cartoons overhead. I talk to her about Jake's fishing and hunting trip with his dad and friends and how he will be gone for another week. She asks lots of questions about him and what he's like and how our house runs. "Mother, we have a tiny little apartment and we both work constantly. It runs like any other house, except we don't see each other because we both have two jobs, plus I'm taking classes."

"You're taking classes? Oh, wow, I am so proud of you. That is so wonderful. What kind of classes, what does that mean?" Her voice is growing softer as we speak, and I beg her to drink from a cup on the tray next to her bed, but she declines.

"I have a writing class to finish before I can graduate. It's just community college, so not that big of a deal."

"Are you kidding me? This is a very big deal. I am so proud. You are doing so wonderfully and I am so happy you're here. You are just like your father, Tommy Lee Jones, he went to Harvard. Maybe you will go to Harvard, too?"

Just as she utters the words, Rob arrives with a bottle of Poland Spring water. I go to pour it into the hospital's Styrofoam cup and she screeches, "No!"

I look back at her and stop. "Okay, what do you want me to do?"

"From the bottle. I don't know what's in their cups. It's not my house."

All I can think is, yeah, I know, this place with all its diseases and germs is still cleaner. I open the cap for her and peer behind my shoulder to see that Rob has left without saying goodbye. She takes a minuscule sip from the bottle; in fact, I'm not even sure she swallowed or that her lips even touched the plastic rim. "Mother, you have to drink, I need you."

She laughs, and then in a very serious tone says, "Your actual father is Tom Brokaw, and he will take good care of you."

"I thought it was Tommy Lee Jones or Tom Selleck or any of the other Toms you told me about. Now you are telling me after all this time it's the guy from the news?"

We both laugh, and I urge her to take another sip, so she pretends to again. We talk for another hour or so and then a short Hispanic woman walks in, interrupting our bonding. My mother perks up and says, "Hi, Bea, how are you? This is my daughter, Shane. Shane, this is Beatrice, one of Vivi's nannies."

"Oh, so nice to meet you," she says with an accent.

I shake her hand, but she doesn't actually seem pleased to meet. I feel funny letting the already fragile Vivi go with her, so I explain that I'll keep her with me and meet up with Simone later.

"No, I was told to come pick up Miss Vivi. Miss Barron told me to."

Rather than argue with the Latina who's developing an attitude, I agree and reach to give Vivi a hug but back off when she climbs down from the bed. "Bye, Vivi, have fun."

She walks away without so much as a wave or a finger buzz, and the sitter follows. I tell my mother she seems weird, but she assures me that Simone likes her and that's all that matters.

"Oh shit, I just remembered I need to get my car. Mother, I need to get my car, do you mind if I come back in the morning? I have to work tonight, too. I'm really sorry, I totally forgot and the day flew by. Will you be okay?" I'm sputtering a hundred words a minute.

"Yes, of course, I'll sleep and catch up on some television shows. They will let me out as soon as they realize I don't have insurance or any money to pay them."

"Oh my gosh, you are stressing me out. Okay, just drink, see you in the morning, and stay until they kick you out or whatever, but just drink, please. Come on, remember how you used to send me for 'vacation' at those hospitals? You know what to do. I will be back, and call me if you need anything. Drink, Mother, drink."

I rush out the door and run down the hall. "Bea, Bea! Beatrice!"

She and Vivi stop and turn around.

"Can you please help me? My car is at the Barnes & Noble near the mall, can you please bring me to get it?"

She looks displeased with me personally, but I'm not sure why. "Yes, no problem, then I take Miss Vivi to the park."

"Okay, thank you. I hope it's fenced, or just be aware of any loose dogs." I laugh to myself, but she doesn't seem to get the joke.

We drive in silence, only stopping when I point out my car. Vivi buzzes me through the closed window but doesn't make a sound as they drive off, cutting our moment short.

I get inside the car, grateful for an old bottle of water, and swig down a pill. I'm getting low and need to catch up with my doctor before Jake comes home. I bolt to the highway, heading back home and hoping I will make the night shift at the bar. When I get to the apartment, the new Mustang is in my parking space again, so I pull around front, parking illegally, and run inside. I throw on some clothes, grab the phone charger, and change Andrew's water, which has a single poop floating in it, before bolting back out.

Empty Seats

When I arrive at the bar, everyone is staring at me. I go to the back to put my purse down and look for Eddie. I find him on the staircase, carrying up food from the freezer.

"Hey you, what's going on around here? The place seems off."

He puts down the frozen bag of french fries on the stair and puts his hand on my arm. "I am so sorry, Shane, but your guy died, you know, the Vet. He got hit by a car and was left, some sort of hit-and-run bullshit. No one knew about it until we saw it in the paper this morning. Ye Ol Doc hasn't been in since. It's really sad, and everyone has been super bummed and are asking where've you been?"

I can feel my body sliding against the wall, but Eddie's strength stops me from falling down the stairs. "Are you okay?"

"Nope. I'm not." I tear up. "My mother's in the hospital and now this. What the fuck! He was the sweetest, and I loved his banter with Ye Ol, what is he going to do? At least he's with his wife and family now. How can some asshole just hit a person? What the freak is wrong with people?" He grabs and hugs me tightly and I lay my head on his shoulder for a good minute or two, feeling the closeness of a true friend. I close my eyes and sink into the arch of his arm holding me tight. "Thank you, I needed that."

I walk out from the back room to find everyone staring at me for a response to our little bar's tragedy. Feeling awful about the whole day and my entire life right now, and this being the cherry on top, I speak up for the whole bar to hear.

"I just heard about our good friend, the Vet, the hero. We are so lucky to have known him. He survived a war protecting this country just for some maniac to have taken his life. May the bastard get caught and may we all drink to celebrate his life, not to be sad." I start to break, my eyes filling with salty tears, and stand up to shout some more on top of a black beer crate. "Life is short, let's live it. To the hero, our hero, the Vet!"

Everyone shouts and yells. "Get us some beers, Shane!" "To our hero and this goddamn weird-ass short life of ours!" "May we all live it until we're full!"

The white-trash little girls who hang around Dave don't

understand and noticeably don't cheer in his memory, and I walk around the bar and tell them to "GET OUT." I'm starting to crack under the pressure of the past week and can't deal with anything petty, even ill-mannered whores. These disrespecting slimy bitches need to get on their way, because they would never understand a man like the Vet. Dave sprints around the corner, physically holding me back as I point and shout at the backs of their bleached blond heads, "Get the hell out. Just get out! No fucking in the basement tonight, girls, get out, NOW!"

I start to cry, and for once in his selfish life, Dave pulls me to him, holding me in his arms and waving them to the door. "I am sorry. I am so sorry. I . . ." I sob into his shoulder, and when I look up everyone is turned around, staring at me.

"It's okay, it's fine. Do you want to go home?" Dave asks.

I contemplate the offer, but the thought of being alone makes me cry harder. "No, I'll be fine. I will be fine. Yep, I will be fine. Can you just cover for a sec?"

Our public embrace unlocks and I head straight for the ladies' room. I stare into the mirror at my sad eyes and how I've aged at least a year for every day this week. My hair is a mess, my face red and blotchy, my lipstick smudged all the way to my cheek. I stand and stare at the mirror, saying to myself, "Get your shit together. You are not that girl! Get over it. Get over him. Get over everything."

Just then Tammy walks out of the stall without flushing or washing her hands and rubs my back. "Guy troubles, baby?"

I'm fairly sure she's a heroin addict and drinks here to pick up the regulars for their blue-collar checks. She's being sincere, and I really should listen to an expert in the field of loose women, since I, too, have entered that category. "Thanks, Tammy, I will be fine."

She walks out and I finish wiping my face with a damp paper towel and leave the restroom feeling stronger and a bit more refreshed and ready for the shift. When I come around the bar, no

one asks me for anything. I can see empty glasses filling the coun-
ters, so I finally say, "C'mon guys, I'm okay. What does everyone
need?"

Finally one of them speaks. "Down here, hot stuff, I need
another." I don't recognize him, but he's in the back pool room
with the Puerto Ricans, who have just shown up and were being
served by Dave.

I continue throughout the night, pouring beers, cleaning and
restocking, filling the time, and keeping myself distracted. At the
end of the night, I ask Dave if we can do shots with the remaining
few, in honor of the Vet. He agrees, and I pour my favorite Fireball
Cinnamon Whisky, and we all toast to the end of his chapter. Dave
surprises me again and tells me to take tomorrow night off. Maybe
I do need the break.

A bit later, I yell for last call, but no one's there to wait and walk
me out. I think about the professor, missing his friend, and the Vet,
somewhere in heaven, missing his seat. I swallow hard and finish
cleaning an empty bar, check all the knobs and doors, and finally
drive home to an empty apartment.

When I arrive, I perform my normal ritual of peeling off smoke-
filled clothes at the door, showering, and eating junk food on the
couch to late-night reruns. I curl up on the other end of the couch,
where Simone and I didn't hook up, avoiding that side like the
disaster it was. It makes me uncomfortable to be near there and
brings back bad memories that I need to distance myself from,
along with all the current promiscuity in my life. Then I think, on
a positive note, at least she didn't try to pay me.

Doctor Wants to Feel Good

W hen I wake in the morning I pop a pill, get dressed, call my doctor's office for a refill, and they tell me it's time to come in and be seen if I want the script. I find this odd since I was just there a few weeks ago.

"Can you come in this morning? We had a cancellation if you can make it in twenty minutes?"

I can't stand the guy, he's touchy-feely, and every single visit requires a new examination with me nearly naked in a johnny. I have two pills left, and my body already knows the consequences of running low come quickly. "Yes, that works great, I'm leaving now."

When I arrive at the clinic, which only takes cash, I pull out one of the hundred-dollar bills that Sebastian gave me, reading "your" in marker on it. The receptionist, whom I am friendly with, makes a funny face, so I shrug my shoulders, pretending not to know. I get in the room, and sure enough, the wraparound johnny is folded neatly on the table for me to change into. I put it on, leaving my bra and pants on. A knock on the door, and Dr. Petucci comes in.

"Why hello there, stranger." He closes the door behind him, placing his chart on the exam table. "All of it, Shane. I need to check the whole alignment of your spine."

I start shimmying the tight jeans off my hips and stop. "Actually, doctor, nothing has changed. The pain is the same."

He ignores my plea. "All the way, Shane, I need to be sure."

I sigh loudly as I slide the pant legs over my socks and put them on the table. I am wearing a thong today, so I tuck the johnny tight around me. He lifts it up, feeling around the frame of my hip bones, then back up to my shoulder blades and one more time down to the dimples right above my butt. I writhe under his hands. "Hold still, I need to check." He has me stand up and put my hands in front of me to reach my toes. This movement allows the johnny to open widely and uncover my butt, with the thong nestled deep between the cheeks. He reaches his hands past the dimples and touches my butt, tracing his cold, bare fingers down the cheek and around to my vagina. I can feel each stroke on my bum, and my anxiety flares as blood begins to rush to my head. I squeeze my thighs together, and he parts them with his bare hands, feeling back up the interior of my thighs, reaching my vagina. He slides a finger over the cotton and back up the arch, ending with a squeeze at my waist. When it's all over, I'm shaking and nauseous.

"You can stand up now. It looks the same, but you are progressing. Have you lost some weight? That will help alleviate stress on your spinal cord. Keep it up. I like you nice and skinny."

I don't respond and sit down on the table, pulling the johnny's fabric over my knees and tucking the rest tightly beneath my legs. He writes the prescription and I find myself relieved that it's all over until the next time. "Thank you."

He hands me the paper and I reach for it, but he doesn't let go. "No, thank you. I will see you in a month, we need to monitor this."

I pull tightly on the script but he pulls back, then the door opens and he breaks free. "Doctor, you are running a little behind," the medical assistant says. "Oh hi, Shane."

I smile back at her and notice that she's put on more weight. The poor thing is getting bigger and bigger every time I see her. The doctor follows her out and closes the door. I pull on my clothes as fast as I can and leave without checking out. There is nothing new about this visit, and just like the first, I want to puke each time I'm here.

I get back in my car and drive to the pharmacy near my mother's hospital. After getting my meds filled on the spot, I feel a lot less anxious about running out of them and free to focus on other priorities.

I enter the hospital, only to be stopped and told she has been moved, yet again. A different receptionist says, "Due to her improvement, we have taken her out of the ICU and moved her upstairs."

I decide to take the stairs, and upon opening the door to her floor, I can hear talking, and at first it sounds like the nurses and doctors chatting away, but then I recognize it's not. It's my mother and Simone. As I get closer, their voices turn to whispers and I overhear what sounds like my mother saying "Are you sure?" and Simone responding with "Yes, don't worry about it." I try to listen from outside the room, but the surrounding noises block most of what they're saying. I walk inside the bright room and they both stop, jolted by my presence. Simone is sitting on the edge of the bed and looks pale with concern.

"What shouldn't she worry about?"

Simone gathers words with perfect poise and says, "Oh, that Vienne is taken care of, that's all."

My mother picks up the television clicker and starts pressing buttons. "Oh, hey there, Shaney bug. So glad you are here, look who came to visit and brought me presents, too!"

I'm suspicious of what they're hiding from me, but I move on from the subject when I take notice of the obscene amount of gifts around the room. I'm not sure if it's the size of her new room making everything look giant, or if it's the preposterousness of celebrating another one of my mother's mental ailments that's worth all the excitement. Taking up an entire corner is an almost life-size brown teddy bear sporting a green T-shirt that reads "Get Beary Well," with at least twenty colored balloons attached to its stuffed arm. In the other corner there's an impressive bouquet of calla lilies in a tall vase placed next to her bed, plus stacks of magazines and a new DVD player in the box with a stack of movies on top of it.

"Wow, this is a lot of stuff. Sorry, I didn't bring anything." I walk past the vinyl upholstered chair that sits empty to get closer to my mother's bedside and almost trip on the piles upon piles of Poland Spring cases, one on top of another, plus more flowers and another stuffed animal. The room is packed with more gifts than Vivi's at the Ritz.

"That's okay, sweetie, I have everything I need right here. I am doing great, and hopefully they will let me out of here today. Simone knows one of the doctors, and she is going to talk to him about letting me go. I need to get back home, I have a lot to do."

I glare at Simone. What is she thinking? She looks away, turning to my mother, and says, "I have something fun to do with Shaney today."

"You do?" I'm as curious as my mother. "Simone, I cannot go anywhere. I need to stay here and find out what's going on, and see if any tests are back."

My mother's frail body sits erect as she points her scrawny finger at the both of us. "No, no, no and more nos. I am totally fine. Vivi is with Beatrice, and you two need some fun. Go with Simone. Patient's orders!"

Simone puts her arm around mine. "She's coming, don't worry, Aggie."

We walk out of the room, Simone's arm still entwined in mine, but I stare back over my shoulder to see that my mother is smiling and waving us on. I am feeling better about leaving and wonder if a fun time out is exactly what I need. "Simone, I seriously hope you do not have some doctor friend who is going to get her out today. She is nuts. Yesterday she told me she was allergic to pretzels. She isn't eating or drinking or anything!"

"Don't worry, silly, I made that up. Your mother is staying, I just said that so she wouldn't go ballistic when they moved her to a different room. I already talked to the doctor, whom I know personally, if you know what I mean, and he assured me that she will be here for a few more days. He told me that he will make sure she gets fluids and back to some semblance of health, with a therapist, too. Don't worry, I knew you would freak out when you heard her say that, but I have it under control." She has an eerie smirk on her face.

"I'm sorry, I am just stressed, like wicked stressed. I had a shitty day at work last night, one of my regulars died unexpectedly, and then seeing my mother like this, especially after being away from her for so long, plus Jake being gone, and the whole Sebastian thing, and even you."

"Me, what did I do?" She gives me her red pouty look made famous in the tabloids, and says as cocky as a man with money, "Sugar Shane, I am as innocent as the day is long, and tonight is gonna be long. Come with me and stop your whining."

The girl has a trance over me, and I can't help but follow her scent. We arrive at the Ritz, where they greet me like a resident, and I welcome the kind attention. Simone breezes by them like they don't exist and yells for me when I stop to ask how they are and when one of the men's cast is coming off his arm. We take the elevator upstairs, and I don't dare talk to the operator in fear she will scold me again. Once inside, I flip off my worn sneakers and she asks me to hang out and catch up. I reach down to grab a pill from my bag, but realizing how obvious, I take the whole purse to the bathroom. From there she shouts through the door as I'm swallowing my little white secret.

"How about we see what the boys are doing?"

I almost choke and cough a couple times to clear my throat.

"Are you okay?"

"NO, actually I am not. You have to be kidding me. I am leaving if that's what we're doing."

"Okay, okay, but he's really sweet on you, and honestly I need every distraction I can get right now. The meetings aren't going very well with the estate's team—that's what they call themselves, an estate team, how lame is that? Fucking crooked lawyers is what they really are. It feels like all I do these days is sign papers that I don't understand and let these assholes drag it out so they can stay on the clock for as long as possible. No one will give me any answers about when everything will be finalized. I'm the sole heiress, it should be really fucking simple. It's bullshit, so I want to go out."

"I don't understand, you aren't getting anything? That doesn't make sense, you are the only family in the Barron estate, and I thought that's been set up since you were a kid?" I feel funny asking her personal questions about money, but it seems strange that such a wealthy girl is shut off from her father's immense fortune.

"Damn right, it's mine. I will get it, whenever they figure it out. You know how people are, they come out of the woodwork and all."

"Well, at least you have the suite to stay in." I say, trying to bring an upside to her spoiled act.

"Of course I have a suite, because they kicked me out of my main home. All my stuff is just sitting there, frozen, getting dusty. They are going to pay all my expenses and anything Vivi or I need until it's cleared, and then things will go back to normal. But living like a peasant is taking its toll, and I need to get out and blow off some steam. So can we please pick a place!"

She is starting to annoy me by mentioning her particularly un-peasant lifestyle, a direct reference to me. I decide to turn it back on her and make it personal, too. "Simone, can't you get a job?"

She looks at me with fury, her plump lips pursed and ready to explode, but with careful poise, like at the hospital, she says, "Shane, I have the easiest job on earth and I'm doing it. I will have everything that's mine just as my father wanted it and will never have to worry about this nonsense again."

I don't understand her overconfidence, so I grab us both a glass of water and sit back down, still pondering her odd response. "Do you mean waiting is the easiest job?"

"Oh my goodness, Shane, you are so naive. It's fucking amazing how you have no clue sometimes. I thought you would appreciate what I am doing. Plus, I thought you needed the money, too?"

"I am not stupid, Simone! Are you saying what I think you are saying?"

"Give me a break, Shane, you would have done it anyhow, I know you. These guys can't get involved with how much they work and who they are. Plus, I know them and they're good people, so there's no harm. Our arrangements serve a purpose, and it's only for a little while. Trust me, I would sell a painting or two at Sotheby's, but all assets are frozen until it's all completely settled."

I take a gulp of water, swallowing hard like there's a tennis ball in my throat. "Again, just to clarify. Is Martin giving you something?"

"Yeah, goofball, of course he is. Why, is Sebastian not paying you? I was told he would, so he better be. Relax, it's fun!"

"I don't even know what to say right now. This is ludicrous. Who else knows about this?"

She flips her blond locks to the side of her tan shoulder and puts her hand in mine. I reluctantly but automatically squeeze back. "No one. Just us. Shaney, that's why I set him up with you, so you can get some money, too. I heard you were struggling but I didn't realize how bad until I saw your place. You don't belong in that nasty bar or that itty-bitty apartment. You deserve better. I promise to take care of you when I get my inheritance, and we'll go on vacation or do something fabulous together."

I rip my hand back and stand up tall. "Simone, I don't want your money, I never have. I am in shock right now, that you, my best friend, or my friend, or whatever the fuck you are, are having me sold to some guy and you just assume that I am fine with it. I am cheating on my fucking husband, for goodness' sake."

"Jesus, Shane, what did you think when they met us out? Did you think they were just nice guys?"

She's right. I had no idea why they were so nice to us. "I am such an idiot and so embarrassed. How could I be so stupid?"

I sink to the floor, allowing the couch cushion to push into my back, and pull a cashmere blanket around my face. A minute or two passes and I realize that I'm not crying like I should be. Maybe she's right, maybe this is what I would have done all along? Does she know me better than I know myself? Simone slides off the couch and sits on the floor next to me. She pulls the blanket from over my head and exposes my sheet-white face. She puts her arm around my shoulder and pulls me down to the lush carpet and lies next to me. She nuzzles her curves into the arch of mine and we lie there amongst hotel carpet fibers, wrapped together as one. She whispers in my ear. "Are you mad at me?"

I don't answer right away, so she hugs me tighter. "No, I'm not mad at you, just at myself. I feel very, very stupid."

"What are you talking about? Don't feel stupid. This is business, Shane. You need money. I need money. We earn it. Definition of a job, isn't it?"

I can't help but smile at the absurdity of Simone Barron's understanding of work. "Maybe it's business to you, but to me it's my life. I don't have anything to fall back on. And what really pisses me off, and I know it sounds dumb, but I actually thought he liked me." Simone leans in, kissing the back of my neck, and rubs the side of my arm with heat and reaches toward my breast. "He does like you."

Royals Belch?

The suite's phone rings, interrupting her hand or any further conversation on the subject. She springs up with a wild burst of energy and says, "Your surprise must be here."

"What surprise?"

She opens the door a few seconds later to reveal Abby, her longtime friend from England who spent time at Simone's house when we were kids. She walks in about as subtle as a sledgehammer, just as I remembered. Abigail is an obscenely wealthy British girl and another friend of Simone's who she met sailing in France. Their grandparents are friends and shared summer homes near one another, so they would see each other every summer until they flew home alone, each in her own jet. She also came from time to time to stay at the estate during school breaks, where I got to know her. As far back as I remember, Abby has always been a part of Simone's clique, and therefore someone I inadvertently knew, too.

She is shorter than us, rather plump in the rear, and has very large boobs that she's proud to show off. Her personality, much like her frame, is boisterous, loud, and funny, and despite an elite upbringing as an heiress to a huge media fortune, she swears like an American truck driver. Her father's side married into the queen's family, and despite their shame of her tabloid recreations as a maniacal party girl, she is quite proud of her royal background. Her father's money and connections always found their way to pay off any real scandal, so she's continued to push the limits, and I've even read about her antics in American tabloids. She is wearing ruby red lipstick, a short green leather skirt that is much too tight, and a men's collared shirt unbuttoned two-thirds of the way down, exposing mountains of cleavage and an unfit bra.

Her first words to our welcoming smiles and hugs are, "Oh my bloody fucker, these booties are killin' me." She flings off the wildest looking beaded and metal torture device–looking shoes I've ever seen. The place where the toes go is melded and curved, not leaving anywhere for toes or a foot to fit. There are marks where the rubbing against her fattish ankles has taken its toll.

"What are those?" I ask as I attempt to slip my much smaller foot inside one of them.

"Stay away, they're Alexander McQueens, and they'll fuckin' McKill ya."

"I cannot believe you are here, this is so great."

"And I can't believe you're here!" she says snidely, but I brush it off, as I am too busy trying to tug this metal hunk off my foot.

Simone is glowing having us all together. She's certainly a billionaire siren, but when it comes to nostalgia, she's a big sappy baby. Unlike many of her other friends, Abby had always been somewhat accepting of me, which is possibly why she's here. She walks over and hugs Simone, saying, "I am so sorry, my darling, how are you doing? What can I do for you?" She looks truly sad and continues to comfort her.

"I will be alright, it's just tough right now, but I will get through it. I really do miss him, though. Anyhow, let's not talk about it. Let's go out! My girls are here!"

It's the first time I've heard Simone mention Mr. Barron in an endearing manner, and I'm a little taken aback. Abby asks to shower and clean up from the trip. She heads for Simone's bathroom, and we talk about old times with her and Simone tells me about her travels to visit her in London a few years back.

Abby walks out refreshed and wearing yet another outlandish outfit that blows both of us away. The dress is highlighter-yellow, flared, and has some sort of multicolored puffballs on it that rise up and fade out as they reach her bare shoulders, plus her notorious Key lime–green eyeliner and traditional bright red lipstick.

"You crack me up, Abby."

"I'm fucking British, darling, I need to be noticed. It's the least I can do as a royal! Well let's get schnookered and meet some stunners." She smacks her chest with a fist, letting out a belch, and says, "See? Representing the royal family." We all laugh, and I can't believe another crazy fated day is upon me, and instead of running for the door I walk into Simone's closet to find something weird to wear, too.

We all find our inner funk following Abby's natural lead, and leave the suite turning heads from elevator to limo, which she has always traveled in, even when we were kids. The attention we've already received means we either look smoking hot or like the Spice Girls on meth. It makes me laugh inside. When I'm with Simone my confidence grows, but with Abby it bursts like a balloon. The night is our oyster, and we are going to put everything from the past and present behind us, including Sebastian. This is our night to be girls.

We head out, stopping first to grab flash-fried appetizers, and then on a whim decide to see the sunset and have the driver race us to the beach. The girls throw off their thousand-dollar shoes, but I lag behind, moving them carefully aside, and then chase after the girls to the pier. They run to the water's edge, screaming when the water hits their feet. I soak in the salty air, leisurely walking toward the waves, shoes dangling from my fingertips.

We're interrupted by a familiar voice. "Hey! Hey lady with the weird kid." What the hell? I look around, but the sun is setting fast and the faded clouds hinder my view of the old man. I look both ways and then behind me to see a huge dog running for me. Before I know what's happened, Good has tackled me and I am on the ground, covered in sand, with the furry beast sitting on my chest. The girls turn around when they hear me yelp and come screaming in fear from the water. Abby's spouting every British, French, and American profanity she knows while Simone gracefully sprints toward me. The dog is literally sitting on top of my lungs, and I can barely budge or talk. For the first time, I hear deep chuckles coming from the homeless man. Apparently, it's hilarious that the dog finds my chest and Simone's very expensive clothes to be comfortable enough to lay its dirty butt upon. I eke out a few words. "Seriously, Good, you have to move."

Finally, Abby and Simone arrive, evaluate the scene, and start laughing, quickly followed by more foul swears toward the homeless man. "Get your mangy bitch off my friend," Abby says.

He stops laughing and looks at them, and his eyes pierce even me, who knows he's harmless.

"It's okay," I say. "Please, it's fine, he'll get off me."

The man pats the dog's leg. "Come on, dog, get off the poor girl."

Just like that, Good rises and I can breathe again. I sit up, brush myself off, and thank him.

"What are you thanking him for? Have you gone mad?" Abby keeps yelling at the man, now even louder. "Get a fucking leash, and while you're at it, a bloody job, too, you Negro dickhead."

"Jesus, Abby, it's fine. I am fine. Look." I show her that I am standing and completely dusted off, but the sun is gone, so she assumes the worst. I feel terrible about her behavior, but I don't need to further an already bad scene, not to mention risk him talking about Vivi in Simone's presence. To my surprise, he talks back to Abby under his breath, and just like that, I can't protect him.

"Knock it off, you entitled little cunt."

Holy smokes, I have never used that word in my life, never mind heard a homeless guy talk to royalty that way.

"Do you know who I am? Do you?" Abby is reared up and angry. She bites her lip and takes off toward him, and Simone and I chase after her.

Wham! She slaps him straight across the face and spits at him, but she's too short for it to hit his face and it slowly dribbles down his shirt. "You're nothing but an evil lying bitch!"

Good growls at her, exposing his pointy teeth and the scars around his mouth, and I try to usher her away. "Enough, you've both made your point. Let's go, the dog's going to bite you."

The man's posture changes, slumping down, and he turns away from us, muttering, "Keep it up, Simone, I am sure your father would be quite proud of the company you're still keeping." He walks away, never wiping the saliva off his clothing, and the pit bull loyally follows behind him into the distance.

"How the hell does he know your name?" I ask.

Simone yells back with anger. "Why don't you learn to drive a car you fucking piece of shit."

"You're a fucking loser wanker!" Abby screams.

They both start laughing, and Simone answers with a shrug of a shoulder. "Whatever, I'm in the papers, maybe the bastard isn't illiterate. He probably saw me there."

We keep walking, but I'm still wondering how in the world he knew those two, and my heart races as I think about Vivi and Good's connection.

Maybe a minute of walking goes by, and we hear the loudest, most primal growl from deep within the man's lungs. He yells as loud as he can without making words—only angry, nonsensical noise bursts from his mouth. We are scared shitless and run to the wooden decking, where the girls find their shoes and I put mine back on in a fury. We don't speak another word of the disgracefulness that just happened and rush to the waiting limo. I know deep down the true colors of my rich friend, but I didn't think she could be that cruel toward another human being. My mother was right, cash doesn't buy class.

We find ourselves at an outdoor bar on the water, not far from the pier where Sebastian and I had docked. I hope to avoid that one like the bubonic plague, because I don't want anything around me that will bring back his memory. We are approached by a couple of very good-looking suits, no doubt on a business trip, hoping to get laid while away from their wives. We play along, striking up a conversation with them, and learn they are in pharmaceuticals and, as we suspected, here on business. Guys like this you can read like a book. Before the drinks have even arrived, Abby is daring them to take their clothes off. Then she turns to us and says, "What? I bore easily." She continues on with the men. "I'll give you my thong if you two do a body shot off each other."

They look disgusted by the idea, and even my eyebrow raises at the thought of her proposal. "You're kidding, right?" one of them says.

I'm not sure I want to see two grown men sucking liquor off each other's hairy bodies, but Abby keeps on. "Nope, I will give you my pink panties—oh, did I mention my hot, wet, pink panties?— only if you two lover boys do a body shot off each other's bellies."

This just got weird for all of us, and we watch their tiny brains ponder the proposal. "Wait, there's two of us and only one pair of thongs? What about her?"

The taller guy points at me. I don't know what to say. I'm not taking off my underwear, but this is too interesting to quit. "Um, well . . ." Just as I start to string them along so we can hilariously watch them do shots off their chubby stomachs, I hear another familiar voice.

"I don't think the lady will be taking anything off. Leave now!"

"Who the fuck are you? This is a private conversation." Abby is fierce tonight and not taking shit from anyone. I look behind me to confirm what I already know: It's Sebastian, accompanied by Martin and another man. The businessmen walk away, and as they do, Abby screams out, "Joke's on you, suities, I'm not wearing any panties."

The whole bar turns around and stares at Abby shaking her oversized booty. This girl and her accent are going to get us arrested.

She takes one look at Sebastian and immediately turns on her British charm. I'm a little surprised by her choice, because Martin has a more masculine look, with chiseled cheekbones and a sleek look about him, which I would assume most women would be attracted to. But there's something seriously sensuous and delicious about Sebastian that all girls are drawn to. "So where did this tall drink of boiling water come from?"

I walk away to refill my cocktail, ignoring the unsubtle hints Abby is throwing like axes. While I wait for my muddled mango mojito, I chat with a beautiful lady sitting next to where I'm standing. She's smoking a very long cigar, which I find odd, but the smell is much better than the bar cigarettes I'm accustomed to. My obvious stare catches her attention.

"Would you like to try?" She has a very strong accent, French, I believe, and I thank her but decline the offer. "Come on, live a little. You are too young to be so tight. Have some. It's Cuban."

Just as I reach for the cleverly wrapped tobacco, I am interrupted yet again by Sebastian, who is speaking French over me. The two kiss each other on each cheek and embrace like old friends. He takes the cigar out of her hand, puffing it down himself, and as he exhales directly at me states, "You know cigars are not good for you," then looks back at her.

"Oh, Sebastian, don't be fresh to the young girl."

My cocktail arrives just in time and I grab the cold glass and thank the pretty lady for the offer.

"Shane, please wait. May I introduce you?" He grabs my hand, so I turn to unlock his grip, nearly spilling my full drink onto another patron. The man sneers at me and walks off completely annoyed, and I don't blame him. Just then Abby walks up to see what we're doing, and within seconds, it is a crowd. I feel incredibly uncomfortable and want him to go or to leave myself. He puts his hand on my shoulder and without a full embrace says, "Shane, this is one of my longtime friends, Catherine. Catherine, I am pleased to introduce Miss Shane Lacy."

Interrupting Abby chimes in. "I am Abigail Bellamy."

The pretty French lady seems intrigued. "Yes, of course, how do you do?" Catherine is dressed in a smart, pure-white tailored suit fitted at the waist, breasts, and bottom. She is sitting up perfectly straight in her chair with a tall martini and has very short blond hair and exotic squinted makeup around her gleaming eyes, colored like an overripe banana. She doesn't seem impressed by Abby's intrusive ways, nor do a few other patrons who look her way. Catherine turns back around and continues smoking her cigar, eyeing me to try it, but I shake my head, declining.

Sebastian is trying to keep me here, but it makes me feel like a bartender trying to appease a drunk customer for a crappy tip. "Shane is a master of the spirits."

"Oh yes, what do you suggest I try next?" Her accent is sexy as hell. I can see why the Richies sail around France instead of around here.

I respond without thinking. "I like bourbon."

Sebastian turns his head sideways and says, "Really? I did not know that."

I ignore him and Catherine says, "I believe there is a lot we don't know about this young lady."

I smile politely at her and say, "I believe you are right." I think she is a lesbian and, to be honest, a very hot one at that. I am sure women and men flock to her sultry ways; she reminds me of a female French Sebastian. We talk for a few minutes about France, and I point to Simone, who is nuzzling with Martin, explaining that she used to sail there, like somehow that makes me cultured, too. Apparently, Catherine also spent her summers in the southern part of her country, in a small village called Saint-Jeannet in the mountains above the coast, where she found peace and tranquility from a hectic life. She is familiar with the areas that Simone and Sebastian sailed because she's yachted there, too. "Small world."

"Incredibly, isn't it?" We continue to chat for a few more moments until Abby comes back and says she's bored and ready to leave.

Sebastian turns and matter-of-factly states, like he's speaking to an infant, "We will leave when everyone is ready to leave."

She looks thoroughly annoyed and remarks, "Aren't you a bit of a cheeky yank." Then she turns to me and says, "Shane, I was talking to you, love. Are you ready or not?"

"Um, we can leave anytime, but let's check with Simone." I offer my hand to shake Catherine's, but she pulls me in, kissing my cheeks, and ends with a big moist one planted on my lips. I must be white as a ghost, because she laughs and says, "My darling, you need to try more things. Sebastian, take good care of this one." She also kisses him on each cheek but skips his lips, and we walk away with Abby pouting.

We meet up with Simone and Martin, who say they're ready whenever we are. I give Simone the wonky brow, knowing now she had reached out to Sebastian in order to get us all together despite my verbal pleas not to. We look around for the friend they brought and find he's smoking with a bunch of other people, including Catherine. When he makes eye contact with Martin, he walks away laughing and pats the backs of fellow comrades as he leaves. "Hey, what's up, are you ready? Wait, I don't think I got a chance to meet all of you. I'm Malakai Ackerman." He waves his hand toward me and says, "You must be Shane?"

I say hello and then he introduces himself to Simone, whose name he's also guessed correctly. Finally, he meets Abby, whom he seems taken aback by, and they immediately strike up a conversation, chatting like new crushes do. I have never seen her anxious, but she speaks a bit nervously to all of us. "How 'bout we get in the limmy and find somewhere to club."

I freeze, and Simone speaks for both of us. "Wait, dancing?"

"Yeah, why, which of yous doesn't like to shake your boots? Come on now." Abby seems completely freaked that someone doesn't want to dance, wiggling her shelf ass as a tease. It's me, and Simone knows it.

I don't say a word until we arrive at the club, when my nerves have spiked. We park in a line of limos and pile out in front of a club called "I." I remember seeing this place on TV when they were following douchey celebrities around town. It's supposed to be very chic, trendy, and difficult to get into according to the show's host. There's a long line rounding the corner, but it doesn't even faze this group, who follow Martin to a side door and are immediately let in. I feel invincible with these people. Then I think of all the others who are usually like me and used to waiting in long lines for hours.

We enter into an old paradise brought back from another era, modern nightlife with a flare of the roaring 1920s. I'm remembering now that this place was converted from someone's mansion on the ocean into a hit nightclub, but unlike in the quick clips on television, this place is more than magnificent, more like a Barron-type mansion. I must be staring in a buzzed state of awe, because the next thing I know, Sebastian wraps his arm around me to look at the same place I'm struck by. The club is bumping with music, crowds, and stunningly beautiful women with unimaginable bodies. Great! A hundred Simones who can dance. I can't move from the beauty of the entrance because it's so crowded with beautiful people. "It's pretty cool, isn't it?"

I just nod my head, and he ushers me inside and the door closes behind us. As I walk, I smear on more hot pink lipstick to give a fresh look and we head outside to where the club opens onto an enormous marble patio. We're on the second level, and the elaborate terrace overlooks the ocean and is held strong by fancy carved banisters. I'm in awe of the decor and ancient architecture and sit in amazement at our private table. Several bottles of champagne arrive, and suddenly a tsunami of surreal comes over me. We drink champagne for the second time tonight, after the first glass on the way to the club. I'm starting to feel pretty good, and my tense feelings about Sebastian begin to loosen. He is nothing but a gentleman around our group and never touches me in an affectionate way. The more I drink the more it bothers me, and I start to crave his attention. My internal pity party is broken up when Abby grabs my hand, yelling into my ear, "Come dance with me, love."

I shake my head no and Simone starts to laugh.

"Whatcha laughin' about? Get up and dance with me."

I shake my head again. "No. I am so sorry, sweetie, I can't."

"Sure ya can, get up and shake your bosoms alongside mine."

Malakai rises from his chair and gallantly takes Abby's hand, kissing it while kneeling, and says, "My royal lady, I would love to dance with you." We all smile at their ridiculous drama for each other, and thankfully they both head off to live it up on the palatial dance floor inside.

"So, if I ask you to dance, will you tell me no, too?"

"Yes," I state with conviction.

Simone nearly spits her champagne all over the table, clearly eavesdropping on our conversation. "Sebastian, darling, Shaney is many, many amazing things, but—"

"Seriously, Simone!"

"It's true, Sugar, and you know it."

Sebastian is curious and enjoys toying with me. "Tell me more. She is what, Simone?"

"Let's just say it's kind of like watching a wild mix of a hippie on acid, Elaine from *Seinfeld*, and someone having a seizure all at once."

Even I laugh, knowing it's completely true. I am the worst, most uncoordinated dancer that's ever existed. I cannot even bob my head to a song without looking like I'm twitching. When Simone and I were young, music videos were extremely popular, so we watched them in her media room and she saw firsthand how absurd I was. Desperately trying to teach me, she had tied strings from my wrists to my knees for the running man. I wanted to learn so bad so I could attend a dance at my school, but I broke the string and fell over, spraining my wrist.

"Oh, well, now we have to see this. What will it take to see Sugar Shane dance?"

I glare at Sebastian and intentionally fire back, "You can't buy this, Sebastian!"

He looks back at me, bewildered and even a little sad. Realizing I pushed it too far, I quickly backtrack by jokingly saying, "It's a gift," and everyone laughs. Inside joke, I think.

We continue to talk and watch all the club's people as they come and go all around us. I can't stop staring at the lights and boats in the distance, entranced by the majestic view.

"Do you see now why I love boats so much?"

I look away and under my breath say, "You mean yachts?"

He laughs and says, "Yes, you got me, yachts. In all fairness, I like boats, too."

I answer his question with honesty. "Of course I do. It would be absolutely amazing to live like that, views of the sea on all four sides, constantly moving and experiencing. If you saw where I live you would understand why I am in awe." I go to continue, but stop myself from opening up further, and he can tell.

"What?" he says.

"Nothing, I don't want to say anything about it. We just live differently, that's all. No big deal."

He looks annoyed.

"Okay, fine, promise me you won't get mad if I'm completely honest about it? I don't want to be offensive, that's not my intention. I guess I always feel better if I tell the truth, and you asked."

His eyes speak for him. "Never."

So for better or worse, I continue. "Okay, here goes. Don't be mad. The staff is overkill. It's not comfortable." He looks at me for more, so I give it to him. "I am sorry, I know you like it, but I didn't. I mean, it doesn't feel good having everyone do everything for you. There's no anonymity to it, and you can't just strip at the door and walk around naked, or eat Cheetos in bed, or answer your own doorbell, or blare the speakers to a great song. I'm not sure what I'm trying to say, but it doesn't feel like home. It has a very homey feeling inside and the decor is spectacular and perfect, but the only thing that truly feels real is the fish tank. All the art, furniture, and perfectly manicured people walking around are fake. I am sorry. I shouldn't be so rude, because I truly appreciate how beautiful it is, it's just not what I am used to. I cannot even imagine living someplace where I couldn't lie on the couch watching old reruns of *I Love Lucy* or *The Honeymooners*, mowing down on junk food in my comfy jammies. Never mind, I should stop. It's beautiful, it truly is an amazing home. I guess because I wasn't raised with it, other than my experience at Simone's, it all feels strange." I feel stupid for my jealous rant and think it's best for me to switch to water. Alcohol is causing too much truth in wine. But he surprises me and is kind beyond words.

"What's your house like?"

I laugh at the ignorance of his question. "Um, the truth?"

"Always." He speaks with a seriousness about him that I don't recognize.

"Okay, then I will tell you. It's four walls and they are thin. I know what the neighbors are doing and what they're planning before they do. I hear Ben, who lives on the left side, every morning at 8:00 a.m. because he jerks off every day at that time like clockwork. On the other hand, no pun intended, he's very nice and always waves to me, so I would never say anything, it's too embarrassing for both of us. On the right, there's my crackerjack, trashy neighbor whose boyfriend just got a big settlement for breaking his back on a quad, but he lied and put in an insurance claim with the pizza parlor where he used to work, and now the mafia is after him for their share. Should I keep going?"

"Yes, please, of course, Shane."

"I use cracked coffee cups for my morning joe because they're Williams Sonoma, and that's the fanciest name brand I've ever owned. I do strip naked at the door, because I work all night at the bar and as you now know, everyone smokes cigarettes and drinks heavily, so I end up smelling how they feel. I have bad furniture that I bought on layaway at a thrift store. I wash my clothes at a Laundromat, and sometimes if things are really tight I use coffee filters for toilet paper or steal rolls in my purse from work. There's one bedroom and a very tiny bathroom with broken tiles that cut your feet if you don't cover them with a towel, and a light that flickers constantly, giving you headaches. There's a whole host of other quirks and I could go on and on. But overall, it's better than I grew up with, and it's all mine. I work two jobs and go to school, all so I can pay the rent and have one place at the end of the night where I can spread out, strip naked, eat crap, and go to sleep. It's an apartment in a very shitty area of town where I hear bullets ring through the neighborhood more than a few times per week. To be completely honest, it's total shit, and the tag-sale curtains over my two foggy windows keep me separated from the outside world. They don't hide the noise or the streetlights, but they keep me safe so at the end of the day, I can go somewhere that's all mine, away from the customers who need me to please their every demand, whether it's because they need a drink or their diamond wasn't sparkly enough. At home, I get to just be me, and most of the time, it is just me."

I can feel the tears welling in my eyes, and he reaches over and touches my leg, spreading all his fingers over my knee as he listens. The cathartic release I just poured all over him feels like weights falling off the round of my shoulders. I have spouted on and on about how poor I am to probably the richest man in the world for all I know, and he just sat and listened. I am dreaming, I swear.

"You're in school?"

"Yeah, why?"

"What else don't I know about you?"

I laugh while wiping a growing tear from my left eye and say, "Lots and lots, but I am not nearly as interesting as you or Simone or Abby or probably Malakai for all I know? Your lives are incredible. Mine is monotonous."

"Actually, Shane, I was just thinking the opposite. Your life is incredible. Yes, we inherited large fortunes, and yes, we went to great schools with real silverware, but we weren't raised by either of our parents and certainly didn't know what home was. I traveled all the time, so home was wherever my nannies were. My mother was a maid when she met my father, working in a hotel that he stayed in while on business in Spain. She lived at home with seven brothers and sisters because her father died and my grandmother couldn't cope and became a severe manic-depressive and alcoholic. During his stay at the hotel, my father was struck by how bad she was at her job, so when he complained, she told him to do it himself. Here's my father, a rich American businessman in a foreign country, and the Spanish maid throws a rag at him and tells him to clean it himself. What I am saying is, that maid is my mother, and she has gotten very used to the lifestyle my father offers her, and of course that is fine, but I think she forgets her roots and doesn't keep in touch with any of her family. But you, Shane, you are real. I can never see you changing. You have seen what Simone has all your life and it never made you different. You don't seem comfortable eating or drinking expensive food or drinks; in fact, quite the opposite. But I think it's because you feel badly that you aren't sharing them with other people who you think are just like you. Instead, you spend time studying them and the room, taking it all in, absorbing all the experiences. I don't. I walk right past those people, because they all look the same to me. You remind me of what I imagine a child would do the first time they see a toy store or presents under the tree. You are full of possibility and wonder, and that is what impresses me most about you. I want to bottle what you have in order to feel again. I want to see again. When I am with you, I do both."

His words are fresh water in a sea of salt. I lean over and kiss him. Right in the open, I push my body into him, and he arranges his chair without ever letting go of me as I move in closer. I grab a chunk of his hair from the back of his head, pulling hard. The passion between us has me literally numb between my legs. His touch gives me shivers, and I want to straddle him on that outdoor couch over the ocean. As we kiss more heavily, not caring about anyone or anything around us, a loud crashing sound breaks our bond. We both look to see a frightened waitress who has dropped an entire tray, and some irate VIP is now screaming at her.

I unlock from him and run to intervene, because I am that waitress and I know what it's like to be treated like shit by a bastard customer. I'm caught by Sebastian, who places an arm on my shoulder to slow my move. I whip it back and keep going, but he urges me to stop, knowing intuitively I'd like to smack the asshole in the face. I bend down and help the poor girl pick up the broken pieces. I can see she is crying, and within earshot of the celeb, I say loudly, "Don't even listen one bit, he hasn't carried a thing for himself ever. If he had, he would have probably dropped way more than this. Plus, his penis is probably smaller than a pencil."

She smiles and sniffles, and says, "He'll make me pay for it. I can't lose this out of my check." Now I know and understand why she's so upset. We finish loading everything onto the tray, and by then a manager has arrived and is apologizing profusely to the table.

He turns in recognition of Sebastian, who says something to him in Spanish, and he nods his head, saying, "Of course, Mr. Kane, of course."

Next thing I know, the table of socialites is being moved elsewhere, and the waitress is reassigned to us. I whisper to Sebastian, "They are going to make her pay for it."

"No, they aren't."

"She said they are. I feel really bad."

"Shane, it's taken care of."

I don't say another word and introduce myself to the girl, learning her name is Sarah and she just recently moved here from some tiny town in Massachusetts none of us have heard of.

"Thank you. Thank you so much. I'm so sorry. I really am. Most people in this section aren't like you."

Sebastian beams, because I don't think he's used to being categorized in that way. He puts his hand on her arm and says, "Don't worry about anything, you are doing a stellar job."

She smiles at his good looks and charming, soft-spoken way, leaving the table blushing. "See, you just made her day. Thank you."

A look of panic comes over his face. "Oh my god, Shane, your hand."

I look down to see blood dripping everywhere, making the marble floor resemble a Jackson Pollock. Sebastian ushers me like a parent with his sick child, asking the first employee we see for the bathroom. The man begins bringing us through the crowd to the public restrooms, and Sebastian says, "No, I want your bathroom!"

The man sighs loudly but walks us through a long hallway and down the stairs to a private and unoccupied restroom. "Get us some bandages, she's hurt."

"I am okay, it's fine." I reach for the faucet, but Sebastian makes me sit down, taking my hand under the cold water, delicately rinsing it and checking for hidden shards. I relax and let him do the work while another man comes in with a first aid kit offering to help, but Sebastian tells him to leave. He gets the bleeding under control and wraps my hand in gauze, reexamining it to make sure he hasn't missed anything. I smile in admiration as I watch him at work. "You should have been a doctor."

"I wanted to be."

"What happened?"

"It wasn't what my family had planned."

I feel bad for him. "There is nothing worse than being pushed into areas of work you don't find interesting." I know this firsthand.

"It's fine, I love what I do, but it's a different kind of rewarding, that's all. My father knew what he was doing. He made the right decision way before I knew what it was."

While I sit in the bathroom chair with my hand wrapped like a mummy, feeling tipsy and already exposed, I decide to ask him what I've been wondering all along. "Sebastian, may I ask you something?"

"Always."

"If you are being truthful about all the things you said, why do you want to pay me, and for what? It doesn't make sense. You can have any girl you desire."

He lets go of my hand and faces the door. "We should let everyone know where we are. It's been a while since we last saw them."

I am lost. He was so tender just seconds ago and now he wants to leave. I feel awful asking the question, but I need answers. It's a mystery to me why he or anyone else would want an unfaithful, unpolished girl from the wrong side of town who can't and will never be able to tell the difference between flank steak and Wagyu beef. I don't belong with him, and I deserve to know why he wants me. "I am serious, Sebastian."

He stops at the door and turns around. "You need money and I have it. You make me happy, and that is rare for me. But remember, Shane, this is not a relationship, it's an arrangement."

I should never have asked, what the fuck was I thinking. Sometimes, you shouldn't ask questions you don't want the answers to. I feel like vomiting in the stall behind me. I squeeze by him under the arch of his elbow that is propping open the door and go in search of Simone. I sprint past the crowds of people and see Abby grinding with Malakai on the dance floor, drink in one hand, his ass in the other. I don't see Simone anywhere, so I leave through the front door and look for a cab. The driver who brought Sebastian and me around the other night yells out my name. "Shane, Miss Shane." I turn and move toward him and he sees that I'm crying. "Come on with me. I'll take you wherever you need to go."

"No, I'll get a cab. I can't do this anymore."

He pleads with me. "Please, Miss Shane, I will get in trouble if I don't look after you. Please get inside. I will take you anywhere you would like to go."

Reluctant and vulnerable, crying in my sleeve, I agree and ask if I can sit up front.

"Yes, of course, whatever you'd like."

I tell him to take me to the hospital. We sit in silence for a few blocks until he finally speaks. "It's none of my business, but are you okay?"

I answer with complete honesty, because I have nothing left to lose. "No, I'm a mess and my entire life is upside down. I don't know what to do. I hate myself. I am a terrible human being."

He doesn't say anything for what feels like five or more minutes, and then he finally speaks. "I have no idea what this is all about, maybe it's the injury on your hand or maybe in your heart, but my boss thinks you're very special."

I start to stop him from going any further, but he continues.

"It is not my place to say this, but he thinks there is something different about you. I never see him like this. He has been acting differently. He hasn't worked much since he met you. Please, Miss Shane, don't repeat this, I would lose my job."

I feel sick to my stomach because I realize now that we both have feelings for each other, but then I remember what he so clearly stated. "Well, he's got us both fooled, because he just told me it's an arrangement." I cannot help crying again and pull a pill from my purse and pop it in my mouth.

"Anything you need, Miss Shane. Just name it."

I thank him without looking at his face and exit the door.

I've arrived at my mother's hospital. When I stop at the nurse's station to learn where they've put her this time, they tell me it isn't visiting hours but allow me through anyhow, seeing how distraught I look. Upon entering her room there are IVs everywhere, attached to her in all directions, pumping fluids into her body. I feel better knowing that she's accepting their help. She looks like she's sleeping, but when I move in closer I can see her eyes are slanted and staring straight ahead. I whisper, "Hi, Mother."

"Oh hi, Shaney, what are you doing here? It's late, honey." I want to tell her everything, lie on her lap and cry my eyes out to her. I assume that's what mothers do for daughters, or at least that's what television teaches us. Right now, I need a movie moment, but that's not who she is. "Whatever it is, you can tell me or not tell me. But I am here for you. I have always been here for you, sweetie."

And just like that, I am sucked back into her manipulative and "kind" ways. "Mother, I'm a bad person. I have no idea what I am meant to do or be. I just know what I'm doing isn't right. I don't recognize myself. I need Jake to be back so everything can be normal again. He keeps things flat and safe."

Her voice is groggy and dry, which surprises me considering the amount her body is drinking. "Sweetie pie, let me teach you something and don't forget it. Just because it makes you feel better, doesn't mean it makes them feel better. Some secrets are meant to be just that, secrets." She lifts her blankets and invites me next to her. I accept the love and snuggle in with ample room under the covers, falling asleep on the extra pillow.

~~~~~~~~~~

From One Cuckoo's Nest to Another

I awake the next day to my mother cracking jokes with the therapy team. They enter the room and speak to both of us about their next plans for her. "We want you to develop a list of safe foods and to read the literature we gave you about the importance of hydration over food."

"Are they releasing you?" I notice the needles and tubes have been removed.

"Yes, sweetie. I'm all fixed."

I go to the bathroom, where I overhear the staff through the walls, talking about how they need to clear the room because she doesn't have any insurance and "that crazy lady needs a lot more care."

Vivi and Rob enter and pack her stuff. I say my goodbyes, buzz

Vivi's finger, and wish my mother well, still grateful for the love she showed me last night.

I drive home to change out of last night's clothes and ready myself for tonight's shift. I listen to two voice mails on my phone. The first is Patti asking me to call her at the store and the second is my teacher looking for an outline of the paper. I had almost forgotten about the fucking paper and am frantically planning how I can get an extension. I wonder if he would feel pity for me because of my mother's illness and give some leniency? He's crazy, she's crazy, he should understand.

My phone rings with an unknown number, and I answer. It's Simone. "Where are you? What happened? I'm freaking out. I have no idea where you went, and I couldn't get a hold of Sebastian."

"Oh, I'm fine. I just needed to go last night, that's all. I'm headed home now. I need to work tonight."

She sounds stressed. "No, come here! I have Vivi's party planned for tomorrow and Abby is leaving tomorrow, too. But you haven't told me where you went? I finally talked to Sebastian this morning and he said his driver took you to the hospital? Or that's what we heard. Is Aggie okay? What's going on? I am literally panicking here wondering what happened! Tell me!"

"Really, I'm fine. I just needed to be alone last night. I spent the night with my mother and this morning they released her."

"Oh good! She'll be able to come to the party tomorrow at the Ritz. They have a banquet area. Please, it's really important, we celebrate it every year."

"Her birthday? How old is she?"

"No, it's not her birthday. It's called Vienne's Day. It's the day I found out I was pregnant. It was a fucking disaster, so I turned it into something good. So now every year, we celebrate Vivi's day. Just come, it's really fun and you've missed all her others."

"Are you serious, Simone, with the guilt? I didn't even know about her never mind a whole day dedicated to a positive pregnancy test." I am being snappy and feeling sorry for myself. Sebastian is consuming my thoughts, and when I talk to Simone, I think about him. "Okay, I'll try and get the day off. It's going to be tough because it feels like I haven't been working at all."

"Just try and get to the party, and don't bring anything. She doesn't need anything. It's at 3:00 p.m. Try to come early so we can catch up."

"Okay, I'll try. I promise."

"Oh, and Shane?"

"Yeah?"

"That's what the money's for. So you can take a day off when you need one."

I don't say anything and we both hang up and I begin the long drive home. I stop on the way and buy food for Andrew. When I get inside the apartment, I perform my usual habit of changing the dirty water and picking up the poop scattered on the mulch and fake sod. He gobbles up two crickets and leaves a third jumping around the tank. My slimy little son is hungry.

I leave for work a couple hours early to stop at the jewelry store to talk to them about tomorrow. When I walk in, I can tell something is wrong. Patti stops what she's doing with her customer and ushers Skylar to take over. We both head to the back room, and I lip "What's wrong?" but she pushes me along with her fingertips on my back. We step into the kitchen area and she peeks around the sides of the doorway to make sure she can speak freely and says, "Sweetie pie, I am so, so sorry."

"Um, about what?" My gut drops to my ankles. I can literally feel bad news coming.

"Honey, they are laying you off."

"What the hell? I have worked here forever. Is Skylar leaving, too? Who else is laid off? What about you?"

She places her hand on my shoulder in a motherly way and says, "Only you that I know of."

"How could this happen? I didn't do anything. I don't understand."

"I know, I know. I am told it's because of the amount of days that you missed."

"What the hell? I thought the people high up approved it?" So many things are running through my head, and I am really scared. I've never been fired from anything, and Jake is going to kill me.

"They did, but no one told the manager, so he thought you were just calling out. I tried to explain, I swear I did. I guess he tried to call corporate, but they didn't have any record of anything. I told him again that it was a personal favor from the owner, but he hasn't been able to reach him. Trust me, I fought like hell over this. I am really mad. I know you had a favor called in, but he thinks you just skipped work." She's tearing up and her Italian hands are flailing in defense of my innocence.

"Thank you, Pattie. I know you did everything you could, but I just got that big order. I thought they were happy with me? I am so sorry. I never take days off but these have been emergencies." I hate bringing up Sebastian, but if it's to save my own ass, I'm willing to sacrifice.

"I know, honey, I tried. I really, really did." Then she whispers in my ear, "It doesn't help that dipshit newbie over here is hooking up with Kenneth."

Honestly, any other time I would love to gossip about our manager, but this is more than bad timing. It's been a week of one thing after another, and I'm not sure how much more I can take. I want to cry and slam things, but instead I ask what to do from here.

"Here's your check. Please come visit anytime. If you need anything at all, I am always here for you. I know you didn't do anything wrong. I am so sorry, honey."

I don't bother collecting my mug from the kitchen or telling them to wish my customers my best. I walk out stunned, beaten down, and shamed by the embarrassment of trusting yet another person who has fucked me over.

Regular Friends

I head for the bar, arriving an hour early. I chew up a pill in my car and take a few long yogic breaths before walking inside.

"Hey, kiddo, did you hear the news?" asks Derek, a seven-days-a-week regular.

I am blindsided, expecting more bad. "Nope, what now? Please tell me something good."

"It's great, actually. Someone donated a bunch of money."

"Money? For what?"

"To hire a private investigator to find out who killed the Vet, and $50,000 to get cars for other vets who need them."

The professor is back, and I couldn't be more pleased to see him sitting at his corner stool. He looks happy, even, when Al, who is consistently drunk and always cheerful, talks about "all the fucking money for our buddy, our favorite hero. We will miss that Vet. Can you believe it, Shane?"

I look to Ye Ol, who has a slight grin on his face and winks when he catches me staring. "I can't believe someone did that," I say. "Does anyone know who it was? It's incredible news and finally a clue that the universe doesn't hate me."

"What's a matter, Shaney? Why is this the only good thing? What's wrong, do you need a drink?"

I smile at his drunken concern as he steps off his stool, ready to head behind the counter. "Thank you, I'm okay. I lost my job at the jewelry store today. They laid me off."

Shouts come from all directions. "Stupid pricks with diamonds stuck up their asses!" "They don't know what they're doing!" "Sucky news, girlfriend." "Fireballs for Shaney, the girl needs a shot!"

I'm laughing at all these characters yelling and screaming for me. It feels good to be wanted.

A young girl I've never seen interrupts the caring chants. "Can you get me a drink? I don't know you, but sorry you lost your job.

Wait, not this one, right?"

I crack a smile and pour her a beer. I look at my loving but sorry group of regulars and say, "Fireballs sound good to me, but sorry, boys, my income just got cut in half."

Ye Ol fingers me over, hands me a hundred-dollar bill, and instructs me to get everyone a shot, including myself, and to keep the change. I tell him it's way too much, but he insists it's what his friend would have wanted, so he'll have two. I appreciate the gesture, and at this point, I'm overwhelmed and scared of Jake's reaction.

The rest of the night goes on as usual, and when Dave walks in, it reminds me of tomorrow's party. If it weren't for Vivi, I wouldn't even attempt to take another night off, especially since learning that Simone inadvertently got me canned. Dave walks by and I grab his arm and ask if he can cover tomorrow's shift for me, explaining I need to spend more time with my mother, who was released from the hospital today. He isn't buying my bullshit.

"You know what, Shane, you have been so stressed lately, why don't you take a couple days off."

"No, that's not what I need, it's fine. I'll be here tomorrow. I can't lose both jobs in one night."

Then his charcoal soul feels sorry for me and he caringly puts his arm around mine. "I am serious. I've known you for a long time, and your job isn't going anywhere. Take my advice, get your shit together and we will cover it."

I reluctantly agree, though I'm still nervous to accept, and we discuss my returning in four or five days. "Will you tell my regulars? I don't want them to think I got fired here, too."

"Yes, I will talk to your friends. Don't worry, we will survive a few days without you. I'm not sure Eddie will, but everyone else will be fine. Go see your mom. Take it easy, whatever, just don't come back for a few nights. I think you need it, plus I probably owe you some vacation time or some government shit like that, so don't

worry, your check will be all set, but without the tips, of course."
He can't stand being so nice to me.

"Thank you, Dave." I hug him tight and he kisses me on the
cheek. Great, I probably have herpes now.

I tend bar for the rest of the night with few disruptions, and
overall it's smooth operating. I do miss the banter between the Vet
and Ye Ol, who left this evening right after the round of shots. I
envied their relationship and am saddened by its tragic end. They
were complete opposites, but their friendship was honest, brought
together by booze and loneliness, like all the great ones are.

When the night is over, I check all the knobs, locks, and doors
like I always do, and it seems Eddie is here to walk me out with the
others. "Thank you, Eddie. You should have gone home hours ago."

"No, it's fine, I always have stuff to do, stocking and such. Are
you all set to get home safe? And hey, is your mom alright?"

"Yes, I will be okay, and thanks, she is doing much better. You
know, we both have crazy moms." He laughs and gets in his Jeep,
driving away, and I do the same.

When I get back home, I follow my usual routine of stripping
at the door, and just as I go to jump in the shower, my phone rings
and I stupidly answer, standing buck naked in the living room.
"Hey you. How are you? What's going on? Where has my wife been
lately?"

"Um, well, all over, actually. Hi. How are you? My mother was
in the hospital, so I've been with her, and then I went out with
Simone and her friend from Britain one night, but besides that,
home." Why did I say that? I don't even believe my own mistruths.

"Oh, I tried to call you, but you never answer, so I got kind
of worried. There's not a ton to do out here but think, so you can
imagine where my mind goes."

I don't want to ruin his trip, and truthfully, I'm too emotionally exhausted to get into a long, drawn-out conversation about
money, deception, and infidelity. So I decide to keep it light and

avoid telling him that we will most likely lose electricity and the entire apartment by next month, not to mention that I'm lying and cheating for money. I have to keep it a secret. He can never know, and just thinking about it floods my brain with Sebastian, which is where I want to leave it all, forever. I don't want his fucking money. "Everything is fine, just tired, that's all. When are you coming home?"

"Sweets, we are doing great besides me worrying and thinking about you all the time. The fishing and hunting has finally taken off. The guys and me are like we were back in the day, having a blast together. I feel good and I would never leave, if I didn't miss you so much. I know I've said it before, but it will be different when I get back. It will be better. I will get you everything you deserve, even if we both have to work three jobs."

I think, Hmmm, only two jobs to go, unless you count my brief stint as a prostitute as the second? "Thanks, Jake, that's so sweet. I miss you, too. What day are you back, so I can plan for it?"

"Oh yeah, it should be four or five days and I'll be back. It all depends if this windfall of bucks keeps up. We traveled a bit farther this year to catch the game out here, but it's been worth it."

"Okay, sounds great, I will see you soon and miss you." We say our goodbyes and both hang up. Then it hits me. I have at least four full days to "get my shit together," to paraphrase Dave, all four of which will not be spent working. That's way too much time on my hands.

We All Need Some Good

I wake in the morning with nowhere to rush to, so I clean the apartment in preparation for Jake's return. I get ready for Vivi's day, and stop by the bank to deposit my last check from Stein's and then get gas before heading out early in hopes of finding something small Vivi might like. Hope is acting up, so I'm nervous about all this driving back and forth between old and new lives. I plug forward, but she stalls in stop-and-go traffic on the highway and overheats. I remember Don telling me to blast the heat when this happens, and it works, so I beg her for a little bit farther.

I arrive safely at the Ritz surprisingly on time but very much empty-handed. I don't know how to talk to Simone about my job, but I tell myself this isn't the right time or place anyway. When I get inside, I follow instructions from the bellman, who is always overly sweet and offers to walk me to the party room. I arrive to see a mini-trampoline in one corner with a child bouncing, a magician in a tuxedo showing tricks to my mother, and a few kids running around playing tag. The room is professionally decorated and there are Disney princesses everywhere who look just like the ones on her covers.

Simone spots me and comes running over to say hello, snagging a glass of champagne from a waiter on her way. I talk to her about how cute the room looks and ask if there's anything I can do to help. She says no, that the planner is here and will arrange for the caterers to start the food and activities shortly. She inquires about the other night, but I brush it off, saying that Sebastian isn't right for me and how I need to focus on Jake coming home.

"But the money is so good, Shaney."

"I know it is, and I know it's working for you, but I can't do it to my husband. Sebastian was really nasty to me the other night, and I just can't deal with the drama. I am sure he will have zero problem finding another girl, trust me."

She drops the subject, still bewildered that I would pass on such a lucrative opportunity considering my current situation. I change the subject to Vivi, which keeps me from exploding about Stein's. "So where's Vivi?"

"Oh, Esmerelda should be here any minute. In fact, I wonder where she is? Oh and Abby is supposed to be coming, too. Did you know she has been with Malakai since the other night? They are crazy about each other. Funny how that stuff happens."

"Well, she certainly doesn't need the money."

Simone snaps back. "He's not paying her, Shane, and she leaves for England tonight, so leave it alone."

I do. A few seconds later, Vivi enters the room and everyone claps. She is wearing the most adorable, fluffy dress, resembling a true royal mute princess if there ever was one. She doesn't crack a smile at the attention nor the scene of her party. Her hair is still wispy, but it appears the nanny has at least tried to comb through it. She has glitter on her cheeks, and everyone is oohing and aahing over her dress, which looks custom-made for today. I walk over to say hello, and she extends her little finger and I buzz her with mine. I look forward to our little chats, and in a way I think she does, too, though who knows, because words are never exchanged.

The food comes out on sterling silver platters, along with mini–spritzer sodas with juice for the kids and assorted craft cocktails for the adults. I order a virgin drink because I need to bolt as quickly as I can to enjoy my time off and work on my paper, or at least start it. Not to mention if Hope breaks down I cannot be slurring my words to a cop.

The food is delicious and even includes tiara-shaped grilled cheeses for the kids and specially decorated foods made to look like wands, jewelry, and other princessy things. The adults feast on a raw bar, pâté, escargot, foie gras, and other French delicacies. While people are chatting and kids are playing, almost everyone stops in their tracks when they hear Abby swearing from down the hall, making a grand entrance. She is wearing another ridiculous outfit and black eyeliner that curves upward around her eyes and ruby red lipstick smeared on her full lips. The almost-glued-on green leather overalls have her ass bulging out the back, and a see-through shirt underneath barely covers her giant breasts. My mother isn't impressed and makes it obvious with a loud sigh, and neither are some of the other guests, who stare and whisper. Despite her embarrassing nature, a few pathetic starstruck fans try to strike up a conversation with the infamous Abigail Bellamy but fail when she states directly to them, "I talk to whomever the bloody fuck I want, and at this particular moment, I don't see myself talking to you people."

I hang around Vivi, who is standing in a corner alone. The other kids are playing games and bustling around taking pictures with the surprise real-life Disney princess, but she still looks unhappy.

"Do you want to go and see the magician?" She doesn't give an inclination toward yes or no, so I take her little hand and usher her to meet him.

On our way, Abby walks up to say hello and notices the little person attached to my arm. She bends down, nearly splitting her pants, and says in her natural British accent, "You must be Simone's mini-muffin?" She doesn't move, not a smile or a budge, just stares at Abby's face. She seems as enamored as the other guests, and I giggle to myself at the most obvious person in the room. I open my mouth to tell Abby she's shy, but she continues talking and Vivi remains silent, unwavering from her stare. Narcissistic Abby takes it personally, moving in closer to Vivi, examining her young face and says, "Are you mongoloid?"

"Jesus, Abby, you have to be kidding me. No, she's not, she's just quiet. Leave her alone."

"Get over yourself, darling, the kid's bloody retarded. Look at her. Aw, poor Simone."

I can't believe what I'm hearing, this bitch has no boundaries. Simone walks over, excited to see Abby, and says, "Oh, you met Vivi, my little princess?"

"Yeah, darling, something's wrong with your young'un. Let's get out of here, I want to have some fun before I'm homebound."

I'm in utter shock and disgust when Simone doesn't react to her poor manners but asks if I'm ready to go, too.

"Um, no, that's okay. I'm going to visit with my mother for a bit. You don't want to stay until everyone's gone?"

"Silly Shane. That's what I pay people for. If you change your mind, just call me, we will send a car. Are you sure you don't want to come?"

Abby leans in, giving me a hug, and I find my arms robotically responding even though she makes me sick. I want to spit in her face for her what she said to Vivi. "Safe trip home!"

"Thanks, darling, come visit with Simone, I'll show you how royalty lives."

I think, if it's anything like you, I don't want to meet another Brit in this world. Then I remind myself there's no way, she's one of a kind, and I feel bad for her country. "Bye guys."

Simone leaves without even a look at her daughter, so I distract her with the magician, who has witnessed the entire interaction. I glance at Vivi, who looks even more miserable, and ask, "You don't want to do this, do you?" She looks up at me and her eyes are welling with water and her lip is quivering. "Come on, pumpkin, let's go. I have something for you."

We walk past the guests and only my mother notices, assuming I'm kidnapping the honored guest. "Shane, what are you doing?"

"Mother, I have a surprise for her. I will bring her back to your house. Does that work? Or should I ask Esmerelda?"

Even she can see through this charade that's obviously for adults and agrees to let me go. "No, honey, my house is fine. I will see you then. Be careful, and make sure she wears her seat belt."

I never let go of her hand all the way to my car and, like before, open her door and she climbs in. We drive to the pier and I tell her, "I hope they're here. It's your special day and you made a wish, right?" She nods her head yes. "Okay, then he will definitely be here."

We move closer toward the ocean water, looking all around, even whistling, but nothing happens. A few more minutes pass, and I talk aloud for them to hear, but I worry my plans are a bust.

All of a sudden, I've lost her little grip and she is running. I look up and there it is, Good and Vivi running for each other. They meet in the sand and she falls down laughing and giggling. He licks her lips, forehead, cheeks, everywhere, all while he romps around her and she keeps giggling. Her dress is covered in sand, but I don't care because this is the happiest I've ever seen her. The homeless man comes from his makeshift house, yelling at first, then, realizing the scene, looks on in his own kind of admiration. His lion of a dog is making a very sad girl *good*. I wave hello but he walks away.

"Wait, please." He puts up his hand in disregard, but I call again. "Please, please wait." I'm running after him, the whole time checking behind me to see if Vivi is okay, and she is, playing like a child. I finally catch up to him underneath the rafters, where his house sits erect, and ask if I can please stay for a few minutes while they play. I go on to explain why, but he wanders inside, so I don't intrude any farther.

"Please, she's a really sweet girl and, well, you met her mother, but I think mostly she's unhappy. Please, sir, I don't think she gets much attention. Actually, I don't know why she's sad, all I know is that dog of yours is the only thing I've seen that even makes her smile. In fact, the only time I've ever seen her react at all is when she sees your dog. We've seen others and she doesn't flicker, but with yours she lights up." I speak louder, unsure if he's listening or can hear me. I need him to understand the odd bond between them. "Please, may we just hang out for a bit? She had a . . . I mean, we both had a really shitty day. Please."

He shows his arm through the flap, handing me something. It's a very dirty and ugly ball of fuzz resembling the fluorescent color of an old tennis ball. "Here, for them," he mumbles.

"Oh, okay, thank you." I run down the beach to where Vivi and Good are running around and give her the ball. I tell her to throw it for him and that he will bring it back. Her infectious giggly laugh has me smiling ear to ear. I love seeing this sweet soul happy, even if what's causing it is a homeless, gigantic, scarred-up pit bull with half its ear missing.

I walk back to the man's home and see he's out, and I'm excited for his company. He's set up a large blanket on the sand and points for me to sit. "Are you hungry?"

"Um, not really, we ate a few hours ago, but thank you."

"Well, it's my dinnertime and I was working on it when you showed up. If you're gonna hang around, then you better eat, but I need her at a distance, okay? They can eat down there."

The request seems weird, but I agree because this whole scenario is strange, and I cannot help being drawn to his obscurity.

"It's about ready, we'll eat out here. Does that work for you?"

"Yes, of course. May I help with anything?"

"Nope, I just don't want her up here, that's all I need help with."

I nod again in affirmation of his request, knowing I can't separate those two if they come up here, even if I try. He disappears for a minute or two and comes back holding a large plate with steam rising from it. Upon closer look, I can see it's spaghetti with shrimp and buttered French bread.

"This is for them. Can you take it to them? The dog will eat whatever she doesn't want. Does she like soda?"

I'm overwhelmed with the food and robotically grab the soda can and head back down the beach. "Look, Vivi, the doggie's owner made you dinner. He said whatever you don't eat you can share with Good." She looks at the food I've laid upon her sandy lap and back at me. She pulls a single noodle from the pile, slurping it up with an exaggerated sound, and without taking her eyes off of me, she places the entire plate onto the sand for the patiently waiting and salivating dog. I laugh out loud because she did exactly what I asked. She drinks straight from the can, even offering some to Good, which he licks from the top. "Oh gosh, Vivi, no, sweetie, doggies have germs that—" And before I can finish, she's already taking another swig. I shake my head and leave it be.

I arrive back at the blanket and there's a matching plate sitting ready for me with real silverware on the side and another can of orange soda. I start explaining what just unfolded between the two, but he seems disinterested in my story.

"You know, I saw you that night you were around here."

"I know, I am so sorry. My friends were total assholes and I am really, really sorry."

"No, not them—and yes they are—but the guy. You need to be careful of him. He's not a good man."

"Do you mean Sebastian?"

"Yes."

It reminds me that I haven't thought about him since I got here. I look toward the water at the sun beginning to set and say, "Are you serious, what do you mean? How do you know him and the girls?" I take a few bites of my incredibly delicious food that would be rude not to eat, but he ignores the question.

He jumps over the conversation, changing it completely, and says, "There's shrimp because I don't eat meat. It's not humane. But the shrimp, I think they're pretty dumb, plus I like them."

"Sir, you really confuse me."

I blurt it out like an idiot and expect a grouchy reaction, but he laughs and says, "Oh yeah, me too."

"I don't think we've ever properly met, my name is Shane Lacy Dell, I live over an hour from here but I grew up really close. Well not that close, not near the ocean. I didn't exactly have the lifestyle that my friends did."

He interrupts. "Not the bad manners, either. My name is Sam." We shake hands and formerly meet. "So, Mrs. Dell, do you like brownies?"

I shiver at the formality and reminder of marriage. "Yes, of course, who doesn't?"

He carries out a small tray of delicious, moist, and densely thick brownies, and I offer to take some below but he stops me, saying the dog can't have chocolate. "Of course. I'm sorry to say, but this is actually the nicest dinner I've had in quite some time. And believe me, lately it has been a roller coaster of experiences, but this food is amazing. Anyhow, why do you live here? Were you a chef before? I'm sorry, I didn't mean it that way. I don't know what to say. I'm sorry."

He takes a couple deep breaths, probably pondering whether to respond to me or kick me out for being like Simone and Abby. "First of all, why are you surprised and sorry that the food is good?"

Before I can choke out more embarrassing and untactful words, he continues. "I live in this exact location because, wouldn't you? It's magnificent. I have an oceanfront home without the taxes or mortgage. But your question is not where I live, but why? Do you mean alone, or because I look homeless? Because, Mrs. Dell, I'm not. I have a home and food and books, even a dog."

"I am so sorry. I feel like I may have overstayed my welcome?"

"Don't be sorry, Mrs. Dell. I will be honest with you. The reason why I am here is because I agreed to be. It works for me and it works for those around me. I will live here in my oceanfront palace until the day I die. This is my home, and besides interruptions, it's fairly quiet."

I smile at the thought of home. The fact that it can be anywhere to anyone has so many different meanings. "Home is a complicated topic."

"Yes, it is, I can relate to that statement."

Just then Vivi runs up with a clean plate in her hands, completely sand stained and dirty from head to toe. I offer her some of my leftover brownie, but I can literally feel Sam's uneasiness with her around.

"Maybe it's time for you to get on your way. The dog and I need to get some sleep."

I look to Vivi's disappointed face. "It's time for him to go in, okay?" I tell her.

She runs over, hugging Sam's legs, then just as fast wraps her skinny arms around Good's wide neck, kissing him goodbye on the nose. "Good. Good boy."

He drops the ball from his mouth. "Wow, Vivi, great job. Look how happy he is when you talk to him." She kneels down on the blanket and whispers more words in his ear but stops when I lean in to listen. He turns and licks her on the face but I tell her we need to get her back. She reluctantly lets go of his neck, and I offer again to help clean up, but Sam ushers me off with his hand.

I wonder how he does dishes or where the stove was? The man is a living curiosity, and I completely forgot to ask him about the sandwiches.

I DRIVE BACK TO MY mother's, speeding the whole way, after seeing how many times she has called my cell. When we arrive, I walk in to her serving dinner to Rob in his lazy recliner. She spots me and holds up a bottle of Poland Spring water and says, "See, I'm doing it."

"I can see that, Mother, but it's not food. What did you add to your safe list today?"

"Honey, I don't want to do this right now, tell me about what you and Vivi did?"

She looks down to a brown-stained child sporting a huge smile on her face. "Oh my God, are you serious, Shane, she is disgusting. Look at the dress. Vivi, get ready for the bath, I will be right in."

She walks away, head down, and her regular affect returns.

"Mother, she's fine and happy, look at her. Plus, you can't give her a bath, there's freaking mushrooms growing in there, seriously. Where's Simone? Or Esmerelda or Beatrice?"

"Oh, I don't know. It's fine, I told Esmerelda I can take her for the night. I like having her here. She's good company, and don't worry, I will just have her rinse off in a bucket. You turned out okay, right?"

"Um, okay? Mother, I've never taken a bath here, not even as a kid. You can't do that to her. Simone would be appalled. Whatever, I'm heading back. Do you want me to get you some special groceries or anything before I head out?"

"No, that's okay. Rob took me to the parking lot of the hospital today so I could try some saltines."

"The hospital, why did you go there?"

"Oh, I feel safer there. If anything happens we're right at the emergency room entrance."

I can't believe the extent of insanity in this home and would love to scoop up Vivi and drive her to my apartment, but I know I can't. "Mother, are you listening to yourself? And you want Vivi to stay here. Does Simone know this? Well, whatever works, as long as you're eating."

"Oh Shaney, stop being so uptight. If you really can't stay, then drive safe, and when will I see you again? Anytime soon?"

"I don't know, Mother. Jake comes back in a few days and I need to get things ready."

"I would love to see him again."

I pause. "Okay, Mother, bye." I walk out the door shouting bye to Vivi, but she comes barreling down the hall buck naked to buzz my finger and hug my legs. Then she runs back to the bathroom, slamming the door.

"Whoa, what did you do with her?"

"She's a very cool kid," I say and walk to my car, ignoring her further prodding from the doorway, waving as I pull away.

Doritos, Doobs, and a Do-si-do

While I'm driving, the phone rings, with no name. I answer, thinking it's Jake again, but instead it's Sebastian. He's soft-spoken and not as confident, so much so that I almost don't recognize his voice.

"Shane, please don't hang up, just listen to me."

I pull over and unload on him, pouring it all out along with more tears. This guy fucks me up so much that I can't hold anything in. "Sebastian, I have nothing to talk to you about. I know exactly how you feel, and I don't know why it bothers me, but it does. I'm not doing this anymore. I made a big fucking mistake and I feel horrible about it. My husband comes back in a few days, I lost my goddamn job, and now I am unknowingly hooking for money. I can't take much more, I don't do well with stress, and I'm not sure what you are used to, but this is fucking stressful. I—"

"Shane, please, please listen to me. Please come here, can you come over? It's very important that I see you. I don't want to beg, but I just might have to."

"Seriously, Sebastian. I'm not doing it. I need to stay away, stop calling me!"

"Shane, don't hang up. Please. I'm sorry to hear about your friend at the bar."

"Wait, are you kidding me? Are you the one who donated all that money? It's a wonderful thing, but . . ." I keep ranting through blurry eyes and a watery mouth until he talks above me.

"Shane, it doesn't matter who did, it's not about you or me. Everyone deserves to know what happened and bring him justice, for Christopher David's sake."

I can't argue because it's kind, thoughtful, and generous and reminds me of the silly banter between him and the professor. I didn't even know the Vet's real name until now. "You are right. Thank you. I appreciate it. I know they do, too."

"Will you come over?"

"Seriously, Sebastian, what could be so important? Why, why do I have to see you? Can't we do this over the phone?"

"Just please come, do you want me to pick you up?"

I pause to think about it, but I know where to go. While listening to his pleading, I have already turned my car around and am heading toward the marina. "Fine, I will come, but then I'm going straight home, no bullshit, okay?"

"Fine, we can discuss it when you get here. I will see you soon. I'll let the guard know you're coming." He hangs up without saying goodbye, an annoying habit that I'm sick of.

My heart palpitates knowing I will see him soon. What was I thinking? I have dirty feet and sandy pants and garlic breath from Sam's homemade dinner. I pull to the side of the road and smear on some lipstick, blot, pop a pill, pull the powder sponge over my nose and under my eyes, and head back into traffic.

When I get to the gate, the man checks me in with a single white flower, a lily, and a handwritten note. I thank him but he says it's from Sebastian. "Have a great night, Miss Lacy."

I break the stem tucking it behind my ear and slide my finger under the shiny blue seal on the back of the note. Inside, handwritten in perfect black calligraphy, it says, "I'm sorry, Sugar."

I go to walk aboard, but he's waiting with a hand perched for me to hold and I can't help but smile. What the hell am I doing?

"I'm so happy you're here. I have something to show you." I don't say a word and follow his lead. We enter the dimly lit entry and I take off my shoes and start to laugh when sand falls out. "You love the beach, don't you?"

If only he knew where I was. "I may need to shower before I start walking around. I'm pretty dirty."

"Oh my, Shane, that's good to know."

I push his shoulder with the tips of my fingers in protest but he grabs them with force, pulling me into his body and hugging me tight. He whispers, "I am so glad you're here."

I whisper back into his rib cage, "Prove it."

He lifts me up, and next thing I know he's carrying me ass over shoulder. I can't help but laugh hysterically since I'm upside down. I can barely see where he's going until we arrive in his beautiful and regrettably familiar bathroom. He turns on the shower with one hand while still holding me with the other and tests the temperature. He carries us both inside, clothes on, placing me on one of the shower seats. He bends to his knees on the mosaic tile floor and begins tugging my tight, drenched clothes off, and my body arches in anticipation. The shower heads are pouring soft, warm droplets of water. The glass doors aren't closed, and I can't help staring at the water gushing onto the floor. "Sebastian—"

He doesn't care and kisses me fiercely. "Um, garlic, huh? Where did you go tonight?"

"Oh my gosh, I am so sorry, this is so embarrassing. I told you I was filthy."

"I know, that's right, my very, very dirty Sugar Shane." He continues to mess with me as he tugs off my undies and then lifts my shirt over my head. I try to rise up, but he pushes me down. Then he picks me up like a bag of feathers and I wrap my wet, spongy legs around his body. He slams me against the tile wall and I squeak in pain. He puts his entire self inside me and I can't help wincing at the shear width of his erection. He pushes me harder and harder against the shower wall, and water drowns my lips and mouth as I scream in pleasure. He holds my bottom with one arm and reaches with the other to cover my mouth, and says, "Hold your breath, Shane." I listen carefully, but the fear of drowning is literally rushing over me and I can barely breathe as the water pours over his hand that's covering my lips. Panic is setting in so I scratch his arm to let me go and at the same time arch my neck and head back, releasing his hold and grunting with an extreme orgasm as the air escapes my lungs. He thrusts me harder a few times but my legs are shaking and the only thing I feel is warm cum dribbling down my thigh, competing with the warm water. He slowly pulls out of me, and fearing I can't stand, he lowers me to the shower seat like a sleeping baby.

I try standing tall to wash off, but an overwhelming sense of woozy and dizzy takes over. I hold on to his waist for stability as he massages delicious-smelling shampoo into my hair and washes me carefully. His scent consumes me, and inhaling his odor has me wanting him back inside of me. He finishes washing my hair and washes himself, and as I watch him lather and tug his still erect penis, I can almost come again. He rinses and exits the shower, closing the glass door securely behind him. There's a huge pool of water all over the marble floors, and he respectably returns a few moments later with a handful of luxurious towels to sop it up.

I also exit the shower, and no sooner have I dried off my body than he calls me to his bedroom. I suspiciously open the door, waiting for some stunning, petite, and bilingual beauty to pop out of nowhere. I enter cautiously and see that it's only Sebastian, and I am relieved and excited for the privacy. He looks sexy as fuck in loose pajama bottoms without a shirt and wet hair going every which way, my favorite. His aroma has spread from the bathroom to my nostrils, filling the air with the smell of sex. The bed is made except for a white cotton dress laid on the duvet. "Jammies?" I ask.

He laughs and says, "Yes, jammies. We can't just lie around watching *I Love Lucy* and *The Honeymooners* reruns in our regular clothes now, can we?"

I run over and tackle him to the bed, kissing him and thanking him, so excited about the rest of the night.

"I have a whole evening planned for us. Go get ready and I will take care of things in here."

Sickly, I love taking orders from him. I slip on a pair of lace boy shorts and the long, fitted sleepy dress. I reenter the bathroom, comb my hair, and explore all the exotic toiletries. I tap my nose with the lightest touch of powder to dull the sheen, and a bit of sweet-smelling deodorant seals the deal. "Are you serious about watching the old shows?"

"Yes, of course I am. You told me that you thought home should be where you can lie around watching movies and eating Cheetos. Well, here we are. I'm not sure what kind of junk food you prefer, so I bought them all."

I walk back to the bedroom to find an assortment of every possible crap food sprawled all over the bed—Twinkies, Ho Hos, Doritos, gummies, Swedish Fish, Pecan Swirls, Junior Mints, and that's only what I can see from the mountain of junk.

"I was also thinking we could try something else, too?"

I'm smiling from ear to ear as I follow him from his bedroom through the silent halls to the place we had dessert only a short time before. It's eerily quiet, and the feeling of walking around in pajamas on a floating mansion has me nervous. Where is everyone?

We sit down to an already prepared bottle of champagne sitting on ice with two glasses and a rolled joint resting in an obviously never used ashtray. "You want to smoke weed?" I start laughing aloud that *the* Sebastian Lincoln Kane wants to smoke pot. This is hilarious.

He interrupts my annoying giggles, obviously embarrassed, and says, "Don't make fun, I haven't done this in years, but when you said Cheetos . . . they kind of go hand in hand. Of course, if you don't want to, we don't need to."

I compose my immature self. "Okay, I haven't done it in years, either, actually since tenth grade I think? The only times were with some people from school, so yeah, it's been a long time for me, too. But if I get paranoid and want to jump ship or something, you have to take care of me, okay?"

"Deal."

We shake on it like schoolyard kids and he lights it up, saying, "If you jump ship, then I'll take that swim with you."

We relax into the sunken deck chairs and pass a doobie back and forth, joking about all the silly things we used to do when we were young. Halfway through our joint, I move to his chair, and he wraps his oversized arms around me. We lie back, staring at the stars, listening to the waves hitting the boat, and I wonder at that moment, what could be better? I don't want to think about anything else.

Time passes, though I am not sure how much, and we head back down the long hallways, giggling the entire time about what junky snacks we're going to dive into. "Where is everyone?"

"Why, are you hungry?"

I respond with a long, pronounced, "Yyyeah."

And just like that, he loops me around to face the opposite direction and we do-si-do back to the kitchen, and I laugh like an idiot as he twirls me. "Where are we going, Sebastian? Where is everyone?"

"I sent everyone home. You said that it wasn't comfortable with so many people, so I sent the staff to hotels."

"What? Why?"

"Because they live here. Where else could they go?"

"Oh."

I'm feeling like the most special girl in the world. We roam the professional chef's kitchen for food. It's obvious he knew we might snoop when we find notes with "Sebastian & Shane" stuck to the glass containers. We pile cold seared tuna, seaweed salad, and some sort of ginger coleslaw onto our plates, and I head to go sit down at one of the tables. Sebastian looks at me with a silly face and a mouthful of food and says, "Are you nuts, we're watching movies in bed!"

For the umpteenth time, we walk back down the maze of hallways to his bedroom and climb under the crisp comforters, eating cold food and drinking beer in bed. I laugh at the irony of the castle compared to now and wonder which one he prefers. But just as I'm about to ask, he eyes the Twinkies and pink SnoBalls and the night is over!

~~~~~~~~

Scribbles Are Sexy

When I wake in the morning, it's dark out and the clock reads 5:45 a.m. Still tasting coconut from the edge of my lips, I can see a handwritten, calligraphy-scribed note from Sebastian placed on the nightstand. "I'm really sorry, I had a work thing come up, but I will be back by 12:00 p.m. I will see you for lunch. No one is here, make yourself at home! Don't leave, and have fun, Sugar!" I read the note again, smiling. I brush my teeth, only to find more clothing hung up and waiting for me. This is a new kind of euphoria, so I pop a pill to keep it all going.

It's early morning, and I don't want to be too snoopy staying here alone, so I head into town, telling the guard whom I've come to know as Hector that I will be back by noon. He opens the gate, agreeing to share my plans with Mr. Kane if he were to return before me. I'm not sure what I'm doing other than wasting time, so I think about picking up breakfast at the cute spot Vivi and I went, despite the long lines. I park without a problem, finding the restaurant to be a lot less busy than last time.

At the last minute and on a whim, I ask if I can double the order and add extra sausage to go. When it's ready, I get back in my car and drive to the secluded area of the beach, hoping to return the favor of food shared together. I whistle for Good, and finally he arrives, almost knocking me over as he aggressively sniffs at the plastic bag. "Hey, good boy. Don't worry, I got you something, too." I call for Sam, and I see his head pop out from under the flap of his makeshift camper. "Hi. I'm here to say thank you. I brought breakfast. I didn't make it though, it's from a place up the street."

He asks annoyingly, "Why are you here so early?"

"I'm sorry. I can just leave it if you would rather eat alone? I was in the area and thought you might like it. I can go. . . ."

Under his breath, he says, "It's fine. The sun's going to be at its perfect rising spot, let me grab a blanket so you can see."

I'm pushing Good away with my elbow to open the containers, finally handing him a piece of sausage to break the incessant begging. Sam climbs out, blanket in hand. Seeing that the containers are open and full of the famous pancakes, he huffs loudly, heading back inside. A moment later he returns with a large metal tin of Vermont maple syrup.

"You continue to surprise me, Sam."

He ignores me and asks where the little rug rat is. "You know, the damn dog whined for an hour after you two left. I think he's really got something for that kid."

"I know, it's super funny. I think the only time that little girl is happy is when she's with your dog."

We work together to set up the Styrofoam boxes and face toward the rising sun, eating syrup-soaked pancakes all while hand-feeding Good more sausage.

Sam starts to very slowly trust me, opening up a little bit more about himself. "I wasn't always like this, you know."

I don't say anything at first because I can tell from bartending he's cracking the door for more questions. "Okay, why are you here then?"

"Because of an unfortunate incident. A stupid and desperate man trying to provide for his family. Never be desperate for money, Shane, and never make deals with uncertain outcomes. It will control you. It doesn't seem that way at first, but over time your soul is nibbled at until finally it's swallowed."

I settle in to listen more attentively. "You had a wife and family?"

"Have. Yes."

He doesn't say anything more, so I lead us in another direction, hoping to keep the information coming. "Sam, I'm learning that every single human has a story. You just have to be willing to listen. Rich ones, poor ones, it doesn't matter. Even sweet Vivi, the little girl, has one, she just isn't willing to tell anyone except for Good." He's staring at the water in a trance-like state. "May I ask how you ended up here?" I point to the sandy blanket we are comfortably sitting upon.

"I told you, it's the best view! Who the hell is Good?"

I laugh because he doesn't know. "Your dog. That's what Vivi calls him."

"Oh, I just call him Dog. Good is better I guess." The side of his mouth curls upward but never reaches a smile. He goes on to tell me about some of the other homeless people he's met on the street and the woman he inherited this house from. "There was a beautiful woman I met when I was still learning to cope with my own madness. She was a genius. I originally stumbled upon her when I was sleeping under the pier for shelter. She threw shells, rocks, and debris at me, hitting me in the head and knocking me out with a block of concrete. When I came to, she was there stitching me up with needle and thread from a sewing kit. At first, I thought she was nuts, and in a way she was, but I loved her for it. It took a long time to break in, but she was exactly the distraction I needed. I learned that she used to work for NASA and had children and a

husband. I thought maybe she was scared of men, abused or something, and that's why she was here. That was until I saw the mouse
carcass in her foil-lined pocket and another wrapped in cloth that
she was feeding crumbs to. There were lots of other odd behaviors
that started to add up, questioning her sanity, and eventually the
mania turned dark and she took her own life. I found her naked
drifting in the tides, and written upside down with a black Sharpie
on her stomach, it read, 'Sam, enjoy the view.' I took that as her
way of giving me the house she worked so hard to make her own to
escape all the demons she was carrying.

"I later learned that she killed her husband and two children
in another state and was on the run. But that was a long time ago
now. Anyhow, I like living under here, away from people except for
outcasts like me. It's quiet, peaceful, and keeps me out of trouble.
I've met some very interesting characters, and they are all different, but Marcy was my favorite. There's the lonely souls, who drink
and drug to forget, but then there's the tortured souls, the mentally
ill, trapped in their own bodies. Turns out that was Marcy. Everyone's got something to hide or run from, but at the end of the day,
we are all selfish, and everything we do is for ourselves. Only in our
minds do we think these relationships exist."

I'm blown away, listening to every single word like it's his last.
"What's your story?"

"Shane, I told you. Sometimes we make bad decisions that we
think are good, or are paid to believe they are. I made a choice and
I am living with it. Just be careful. You are young and you don't
want to get caught in the trap of those who feel nothing because
they can afford not to."

It gives me shivers and a wave of nausea, reminding me that
everything with Sebastian isn't real, and our fairy-tale affair comes
to an end in a few days.

Sam invites me inside his home, and I reluctantly crouch at the
flap, deciding whether it's safe to follow. "You can come in, ya know,

you already barged in before, at least you're invited this time."

"Um, okay. It's not like I can call."

With the sun shining outside, I can see how incredibly clean the interior is. The thousands of paper bags are all facing the same direction, creating a type of paper art within the structure. I want so badly to ask about the bags, the bank, and if these are them, but we've already talked so much, I don't push it and instead admire the sea of brown paper waves he's made. His clothing is neatly folded in perfect stacks. In another corner, there's a cooler, with food I suppose, or maybe Marcy's dead mice? There's a cabinet hung up, presumably where his condiments are kept, like real maple syrup and spices for dinner. The entire space is incredible in all its hipster weirdness, but what really surprises me is the military-style tucked and tidy bed with mounds of books piled all around it. There are books from floor to ceiling. He has cups on one stack and a cactus plant on another. They are everywhere.

"Here. Read this." He hands me a copy of a book titled *Slaughterhouse*. Then he pulls another book from under the bed called *The China Study*. "Finish *Slaughterhouse* and then come and see me and I will release this one to you, you aren't ready for it yet."

"Okay . . ." I'm incredibly confused. "Where did you get all these books?"

"You're joking, right? The library, of course. You'd be surprised the linguistic gems people abandon or throw out. Some I rent, others are gifts. Don't you read?"

"Well, a bit since I am in school, but I guess I don't really have time to."

His voice is stern. "Make time!"

I take the book and thank him, heading out of the structure to the sunny beach below. I proceed to pick up the containers that Good has licked clean. Sam shakes out the blanket, folding it into a perfect square, and I ask if I can visit again.

"Yeah, yeah sure, whatever. Don't lose my book."

I wave to him, but he ignores me. I tuck the book under my arm and head for my car.

I drive back to the marina and Hector says, "Mr. Kane hasn't yet arrived," and he offers to park the car for me. I decline and go back into the yacht to check out all of the clothing that was left for me. There are four bathing suits to choose from. I put on the sunflower yellow one, grab a rolled-up towel, and head to the deck, where I find the ashtray with a joint in a clip dangling on the side. It feels oddly quiet and all alone in such a wide-open space. The feeling fades and I lie on an elongated couch, propping my head up with a pillow, and open the book. I read for a long time while my heart and head try and work together to handle the most inhumane topic I've ever come across. I place it down for a while and head to the built-in wine fridge, pouring from an open bottle. A little alcohol with a crunched pill will help numb the pain of these awful words, and I keep reading.

I'm awoken by a kiss on my forehead. I'm startled but excited when I see it's Sebastian standing over me. He slips the book out of my hand and asks why I would choose to read such a grotesque genre. I can't tell him where I got it, so I lie, telling him a friend from the bar told me to read it when I had time.

He places it on the edge of the table like it's rotting cabbage and kneels next to me. He smells so delicious and masculine, I have an urge to tackle him right here. "What would you like to do today?"

"Um, I haven't really thought about it. I didn't even know I fell asleep. What time is it?" I rise to freshen in the ladies' room but he catches me when I stumble.

"Someone found my favorite rosé." He laughs.

"Oh really? The bottle was open, and I could barely handle what I was reading, but I was trying to get through it. I guess I'm just not used to drinking during the day." I excuse myself, following the hallways to his bathroom to pee. When I glance in the mirror, there are black streaks around my eyes and partway down my cheek that must be from tears, though I don't remember crying. I crease the abnormally soft toilet paper and wipe under each lid, removing the run mascara. I fix my hair, blot my face with powder, and head to his room to grab a pill from my purse and apply some much-needed lipstick. I hear his footsteps coming, so I hurry and break the pill in half, hiding it inside my cheek to talk. I scan the room for something to drink, and there's a mini-fridge that I hadn't previously noticed. I bend down, grabbing an artsy-looking seltzer to swallow the secret tucked in my gum.

"I have an idea for you."

"Um, okay, what is it?"

"Hold on, I will be right back."

A few minutes later, Sebastian returns with a sinister but notably excited look on his face. "Which hand?"

"What?"

He has both hands behind his back, and the definition from his muscular arms mounds from his shirt. I point to the left with a grin of my own, and he hands me a crumpled piece of paper with a picture of a hand, the kind you would sketch to make turkeys in kindergarten.

"What does this mean?"

"Oh, are you thinking you should have gone with the right? Do you want to switch?" He grabs the wrinkly hand picture from my fingers and stuffs it in his pocket. I giggle at his adorably childish ways.

"Yes, I do. What's behind your right hand, please?"

He pulls out another piece of crumpled paper, this one with a terribly drawn animal. I laugh. "Um, now I'm really confused. Am I only allowed to choose one?"

He grabs me, throwing me roughly to the bed, and lies carefully on top of me. "I suppose if you're good, we can do both."

I am beginning to love playing his games. "Oh yeah, but what if I'm bad?"

He abruptly rolls off, saying, "Then you get nothing!" and spanks my right cheek.

"Okay, okay, I will be good."

He climbs back on top of me, gently kissing me, moving his mouth down to my cleavage, and I can't help but arch my back in anticipation. In one swift move he rips my yellow bathing suit bottoms off, and before I know what's happening, he is filling me up. He thrusts fast and harder than ever before, and I am writhing in pleasure and pain as he grabs my legs, holding them straight into the air, nearly touching my knees to my ears. I've skipped over the pain and right into orgasm, so I give him the tiniest smirk of a smile and he plunges harder and harder. I don't even have time to practice holding my breath as I squeak and squeal in his grasp. He grunts as he comes, letting out his own held breath, and lowers his massive body on top of mine. He is panting loudly but holding his weight with his elbows to avoid crushing me, all while keeping his slightly erect penis inside me as I squeeze tight.

"Are you messing with me?"

"Can you feel that?"

"Yes, of course I can." He thrusts one more time, then slowly pulls out when I exhale in frustration.

"Come on, we need to go and you need to pick. What're we doing?"

I almost forgot about his drawings, but then I look at the floor, where the weird little hand is peering back at me. "I choose both."

He agrees without hesitation. "Okay, which one first?"

"Um, the animal, I think?"

"Oh, I think you will like that. Do you have any allergies?"

"No, not to animals. Are we going to the zoo?"

He becomes the assertive guy I'm growing to like and says, "No more questions."

I quiet and ready myself in the bathroom, quickly rinsing off and tossing on a sundress, and meet him in the bedroom to leave.

When we're finally outside, he opens the passenger's side of his car and I graciously climb in, thinking, no wonder Vivi makes me do this. We drive through the gate, and I wave to Hector as we go by, but Sebastian glares my way.

"What?"

"You don't need to talk to him, there's no reason for it."

"He's nice. What's the problem? When I left today, he let me back in and offered to park Hope. He's a nice guy."

It's tense for a few minutes, but eventually he caves, sparking conversation over the jazzy music playing on the stereo. After at least an hour's drive or more, we pull down a long dirt road that's densely wooded on both sides. I haven't seen a single sign to clue me in as to where we are going, and now this mysterious dirt path has my curiosity bells ringing. Sebastian looks excited.

"Are you ready?"

"I think so, even though I'm not sure what for?"

We pull up to a ridiculous amount of fencing. There's a mixture of stockade and chain-link, some metal, others weathered wood and painted. A fairly nice home sits dead smack in the middle of the property and is much nicer than the one I grew up in, with beautiful flowering trees all around. I open my door, and the outside commotion and unfamiliar grounds make me incredibly wary. With anyone else and in any other circumstance, this type of property may feel normal, but this isn't Sebastian's style.

A very pretty lady with wavy brown hair flowing from a baseball cap, wearing cut denim shorts and a tight tank top with no bra, comes from the house carrying something. Thrilled to see Sebastian, she gives him a huge hug and a kiss on the cheek.

"What are you doing here?" she asks.

"Shane, this is my good friend Lauren. Lauren, this is Shane. We are here to get some love."

She chuckles, seemingly knowing what that means, and says, "Well, there is plenty of that here. Come on in and I will show you our new additions."

I wish I had picked hand only, this has me freaking out inside. Who are we getting love from, I wonder? We walk through an overly tall, latched fence, and like magic it unleashes an enormous amount of acreage of green, pastoral property behind it. The majesty doesn't end at the house, which is decoratively covered in ivy and is even more charming up close.

Once inside, we are greeted with squawks and barks. I wonder if she's some sort of hoarder of all things animal, since I still have no idea what is going on. An elderly gentleman greets us, offering some homemade lemonade, and we gladly accept. I'm thinking about taking a pill but can't sneak it until I know this is safe. Sebastian and Lauren speak quietly for a few moments, and I gather from eavesdropping that it's something about donations and additional land. I'm half listening because looking around for clues is more exciting. Then Sebastian points toward me and says, "So Shane here is reading a book her friend gave her called *Slaughterhouse*."

Lauren stops him with her hand and reaches for my shoulder. "Jesus, sweetie, it's a killer, but you gotta get through it. Oh shit, did I say killer? Bad choice of words, but whatever, it's worth it. Just try. I know it's awful, but so worth the read."

I can't stop staring at her crystal blue eyes and hope she talks more so I can look at them, wondering if they're contacts or natural. "I just started it today and it was brutal, but I'm always happy to learn about new things. I'm working on a paper for school and it's giving me all kinds of ideas."

"Well why don't we cheer you up by showing you what we do here to save our animal friends, not eat them. I'm a vegan if you can't tell, and this is my sanctuary for any animal that can't be taken care of or just needs a better place to call home. Sebastian even helped me rescue some alpacas. That was a crazy night." She starts laughing, and he smirks, looking toward the field. I'm envisioning him wrestling those big furry beasts into a trailer and hauling them down the dirt road in the middle of the night.

He shakes his head at me. "It was a crazy night, indeed. But they're doing well, right?"

"Come see." Lauren brings us to one side of the pasture, where a makeshift fence is separating the land into two distinct plots. There stands the cutest, sweetest, little fur-matted animal I have ever encountered. There are two larger ones in the near distance grazing.

"Oh my goodness, is that their baby?"

"Yes, and if it weren't for Sebastian, they all would have died. They were unable to walk, stuck like cement in their own filth, never mind start a family." She points them out. "The big brown one is Tiger, and his wife, Tigress, and their baby, she's named Kitten."

We all laugh, and Sebastian says, "What, are you serious with those names?"

She smacks him flirtingly on the arm and says, "Yes, I am. The two parents were as tough and strong as wild tigers and as mean, too, but their sweet angel of a baby is like a cuddly kitten. She is happy here and very good around people. Actually, they are all pretty good now. I can even hand-feed Tiger. For a long time they were terrified of me and had awful marks all over from when they were whipped. But those have healed, and the fur has covered the scars, and now they have something incredible to share together. They are survivors. Come on, there's more."

I think about all of the scars in my own life, new and old, and the people who've made them or helped them heal over. We walk back to the house and out another fence to a large open-air area that is caged from top to bottom and at least twenty or thirty feet tall. There are birds playing, chewing, bobbing, and flying around. "Wow."

Lauren hands us some long sticks with treats on the ends, instructing us to hold them out. "They will come and see you." We do just that, and a beautiful green parrot with only one leg hops out from underneath a branch and pulls the entire stick away from me. He proceeds to slam it against the side of a large piece of driftwood and peck at the seeds like a chicken. "Usually, the birds hold on to it, but you've met Grifter, our resident thief, and as you can see he has only one foot. It doesn't bother him one bit. He's smart."

"What happened to him?"

"Well, as you are seeing, every animal here has a story, and this poor guy had his foot caught in a cage door at a horrible pet store, and when he came to us, it was dangling by a thread and needed to be amputated. But he's a good eater and will steal just about anything you leave out. So all in all, he seems happy."

We sit on a bench watching the beautiful birds sing, play, and fly around. Sebastian hands his treat to a parakeet, who very carefully, one step at a time, approaches by sliding his body closer and closer until he grabs it and runs off. I could sit in here all day watching them play.

"Shane!"

I must've spaced out. Sebastian and Lauren are outside, waiting at the door. "Come on, there's more."

We walk through more of the huge yard to more animals, and along the way see turkeys plucking at the grass. There are loose bunnies running all over, hiding in mini-houses when they see us coming. We keep walking, and Lauren ushers us along and into another segregated area of the yard. This one has walls all around it and is made with the taller wooden fencing. She reaches to open the door but stops on the gate's lock and says, "Okay we are here, but Sebastian made a request, so I will be right back, just one sec. I almost forgot."

She comes back a moment later and Sebastian tells me to turn around and to trust him. Another one of his games, I wonder? He takes a piece of fabric from his pocket and wraps it around my eyes and holds my hand. "Come with me. I am going to help the whole way, just a few more steps. Okay, now we are going to get onto our knees. Hold on to my shoulder and get ready!" He lowers me onto what feels like a blanket, and we lie down onto our backs. Not a second later, we are mauled by hundreds of licks all over our faces, arms, and legs. I can't stop giggling and I need to close my mouth to keep them from licking inside, but it's too cute, whatever it is. They are climbing on top of us, over our legs, on our torsos, and I can even feel one nestling onto my head. I feel Sebastian's touch, and he is unraveling my blindfold to uncover at least two dozen puppies running all around us.

Lauren arrives just in time for my surprise with treats for us to share. She offers us both a hand to lift us up. I grab hold because their wiggling bodies are causing me to almost trip on top of them. I see a beautiful tapestry beneath us where we had just been lying, and the pups are jumping all over our ankles, begging for treats.

"All the little guys with black and white spots should be named Miracle. They were found on the side of a highway inside their pregnant mom, who had been hit by a car, and by some miracle these pups were kept safely inside her womb, unscathed. We only lost one, the runt, who refused any milk, but there are twelve strong ones left. The other litter, the bigger brown and black ones, was dropped off last week by the local police, who found them in a house of a drug dealer, who was already putting chains around their baby necks."

"Oh my goodness, I can't even imagine. They are so lucky that you took them in." They all look like little hamsters and guinea pigs, in different colors, shapes, and sizes. "We know the little guys are about six weeks or so now, but the others we aren't sure about because the mother was too vicious to bring here. It wasn't her fault she was taught to be cruel, and the cops didn't know, and we couldn't exactly ask the asshole who did that to them. They are all happy babies and will be up for adoption soon. But for now, they get to just play and run around and be one big family together. Do you want to name one?"

I look at Sebastian and he smiles at me. "I would love to." I choose the largest black puppy with a white stripe down her nose who hasn't left my side since we came in. "Lily."

"Perfect, I will remember that for when she's adopted. Puppy Lily it is."

I can't stop smiling. I want to grab one or five and wrap them up for Vivi, just to see her smile. Then again, her affinity for Good is uncanny, and she would probably walk right past these adorable puppies, buzzing my finger to leave.

We continue our tour to see more abandoned animals that this amazing woman has taken into her home. The habitats she's created are homey, comfortable, and natural to their environments. I wish all zoos could mimic Lauren's incredible philosophy.

We finish the day in the middle of the alpacas' home, where a couple resident sheep and a goat nibble at my dress. I'm smiling inside and out because it's so special to sit in the middle of nowhere with absolutely nothing to do but admire Mother Nature's gifts. Life is good right now.

Lauren hands me a mason jar and asks me to join her cutting fresh flowers for the table. I follow her lead, picking out an array of sweet-smelling, brightly colored wildflowers and some mint for aroma. As we approach the picnic-style farm table, caterers of some sort wearing neon green uniforms reading "Oggie's Organics" arrive with trays of food. Sebastian places a bottle of wine and a marble canister of ice on top of the table. He uncorks the bottle, pouring rosé-colored wine into our crystal glasses, while the neons set the table with varying kinds of produce, fruits, and mixed salads. Without a word and in awkward sync, they tip their heads at Sebastian and walk away.

I have almost completely forgotten to take a pill and can feel my nose starting to drip. With terrible timing, I excuse myself to the ladies' room to wash up, quickly swallowing a pill with a hand-ful of the sink's funny-tasting water. I come back to the table and Sebastian rises until I sit, and Lauren says, "Let's eat!"

She makes a point of saying that this is a vegan spread, and we will under no circumstance be consuming anything to do with our lovely animals on the farm or their extended families. "Anything you do outside of here, you are welcome to do, but here, today, we don't eat friends."

"A good philosophy to live by," Sebastian says. We all chuckle and dig in.

The crisp, cool wine is paired perfectly with all the incredible-tasting greens and interesting salads. We talk and laugh together and I learn how Sebastian and Lauren formed their long friendship together. Her parents were close with his and they grew up seeing each other at parties and school. I nervously ask if they were ever together, but she hysterically laughs, nearly choking on the wine in her mouth and throws a cherry tomato at me. "No, silly girl, you're more my type than this guy. I just use him for his money. My real loves are the animals."

I feel so dumb for having asked and say, "Oh, okay, that's so nice."

Sebastian proceeds to tell me why he brought me here. "I wanted you to see the other side of that book you're reading. The rescuers. Lauren is one of many who care about supporting her cause. Since she started, which was about ten years ago now, with her first rescued rooster—"

She interjects, "My parents don't exactly like what I'm doing here. I was supposed to be a doctor, ya know, but I didn't feel that taking care of humans was my calling. This is definitely more me. I am a doctor, though, just the animal kind. It's handy to be a vet with all these guys running around getting into trouble. I am so grateful for Sebastian's help and that of my other friends, too."

Sebastian says, "Who cares about the animals, it's a great tax break!" She throws a tomato at him, too.

Another bottle of wine is consumed, along with more stories and laughing. Soon, the day turns to night and it's pitch black. We can only hear the sounds of the animals we saw and are swatting at bugs that are surrounding all the candles. Sebastian nudges me that it's time to go, so I stand up, grabbing dishes in my arms, but he shakes his head no. "But—"

"They will take care of it."

"Who will? I'm happy to help," I say, but set the dishes back down and instead hug Lauren and thank her for the most amazing day and for opening my eyes to her lifestyle. Inside, I am thoroughly impressed and in even more awe of Sebastian for showing me another tiny slice of who he really is. The more he gives the more I crave him. We walk to the car, and as soon as the gate opens, I see the Oggie's Organics caravan and realize they've been waiting this whole time for us to finish. Sebastian allows them in, and like worker bees they pile out of their hive with rolling carts to clean our mess.

Moo, Goo, and Green Teeth

I'm feeling a bit tipsy when Sebastian opens the door for me, so I recline in my seat facing the driver's side. He starts the car with a roar of the engine but it doesn't move. "Would you like to go somewhere else?"

"Um, is this the other picture, the hand?"

"No, we'll save that for tomorrow."

"Okay, then sure, why not?"

We drive for a while, getting farther and farther into the darkness without streetlights, and I can barely see the farmland around us. He slows down, and the only thing I can see in the far distance is a large home illuminated by window candles and a few random lights. We drive up another long dirt driveway to a huge front porch filled with at least a dozen rocking chairs and more lit candles. Sebastian opens my door, and upon stepping out I can see it's an incredibly charming and quaint farmhouse. I wonder who Sebastian knows here?

We enter without a knock and I now see this is much more than a house. It's chic but old and smells of fresh-baked cookies.

"Do you have room for us tonight?"

"Well, yes we do, just the one night?"

"For now."

I look at Sebastian in confusion, but he pays no mind and hands the lady a credit card. She reaches for the keys, turning only to me, whose pinky finger is loosely draped on Sebastian's back pocket, and says, "Are you married?"

I think, yes, yes I am, but I assume she means us, so I wait for Sebastian to respond.

"Nope, siblings."

She grabs a different set of keys, putting back the other, and we are escorted upstairs. She unlocks the door and it opens into a huge loft with a beautiful, white antique tub sitting directly in the center of the room. I've never seen anything like this and walk around to take it all in. The elderly lady tells us to feel free to use anything in the room and that she will see us in the morning when we wake for breakfast. She goes to close the door behind her, stopping, saying, "I almost forgot, silly me. I will be right back."

I continue to walk about the room and see another bath with a shower but it doesn't compare to the oddly placed tub in the center. Sebastian laughs when he takes off his shoes and sees that behind the antique wooden bifold, set up as some sort of privacy barrier, there are two twin beds. "Well, sis, you better sleep here, and I will sleep there."

"Yes, of course, I need to listen to my older brother."

Just then there's a knock at the half-opened door and I run to let her in. She is holding an old-fashioned picnic basket filled with two glass bottles of milk and a heaping plate of cookies. "Good timing, they're still warm. Have a good night, you two."

"Oh wow, thank you. You, too."

We both sit cross-legged on our own bed eating warm cookies and drinking fresh milk from the jars. When we're finished, we find carved wooden toothbrushes with thick herbs for bristles and other homemade hygiene products in the bathroom, including baking soda–tasting toothpaste with crushed mint leaves in it. I smile a big smile and say, "Hey, brother, do I have anything in my teeth?" Knowing full well bits of green are all over as I smile widely.

He smiles just as wide, exposing his freckled green teeth, and asks, "Do I?"

We both laugh, almost spitting the paste everywhere before it hits the sink. We finish getting ready, blow out the candles, and climb into our own beds, reaching each other so the tips of our hands can touch. We face one another in the dark room and I tell him what a wonderful day I had and thank him for the amazing experience with Lauren and the animals. We chat for a few more minutes and fall asleep to a cool breeze blowing in from the windows without any screens.

In the morning I wake to the feeling of being suffocated. Sebastian's whole body is enveloping mine. We obey the innkeeper's expectations of brother and sister and never have sex; he just snuggles me in his arms. In a strange way I am proud, like we are better than sex.

The breakfast spread looks delicious and includes warm chocolate croissants, thick oatmeal with heavy cream, and freshly picked peaches, pears, and figs. A few other guests join us in the atrium but I can tell we stand out. They are all much older and seem put off by our joking around. I wolf down tasty crepes with real maple syrup tapped from the inn's trees but pass on the bacon. Sebastian has several cups of coffee but only nibbles at his plate. When I quiz him on his lack of appetite, he tells me he prefers the staff cooking over this. "It's mediocre."

I couldn't disagree more.

~~~~~~~~

Many Hands

We spend a fair part of the day in the car, reminiscing about our adventure. Sebastian makes fun of me, recalling that I asked if the old fireplace was an old-fashioned pizza oven—nope, that extra brick shelf is just for the wood. We joke about our kinship as siblings and the nosy lady who gazed at our hands for rings. Having only seen mine, and the way we naturally acted toward one another, I can only imagine what kind of incestuous relationship she thought we had brewing.

We arrive back at the yacht and Sebastian explains he needs to make some calls. I overhear him talking in a couple different languages, probably to the who's who about who knows what. I start to ready myself for the day, gathering my things, but he raises his index finger in protest while still in conversation. I look at him, putting my hands up, but he waves his finger harder at me and points to the couch to sit. With spare time, I check my phone and see there are four missed calls. I listen while he continues to talk business. The first three are Simone asking where I am, and the other is from the bar, Eddie checking in on me.

After the phone calls, Sebastian searches around the bedroom's floor, and with an "aha" he picks up the crumpled piece of paper. "You still have one thing to do, remember? I meant for us to do it yesterday, but the day got away from us." He leans in and kisses me when he speaks, opening the little square of paper and exposing the roughly drawn hand. "You know why I adore spending time with you? Because time doesn't exist."

I'm completely enamored by this man and feel the exact same way.

"Don't bother showering, I have something planned for us. Throw on anything comfortable, it really doesn't matter, just grab whatever. Are there enough clothes for you? Since the staff is on hiatus, it is slim pickin's around here, so tell me if you're missing or need anything."

I look around and smile. "What else could I possibly need?"

He speaks quietly while he ties his shoes and says, "You're right about that, compared to what you're used to."

"Excuse me?"

"Nothing, Sugar. Grab something comfy to wear and let's get going."

I feel awful about what he just said because I know it's true, but feel worse knowing that I've opened up to him only for it to be thrown in my face. This is not what I'm used to, and I didn't do anything to deserve it. It's an overwhelming reminder of Jake coming home, missing my regulars from the bar, and even Patti at the jewelry store. I'm not used to this lifestyle, and he is making it entirely too easy for me. I am living a dream and feel like I could wake at any second. Like an immediate epiphany, I want to swallow it whole and spit it all out at the same time, ending our relationship.

He walks over, seeing the despair on my face, and hugs me. With a tight squeeze of affection and a kiss on my forehead, I feel momentarily better. "Are you okay?" he asks. I don't answer. "Come on, Sugar, let's go. I need you to have a good day."

I concede but am still glum. I try walking away to get ready, but he pulls me back, tossing my limp body to the bed and climbing on top of me. He kisses my lips, then down to my belly button, and out of nowhere tickles me under my arms, making fun of my apparent sadness, saying, "Whatever you do, don't laugh. I mean it, Shane, no laughing."

I can't keep them in, and the giggles fly from my mouth like bubbles. I yell out, "Mercy! Uncle!" and he stops.

"Are you better now?"

"Yes."

"Okay then, let's go. Or do I need to tickle you again? No laughing!"

I run from him to the door, and he nearly falls over rushing to put his shoes on for the chase.

WE ARE ON THE ROAD for another who-knows, random, crazy experience of a lifetime, and I'm giddy again with anticipation.

We drive far from the marina, deep into the old part of town where wealth has no limits, and eventually reach an arched gate. Sebastian presses the button and we are buzzed in as he announces his name over the speaker.

The grounds are reminiscent of the Barrons', except the property is much larger. We follow the curvy drive that leads to another magnificent estate and I look at him inquisitively, but he doesn't respond to my pry or wonky eyebrow raise.

"Well hello, Mr. Kane." A tall, red-haired woman in a tailored suit with high heels opens the door to another monstrous building/homestead and kisses Sebastian's cheek, welcoming me with only a smile. "Would you like anything beforehand, something to drink, perhaps, or maybe a bite after your drive?"

"No, we are fine, thank you."

"Okay, as you desire, Mr. Kane."

We walk down a long, glass hallway like nothing I've ever seen, showcasing the outside of the estate, with endless views of beautifully straight trees and manicured flower displays.

We reach the end of the hall in front of a single red door. The woman opens it for us and disappears. Inside is a dimly lit room with at least one hundred white candles burning and the faintest sound of a piano in the background. There is plum-colored fabric hanging on the back of the door, which Sebastian reaches for and hands to me. Its slippery texture falls from my fingers, but he swoops it up before it hits the floor and hands it back to me. "Come here." He lifts my shirt over my head, one arm at a time. Then, while breathing in my mouth, almost kissing me, he unbuckles my bra, then kneels to the floor, pulling off each pant leg, and eventually my undies are around my ankles. He breathes heavier onto each newly exposed piece of flesh. He wraps the silk fabric directly above my breasts, never actually touching them, and tucks it into place. I try to reciprocate as provocatively as him, but he stops me by slipping off his own clothes purposefully without my assistance. I'm standing barefoot, draped in purple silk, arm in arm with this beautiful man, and we walk together, looking like guests at a lavish toga party. We walk through a second exit in the back of the room leading outside.

It's astounding to see, hear, and breathe. The entire area is covered top to bottom in sheets of glass with water pouring down on either side. The mist is flying everywhere, coating my skin, nostrils, and the silk as they soak up the moisture. I look around, feeling like we are the fish inside a bowl, and a bit of panic overcomes me and I squeeze Sebastian's arm. The glass water box opens at the ceiling and I see birds flying above, warm sun peering down, and

I can breathe again. There are tropical-colored fish swirling about in the pools beneath the glass wall waterfalls. I stand still, taking it all in, closing my eyes and imagining what's next. My senses are blasted when the glass begins to darken, and the only light is from the open air above as four people walk in, all female and dressed in matching plum robes. The women separate into two groups and escort Sebastian and I onto flat, soft couches without backs or cushions. We are told to lie face down for sleep and face up to wake. I listen intently to their accents, still unsure of what's happening, but just then Sebastian whispers to me from his private couch and shakes his fingers, saying, "Remember the paper."

I nod my head yes and he puts his face down in the headrest. I keep my head up and watch two ladies pull the silk off of his body, then one starts to rub his hands and the other his feet. I feel a delicate push on the back of my head, urging me to rest mine, and I nervously let go, obliging the bossy masseuses. The two ladies drizzle me in beautifully fragranced oil and each one of them rubs and tugs opposite ends of my body. With each deep pulse of pressure, I feel the stress leaving my body, disappearing into beads of mist and floating into the sky above. I don't say anything because Sebastian hasn't made a peep, so I follow his lead and allow myself to completely let go as the women rub and rub, and I sink farther and farther into the cushions. I forget about Jake and my mother and this crazy week. I imagine living with Sebastian, being married to him instead of Jake. I'm melding myself into someone else, bringing the fantasy alive, and these hands are pushing further into the imaginary.

A long while passes, then a tiny little bell rings and there's a whisper to awaken. I don't move, and she nudges me to turn over. I must have dozed off because I'm lightheaded and confused. I spot Sebastian's tousled hair, remembering I'm not alone for this blissful experience. He wiggles his fingers, whispering "hands," and I smile back at him. I lie on my back, staring at the clouds and birds, then close my eyes forcefully back into the dream where I imagine never leaving Sebastian. The two ladies' four hands work their magic on every inch of my front, with particular attention to my breasts and nipples, and strangely I'm not afraid.

A while later another soft bell rings, and when I open my eyes it's only Sebastian and me. He smiles, asking if I enjoyed it.

"It was incredible. This place is incredible."

He stands up, completely naked, and confidently walks to my couch, where I'm lying faceup, also nude and covered in scented oil. He pulls my legs off the edge of the rectangular furniture until my butt hangs off the end. He takes my legs, placing them on his shoulders, and ever so slowly eases his already erect penis inside of me. I'm so relaxed, like Jell-O, I can barely move along to any kind of rhythm. Just as I feel myself getting more and more wet, I worry about my lazy lack of participation, when he says, "Hold your breath, I don't want you to move." I do exactly that, and with every gasp of air he pushes a little more until he's finally thrusting hard and deep inside me. I hold my breath until the very end, when I can feel myself ready to scream. I cover my mouth with my arm and yell into the crease of my elbow, exhaling hard into my skin and biting my arm. My heart is pounding fast as Sebastian lifts me, sitting me back down on the couch. I'm so lightheaded I nearly fall over, but he catches me with his arm. "Hold on, let me get you some orange juice."

"No, I am fine, I'm just, um—"

"I understand, me, too."

He wraps the purple toga around my body, walking toward one of the glass water walls. It magically widens, and the water stops flowing as we step barefoot over the moving fish onto the grass outside. There sits a private wooden hot tub with two glasses of champagne and blackberries in each glass. He picks me up, and the fabric falls off, and he lowers us both into the excruciatingly hot water. I gasp in pain, but it soon fades as we sit together, wrapped in each other's arms, silently sipping champagne. I cannot imagine a drug making me more comfortable than this one. If only I could pop a pill like Sebastian.

We step from the tub, experiencing the lush, cool outside air. We head to the wooden shower and wash our bodies together, then grab the dangling loose fabric robes to drape over our clean bodies. Another ding and we are brought back through the maze of doors and paths to the original room, where our clothes are found neatly hanging on the back of the door. There's a basket of makeup and other products, which I use to dust my face, smearing on my favorite lipstick. I dig into my purse to pull out a pill while Sebastian's back is turned, swallowing it whole. It gets stuck in the back of my throat and I start to choke. He immediately turns, running the water, and cups his hands for me to drink from. I move past him and duck my face under the running faucet, letting the water lubricate my throat, and the pill passes. I'm embarrassed, but I act like nothing happened and thank him anyway. "Sorry, I don't know what happened."

"Let's get you some lunch and something better to drink."

We walk out to a bright hallway and I glance at the time. I can't believe an entire afternoon has flown by.

We sit outside in teak chairs, and a man and lady give us tea, champagne, and tiny plates of various mini-sized appetizers. We sip and eat as our blood sugar rises, along with the reminder of real life. I thank Sebastian over and over but he stops me, only asking if I enjoyed the experience. I would have to be a complete orangutan not to have loved every second of it.

"Yes, of course, I've never had a massage before."

He seems pleased but not shocked.

Two Days . . .

We drive back to his yacht and I feel myself fading. As we drive, he pushes a button and my seat reclines fully flat and a radio turns on.

I awake to a slight jostle and a whisper. "Honey, we're home."

Still sleepy, I accept his hand as I robotically follow him toward the bedroom. "I think you should take a nap." He pulls back the covers on his bed and fluffs two pillows, hitting them with the side of his hand.

"I can't take a nap, I just took one, I think?"

"Snuggle up, Sugar." He throws me over his shoulder and lowers me down onto the bed. I land in a sea of crisp comforters, and before I object any further, I'm wrapped up like a grape leaf and fall back asleep.

I'm awoken suddenly by a telephone ringing. I groggily answer, listening to Simone's bubbly voice on the other end. She can't believe that Sebastian and I have been together this whole time and that I'm on the yacht. "Wow, he must really like you. I am so happy for you, Shaney. Martin and I are going to get dinner, would you guys like to join us?"

"I'm not sure, he had some work to do, so I'm just hanging out here until he gets back. Actually, that's a lie, I was totally sleeping. What time is it?"

"It's seven o'clock, my dear, time to wake up."

"Holy shit, it is? No, I think we will pass on dinner, but another time sounds good."

"Okay, well, call us if anything changes. I need a good night out, just us girls. Things are so stressful around here." Her voice slumps.

"Still your dad's stuff?"

"Yep, there's another issue."

"Oh no, what? Is there anything I can do to help?"

"I don't want to get into it, but I'm working on it. No worries. Have a great night and be good. Nothing I wouldn't do, okay?"

I laugh and say, "Um, I've kind of crossed that bridge and have landed on the other side."

She giggles a cute Simone laugh and we hang up.

Now up, I wander about the yacht for a few minutes, exploring. I peek in to where the staff sleeps, but I feel sneaky looking at their cramped rooms. Funny, because I usually know the feeling. The mechanical area scares me with all its noises and gauges, so I don't even finish climbing down the stairs and head back up. Bored and feeling weird about lurking around alone, I decide getting Sebastian and I some dinner is a good idea. I drive out of the gates, waving goodbye to the guard, when my phone rings again. "Hello?"

"Hey, sweets, it's me. How are you?"

"Oh my gosh, hi! How are you? What's going on?"

"All is good, we are just starting to get everything packed up and gonna get on the road tomorrow. We have a few more spots that some locals told us about, so we're going to explore them and then head back. We will probably be home in a couple days. I will call you when I know more, but I assume it will be night. You might be working and I will be wiped, so I will see you when you get home from your shift."

"That sounds great. Did you get some good quality time with your friends and your dad? Are you ready to be back?"

His voice rises in surprise. "Yes, of course I'm ready, aren't you ready to have me back?"

"Yes, of course. Things are good. I'm just about to buy some food for dinner. Dave gave me the night off, so I'm on my way to grab some takeout."

"Shane, you have the night off and you're buying dinner out?"

"Yes, I am. Are you serious, Jake, you are going to give me a hard time about money?"

"I'm not going to do this with you right now. I'll be home soon. I have a shitload of bills to catch up on, and your car needs fixing, plus I haven't worked in two weeks, so everything is going to be tight for a while. So eat your fancy dinners out now, because when I get home that's going to stop. You will eat what I killed and that's that."

"I will make it up, Jake, it's fine. Stop being an asshole."

"I'm just saying, you should really think about this. If we are going to work on all the things we talked about, we need to start being more serious about spending less and working more. Plus, I have a ton of laundry. Do you have the quarters saved for me from work?"

"Yes, I do. Jesus, Jake, I don't want to fight. Get home safe and call me if you need anything. I can't go back into work after he gave me the day off, so I will make it up other ways. Don't worry, our bills will be fine. The tips have been really good lately."

"Okay, Shane. Love you."

"You too, and get home safely, it feels like forever."

We hang up and I'm thoroughly annoyed by his remarks about money while he's on vacation for two weeks and I get to keep working and going to school. It brings back everything that I've pushed aside while being around Sebastian. Now all I can think about is going home to a stack of bills, rent due, an empty fridge, losing my job, and poor Hope, who's running on gas and a prayer. Why the fuck did he have to call and start a big fight with me? Just as I can feel myself getting worked up, the way Jake does over money, I think about the five grand I have in the bank. I may have earned it unethically, but it's all mine. My mind slows and I begin to think about the incredible time I'm having in la-la land with Sebastian, so I make a conscious decision to not get myself stressed out and just focus on the next two days of happy.

I pull over and park in front of a fresh, homemade pasta place I've always wanted to try. Sebastian hasn't called, so I assume he's not back, and I decide to grab another order for Sam, with extra sausage on the side. When I reach the parking lot near Sam's fort, I carry the to-go bag filled with breadsticks and fresh pesto linguine through the dark alley, finally reaching the secluded beach. I find my way to the underground pier and can barely make out his house in the darkness. "Good? Sam?" I call out louder and louder, but it's quiet except for the crash of the waves. "Sam, are you home?" I dangle the bag from my arm toward his fort when I almost trip over something in the sand. It's Sam.

I drop the bag and scream hysterically for help. "Sam, oh my gosh, are you okay? Can you hear me? Please, Sam!" I look up to see two men in the distance walking away from us. Good is nowhere to be seen, but I call for him anyhow.

Sam grabs my hand, squeezing it tight, and with a hoarse voice says, "Get the dog." He tries to rise but immediately falls back and his head hits the sand.

"Okay, where? Are you okay?"

"The dog, now!"

I listen to his demand and begin calling him again and again, louder and in a high pitch to attract him. "Good, where are you, boy? Come on, sweetie, where are you?"

All of a sudden, through the light from the moon and Sam's house, I barely see an object moving slowly, army-crawling toward me. I run to him. "Oh my gosh, sweetheart, are you okay?" I hug him like Vivi does and try to urge him to his feet. Sam's beside us and holding my shoulder for support. "The motherfuckers kicked him hard. This was about me, not him."

"Jesus, Sam, what happened? Who are they? Who'd do this?"

"Shane, you should get out of here, there's nothing you can do."

"You're nuts, I'm not going anywhere. We need to call the police. I'm bringing you to the hospital, and Good to the vet."

"Absolutely not! I am not going anywhere. He is tough and we will both be fine."

"Sam, I don't think so, he seems really hurt. Who the hell kicks a dog, what the frick is wrong with people? What do they want from you?"

"He was trying to protect me from those fuckers, and to keep him from biting again, one of them slammed their pointy fucking shoes into his chest."

"Okay, I'm bringing him with me, let's get him to the vet."

"Shane, I said NO."

I can feel the seriousness in his voice and I back off. "Okay, okay. But what about you, are you hurt? Can I get you something?"

"Nah, I will be alright. They are just bullies and think roughing up an old man is their way to get a point across. Well, I got it and you shouldn't be here. You will make it worse."

"Wait, you know those guys? Why would I make it worse?"

"Shane, you need to go. I'm not a good person, and I did things that I can't come back from. They are just trying to make sure I stay quiet, so please just go." He is practically crying, and his voice is tired and defeated.

I walk with Sam holding my shoulder for support, and Good slowly limps behind us. We enter through the flap of his house and he sits down on the bed. I go behind the home, where he has a cooler, and grab a cup of water from the melting ice and hand it to him. I pull four precious pills from my purse and place them inside his palm. I know I will suffer when I run low at the end of the month, but he needs them more than me. "What are you doing with these? These are not good for you. You shouldn't mess around with this crap."

"Sam, don't worry about it, just take one, it will help with the pain." He swallows them all and lies back down on the bed. "Not all of them!"

He ignores what I said, so I cover him up with a blanket and turn to care for Good. He is panting hard on the floor. I sit with him, petting his bruised and already scarred body. I leave them be while I head back outside to try and find the takeout I'd brought. It's lying in the sand exactly where I'd dropped it. I bring it inside and hand-feed Good little bites of sausage. Then he slurps noodles from the open box, and I know now he will be okay. It makes me laugh, because ironically, my mother always said, "If you're eating, then you must be healthy."

Sam watches us with a raw gaze and asks what I think he's been wondering for a while. "Why are you so nice to us? I don't deserve it. You shouldn't be here. I'm not a good man and I don't need you mixed up in this any more than you already are." He's starting to get drowsy and his words are slurring and sound funny to my ear.

"Why, Sam? What did you do that was so bad?"

"Because, Shane, I was in the wrong place at the wrong time and took a deal that I thought was the right thing."

"What kind of deal? I don't understand."

He is groggy and his eyes are closing before me. "A deal with your boyfriend."

His eyes are closed completely. Does he mean Sebastian? I need more information to know what happened that was so bad, and why Sebastian? I urge him for more.

"He's a bad man, Shane. They are bad people. Don't go with him, do you understand me. He will hurt you. Keep her away from me. Don't bring that girl here again. You stay away from me, do you hear?" Tears are slowly streaking from the corner of his eye, falling onto the waiting blanket.

"Vivi? Sebastian? What are you talking about? What did you do, Sam? Sam, please tell me what you did. What did he do? Why is Sebastian so bad? Please, answer me." I shake him to wake and he swats at me, striking my face, and I scream in reaction.

"Go! Go away. Leave me alone. Don't come back. Don't bring her, and you don't come around me." He is barely conscious and I'm scared to leave him, worried he's either a murderer of some kind or that I might have inadvertently overdosed a man. I pick up the empty box and leave some water for Good, who is now sleeping. I get back into the car, driving straight to Sebastian's.

When I walk inside, he welcomes me with an inviting smile. "Whoa, what happened to you? Is that blood?"

I look down and my clothes are smeared with a mixture of red, brown, and sand. "Listen to me, Sebastian. Please tell me right now. How do you know the homeless guy?"

"Shane, what are you talking about?"

"The homeless guy, Sam. The one with the huge dog. I've seen him at the bank, the same one I now have an account with. How do you know him?"

He walks away from me, completely ignoring the seriousness of my question.

"I'm not kidding, Sebastian, how do you know him?"

"Shane, he's a bad guy, and you need to not bother with him. Did he do this to you?" His temper is rising, and the volume and tone of his raised voice makes me cower, and I sit.

"No, of course not. I was bringing him some food—"

I can't even finish when Sebastian slams his hand on the dresser. "You did what?"

"I was bringing him dinner, and Good, too."

"Are you nuts? Stay the fuck away from him. Do you understand me? Stay away. He's dangerous. I made it very clear I don't want him around you."

"You made it clear? I need to know why. If you tell me why, I will do it, but tell me, goddammit."

He approaches me sympathetically. "Yes, I know who he is. There is no reason to go near him or talk to him, and if you can't handle that, then you need to leave. Do you understand what I am telling you? He does not need food or anything else from you. He is fine where he is, and we all know where that is. Just leave him alone. Promise me you will do that. Please, Shane, promise me." He is stroking my arms, but my brows are furrowed so tight my head is pounding.

"I don't understand, Sebastian. He's not bad."

"Stay away from him. End of story, Shane! Now go and shower and throw away those disgusting clothes."

"Someone hurt him tonight, and the dog, too. I still don't understand how you two are connected? He knows who you are."

"Of course he does, and I don't give a fuck about him or the dog. It doesn't concern you, Shane, but he really doesn't need your charity or anyone else's. He is fine on his own. He should not be talking to you about me or anyone else, do you understand, or it will get worse for everyone."

I'm not satisfied with his vague explanation and unsure whom I should trust. Someone is lying to me. I hate the idea of leaving, but I can't stay not knowing what happened. I need to figure this out. I go to the bathroom, ready to strip and climb in the shower, but I stop and turn around. I make a quick decision to grab my purse and walk past Sebastian, who is taking off his tie. "What are you doing?"

"I'm leaving. I want to go. Nothing makes sense, so I want to go. Someone is lying to me and I need to know the truth." He grabs my arm to stop me, but I rip it back. He blocks the door with his large frame and tries to grab me again. I attempt to escape him by crawling underneath his legs, but he holds me back and pulls me into his chest. I can't help but start to cry. "Nothing makes sense. My life was so boring, and the last couple weeks have been absolutely insane. I don't know what to do. And it's all going to end soon." My heart and brain are fireworks on acid and I can feel myself ready to implode with emotions.

He rubs my back and I sob tears and snot into his shirt. "It's okay, it's okay. I know you are scared. I'm so sorry. I shouldn't have yelled at you, I just don't want him near you. I want to protect you."

"I have to go home and I don't want to. Jake is back in two days, and I'm scared shitless. I have to go back to work. I mean, what work I have left, and for fuck's sake, I have school to finish, too. Plus, Simone's having issues with her dad's thing and my mother is seriously sick and I just don't know what to do anymore. This place is magic, and I don't want it to end. You are magic, and it's all ending."

He keeps rubbing my back and then pulls me into him to kiss me and says, "It's going to be okay. Hey, whatever you do, don't laugh, okay. Whatever you do in this whole wide world, no laughing."

I can't help but crack a smile through the tears at his constant silliness. He hugs me tight and comforts me again with another kiss to my lips and one to my head. I unclasp his grip and head to the bathroom, climbing into the shower and allowing the water to wash my sins and sadness down the drain.

DAY 13

Adventures in Wealthy Wonderland

The next morning when I wake, I find a note from Sebastian on the side of the bed. I open the blue seal to find the handwritten calligraphy I've grown to appreciate, and inside it reads: "Good morning, Sugar. I needed to run out for a work emergency but will be back as soon as I can. Make yourself comfortable. Are you ready for the staff to come back? I need breakfast! ~ SLK."

Spoiled brat, I think. I take my time getting ready, but he's right, the boat feels empty without any noise, and I am starting to miss the hustle and bustle of people. My only friend is Hector, and we just wave when I pass through the gate. I hop in my car, wave to my buddy, and head toward my mother's house.

Upon arrival, I knock, but no one answers, and I can see the chicken through the window, plucking underneath Rob's chair. I get back in my car, and from the driveway I call Simone, but there's no answer from her, either. I head back to the boat, but not before stopping at the drugstore to grab some medicine for Sam and Good. I don't care what Sebastian says, I need to know what the deal is with them.

I arrive at his home and yell for him, but no one comes running or calls back. Uncomfortable about what I might find, I let myself in, but no one is there. I put the little bag of aspirin, bandages, and ointment on the bed and head to the beach. I stretch out on the sand to wait and read more of the gruesome book he gave to me. An hour or two goes by, but there's still no sign of Sam or Good. Hot from the sun and curious, I drive by the bank, but he's nowhere to be seen. I contemplate asking questions of the manager but worry Sebastian will find out.

I begin the drive back to the boat and the phone rings. Finally, I think, someone knows I'm looking for them, and it's Simone. "Hey there. What's up?"

"Hi. Nothing, except running around trying to figure shit out. The attorneys are meeting with me this afternoon, and hopefully everything will be straightened out and I can get back into my fucking house or sell it or whatever. I am so sick of the hotel."

"I'm so sorry, Simone. I hate that you are going through all of this. I'm in town if you need anything, and Sebastian's at work."

Her annoyance turns to a giggle. "Seriously, you're still with him, huh? How's it going?"

"It's going nowhere. Jake comes home tomorrow night, and I'm honestly freaking out. I don't know what I'm doing with him, anyhow. He's amazing and I don't want to leave, but I need to face reality and go back to the monotony of a life at home."

"You've got me, sweetie. You aren't going anywhere. Not again. You are stuck with me for life and always have been. Hey, what are you guys doing tonight? Martin and I were supposed to have some time together last night but he had something come up and couldn't. Do you want to go out for dinner, a farewell sort of thing? I should be done hopefully by six, if these dickhead lawyers get their shit together and give me what's mine."

"Um, sure, that sounds great. I will ask Sebastian, but that would be really nice. It will be my last hurrah before heading back home. Geez, I sound like such an asshole. I'm celebrating the end of an affair to go home to my husband. What is wrong with me?"

"Nothing, sweetie. You are just finally realizing what life's all about and enjoying it a bit!"

"Hey, by chance, do you know where my mother is?"

"Yeah, she and Esmerelda took Vivi somewhere, I'm not really sure where, though."

"Okay, I will call you once I hear from Sebastian." We hang up and I drive up to the gate. I can see Sebastian's Maserati in the distance pulling in, too. He's talking to some other people, so I walk past the dock so as not to draw attention to myself.

"Shane, come here." He waves me over. "These are some of the guys who take care of my boats." He introduces me as his friend Shane Lacy, and we all say hello. They're a gorgeous group of rougher-looking guys, the type I'm usually seen with, and from far away it could have been Jake standing there. I say goodbye and other pleasantries and walk inside to wait for Sebastian.

"Simone called and said that she and Martin are going out tonight and wants to know if we want to join?"

"Sure, sounds great. I know a terrific restaurant that my friend just opened. Well, he says it's terrific, but I think it probably is. It's supposed to be kind of funky. I'll give him a call and set it up."

"Awesome, I will call her, too."

We spend the rest of the day lying around on the outdoor furniture with a skeleton crew of staff he's brought back serving us crisp white wine and snacks while we read books and lounge about, him working and me relaxing. I sunbathe in one of the new suits he gave me, and he spends the majority of the day on his laptop or speaking some other language to another human on the phone.

"Is there any language you can't speak?"

"Mandarin."

I laugh. "Oh okay, so you can't speak Chinese?"

"Nope, but I speak a little Japanese."

"Of course you do." We play around while he tries to teach me some Spanish, French, Italian, and Japanese, and it all ends with both of us laughing hysterically at my terrible American accent.

"Everyone should at least know how to say hello in every language."

"I agree with the concept, but my brain and linguistic skills aren't in sync with my desire to learn. Sorry."

Alice Would Be Jealous

In the early evening Simone and Martin arrive at the yacht, both sporting gorgeous outfits and looking like the beautiful super couple they are. Simone, no surprise, is drop-dead gorgeous, and it makes me feel insecure standing beside her, but Sebastian seems disinterested, so I don't worry too much. We leave in a private SUV limo with tinted windows, drinking champagne the entire way to the restaurant, joking around as if we were seniors on our way to prom.

We arrive after a long drive to a strange and actually quite frightening-looking building. No one would know what it is or where we are until Sebastian spots the letter X on the door, marking the spot. I wonder if this is some kind of treasure-themed restaurant and we will be searching for gold with mighty pirates, but I remember the company I'm with and laugh to myself. As we exit the car, the driver hands each of us a beautiful blue egg and a rubber band.

"Um?"

"It's to get inside."

I think about how hilarious it would be at my bar asking customers to bring strange items with them to get their alcohol. My regulars would chuck the eggs at the windows and fling the rubber bands at my head.

We walk through the first door and show a man covered in tattoos and piercings the blue eggs and the rubber bands we've placed around our wrists. He takes them all and hands us a single egg back, but this one looks typical and white. We enter through another door, but it's much smaller than the first and we need to crouch down to enter. Sebastian, Martin, and Simone are crawling on their knees, but being shorter than them, I creep along. It feels a bit like *Alice in Wonderland*, as we hover even lower through a third door, all of us now crawling on all fours, butts to heads. Just as the feeling of claustrophobia sets in, a man lying on his belly greets us with a smile. He shines a purple light on the egg, and it illuminates the letter X and we are waved through. We rise from the floor brushing ourselves off and take in the insane surroundings.

Serving the patrons are stunning Asian women with hair down to their waists, wearing high heels, short, flared fluorescent orange skirts, and no tops. The room is dim and holds only ten or twelve tables and a circular bar. Simone says, "Oh, this is interesting. I think I like it" and squeezes Martin's arm. Sebastian looks at me for approval but I don't waver, and we're escorted to a table by a sharply dressed man. We are seated and approached by Sebastian's friend, a very skinny, geeky-looking Asian man with dyed orange hair that matches the skirts of the topless waitresses walking around. Sebastian speaks a bit of Japanese with the man, and Martin interrupts, showing off his own linguistic versatility. Simone and I are too busy in conversation about the girls' bodies to guess or really care what they are saying.

A very tiny woman with straight jet-black hair that rests on the nipples of her tiny breasts approaches Sebastian, and after a few minutes of unrecognizable conversation, I think he's ordered for the table. There are no menus, and because she ignored us, there's no way to ask questions. Within twenty minutes or so, tiny plates are placed in front of each of us at the same time by four different hot Asian ladies. The plates themselves are bizarre shapes, and on them sit globs of colored bubbles off to one side. I look at Sebastian for an explanation and he responds, "Cocktails, I think?" We all shrug our shoulders, and with nervous excitement pop one in our mouths, unsure what to expect. The gelatinous balls are difficult to hold between our fingers and wiggle and wobble in our hands like teeny-tiny waterbeds. We share the flavors with each other, offering the plates around so we can try all the different colors. The taste is unusual and they burst in our mouths, reminding me of sex with Sebastian. The popping sensation and incredible erup- tions of liquid fruit are strange to get used to, but the potency soon becomes apparent. Within a few moments of sucking and explod- ing our globular drinks, we are chatting and laughing at practically anything. I'm not sure what's in them, but the feeling is amazing.

The dinner arrives over discussion of one of the server's inor- dinately perky breasts that actually flip up to the sky, and we all wonder how gravity could work in such a way. Extremely long and skinny rectangular dishes are placed in front of us, each one as unique as the next. Mine has a long, thin strand of what looks like maple cotton candy—or tan insulation—poking upward at least four or five feet high, and beneath is a less interesting minus- cule blurb of a fish with teeth showing. Simone's plate is equally impressive: a tower of sideways noodles, which causes Martin to bitch about moving his chair to avoid it. It's a spectacle of food creativity, and I love every second of it. I wish I could tell Eddie all about it.

The rest of the night goes by flawlessly, and with more cre- ations landing on our table and the various sensations we are all feeling, I begin to wonder if we're being drugged? Feeling loosey-goosey and extra weird, Simone and I tease our waitresses by yanking down our dresses and serving the boys little bites from our mouths with our own breasts popping out. Sebastian and Martin sit back and watch as Simone and I act silly and kiss each other. I start to dance around the room, but within seconds Sebastian stops the embarrassment of my flailing arms and legs by picking me up and carrying me back to the table, where I sit inappropriately on his lap. The entire restaurant is filled with delicious sexual meals and couples joking and laughing. The topless Asians keep the food and molecular, gelatinous cocktails coming until the whole room is feeling good.

When the night comes to an end, Sebastian and Martin stay behind to say goodbye to his friend while Simone and I leave doing the cancan with our knees all the way through the triple tiny doors. I don't remember anything after that.

DAY 14

———— ~~~~ ————

Naughty Yachty

I wake in the middle of the night, confused and sweating, with Sebastian's heavy arm draped over my naked body. I ease out of bed and move about the dark room quietly, looking for my purse. I can't find it anywhere and try not to panic, but the feeling of my nose dripping reminds me that the symptoms of withdrawal are hours away. He turns over and grumbles to me, "What are you doing?"

I whisper back even though he's now awake. "My purse, I can't find it anywhere?"

"Oh, it's probably in the front entry. Simone called but you were asleep, you had left it in the car. The driver dropped it off."

I stop listening, throw on a T-shirt, hurry down the hallway, lightly waving to a passing staff person, and find my purse sitting on a different stand like a trophy on a mantle. I reach inside, finding my pills in the zippered pocket. Thank goodness. I immediately feel better, taking one out and crushing it between my teeth.

"Shane, what are you doing?" Sebastian is directly behind me.

"Oh, nothing, I just needed to make sure I had everything. I'm coming now."

We walk back together and I tuck my purse in the corner of the room within eyeshot, remove the shirt, and nestle back into bed. Soon he is snoring peacefully and we both fall back asleep.

In the morning, my head is pounding and all I can think of is another pill and a hot cup of coffee. I don't see Sebastian, so I call out for him but he doesn't answer. The door jiggles, and it's Sebastian with a tray with fresh coffee, hot tea, and various fruits. "I have Tylenol for you, too."

"How did you know?" My voice sounds terrible, sleepy and sickly.

"You had fun last night."

"I did?"

"It was a blast. My favorite part was getting to see you dance."

I put my head down in complete embarrassment. "Oh my gosh, burn it out of your head. I'm the worst. I can't believe I danced. I don't even remember it."

He laughs. "Well, I would love to argue with you, but, um, like Simone said, you are good at all sorts of other things, right?"

I shake my head, imagining what else I did to make myself look stupid. He places the tray on the bed, pours me a coffee, and I drink while lying back against the pillows.

"So, what would you like to do today?"

"Wait, what day is it?"

"Why?"

"Fuck. Sebastian, I have to go home tonight. Jesus, I have to make night shift, too. I can't believe this. I have work and I need to get food for Andrew and get everything ready. Oh my goodness, I can't believe this. It's my last day." My head is throbbing, but he pulls me back from my spring-like posture and I nearly spill my coffee all over the duvet.

"Calm down, it's fine. We'll make the most of whatever time you have. Please, let's enjoy every second of it. Plus, it's early."

I nod my head in agreement, though I'm terrified inside. I'm also annoyed that he can calm me down within seconds and make everything better.

We finish breakfast and he instructs me to put on a bathing suit and leaves the room. When he returns I feel a rocking motion. "What's going on?"

"Well, you've never actually been out on the boat, have you?"

"No. Are we going out?" I then hear a horn coming from outside.

"Yes, but not on this one. They're bringing another one around for me. It's one of my favorites. I hope you like it. But first, are you sure you're well enough to go out on a boat?"

My pill's kicking in, and hopefully the Tylenol will, too. I'm not feeling particularly well, but I can't imagine missing one second with Sebastian. "Yes, I'll be fine."

He grabs my hand, and barefooted we walk to the pier and board a much smaller but still substantially sized yacht. There are a few staff members both on the vessel and still on the dock, piling supplies on for us. I can see baskets filled with towels, food, drinks, and other assorted items. We board with the careful guidance of Sebastian's hands, and the staff retreats upon seeing us.

"Where are they going?"

"It's just us, Sugar Shane. I'm driving." He gives me a sinister look and his mouth barely smiles, unveiling the tiniest glimpse of his crooked canines.

We take off into the open ocean, and the wind whips through my hair the farther and faster we go. It's too loud to talk, and the time flies as I close my eyes and let the sea and salt bounce off my skin. An hour or two may have passed when we stop and dock near a tiny remote piece of land in the middle of the sea. I look around but can't see anything but blue water and the lush tropical fields of an island. I don't ask any questions, because I've learned how much Sebastian likes keeping things a surprise.

He pulls out snorkels and fins for both of us, showing me how to use them. I figure out the fins fairly easily and play around like a mermaid with her tail. He has me practice blowing air in and out of the tube before we get in the water, but I feel absolutely ridiculous and ugly as ever with a giant mask around my face and my nasally sounding voice. Sebastian doesn't seem to care, and as usual is more interested in teaching me how to breathe than how I look. "Shane, breathe normal. Don't hold your breath at all. In fact, forget everything I've ever taught you and do exactly what you were born to do."

He snickers and continues with more instructions as we lower ourselves into the warm water, pushing away from the boat. He grabs my hand and I lower my face, viewing the most beautiful creatures swimming right below us. I had no clue about the world beneath us, having mostly admired the ocean from the television or a very rare swim, but nothing like this. My confidence grows and I unleash my hand from his, wandering around the coves and mangroves that spread from the island's surround. I want to slip away, see it all, but Sebastian is too close and barely lets me roam. He points to the boat, signing to surface, but I shake my head vigorously underwater. He grabs my defiant arms, lifting me to the surface. "Do I need to force you onto the boat?"

"Uh-huh."

He throws my body, bum side up, onto his shoulder and lifts us both aboard, fins and hands waving frantically in a playful protest not to leave.

He sits down in the captain's chair, still dripping wet and looking sexy as fuck. I stand over him while he pulls the mask and snorkel off of my face, pushing my salty hair to the side. I climb on to him, straddling his body, and my legs automatically lift off the floor. He pulls down my bikini bottoms and, in the same

movement, his swim trunks. I lower myself slowly onto his perfectly hard penis with sloth-like timing. He moves to put his hands
around my hips to take control of my slow speed, but I grab them,
pushing them behind his back. I lean in, pressing my boobs into
his chest, breathing heavily into his mouth. We are both still wet,
and the taste of salt lines our lips and tongues. I move with careful
ease, teasing him with very fast then super slow hip motions. I can
see my reflection in the glass, and the techniques are turning me
on. He can't take the teasing any longer and picks me up while I'm
still riding on top of him, flipping around and hugging the back of
the slippery white chair as he pounds harder and harder inside me.
I squeal with pleasure as our slick bodies hit each other with tre-
mendous force. He whispers into my ear, "Louder, louder." I have
been teaching myself to hold my breath to orgasm, but this time I
let it all go and scream at the last thrust inside of me. He is panting and rests his still-standing body over mine. We collapse with
exhaustion, with him leaning on me and me on the chair, when
another boat flies by, shouting and whistling at the passionate and
naughty sex they just witnessed. We laugh and he tickles my belly.
He comments on seeing his reflection pounding me from behind
and I tell him that I saw it, too, and how much I liked it. He kisses
me hard.

We pull our clothes back on and I catch the time from a clock
on the lower level. It's noon! He sees my panicked face and says,
"Let's just eat something, okay? I know you need to go, but I have
you for a little while longer."

We sit on the boat cross-legged in our chairs and enjoy a full
picnic lunch together. We sip fresh fruit juice and munch on
petite sandwiches filled with dill, cucumber, and smoked salmon.
It's delightful, and I can't bear thinking about ever leaving this
spot. I even imagine drowning here, because that means it all just
ended right here and with him. Every single unique experience
that I share with Sebastian makes me realize how much I rely on

him. He is my escape, and without him, I fear my other life, my actual life.

We pack up anything loose to protect it from the wind and head back. Upon arriving at the pier, I'm offered a hand to help me off, and the people standing around waiting quickly take the boat and clean it or whatever they do. I thank them before they scurry off and apologize for the mess of dishes and used snorkel equipment we've left behind. They pay no attention to my apology and nod their head to Sebastian.

Inside his yacht, I shower the sea's salt from my body and search for my old clothes, the ones I bought a long time ago. I find them laundered and hanging in the bathroom closet. Sebastian points to the four chic burlap totes filled with clothing sitting by the door. "Shane, those are for you. I want you to keep everything. They were picked and bought for you and only you. Please keep them and enjoy them."

I love the idea of keeping all the incredible outfits and the memories they carry, but then my mind wanders to life with Jake and I want to burn them. My eyebrow raises in dismay and quiet protest.

He pleads again. "Please, they will just get donated if you don't take them."

I shake my head but gratefully grab the bags and other personal items to put inside my car.

"No, no, I will get someone to take care of it. Just leave it."

"Okay. Thank you."

All the Holidays

I'm feeling incredibly sad about our ending and fear I haven't given him nearly as much as he has given me. "I have an idea, just one last thing, okay? We have a couple hours, so please let me do this. I will be right back."

He looks so nervous with me in control. I run through the halls as fast I can, finally reaching the chef. I ask him about making a Thanksgiving dinner, minus the big turkey but with some sort of clever substitute, and then run back through the halls out of breath to find Sebastian.

"Come on, let's go. If we hurry we can make it." I grab his hand for a change and pull him out to the dock. I make him race with me down the pier to my car.

"What are you doing, Shane? We can take mine or I will call for one."

"Just come on, we don't have time for that."

He reluctantly gets in on the passenger's side, and thankfully Hope starts up with a growl. There's a fierce rattle that we will need to talk over, but she's started. I throw her in first and we're off. I rushed him so quickly, I laugh out loud when I see his bare feet. He smirks back now, curious about the spontaneous rush out the door.

We pull into a low-end shopping mall that I'd noticed on my travels out and about when he was gone. There's a nail salon, pizza place, Laundromat, and a few other random low-end shops that I know all too well. I get out in a bound and Sebastian waits in the car. "I don't have shoes."

I reach to the back of my car into the bag of work clothes from a few days ago and yank out a pair of white socks. "Here, throw these on."

He looks at me like I'm nuts and rolls his eyes. It's the first time I feel snobbery oozing from him.

"C'mon, please."

Annoyed, he pulls on the dirty pair of socks and gets out of the car, running over the hot pavement. He follows my lead to the front entrance of a dollar store, where I reach in my purse and pull out the ten dollars of emergency money I keep hidden in my wallet. I hand him a five-dollar bill. "It's May, and I have no idea how this will end, but all I can think is that this is it. No celebrations, no special occasions, and no weekends or holidays with us together. Today we celebrate them all." I pause, as my words are coming out as fast as I can think, and a tear comes to my eye. I try to continue without completely losing it. My voice cracks as I talk. "You and I each have five dollars and we need to buy Christmas presents. This is our budget. We can each get five things. Please pick something out for me, and I will do the same for you."

Sebastian grabs my shoulder in protest and strokes the tear that's slid down my cheek with his finger. "Shane, this is crazy. I can get you a real present. This is shit, why are you doing this?"

"Come on, Sebastian, please do it for me. I need to know what I did wasn't in vain. This way, in my mind, we spent a whole year together."

He leans in, and with a very serious face kisses me on the lips, and we walk inside the store. A few people make eyes when they see this beautiful man walking around in socks. I overhear him say something but I don't understand. We split up, both going our separate ways down the aisles and carrying green baskets to hide our secret presents. I remember to grab wrapping paper and tape, which unfortunately uses up two dollars, so I need to be conscious of what I pick next. I search the lanes with speed and precision, thinking carefully about our time together and what will make the best gifts. I can see Sebastian is already at the cashier. I wonder how quickly he could have chosen something? I continue making my selections, and when I see he's exited and is waiting outside, I pay for my order with the help of quarters and nickels at the base of my purse.

We drive back to the yacht, and almost the entire way he tells me how silly this is and that he can buy me whatever I want. "I know you can, and it's amazing, but that isn't the point. The point is, I will probably never see you again, and at least this way we can spend the holidays together, even if it's total make-believe." He leaves it alone with a childish grunt, stating he doesn't agree with it.

We board the boat, and immediately Sebastian pulls off his filthy socks that are now a white-gray with black bottoms, and before they hit the floor someone walks by and swoops them from his feet. He is more at ease now. His comfort level is rising and he's back to the silly Sebastian I adore.

"So, Sugar, I need to wrap my presents for you, but I need to ask around if they have any paper or I will send someone out to get it."

"Actually, it's fine, I bought some." I grab the wrapping paper, carefully cinching the bag to keep him from seeing more.

"Birthday-Christmas is it?"

We both laugh at the birthday paper with toy trucks printed all over it. "You do your stuff first and I will be right back and wrap mine. No cheating!"

I run down the hall, stopping all the staff I see, asking them to come with me. Like trained puppies they follow me to the hall outside the kitchen and I ask for their help. "First and foremost, thank you so much for being so kind to me during the time I've spent aboard. You truly are a wonderful group of people and I know how hard you work."

The pretty, somewhat bitchy girl I was introduced to the first time I boarded the ship says, "No, we thank you. We all got a couple days off for no reason. Thank you, sweetie. Tell us what we can do!"

I smile with only my lips and proceed to thank them in advance for their volunteering and they all happily nod with enthusiasm to participate. "So I am throwing a very, very fast party with Sebastian, and I know it seems insane, but we are going to celebrate all the holidays at once, in like twenty minutes. So if you can help me set up that would be amazing. I want to use the outdoor living area at the front of the boat. I need something for Halloween, and maybe some lights for Christmas, and anything else you can come up with. Please hurry. I know the chef is working on Thanksgiving dinner, and I would love for everyone to come and join in if you can? Please, anything you can do to bring the festivities together would be awesome."

To my surprise, they all looked excited. Only one of the men exits the interruption, explaining he's security and can't partake, but wishes us well and says it sounds fun. Then all at once, everyone scatters. I run back down the hall to Sebastian's room, knocking in a playful rhythm on his door. He answers, opening the door widely to allow me in, but realizes I can see the shapes of wrapped presents and rushes to hide them. Normally, I would love to watch him squirm, especially over something so sweet, but I need to get mine done, and time is precious. I jokingly snap at him, hoping he will leave the room, and say, "It's the holidays ya know, you better get something decent on."

He shakes his head and walks toward the closets in a separate part of the room. Before leaving the suite he says, "Wait, I need to get my stuff. Close your eyes, I don't want you peeking, those are priceless gifts, ya know."

I laugh and close my eyes, hearing the door close. After a few minutes and an argument with the cheap tape that's sticking to everything, including my fingers and clothes, I gather the badly wrapped presents and open the door, inviting Sebastian back in.

He looks like a man ready to accept an Oscar. Sebastian is in a full black-tie ensemble, with a slightly unshaven face, tan from the sun today, and looking gorgeous with his hair tousled and messed about. What strikes me most is not how handsome he is, but how sad he looks as I open the door. I look down and smile because I know if I look straight at him, I will burst out crying. I need to keep the pace going, which is also serving as a distraction because my time with this amazing human being is coming to an end. With no time to change, I powder my face and gloss my lips.

I load my presents into the dollar store bag and carry it around my wrist and down the halls, interlocking my arm with his. One of the staff sees us coming and quickly turns around, rushing ahead to get there before us. He's shouting in the distance, "Operation Holiday, Operation Holiday!"

We both laugh, and he says, "Was that a code word?"

I shrug my shoulders, smiling the whole time. We don't see another soul until reaching my favorite place, the outside portion in the front of the yacht. Before we step into the fresh salty air I pull him back to thank him. "Sebastian, I have never experienced anything like you before. I . . ." I'm choking up, and he grabs and hugs me into his beautiful chest.

I can feel myself ready to bawl, but he grabs my hand and says, "It's Operation Holiday. Sugar, there's no crying on Christmas!"

We walk outside, and the head staff run to the edges of the boat. It's as if a bride and groom are entering the ballroom for their first dance, and like a wedding they all start clapping and smiling at us. The sight is magnificent, better than I could ever imagine. They have draped stunning, billowy silk tapestries as a backdrop, with tea light candles lit in every direction and on every flat surface. Tiny white lights are strewn across the overhang above the main dining table, which is set with a scarlet red cloth and matching silver. An oversized butternut squash is carved into a jack-o'-lantern and illuminated with yet another shining candle. There are petals reminiscent of Valentine's Day guiding our path to sit, and party hats and blow horns for a New Year's Eve celebration. I tear up at the beauty of it all and the care that the hardworking people in Sebastian's life have put into my silly little idea.

Sebastian seems even more taken aback than me, and just as he is about to say something, servers arrive single-file from the kitchen with trays of items for our Thanksgiving feast. The chef follows the line, stopping in front of us, points to the largest silver tray, and says, "Braised lobster with a tarragon *limone* sauce. But in honor of a true Thanksgiving dinner, it is accompanied by a roasted organic chicken, cranberry compote, and fresh clover greens. Please enjoy, and I will see you soon when you are ready for a special dessert celebration."

There is so much beautiful food, and everyone is standing at attention, waiting for us to drop something and ready to scrape the table of crumbs. I can't stand the formality, and even though I'm nervous that Sebastian will disapprove, I invite them to share in the festivities. Nervously, they accept once Sebastian nods okay, and everyone sits down, joining us around the table for dinner, using the side dishes for plates and piling them with slivers of chicken, crustaceans, spinach, cranberries, various butters, and decadent breads. We talk and joke like family, and everyone seems more comfortable than I've ever seen them, all but Sebastian.

Nearing the end of our meal, and being the extraordinarily well-trained staff that they are, they begin piling dishes and removing items as fast as a greyhound. Sebastian and I just stare at one another, excited to experience the next event. Suddenly, sounds of stunningly beautiful Celtic music for Saint Patrick's Day play over the speakers and the chef arrives carrying a large white chocolate egg with hot sparklers shooting from the top. "I'm pleased to offer the Fourth of July's Irish Easter! Ta-da!"

We laugh and clap for the hilarious and special moment we are having. Warm, molten dark-chocolate lava trickles from the egg that's purposely heated by the fire from the sparklers. We chunk it off with our hands, and Sebastian welcomes everyone to grab a piece and dip it into the lava sauce below.

Once the dishes are cleared and we are so full beyond any party I've ever attended, Sebastian asks for a few moments alone with me, and like that, everyone disappears. He grabs my hands, stares into my eyes, and thanks me for being me. "Don't ever change who you are, Miss Sugar Shane Lacy."

"You either, Mr. Sebastian Lincoln Kane." He pulls out my first very neatly wrapped present. It's the complete opposite of my oversized wrapping mess, with its many folds and assorted rips and tears of tape all over the package. I excitedly open it, and inside is a champagne bottle–shaped container of bubble bath. "For my princess, who in a castle knew a fine champagne when she tasted one."

I'm blushing and tingling all over. I hand him his first present and put my head down in embarrassment over the ridiculous wrapping job. He shakes his head, opening it in a fury. It's a card game called Truth or Dare Ya! He starts laughing with a deep chuckle and says, "My favorite, how did you know?"

Then he hands me my next present, which is a very cheap pair of swim goggles, whose green frames are larger on one side than the other, evidence of their quality. "For all your snorkeling adventures!"

It's hitting me how much I'm really going to miss him. I want to start crying, because it feels so natural to do so, but I hold myself back, handing him another present. The next one is a container of play money, similar to the kind in Monopoly. I wrote on five of the hundreds, "For My Time With Sebastian." He doesn't even smile and hands me the next present. I may have gone too far, but he must know I'm kidding. I can tell it made him uncomfortable, and I play it off like a joke so as not to ruin the mood.

The next present is another perfectly wrapped one for me. It's a man's hat with a giant fluorescent green marijuana leaf on the front. I start cracking up, and thankfully, the tension between us breaks. He laughs after unwrapping his next present, which are Twinkies. Then I make a frowny face, saying, "I spent the other two dollars on the paper and tape, I'm so sorry, I don't have any more for you."

He doesn't look at all disappointed. "But I have another for you." He hands me a funny-shaped package, and when I open it, I smile wide in remembrance of all our incredible times together. It's a stuffed animal, a puppy.

"Oh my gosh, it's puppy Lily."

"Here's your last one."

I rip the tape very slowly, never taking my eyes off of his, and when I do to see what it is, we both kiss. It's a toy replica of a life-guard stand, just like the one we drank wine on and played by near the ocean. We hug each other, and with stuff still in our hands, the staff arrives carrying bottles of champagne and wearing silly hats. Sebastian grabs a pointed party hat and puts mine on for me, then his. He takes the first bottle of champagne and pops the cork, which flies across the floor, and we all cheer in celebratory fashion. I take the first swig from the bottle, and we pass it around to every-one else, who does the same. Then, like we've done it a thousand times before, we all join together in chanting: "10, 9, 8, 7, 6, 5, 4, 3, 2, 1. Happy New Year!!!!"

Sebastian kisses me with intention and care, arching my back as my leg naturally lifts off the ground. Everyone cheers and whis-tles as they watch. His lips are soft and parted, just barely touching mine, when he whispers "thank you" into my mouth. There's yell-ing and noisemakers going off all around us, but this moment right now for him and I, it's as quiet as a church. He leans in and says, "Happy New Year, Shane. I can't imagine a better one."

A tear falls from my eye. Sebastian wipes it from my cheek, and then I panic when I hear someone say the time. I still need to get home and prepare for work, make the house look like I've been there the whole time, and grab food for Andrew. I don't want to leave, and I imagine abandoning my entire life if it means just a few more minutes with this magical man, but I have to go. We would never work. I need to go home. Everything is a blur and our moments are over.

It's a rush of goodbyes and thank yous as I thank every single staff person I see and hug a couple of them. They look concerned and even worried about the urgency of my exit. To avoid a very painful explanation, I head directly to Sebastian's bedroom, grab-bing my purse and any other belongings that aren't already col-lected. He's waiting for me inside. "Do you have everything?"

"I think so?"

"It should all be in your car, if not, please tell me, I will get whatever is yours to you. I also had them fill up Hope and check the oil, and your deposits are done."

Are you fucking kidding me. Don't ruin this, don't kill my love for you with this prostitution bullshit. How could he. I can't even respond to those horrible words, and I walk to the door. He grabs my hand and I pull back, determined to leave, but I melt with his touch. I speak under my breath as I spin around, "It was never about the fucking money. I don't want any money, this is crazy."

There's a choke in his voice as he tries to talk to me, and I want to drop to my knees and beg him to let me stay. I want to feel him one more time inside of me. I want to have one more exciting adventure alongside him. I would have killed myself right now knowing life couldn't possibly get any better than it is with him. But it's all fantasy, and I know what I need to do, and it's time. He lets me go without ever saying goodbye, and I walk alone to my car. I regrettably look back, but the door is already closed.

Here Is Home

I wave to Hector, and in a crackling voice that's ready to explode with sobs of sadness, I thank him for his hospitality and drive off, tears flooding down my face. It's over. For the first time in my life, I fell head over heels for a man, for no reason at all. If heartbreak could kill, it's murdering me.

I listen to country music, and the long sappy tones of Patsy Cline help calm my pain, allowing me to space out and stop thinking a few seconds at a time. The entire drive home has me in a trance of nothingness, a body without a soul. I find myself in a daze as I stop at the fish store for crickets, and the woman who sees me asks if I'm okay. It's kind of a trick question, and I'm not ready to answer. I tell her I'm sick and leave the store in tears.

I park and unload Hope's trunk, carrying all the evidence of my affair into the apartment and plan to hide it. The contents remind me of different experiences with Sebastian, and just seeing it all causes me to drop to my knees and cry. Closing the door to my tiny little apartment behind me, I gather my composure, pop a pill, and wash my face, ready for reality.

I mix the neatly hung clothes on hangers into the bin on the floor for the Laundromat. I stuff the olive wood hangers into the trash and tie it to drop in the dumpster later on. I do the same with the shoes, which get thrown into the closet, and unload makeup into a basket in the bathroom. Finding the bag with my sweet little presents from Sebastian, I decide it best to keep them hidden in Hope's trunk and place it next to the trash for when I leave. Next, I look in the mirror, pulling in a few deep breaths, and out loud tell myself, "You belong here. You are not that girl. Knock it off. It's over. Move on. Here is home." I keep repeating it over and over until I'm choking on the words, forcing myself to believe them. After a while, the tears stop flowing and only puffy red circles remain. I stand in the shower, too exhausted to move, and let the water run down my naked body. I have no energy and sit down, sobbing into my hands, but nothing comes out. I'm dried up. I sit for a while on the shower's floor, listening to the rushing water fall over me, but it's getting cold and the temperature shocks me into turning it off.

Sort of awake, I dress and cover up the blotchy red patches that make up my face. I spend a full hour both messing and tidying the apartment to show I've been living here until it looks believable. I leave for work. As the door shuts, I swing it back open to write a note to Jake. After all, this is my life, and he expects a welcoming wife to come home to. "Welcome home! See you tonight. Sorry there's no food . . . it's been a little hectic. Love, Shane." I leave it next to the television controller, where he's sure to see it.

I drop the trash in the dumpster and presents in the trunk and climb into Hope, whose back-and-forth driving is wearing on her engine. With some caressing and multiple turns of the ignition, she finally starts and we are off. I promise not to drive that far ever again, and she reciprocates with an easeful ride to work with no stalls at lights.

The bar is business as usual, and the same regulars are in the same chairs slopping down the same drinks. Everyone says hello, asking where I've been, claiming their tips are "too high if I was off on vacation!"

I laugh because it's funny and say, "Yes, it's been tough living on a yacht, eating lobster by day and visiting castles at night." They stop listening when they feel I'm just fucking with them. No one ever believes the truth, ever.

The rest of the night is uneventful. I pour, clean, stock, and talk as normal as the time ticks on. Eddie fills me in on all the extra sluts Dave's been hooking up with while I was gone. He even caught him doing lines off some chick's stomach in the sex cave-slash-office where he keeps the spare kegs. "He isn't working much. He was in and out at times, but mostly he was acting nuts. The second night you were gone, he let Cherry work and gave her the keys to lock up."

"Are you kidding me, crazy Cherry, the one with the fluttery eye? She can't even drink a beer without spilling it on herself."

"I told you, he's nuts. I stayed late and ran the bar, so I had to close down the food for the night, which everyone was bitching about, but we got through it. After a while she found herself back on the stool, so I gave her free drinks to offset what she thought she lost in tips."

"He's such a dirtball. If I notice anything, I will let you know. I'm back for good now, so I will try to keep the jail-bait bitches to a minimum. I'll start carding anyone I don't recognize."

Eddie agrees and reiterates how nice it is to have me back and asks about Jake.

"He's home tonight. It feels like forever, I can't believe it."

"I am sure he will be glad to be back. I bet he's missed you like crazy. I know I would. But then again, I never would have left you."

"Aw, thanks Eddie, that's so sweet. We will see. Actually, can you do me a favor? If you do see him, please don't mention the days I had off. He gets weird about me not working and nervous about money."

He looks concerned but says, "No problem, of course I won't."

I leave Eddie in the back room to follow the yelling of Ye Ol, who's drunk and noticeably pissed off about the newspaper he's reading and letting everybody know it. But if I'm honest, I'm glad to see his face, though it immediately reminds me of the loss of our friend.

"Shane, did you see this, they are fucking arming babies with bombs now. If you get near the little ISIS spawn or try to help it, you both blow up. Can you imagine arming babies, what the fuck is wrong with them? These goddamn terrorists should be burned alive. I would slit their throats with broken glass." He bangs his beer bottle on the edge of the bar in a dramatic fashion, so I come around the counter to intervene. I've never heard him talk so violently about anything.

"Hey, it's nice to see you. What classes are you teaching next semester?" He turns to me beside him and, with a smile, changes the subject to his course load and the spoiled rotten students he "takes care of." In the midst of our light conversation about classes, a latecomer eggs him on in an effort to rile him back up for what us behind the bar call drunkentainment, but I promise him a free shot if he leaves it be.

The rest of the night goes on, extinguishing boozy little fires when they arise. When I yell for last call, I'm rudely interrupted by the biggest douchebag of them all.

"Look who's here, everybody, Shaney's back. Look, my sweet little Shaney's here!" Dave has a bleached blond bimbo around his arm who can't be more than ninety pounds and less than five feet tall. I walk over to talk to him about closing up and getting everyone out, but he slobbers my cheek with a wet kiss and tries to dip me like we're dancing, and his breath nearly knocks me unconscious.

I rise up to laugh it off and turn to the girl. "I need your ID."

"What?"

"I need to see your ID."

She looks at Dave and begins to walk away.

"Give me your ID or you need to leave."

"Listen, you bitch, I am not giving you an ID. I am with the owner, you know."

"Yes, I do know, you and most of the town are or have been with the owner. So give me your fucking ID or I'm going to call the cops."

Dave puts his arms up in lame resistance, saying, "Come on, Shaney, give her a break."

"No, Dave, I need an ID or she needs to go." I look around to see the whole bar is watching.

"Sorry, babe, she's the boss. You gotta show her."

To my surprise, he defends me. She digs her puny hands into a red patent leather purse and pulls an ID from a zebra wallet and it's a freaking learner's permit. "You're joking, right? Get out of here before I call your parents." I turn to Dave. "Are you a complete fool?"

He's hysterically laughing, and after seeing it for himself says, "Oh shit, see ya. Good call, Shaney."

Her eyes water in embarrassment as everyone continues to watch. "I need a ride. I can't go home and I'm not allowed to drive alone yet."

Eddie walks over and, being the consistent gentleman he is, offers her a ride home. She looks him up and down and says, "Okay, now we're talking."

He tells her to knock it off or he'll tell her parents, too. She quiets and I pour her a club soda, assigning her to a table in the corner until Eddie's ready to go. Dave disappears, most likely to pass out on his office mattress, and knowing everyone's set and I'm done herding drunk kittens, I yell for the second time, "Last call."

The night's ending and reality is setting in. I check the plugs, outlets, and door locks a half dozen times, walk out with Eddie and Paula, the tiny teenager, and drive home after a long night. I pull into the apartment complex and my heart is pounding with anxiety, knowing Jake will be there. It's too much, especially after an exhausting night, and during every free second, I thought about Sebastian. I'm sick inside missing him, and nothing about my life feels right. I walk up the stairs, and just as I'm about to reach the door, my white-trash neighbor yells, "Hey girl, where you been?"

I want to slap the hush right out of her mouth. "Shhh, it's late. I've been working a lot."

"K, nighty night, girlfriend."

I walk in, stripping my clothes off, and start the usual routine of showering and eating on the couch, getting sleepy to old reruns. The shower must have awoken Jake; he appears looking more adorable and bulkier than I remember. My heart softens when I see him and he smiles at me. I bend my head as he lowers to kiss my forehead. His voice is sleepy. "Hey, sweets, when did you get home? Why didn't you wake me up?"

I am too tired to answer, so I show him the blankets and he curls up with me and we both fall asleep to the sounds of *Mama's Family* playing on the tube.

In the morning I wake up to Jake frantically shaking me. "Wake up for work, Shane. Shaney, wake up," and in my sleepy haze it comes to me that I still haven't told him about Stein's.

A huge argument erupts, and he orders me to go there and beg for my job back. "What the fuck do you expect me to do, Shane? Seriously, you can't have it all."

"Jesus, Jake, I am doing the best I can. I work, I go to school, how much more can I do? I wasn't the one off for two weeks shooting innocent animals with my friends."

He walks away to ready himself for work. I feel badly about snapping at him, and in general feel very guilty and follow him to the bedroom, where he's sitting on the bed, face cupped in his hands. "Jake?"

He utters in barely a whisper, "Shane, I don't want to do this with you. I just got home and I don't want to fight." He reaches for me as I move closer, sitting beside him on the bed, mentally settling back into my own reality of home. He kisses my cheek and smiles at me. This has become unfamiliar territory, and I'm trying to hide my nerves because all I can think of is Sebastian. He moves down my neck, kissing me again and again, finally reaching my pants. I squeeze my legs together and he looks at me funny, so I loosen them enough for my pants to come off. I lie there on my back, his torso between my legs, as he penetrates me, and I wait for it to end. I've forgotten what he feels like inside me, and the difference between his and Sebastian's touch is black-and-white. A teardrop rolls from the corner of my eye, and I turn my head to the covers to soak it up. I close my eyes tight, still waiting, and he sighs loudly, giving me the cue that he came. It's over. He pulls his penis out from inside me and rolls over to standing position, heading for the shower. No snuggling, smooching, or post-sex hugging. I'm just a hole with a body attached, disguised as a wife.

I want to run for the door, start Hope, and drive to Sebastian's, heart in hand, and beg him to be with me. I miss him so much it's making me sick, and thinking that being home with Jake will change that is just plain naive. I grab a pill from my purse but it slips between my trembling fingers back into the abyss of my dark, messy bag. I'm elbow deep in purse litter, trying to find an oblong little pill that's in there somewhere. I hear the shower still running, so I'm not worried about Jake catching me as I sift through the papers and bizarre tidbits I toss inside but never clean out. I come across an unrecognizable shape, not the normal oddly shaped crap I generally feel, so I pull it out for closer examination. Aha, I see the pill sitting right below it and grab that, too, chomping the little bastard between my molars. Looking more closely, my heart flutters when I see the birthday paper with toy trucks that Sebastian and I used yesterday. Did I forget to give him one of the presents?

Just then, Jake walks in, startling me. I place the curious little surprise back inside the safety of my purse and direct my attention to him. "What's wrong? You okay?"

"Oh, nothing. I dropped some Tylenol at the bottom of my purse and was trying to find it when you walked in, so you just scared me, that's all."

"Oh, okay. Since you're home this morning, would you mind unloading the meat and getting it ready to freeze? Oh, and we really need some groceries. Do you have any last checks from Stein's or tips from last night that you could use? I have a shit ton of laundry to do, too. Can you help me out? I'm doing a double tonight to try and catch up."

It's already starting. I want to crawl into a cave and cry for Sebastian to rescue me. "Um, sure, I will do my best, but I'm at the bar tonight, and Dave's being a nutbag, so I need to keep an eye on him. Last night he brought a sixteen-year-old girl in there."

"He's a sick fuck, isn't he?"

"It's fine, Eddie brought her home."

"I bet he did."

"Whatever, Jake, he's a good guy."

He ignores me and pulls on his boots and points to the meat in a cooler in the kitchen. He shouts bye, and with the sweet slam of the door, I take to the couch and pull out the little mystery box.

I'm nervous to open it, and still not sure how it got there, but even the thought of Sebastian hiding it from me is just a reminder of how sweet he is. I take a few deep breaths, stare at it like a blooming poppy, and grab a glass of water. I need this one last piece of him to stick with me all day, so I can drag the feeling out as long as possible. I gently unwrap each piece of carefully placed tape, thinking of him touching it, and hold it up to my nose to see if I can smell him. Underneath the toy-paper garnish is a small decorative box that I remember passing by at the dollar store. I open it carefully, then close it immediately, pinching my finger on the cheap hinge. I take more deep breaths, but this time they're rapid, and I open the box again, pushing against the couch cushions. I cannot believe what he did. Inside are the most incredibly beautiful turquoise blue Paraiba tourmaline stud earrings set in a presumably platinum scroll design with screw-back posts for safe wearing. They are the same stones that were supposed to be made into cuff links, except they're the most stunning earrings, all for me. I hold them against my bulging heart and read the tiny crumpled note inside. "For our time at the ocean! Oh, sorry . . . I used one of my own dollars. SLK."

I want to jump in the car and thank him in person for the most beautiful gift in the world. Never mind that not in my wildest dreams did I think I would ever own or have the ability to wear real Paraiba tourmalines. I wash my hands, making sure the box is a safe distance away from the sink, and take each stud out, shakily placing them in my ears, screwing the posts tight. I look in the mirror at my glassy eyes filling with tears, then back to the beautiful blue earrings, and think of the ocean and Sebastian and everything that came with our time together. But my face and mood change when I think of Jake and what he'll say about new jewelry. I know him, and he will take notice and no doubt inquire about them. I remove each perfectly created stone from God out of my ear and wrap them individually in tissue paper and place them inside the bottle with my pills, where I know they'll be safe. Someday I hope to wear them for Sebastian, and the thought of a someday has me beaming inside. It can't be goodbye, it can't.

I have so much extra nervous and excitable energy. I start cleaning the house, preparing the clothes for the Laundromat, and pack my book to read while I wait. I'm in adrenaline mode and can barely relax, I'm so happy.

I arrive home with our clean clothes, but I'm still in manic mode. I walk into the kitchen to get a drink for my pill, and there it is, the cooler. The still-dripping carcasses with patches of fur and bone attached are overflowing out the sides. I put more ice on top to hide the sight, but it just makes the wet blood pink. I cannot contribute to the slaughter of wild animals or, for that matter, any animals, not after reading this book.

I spend all day in a nervous state busying myself to waste time, all the while hoping and praying that Sebastian has called or texted, but nothing. Now that Jake's home, and since we share the cell, I worry what would happen if he were to call. I know he won't, and it kills me.

The night is here and I am grateful for more busywork to keep me distracted, and the bar is the cure. Back home after a long night, I walk in the door, ready to strip the smoky clothes from my body, when Jake starts screaming at me.

"Why didn't you do this, Shane? What the fuck?" He rises up from the kitchen stool, pointing to the cooler that's leaked the bloody pink water all over the floor. I start to gag, but he won't tolerate my aversion and scolds me like a child. "It's been like this all fucking day and now I'm not sure it's good anymore. How do you expect us to eat this if it goes bad? Seriously, Shane, what were you thinking? Where is your head at?"

I'm quick to defend, because being yelled at after coming home to the life I hate is exactly what's going to send me over the edge. "I was thinking, I don't want to eat meat, that's what I was thinking!"

His temper flares. "You love venison, what is wrong with you? It's like you're a whole different person. I don't fucking understand you, Shane."

"It's cruel, and I don't want any part of it. If you want to eat blood, bones, and flesh, then you can put it away yourself!"

"You've been hanging out with your mother way too much, you've gone fucking bananas just like she is."

I sprint to the shower, stubbing my toe on the couch, but the pain escapes me because I've stopped feeling. I choke on my tears and sob hysterically into the shower's drain. It's all hitting me, and I realize at the end of the day, this is my life. This is who I am, where I'm from, and acceptance is my only salvation.

I walk into the bedroom draped in a towel, hiding my body from Jake, who's sitting on the edge of the bed waiting to talk. I want to get dressed, but he's trying to apologize, and I can't listen if he's going to stare at my naked self. I grab clothes and change in the bathroom, but he follows me, waiting outside the door. "Shane, I'm sorry. This is the healthiest meat we can eat and also the cheapest. You're not crazy, I'm sorry I said that and I'm sorry I compared you to your mother. Please, Shaney, talk to me."

I ignore his incessant pleas for forgiveness and hide my face in the wet towel. I go to bed, fall asleep, and in the morning awake to his arms wrapped around me.

Same Ol' Life

The weeks go by, and I work harder and harder to become more comfortable in my routine. I keep busy during the day living normally, cleaning, working, and reminiscing about Sebastian. I get by but feel ill with sadness and guilt most days and don't enjoy anything like I used to. Eddie does his best to cheer me up with his specialty soups. My mother and Simone try to call but I ignore them, too. I miss everything about my fantastical life where I felt like a princess. I miss Sebastian so much and deeply crave him, but it's also Simone, Vivi, Sam, Good, and even my crazy mother who I can't stop thinking about. I can't focus on anything but the rote days of work, sleep, and trying to accept Jake and our monotonous life, and it's making me miserable.

My depression deepens when I receive a letter stating I'm bordering on getting an incomplete and risking graduation if I don't finish my final assignment. I call the professor and beg him for a month's extension. He spouts nonsensical crap about living and working like Nietzsche.

"Shane, my fragile little weed, I will give you two more weeks, no more. I know you work like a hog for slop, so I will allow you the extra hours to make your paper unique and untraditional. I don't want some fag hag story or something dumb about your place as a woman in society. I want raw fucking words. Don't waste my time, and get it to me by the ninth." He hangs up before I can thank him. I appreciate his gesture but also realize I have nothing to write about. I think about Sebastian and following his family, particularly his mother's rise to fortune, and how it could be the exact excuse I need to visit him. I think about how it would feel to pop by his company's headquarters and get a glimpse of his father or him knee-deep in work at a desk with hair floppy and wearing a designer suit. I decide that it's wrong and not how I want to see him, and it makes me feel empty again. I'm sick missing him, and any excuse is worth writing a thousand pages, but getting to see him that way isn't the right way.

I leave the apartment to buy groceries and drive, shop, and return home still pondering what to write. I can't worry about it anymore and need to get ready for work, a long-ass double. Jake's waking up from the night shift and wandering around the apartment, ruffling drawers and tossing cushions looking for a pair of pants he can't find. "Where are they, Shane? They couldn't have just disappeared? Maybe you left them when you did the laundry? You should stop by and see if they have them. I need them for work. I can't buy another pair, the company doesn't reimburse anything anymore."

His annoying on-and-on drawl about the pants is getting to me. "Okay, fine, what do they look like?"

"They have patches on the knees for protection and are a brown cargo, you know the kind I wear for work. Just stop by and check, it's right on your way, and you probably lost them anyhow."

I've stopped listening because his voice and accusatory tone is getting on my nerves. It's another reminder that I've settled back into my regular life and it into me. I'm unhappy, unsatisfied, and so, so sad inside. I can barely eat, and all I think about from the moment I wake until I finally fall sleep is the incredible man I met and the experiences he gave me. I dream about living happily ever after with Sebastian on a boat, free from the world of laundry, dishes, and cargo pants.

I walk from the shower, drying off, when Jake yells to me in a nasty tone, "Who's Sebastian?"

I gulp so hard, I think I've swallowed my tongue. I wonder if he's called? I don't know if I'm walking into a knife to my heart or one to my throat. I can only imagine how Jake would dismember me like a Winchester shot deer if he found out about us. A screechy pre-pubescent "Why?" ekes from my mouth.

"Because it's written on this hundred-dollar bill you have in the drawer, plus some other shit I don't recognize."

Oh my gosh, the money, he found it. "Why are you going through my drawers?"

"Looking for my pants, and seriously, Shane, you have hundred-dollar bills and you are asking me why?"

I impress myself with how quickly I think on my toes. "I got them from work as an advance from Dave, when you were away. We were so broke and I didn't think Hope was going to make it. If I had to bring her to a mechanic, I would be able to pay for it."

"What does that scumbag expect in return?"

"Nothing, Jake. I will give it back. Who do you think I am? You said Don could help fix her anyhow, but she's been getting by. Give me the money, I'll bring it back tonight." His suspicion and temper are rising and I try to grab the bills from his hands.

"Why does it have words all over it? This is fucked-up, Shane, and you know it. What happened when I was gone?"

"I have no clue, I didn't even notice. I just took the cash and put it away. Honestly, Jake, I'd forgotten all about it because I didn't need it."

"We don't need his goddamn charity, Shane. You better not have gotten on your knees for that bastard. I will kill you both if you did."

I can't even believe my ears. I wonder why Jake's being so testy and mean. Even with all his faults, it's still unlike him. "You're disgusting! Have some respect for your fucking wife! If you hadn't left, none of this would have happened and Hope wouldn't buck and sputter every time she starts. A real husband would have gotten it fixed." He walks away from me, ignoring the rebuttal because he knows I'm right. I tuck the money deep in my purse, knowing I can't give it back to Dave, who knows nothing about it.

Work is normal, with most of my regulars sitting around getting drunk off of cheap beer. Billy Joel songs blare from the cracked jukebox and a couple sways to the tunes. Eddie surprises me with a big salad with extra cucumbers, knowing I've sworn off meat, and explains that he specially ordered them for me. That sweetheart of a man listens to every single thing I say, no matter how unimportant.

My nerves are shot, I can still barely eat, so I sneak the leftovers near where I hide my purse, while he's busy cooking for someone else. I finish up the very long day and night, and when I finally get home, Jake's already sleeping. I strip at the door, removing the smoky clothes, pop a pill, take a shower, and watch reruns on the couch. This is my life.

I wake up to another morning with my husband and another fight behind us. I scramble some eggs and toast for Jake, telling him about my plans for the day. He's working a double today and won't be home until tomorrow morning.

"Okay, no problem. I will clean up and stop by the Laundromat to see about your shorts."

"They're pants! Pants, Shane, not shorts. When do you think you will get another job? This housemaid stuff is great, but what we need more than clean laundry and dishes is money. Shit's going to get tough on both of us."

I'm overcome with a sick desire to slap him across the face. *Whack!* I can picture my hand smacking his skin with a loud thump and running for cover. "I need to finish my paper and then I will have my degree and can try to get a better one. Or I may go back to school. I don't know yet, I'm not really sure what I want to do."

"Are you serious, school again? We can't keep this up with you working only at night and me doing doubles. Who knows how long it will stay busy at the casket place. I can't rely on that. You need to figure this out."

"People are going to keep dying, Jake, of course you'll stay busy. Do you need someone to die to keep the numbers up? We can start with our trashy neighbors. And I did a double yesterday, what the hell?"

He doesn't appreciate the sarcasm and finishes by saying "Figure it out before it gets too hard not to." He leaves, allowing another ridiculous fight to fizzle and die. I don't have the anger in me to keep this going, only sadness. I can only think he's acting like this because of how I'm feeling? I keep thinking about the money Sebastian put into the bank and how independent I could be on my own. Money is strength, and with it, I could leave Jake. I'm depressed, living the life my mother and I lived without even a house to show for it. I can't become my mother! I throw the dirty pan in the sink, get myself ready, and head out to see her.

I'm almost to her house when a nervous feeling comes over me. Even being closer to Sebastian than I was only a couple of hours ago has my heart pounding wildly with anxiety. I stop for gas, and take deep breaths the whole rest of the ride. I pull into the driveway of the shack, which looks even more run-down than a couple weeks ago. Vivi's here and alone, playing with dirt by the mailbox. "Hey, sweetie pie, whatcha doing out here?" She doesn't say a word and gives me a bzzzzzz with her finger and returns to the dirt. "Hey, want to go for a ride?"

She looks at me with her bright green eyes and frazzled,

unkempt hair, and says, "Good?"

I smile wide to match her excitement. "Yes, honey, Good. We can take a trip to visit him. Maybe pick up some treats, too?" I walk inside the house, Vivi attached to my hand, and my mother scatters papers for me not to see. "What's all that?"

"Oh, nothing, sweetie. Just some documents, that's all. Nothing for my cuckoo monster to worry about. Hey, I'm so glad you're here. What a surprise! Do you want me to make you something to eat?" She opens the fridge as she talks. She's in a frantic, nervous state so I decide not to bring up the fact that Vivi was playing in mud next to speeding cars.

"No, I'm not hungry. Actually, I want to take Vivi out for lunch or ice cream. Is that okay?"

"Oh, sure. I think Esmerelda or Simone will be back later, but I'm not sure what time. Simone will be so happy you're spending time with her, so yes, of course, go ahead. Do you need some money?"

"Nope, I got it."

I open the rear door and Vivi climbs in the back, where I buckle her up. "Let's stop by the store and get Sam and Good some lunch, what do you say?" She nods her head yes and we drive off. I tell her that Good wasn't feeling well but that he will feel a lot better when he sees her. She smiles wide, and her little legs move rapidly in anticipation. When we arrive at the grocery store, she takes off her seatbelt and nearly leaps from the backseat.

Inside, we pick out a few different types of bones and toys for Good and I put together a to-go container at the salad bar for Sam, Vivi, and I to share. We make our way to the deli counter and order turkey for Good, and Vivi eats a piece of free cheese that is offered. We take all the snacks and treats, pile back in the car, and head to her favorite place.

My heart flutters the closer we get, and I barely hold it together as we pass the marina. I drive slowly and can faintly see there's a different security guard checking IDs, and I proceed to tell Vivi about a friend of mine who lives there. She doesn't seem interested or impressed by the story and keeps kicking the seat with her excited little legs, knowing we're getting close to Good.

A few minutes later, we approach the bank on the right side of the street and it immediately reminds me of Sebastian, and for a moment I think about stopping. It ties Sebastian and I together, and the nostalgia and memories of him hold me captive. I wonder if I would see him there? The mere possibility of seeing Sebastian doing something as mundane as a deposit has me reaching in my purse and smearing on lipstick and pulling a U-turn to check. Vivi kicks my seat so hard, it pushes me forward and I yell inadvertently, "What the—Vivi, you can't do that, it scared me."

She is thoroughly annoyed by the change of plans, and when I look back to her, she kicks the seat again.

"Sweetie, remember, sometimes Good comes here to get his sandwich. We can check here first and if he's not here, then we will keep going to the beach."

I find the perfect spot in front of the bank and I'm convinced it's fate, an omen that we are meant to be here right now. Vivi waits for the car door to open and walks inside the bank with me. The manager looks up from behind his desk and glass cage, flagging me down with a wave of his hand.

"Excuse me, Ms. Lacy, we should talk."

I look around to make sure he is talking to me. "Um, okay?"

His voice is secretively low and he urges us to follow him. He talks as we walk in a line. "Accounts with your size deposits can be invested in other ways. I would be a fool if I didn't offer to guide you in a more profitable direction. Would you like to talk with one of our financial advisors?"

I start to laugh. "You're joking, right?"

"Do you have your accounting book with you?"

"No, I didn't want that thing."

"Okay, no problem at all, Ms. Lacy. I will get the balance for you and see if our head financier is available to meet."

"No, please don't. I'm not comfortable with any services, and honestly, I can't afford that kind of advice, but the balance would be great." He looks deflated walking away. When he comes back, he hands me a new, clean book to preview. I almost pee myself when I see $105,000.00 neatly typed across the paper booklet. I must be raising my eyebrow in wonky fashion, because he looks just as surprised as I am at my reaction to the amount.

"Does it seem incorrect to you, Ms. Lacy?"

"No, I'm sure it's right. Thank you. Is anyone else on this account?"

He steps back behind his desk and clicks the keys on his computer and says, "No, Ms. Lacy, only you. Again, we are happy to help with anything else you need, and if you change your mind about meeting with an advisor, it's free of charge."

I laugh again. "No, that's fine. I don't expect any further deposits, but thank you."

"Okay, good day then, Ms. Lacy."

We're walking out of the bank and Vivi tugs on my hand. In the commotion of learning I'm super rich, I'd almost forgotten about Good. I go back in and find the manager.

"Excuse me, this may sound strange, but I was wondering if you've seen the man with the dog? Um, I've seen you give him a sandwich before?"

He looks at me with an odd look, not the kind, helpful one from just a few seconds earlier. "How can I help you with that?"

"I was just wondering what his story was? It seemed odd giving a man and his dog a grinder, that's all?"

"I'm not at liberty to share our customers' information or their connections to this bank. He's a loyal customer, as are you, Ms. Lacy, and that is all I can comment. Good day." He walks away without looking back.

Within a minute or two I went from the VIP customer being offered fancy banking services to my questions surrounding Sam seeming like kryptonite to the bank's manager. Vivi is tugging so hard on my hand, I can't ignore her any longer. "Okay, okay, we're going." I tuck the blue book deep in my purse and we are on our way.

We drive farther down the busy downtown street to find a not-so-great parking spot but snag it anyway. We walk a distance to the secluded beach, and Vivi drops her bag of groceries as Good appears out of nowhere and tackles her little frame to the sand. "Good, it's you, boy, it's you." My heart lifts and the first real smile in a long time comes across my face as they roll around in the white sand.

Sam comes from under his home's flap and sees me standing there, admiring the two playing like long-lost siblings on the beach.

"What are you doing here? Why is the girl here?"

"Oh, I brought food. I was hoping we could have lunch?"

He seems aggravated, but that's his usual response, so I don't pay any mind to it, mostly because I'm selfishly so happy to be here with all of them. He huffs a few words under his breath and disappears under the flap. I sit down, nestling my butt into the sand, and watch the two run around like maniacs, chasing each other while Good slobbers all over Vivi and she returns for more.

Sam yells for me to help him and hands me a blanket. He carries a basket of silverware and plates onto the beach. "There better not be any steak. You know I don't eat that shit. Do you have my book?"

"Oh my goodness, no, I forgot it. I'm so sorry. I will bring it next time. I can try and come tomorrow or the next day, is that okay?"

"Yeah, that's fine, but I need it returned to my library, okay? And come alone, no kid."

"No problem at all."

We set up our plates and spread the bag of food out on the

blanket. I show Sam all the bones Vivi chose for Good. He takes one and throws it far onto the beach. Vivi and Good ignore it, continuing to run around, playing one-sided tag with each other. She gets close to him and he runs the other way, then he gets close and she runs, and she giggles hard the whole time. We open our containers, eat, and talk. He thanks me for the medicine. "I assume it was you who dropped it off. I couldn't figure who else, even though I thought you would return my book at the same time." I glare in a joking manner and he continues. "It helped, Shane. We are doing better."

I smile at his honesty and willingness to share it with me. Feeling like he's in a chatty mood, I inquire about that night, trying to wrangle more details out of him about the connection to Sebastian, but he changes the subject. I don't pursue it, though all I want to do is talk about Sebastian and reminisce about him, no matter what the topic.

We spend a couple of hours sitting on the blanket, talking and watching the most beautiful view and happiest kid and dog play on the beach, soaked, dirty, laughing, and barking. I ask Sam about his connection to the bank, but he doesn't answer and asks only what they said. "They didn't say anything. He wouldn't speak to me about you. He just said you were a loyal customer, no more, no less."

"Good, then. Let's leave it at that."

"Can you tell me what that means? I don't understand. Sebastian told me you were a bad man. You told me *he* was a bad man. Then the bank is secretive about you, and I saw you with those sandwiches. Why does the bank give you sandwiches? Who are you, Sam?"

"Shane, I'm no one. That's why I'm here. Because I'm a nobody. A long time ago I guess I was someone, but that soul was sold and my body remains." His voice and posture droop, and I feel bad prying, but I need to know more. "Some other time, I will tell you. Just not today, okay? Today isn't a good day. Maybe when you bring me back the book I can tell you a little more."

I'm excited about the opportunity to share more conversations with the mysterious man named Sam and thank him. Feeling satisfied, I try not to be outwardly happy and instead tell him I need to gather Vivi to go home. He appreciates the talking and calls for his dog with a whistle and a clap. The dog flies up the sand like a bullet with a fast turn as Sam points to the flap, and he runs inside. Vivi tries to follow him but Sam asserts loudly, "NO!"

She starts to cry and he says, "It's time to go, Shane. Thank you for lunch." He looks at Vivi, whose tears are flowing, and obviously feeling guilty for yelling says in a much softer tone, "Good needs to take a nap now."

She nods her head, understanding, and wipes the tears with the back of her hand.

We leave the beach carrying the leftover trash. Upon reaching the street, I remember why I wanted to come here. "Hold on, sweetie, just one second." I dig in my purse and run as fast as I can to the shack, yelling for Sam. He comes out of the flap, grumbling in annoyance. "Sam, please take this. I want you to have it."

He laughs an absurd laugh and says, "I don't want your money, Shane. I don't need it. Is that what you think of me?"

I push harder, but he refuses again. I look back to see Vivi wandering aimlessly. She couldn't care less about what I'm doing. "Okay, fine. Can you please just hold on to it for me, or use it. Whatever you want. Thank you. I have to go. Please, Sam. I can't have it in my house." I hand him the four leftover bills I have and a couple twenty's and ten's, all from the original five hundred that Sebastian gave me. The rest of the money, in particular the hundred that read "For," I'd spent at the grocery store buying our lunch and bones for Good. I race off to find Vivi, who's already started the trek alone back to the car.

We drive past the marina for the second time today, and all I can think of is the fortune sitting in the bank. If I only had pennies left, I would keep the account open, knowing it connects me to Sebastian. I fantasize about the opportunities this literally affords me and about leaving Jake and starting a new life. I could start over alone, or we could stay together and I could buy us both a house to live in, or at least a mobile home. I could help my mother with her medical bills. Or I could run back to Sebastian, handing him all the money in that little blue book, and return to right where we left off. My mind is rampant, thinking hard about what to do next.

I drop Vivi at my mother's house and ask her to say hello to Simone for me. I rush out the door and surprisingly make it to work with a few minutes to spare. For a brief moment, I sit in my parked car, wondering if I should even go in, but tell myself to keep acting normal until I decide what to do.

Burned

I barely make it over the door's threshold when Ye Ol pulls me aside. "Shaney, I was contacted by the private detective working on the Vet's case. There's footage from a surveillance camera and it shows exactly what happened."

My first thought is *Thank goodness, now we know something,* but his face quickly drops and he grabs me tight, hugging hard, and I instinctively squeeze back. It's a comforting but odd feeling, like a grandpa hug, because I've never been this close to a regular before. "Oh my gosh, what happened? Please tell me he didn't suffer. . . . I'm sorry, I am just so worried. What did you see?"

We release at the same time and he reaches for his Brooks Brothers cuffed jacket, wiping one prominent tear from his left eye. "He gave up, Shaney, he gave in and gave up." My eyebrow won't stay down, and he continues to explain, trying to soften the hurt because we both know there's comfort in truth no matter how awful it is. "I saw the video myself or I wouldn't believe it. He must have

been planning his suicide for who knows how long, or I don't know
what he was thinking, but he just couldn't live so sadly anymore." He
takes a deep breath and continues. "It showed him deliberately making himself fall in front of a speeding car. It was so obvious he did it
on purpose. He wanted to die. Fucking pride on this guy, keeping it
all to himself." He stops for a second and stares at me for a response,
but before I can absorb the words that are coming from his mouth I
selfishly think about myself. Our pain is different, but pain is pain is
pain. I understand. I want to give up, too.

"It's like the beginning of a bad joke, Shane. A lawyer, the PI,
and the police all call me in at once. Apparently, he made me exec-
utor of his estate and left instructions in a huge envelope at his
house. The police took me there. I had never been inside, and you
don't even want to know what he was living like. It was enough to
make any sane man mad. The charred walls, the mold from where
rain poured in through the burned and missing parts of the home,
and the most horrific odors you could ever imagine. It was death in
there. It was what I think hell must smell and feel like." He takes
another deep breath—we both do—and he tells me about the envelope and his will. "You know the Vet, crazy bastard with his stub-
born ways. He left strict instructions that I have to follow to a T,
his words. He wants his house torn down and said for the land to
never be built on again. He said his wife liked the spring and all the
flowers it brought, and he'd rather have dogs pissing on tulips than
for someone to cover his family's grave with some bullshit new construction. He also wanted me to leave all his cash, almost $230,000,
to whoever hit him. He wanted them to know he appreciated what
they did for him and to never feel guilty about it. He said to tell them
guilt will eat you alive from the inside out. He made it very clear that
everyone involved in any ridiculous investigation was to know he did
it, not the person who hit him, and that the money was for their family. Oddly enough, I just found out it was a single mother who lives
in the projects, near you I think. She had gone to the convenience

store to get her daughter cough medicine and had left her alone in her crib, not wanting to wake her. She was rushing back home when it happened. She cried and cried until I read the letter he left for her explaining his wishes."

"I cannot believe this. To go out that way is so strange. I cannot even imagine. I feel awful thinking back that he was probably planning his demise this whole time while we were all going along, not knowing a thing. I guess I just miss him. Your guys' bantering made my nights."

"Yeah, I miss him, too. I think he wanted it to hurt. I think he wanted to physically feel it. He'd hidden behind those drinks and charred walls for so long, he just wanted to feel again, even if it was for the last time. He thought he deserved it."

He looks up to the ceiling to hold back another tear from falling. "He left me one last note in the bottom of the envelope along with a wacky scavenger hunt to find this old suitcase." He points to a leather case with tarnished buckles and writing on the side sitting on the floor next to his feet. I realize it's military issued but don't say anything, and he pulls out a piece of scrap paper with ripped edges from inside his blazer. "Doc, thanks for being my friend. You kept me going for a good while. Don't forget to give Shane that suitcase money because you tip like shit and she's gonna need it when she finally realizes she's better than that piece-of-shit bar. Thanks for taking care of everything. Fuck off for now, friend, it's time to be with my family. —Vet"

I smile in admiration of him and his thoughtfulness in mentioning and even thinking of me in such a progressive way, like I deserve more. I feel nauseous just knowing I've already disappointed him because I'm still here. Ye Ol snickers after reading it to me and asks if we can keep the seat next to him empty for a little while. I nod and walk around the bar, grabbing Eddie's fancy sharp knife from the kitchen, and carve "Vet's only" into the seat of the wooden barstool. When I come back from returning the knife and putting my purse away in the back room, Ye Ol's regular stool is empty, and the only thing remaining is the suitcase with the note where the Vet should be sitting.

It's a really slow night, so I ask a shockingly alert Dave if we can close early. There's no need to say "last call" for an empty bar, but I whisper it for fun and go through my usual routine of OCD behaviors.

The Power to Destroy

I drive home to find that annoying little fucker is in my parking spot again. This guy thinks he's such a hotshot with his Mustang that he can park wherever he feels like it. Thug life isn't for me. I want to go back to the yacht. In fact, I want to turn around and drive straight there, but I don't. The lot is full and I don't feel like searching, so I drive all the way around back to an empty space. I walk up the dark staircase to the apartment stairs through the back of the complex.

I approach the door and can hear a girl laughing along with Jake's voice. I stand outside for a moment listening but cannot believe my ears. I'm in utter shock. I open the door to find Simone sitting next to Jake without an inch between them and her hand resting on his thigh. He flings her hand off his leg and she rises to hug me.

"What the fuck, Simone?"

"Holy shit, Shane, you're home, hi. It's not what you think."

"Shut up, Jake, you don't get to speak!"

She is so excruciatingly beautiful. Standing next to her makes me feel even more ugly and worthless than I already am. Her blond, wispy hair is long, hugging her breasts, her black skirt is tight, showing off her five-foot legs with designer ankle boots, and glossy red lipstick plumps her pouty lips. She's invading my privacy, risking Jake's innocence, and ruining my chance to escape this place.

"That's hilarious, Shane, you are going to give him a hard time after all you've done? Chill out, we are just talking. I was catching him up on all that we've been up to. I can't believe how little you've told him. I mean, come on, remember this couch?"

"What is going on, Shane? What is she talking about? I fucking knew you've been different, I just couldn't figure out why. Now thanks to your friend, I know you're hiding something." He rises with conviction and vengeance in his eyes and comes toward me forcefully but I block myself with the still-open door.

"I didn't do anything. Don't listen to her."

"You didn't do anything? That's hilarious, Shane. I guess I never really knew you, did I? You spoiled bitch, I gave you everything. I married you because I loved you despite who you were and what you did."

Simone laughs as Jake's words tear me apart. I drop to my knees and start bawling. Did she tell him? How could he know? Simone is smiling. The admission of guilt barely leaves my lips. "You told him?"

She doesn't answer, but Jake says, "I already knew what you did back in high school, everyone talks, but I loved you anyhow, that's why I married you. I helped you escape your supposed hellish life back home or was that all made up, too? What else are you lying about? Tell me, Shane, what the fuck else are you lying about?" I tuck my knees between my arms and cry into my sleeve.

"Yeah, Shane, what else are you lying about?"

"Simone, what the fuck! Why are you doing this? Leave me alone. Go. Leave us alone! I'm done! You win. You are right, Simone, but I bet you already knew that. I can't handle your Richie lifestyle. I'm not like you, I never have been, so stop fucking torturing me. I am sorry, so, so sorry, but you already know this, so just please leave us alone. Why can't you just leave me alone?"

Jake keeps turning his head from me to Simone, confused by the dialogue. "Will someone tell me what the fuck is going on?

Shane, what exactly did you do? Someone tell me!" He's shouting at me and a mist of his spit lands on my face and there's a bang on the wall, our neighbors alerting us to knock it off.

"Oh c'mon, Shane, you can't change who you really are, so why don't you tell him. Tell your husband who loves you so much what you've actually been up to. I didn't want to ruin the surprise, but I can."

I want to slap her across the face, but I can't muster the courage because I am so heartbroken by her revenge. Jake is fuming and his breathing is erratic. "Jake, please. I'm sorry, it's nothing." His nose is dripping and his eyes are bloodshot. "I didn't do anything. Simone, tell him I didn't do anything." She doesn't say a word and smiles on one side of her face. "Tell him, Simone, tell him I didn't do anything," I repeat.

"Of course not, Jake, she's a good girl, just like me," she says both sarcastically and cockily.

He stares at both of us, silent, breathing heavily. He yells in a gritty tone I've never heard before and the corners of his mouth froth. "WHAT DID YOU DO, SHANE? I FUCKING KNEW IT! TELL ME NOW!"

I look to Simone again, expecting our long friendship may somehow protect me, but she snickers and says, "Oh, Sugar, come clean. It was only fucking. Sebastian doesn't want you, he owed me a favor, that's all, nothing more." My heart drops and I'm dry heaving air from my gut.

"Sebastian! The fucking guy's name on the money, you fucked him? Oh my God, oh my God."

I ignore Jake, who is now pacing back and forth, and look at Simone's pleased self. "Why?"

"Oh c'mon, Shane, like you don't know why. Oh, Jake, I tasted her, too. She seems to get around when you're not around." I stare at her eyes, looking for answers, but her smile turns to a laugh.

"Look at me, you whore!" I turn my head and tears are flowing down Jake's face and he's pointing his hunting rifle directly at me with one eye staring down the barrel. Simone makes a frantic move in front of me, blocking his aim, and he waves the gun, wiping his salted face and trying to regain his sight. "Shane, look at me."

I rise from the floor with Simone covering my frame, grab my purse, and run out the door and down the apartment building stairs, escaping both of them. I'm crying and shaking and sprinting as fast as I can and trip on the gravel, skinning my knee, but keep going. I'm going so fast that my body slams into Hope's door, and like her name, we are finally free. I fly down the highway with my foot to the floor but she still putters along to her own tune. I need Corvette fast and she's tinkering about. It's 2:00 a.m. and I have no idea where I'm going or what I'm doing. I can't think, I just keep pressing the pedal to the car's carpeted floor. I don't know if Simone is dead for being an accomplice to what I've done or if Jake's following me. I can only assume she's told him everything now or is trying to fuck him just because she can. I want to head for the bank, withdraw my money, and leave this awful fucking nightmare for good.

I nearly hit the lamppost at my mother's house, then I fly inside, almost hyperventilating and barely able to speak. Rob's at the door, gut hanging out over his sweats' waistband and a gun at his side. My knees give out and I throw up all over the entry and a little on Rob's filthy bare feet.

"What the fuck, Shane?"

I wipe vomit from my face, and my legs curl beneath me. I cry into my hands, and the smell of puke and tears overwhelms me.

"Oh my goodness, Rob, put that away. Go. Go on now. It's my Shaney." My mother tries pulling me up, but my legs won't work and her weak arms barely budge my shocked body. She pulls on me hard, huffing aloud, drags me through the vomit, and closes the door. I lay my head onto the filthy floor, sobbing into the carpet. I've completely given up and can't breathe. The smells and textures are

all-consuming, and it makes me sob harder. The chicken is pecking at the bits of puke around me, but I can't muster the strength
to push it away. I can hear my mother in the distance, asking Rob
if I'm hurt and if she should call an ambulance. "I think I'm gonna
call 911."

"Mother, Mother!" I try and utter her name, but it's muffled
and soundless from the carpet. "I'm not hurt."

She runs over to me and grabs my arms, dragging me to the
bathroom. I don't want to leave this dirty floor. I deserve it and
more, Jake is right. I'm catatonic, lying here defeated, staring
into space and listening to the panic in my mother's voice and
the absence of it in Rob's. I think she's left, but just then she
bends down and slides a pillow under my head. She's brought
one for herself, too. The smell of the pillow is a mix of sour and
musty that's all too familiar to her bedroom and this house. I
don't care, because it's who I am and where I'm from. Those
smells are me.

We lie together on the bathroom floor and she rubs my back,
which is uncharacteristic and caring, making me even more aware
of the severity of my situation. We don't say anything for a long
time and I can feel myself calming. "Why? Why is my life like this?
How did I fuck it up so much?"

"First of all, I didn't raise you to speak that kind of language.
But yes, I know, sweetheart, this wasn't the plan I had for you
either. It wasn't the plan for either of us." She continues rubbing
my back and in a sad tone says, "I've always wanted more for us.
The Lacys don't give up. We will get what's owed to us. I've waited
too long and given up too much not to."

I'm not sure what she's referring to, but it could be any number
of delusions. I nod off from exhaustion to the sound of her voice.
As I drift, loose thoughts enter my mind of what happened tonight,
and I worry about Simone or even Jake showing up. I worry that
my car is out front and can be seen from the street. I should find

out where Rob put his gun in case we need it, so I can access it easily. I wonder if Jake will kill me? So what if he does kill me, I deserve it. So what if she tells him, I deserve the punishment, all of it. God, I fucking miss Sebastian. I hate this. I want to be back on the boat where life was bliss.

Eventually, exhaustion overcomes paranoia and my mind races with fleeting thoughts until I must have dozed off.

I'm awakened by Rob scooping me up from the bathroom floor, but I lie limp in his arms as he lowers me into the bathtub and walks away. I put my head on the porcelain side, dust and pink scum rubbing against my hair, and stare at the toilet. I wonder where the mushroom went?

My mother breaks my concentration, saying, "Come on, my little padiddle hopper, let me help you." She shuts the door with the side of her slipper, peeling the vomit-stained clothes off my body. She pulls me up with all her might, accompanied by aching noises. She starts the shower, flushing freezing-cold water onto my half-naked body, and begins pouring shampoo all over me. I'm wide-awake from my self-induced pity coma, and the cold, fresh water snaps me into reality. I take the bottle from her and close the plastic curtain. "Sweetie, are you sure you can do it alone? I will wait right here in case you need me."

I mutter into the water, "I don't have the energy to talk or do anything."

"Okay, pumpkin pie, then I will just leave a towel for you, and when you're ready I'll be waiting right here."

I can only take so much cold water on my already numb body. I turn it off, shaking the towel, and a spider flies across the room. I learned the lesson of hiding biting insects very young and have never stopped shaking towels. My mother laughs and says, "That's Henry" and hands me an old pair of pajama bottoms and a yellow-stained tee. I shake them, too, and dust flies wildly, making me cough and hack in the crowded bathroom.

She grabs my hand and I follow her tiny body to the couch, where she's cleared a section of junk, piling it onto the floor. There's a semi-clean-looking sheet covering the area along with a pillow and puffy dog blanket. They both smell terrible, but I bury my face in them and my mother tucks me in like the child I am.

Human Trap

I wake in the morning to a wave of panic. Yesterday's events are stirring like thick soup through my mind, and anxiety has me jumping off the couch to find my mother. She's in the kitchen with cardboard packages of processed foods spread over the whole counter, and I can see she's making another heart attack breakfast for Rob. She startles when she sees me and drops the frozen sausage on the floor. Looking around and seeing only me, she wipes the hairy fuzz onto her apron and throws the sausage in the pan, shrugging her shoulders and whispering, "It's for Rob, who cares."

I can barely crack a smile, even though I want to. I walk away, looking for my purse—or, rather, my pills. "Mother, where's my purse? Have you seen it?"

"Oh, yes, of course. I put it near the couch, sweetheart. You were sleeping and had left it in the doorway." Rob's chair rests against the couch but his eyes never leave the television, so I sneak a pill from my purse and carry it in my cheek until I reach the kitchen.

All I can think about is Sebastian. I'm relieved to see that neither Simone nor my newly psychotic husband have shown up. I can barely swallow the coffee my mother's put out for me because my throat is swollen with nervousness. To calm myself and relieve some anxiety, I shower, freeing my body of the stench of the couch. I ask my mother if I may borrow one of her now-vintage sundresses. From the base of the closet she pulls a cute, fitted yellow dress just like the one I'd seen in one of her photos from when she was so strikingly beautiful. I find some very old makeup under the sink from when I was a teenager to blot the shine from my nose, and smear on the reliable lipstick from my purse. I prop my hair into a loose ponytail with wispy bangs and throw on a pair of borrowed red wedges, another treasure from the closet. I walk to my mother's mirror in the bedroom to check my appearance. Convincing myself that this pathetic look could pass for vintage chic, I head out the door. Before exiting, I yell to my mother that I'm checking on something, but no one responds or is listening. I get into Hope, start her up, and the engine shakes with vibrations, making steering tricky as I drive into the city and toward the marina.

I crank the radio to distract my wild thoughts. Anxiety surrounding what I might say, how I should say it, and how to act around him has me paranoid and nervous. My heart's pounding, my hands are sweaty and trembling, and my foot's tapping the gas like a drum.

I arrive at the marina after what feels like an eternity, and my nerves are so shot, I'm scared to pull in. I turn the music down, take one last deep breath, and pull slowly to the gate. Hope rattles loudly, so I throw her in neutral. A guard I don't recognize asks for ID, and I explain to him that I'm here to see Sebastian Kane and have stayed here with him and point to the yacht. He acts exhausted, explaining how he doesn't care if I'm there to see the Pope, he needs identification in order for me to pass through. I point again to the largest yacht in the distance and explain that

I'm here to see Sebastian. He shakes his head, looking back at the monitor. Feeling frustrated with his ignorance but knowing he's doing his job, I reach to the passenger seat to grab my license, but my purse isn't there. I put Hope in park and twist over the seat, searching for my bag. "Shit, shit, shit!"

"Is there a problem, ma'am?"

"Yes, I don't have my purse. I must have forgotten it. Fuck, I don't have my phone, either. Please, if you could just call him. Please, can you just—"

He stops me from speaking any further with a wave of his hand and orders me to turn around and exit the "private property" or come back with a license and permission to be there. Just as tears fill my eyes in defeat, Hector, who's sporting giant blue headphones and tending to the landscaping, sees my car and waves to me. The guard reluctantly opens the gate, and I push my luck, saying, "See, I wasn't lying."

"Ma'am, I can stop the gate from opening if you'd like, since I still don't have your ID." I smile, say thank you, drive through the gates, and park.

Before approaching the magnificent boat, I check the mirror, adjust my mother's vintage dress for optimal cleavage, and walk with a facade of confidence to the pier where the yacht is docked.

For the first time, I have to knock on his door. The waves of fear and anxiety on my way here don't compare to this very moment as I wait for a response. Finally, the door opens. A little blond boy, maybe Vivi's age, answers with a smile and says, "Hi."

"Hello," I say back, looking behind me to ensure I'm at the right spot. "Um, excuse me if I am at the wrong yacht, but I am looking for Sebastian."

He steps back inside, waving me in with his little fingers. "Mom, someone's here."

I'm literally shaking as he shouts to a woman. Oh my fucking word. I think of his mother's description and her Spanish heritage and pray that's who will appear. I'm going to vomit again. I begin to walk out, but she arrives, and she is certainly not Spanish. She's tall, her skin very pale, and her hair red. A female staff member I recognize is behind her, busying the boy. I wave to the girl, but when she sees me she takes the child out of sight.

"Hi, may I help you?"

"Hi, I'm sorry to interrupt. I'm looking for Sebastian. Sebastian Kane."

"I see. Well, there's nobody here by that name."

"I just saw a girl I know from this ship. She was with the boy. She worked here on this boat for Sebastian, the owner." I point to the marble floors and salt water overflows from my eyeballs.

"I'm really sorry. There's no one here by that name, nor is he the owner."

I turn around, speechless, and with my head in my hands run sobbing to the car.

The lady yells with a kind plea to her voice. "Miss, please stop!"

My feet brake out of instinct and tears glide from my face. I whisper, "What?"

"I can call the gate and check the roster. It was rented for a few weeks and that's why we are using it now instead of a couple weeks ago when we wanted to."

I turn around to hear more clearly. She continues to shout, but I start to move closer. "I will see who my husband lent it to. He does that sometimes. Just hold right there, I will call for you. We will track down this Sebastian, don't you worry."

The sound of his name nauseates me. Droplets fall off my chin, hitting the wood, and pool next to my feet.

I arrive back at the door, and the little boy, with his caring hands, touches my knee, telling me to have a seat. "It's okay, miss. I get really sad sometimes, too."

I can taste the tears in my watering mouth and look everywhere in sight to try and spot the staff, but no one is around. Everything and nothing is familiar. The little boy pats my shoulder, one thump at a time, until his mother returns. With a sad face, she says, "I'm so sorry, honey. The only name on the roster is Barron."

"Excuse me? Barron?"

"Yes, that's what they said. My husband works so much so we don't get to enjoy it as often as we'd like, so he occasionally lends it to his elite clients or friends. Does that name mean something to you? Did you know Bill Barron? Actually that does seem odd, because I heard he had passed? Maybe it was that sweet daughter of his? I'm not really sure, but when my husband returns I could find out for you?"

I feel faint and must look as much because the kind lady calls a staff member with a button I never noticed and asks her to bring water immediately. When I come to, the red-haired woman is sitting on the floor with me.

"Are you okay? Is there someone I can call for you?"

"I don't know. I don't know anything."

"It's okay, honey, take your time. I've had bad days and bad boyfriends, we all have."

I barely piece logical words together for a response when I see more staff scattered about, but they look different than Sebastian's, and I don't see the girl. "May I ask if this is your regular staff? I saw a girl I know, but everyone else looks different."

"Yes, they are. We took them to the Caribbean on our sailboat last month. Most of our guests bring their own staff. Maybe it was Louisa who looked familiar to you? She stayed in town to handle some things for my husband and has always been a regular on our boat. Do you want me to get her for you? Oh, and I'm Kay, by the way, and this is my son, Lucas."

I look around, reminiscing about every square inch of paradise that Sebastian and I had celebrated here, and back to the kind woman before me. I stand up quickly, but feeling lightheaded again, I nearly fall down.

"Here, sit here. It's okay."

She shoos Lucas away with a wave of her hand. I sit down, embarrassed and stunned, and apologize.

"Would you like to call someone?"

I think about that question for a moment and contemplate who in this world I would call, and start to chuckle. She looks nervous, but I'm thinking of my mother and her insane words of wisdom. "Shane, get mad, not sad." I say yes and thank her when she returns with a cell phone. She offers me privacy, exiting the entryway. I've memorized Sebastian's number because saving it on Jake's phone would have been disastrous. I dial and wait for the rings.

My hands are shaking so much, I can barely hold the phone to my ear. He answers and I nearly lose my grip from my clammy fingers, but I keep thinking of my mother's words.

"Hello?"

My voice quivers into the phone. "Sebastian?"

"Yes, this is Sebastian."

"It's Shane."

"Hi, Sugar, how are you?" He sounds jovial and overall excited, throwing me off guard.

"Not well, actually. I'm at the marina. Um, yeah, I'm standing inside your yacht."

"Oh." He pauses, sighing into the phone. "I really should go, Shane. I am so sorry you went there, and I would love to explain, but I can't."

"NO! You don't get to hang up on me. I need to know what the fuck is going on?" The woman comes from around the corner, shaking her head at me, and I nod mine in apology for swearing. "I was going to give up everything for you. I don't understand. They are telling me the boat was rented in Simone's name or her father's, I really don't know? Nothing makes sense to me. I found Simone with Jake at my apartment. Is there some kind of sick coercion going on? I can't deal with this and took off to my mother's house.

Honestly, I have no idea where Simone is or what is happening. She was acting all nuts and laughing with amusement when I saw her. I left her and Jake, who found out about us and pulled out his rifle. Then I come here to see you and tell you how I want to leave him and I find out it's a big fucking lie. I don't get it. Please help me understand. I am breaking down here, what is happening? Is this what you Richies do, you guys fuck with people's lives and it's fun?" My voice breaks from weakness, and tears drench kind Kay's phone.

"Shane, I am so sorry. I didn't mean to hurt you. It wasn't supposed to happen this way. I am so sorry, I really am."

"If that's true, then why did you?"

His voice softens to almost a shy whisper. "Shane, I was helping out a friend. I never expected what happened between us to get so serious. I am very sorry, this is hard for me, too." I swallow up his words, clinging to them, knowing he does care for me.

"I don't understand, why did you lie to me? How could you pretend like that? How could you toy with me? Please, Sebastian, make me understand. I was falling for you like an idiot because I had no idea that everyone was scheming behind my back. I feel so fucking stupid and hurt and . . . just plain stupid."

"Shane, don't take this the wrong way, but I need to be honest with you."

"I would love some fucking honesty!" Kay comes around the corner and puts her finger to her lips, glaring at me to knock it off. I look the other way.

"Shane, I am so sorry, I really am. But seriously, look at your life. You're married and a pretty serious drug addict and, given the opportunity, prostituted yourself without a whole lot of nudging. You stepped perfectly into the traps that were set for you."

My legs weaken and my knees buckle from the pain. I can barely talk with the giant lump in my throat. "Why? How? Who?"

"The same reason anyone does anything. Money, revenge, I

suppose. It was supposed to be a simple favor, just a couple of dates, and honestly I never thought it would go where it did. It was supposed to be fun, and it was. You are incredible in so many ways and will always mean something to me. You got the money, right? Simone wanted you to have it."

I'm starting to hyperventilate, and breathing is no longer automatic. I can't comprehend the words he is saying. Who is this guy? He isn't the Sebastian I know. "A favor? A favor for what?"

"You know what, I am so sorry, Sugar, I can tell you are really upset, and it was never my intention to hurt you. It was something from a long time ago. Honestly, I should never have gotten in the middle of it. Really, Shane, I don't want to say any more because I don't know that much about it other than she wanted to get back at you for something, her dad maybe?"

"Tell me this, Sebastian, was anything real? All the experiences, the amazing adventures, the last day together, not even the earrings?"

"Um . . . no, Shane." He pauses, presumably with some guilt, and speaks with a less confident tone. "I think she had a friend there, someone from school or something? She arranged it. She arranged everything."

I drop the phone and buckle to the floor. I try to take deep breaths, but I can't breathe. I'm devastated. I keep thinking about the words he said, "She arranged everything . . . traps were set for me." What does he mean? My mind rushes to Sam and I think of the connection to Sebastian and suddenly feel that I am the center of a much larger conspiracy. I place my hands on the ground and push myself up, leaving through the same door I had entered only a couple of weeks before. It's no longer a mystical place where romance and dreams are made, it's just a gas-guzzling boat for the pretentious lying fucks it houses. I want to thank kind Kay for her help, but I leave the phone and run to my car.

Inside, I wipe the stupid lipstick off on my arm, feeling

ridiculous for putting it on. I'm so embarrassed. Hector must know, and he ducks his head in pity as I back up. I know now that he never meant to wave me in, he was only saying hello. I am leaving the marina, and before I do, I glance back to the boat, still trying to comprehend what just happened. There it is, maybe there the whole time: "Sweet Lady Kay" written in beautiful navy and gold font across the back. I had never even noticed it before. SLK, the blue waxed stamps on Sebastian's notes. What a fucking coincidence. I wonder if Simone planned that, too. I feel like dying.

I drive about one block down the road and pull into a shopping mall to compose myself. I rest my forehead against the ripped steering wheel and sob snot and tears into it. They pour like a waterfall onto my bare knees and I watch them stream down my leg, eventually absorbing into the carpet. I wipe my face on my collar that stinks of my mother's house and pull my shit together to go inside the grinder shop. I hide my face, asking to use their bathroom. The high school boy behind the counter looks too freaked to say anything.

I rinse my face, rubbing my pink lips with hand soap, trying to get every part of my ridiculous attempt to impress off of me. The mirror reveals exactly what I expected, the pathetic girl that I am: red, blotchy, and always sad. My mother's voice echoes through my head again, and her lifelong mantra of "get mad, not sad" shifts from being about Sebastian to Simone. I wonder if she taught her as well, and I start to cry, knowing now I was the "get mad" part of her sick plan.

I startle myself peeling out onto the street. I crush a pill between my teeth and smear fresh lipstick back on my lips in an attempt to portray confidence. I arrive at the Ritz, and the gentleman waves hello, treating me as joyfully as before. He looks concerned when he sees my distraught face, and I smile weakly. I enter the elevator, my hands and body shaking, and I cannot face the man controlling it. We arrive at the top floor, and without thinking too much I pound on Simone's door over and over, screaming for her. She doesn't answer. I look back at the elevator, expecting it to be closed, but the bellman is still there, waiting and watching my frantic scene. I want to scream at him, too, but the weakling already looks terrified and probably nervous that he's next. He fingers me back to the elevator, and like a defeated dog I listen and we ride all the way back to the lobby floor. I ask the front desk, sharing identification, and receive verbal confirmation from a familiar bellman that she's not there. "Ms. Barron checked out a few days ago, stating that she will no longer be requiring the residence." My stomach drops. Of course she doesn't, she's too smart to be anywhere I can find her. Why did she do this to me? I cannot stop wondering why? I thank them a final time and get into my car, determined to get answers. If she's mad, I'm fucking angry. I need to find her! I need answers! Who am I kidding? I'm so weak. Tears stream down my face. Sad is so much easier.

The True Puppet Master

I turn off the music, concentrating on the questions I'm creating in my head to find out why she's done this to me. The entire drive I play them over and over in my mind, trying to solve the puzzle, but I can't figure it out. Just as I turn the corner to my mother's house, I know at this very moment that I will receive my answers. I hit the gas hard, grip the wheel, and almost lose control with Hope balancing on two wheels as I turn into my mother's drive, slamming into the rear of that cunt's BMW.

I can hear arguing from the driveway. "I told you that it's different now. The attorneys are all over me about this, you have to let it go."

I can't believe this. None of it makes sense. I burst open the front door to four stunned faces.

"Are you fucking kidding me, Simone? You goddamn crazy bitch. How could you do this to me?" More automatic tears flood my eyes.

"Knock it off, Shane. Cut the language, okay, sweetie?"

"No fucking way, Mother. I need to know what's going on. She set me up! Was it because of your father? I'm so very sorry for that, you know this, and I would take it back if I could. I've regretted doing that every day since it happened, but I did it for you, Simone, for fucking YOU!" I'm screaming at the top of my lungs, my heart is pounding out of my chest, and froth is foaming from the corners of my mouth. I can see now that Simone is as red as a beet and keeps shaking her head while glaring at my mother.

"I know."

"That's not good enough, Simone! You have always had everything and I've always had nothing. So now you take what little bit of dignity I have left. Make me look like a whore, set me up, try to pay me off. Is this a game to you? What, you're bored or hurt or who knows what so you decide to fuck with a friend from the past? You're sick, Simone, do you understand? You are sick! What the fuck do you want from me? I moved away for you. I left home and got married because of you! Anything I could do to forget you and what happened is what I did, all for you. That's not enough? You need to fuck with my ridiculously pathetic life, too?" I look at my mother and yell at them both. "I have lived every single day just as poor as the way I was raised, working as hard as I can, going to school, filling my days with nonsense just to forget what happened. I left everything—you, my mother, my reputation, my whole life. I left it all because of you. And then you pull this bullshit on me. You have no fucking idea what it was like living here. You were born with a silver spoon while I was choking on a filthy plastic one."

"That's enough, Shane, cut it out and leave her alone."

"No, Mother, I won't leave her alone! She just twisted and turned my life upside down. She manipulated it so she could fuck me over, just the way she thinks I fucked her over." Simone doesn't say anything. I want to slap the words out of her mouth, but she remains stoic and silent. This has been building for years and I'm about to explode. My mind and body cannot take one more second of lies, manipulation, or heartache. I walk over and with all my strength push her right in the chest. She falls backward, catching herself on the side of Rob's empty chair.

My mother charges and slaps me across the face. I stand there paralyzed, and more tears cascade down my cheeks. I cannot understand what is happening. "Come on, you fucking bitch, speak! Why did you do this to me? Tell me. Speak, Simone, speak!" I run toward her again, ready to take her down, but my mother grabs me and I fling her frail body away without any effort. "You are going to tell me why. Do you understand?" I am on top of her with my hands over her supple neck.

"I'm sorry. I know it was wrong. You don't understand, I didn't know anything then, but I do now." She looks at Aggie with her fierce blue eyes and purses her quivering lips.

"That's it? You're sorry? You think I ruined your life, so you want to ruin mine—*again*?"

"You're right, I set you up. I wanted you to have the money, but I was hurt. I am sorry, I truly am. But you don't understand, everything else wasn't me."

"Fuck you, Simone."

"Shane, it wasn't me." She is gurgling through her words and I loosen my grip to hear.

Whack! My mother slaps me across the back of the head, screaming bloody murder. "Get off of her! You're going to kill her!"

I rise up from on top of her, then collapse to the floor, hunched over and sobbing into my hands.

My mother and Simone are both crying, too. "I am not doing this anymore, I am not lying to her anymore. TELL HER! Tell her or I am going to!" Simone screams at my mother.

I pull my hands from my face. Simone stands up with her beautiful posture, straight as a dancer, wipes the tears from her perfect face, and hisses in a low, even voice to my mother, "I am done. Do you hear me? I am done with your games. I am finished, just the way my father was done with you."

My mother stands perfectly still, staring her down. I have never seen this look from her before. She responds in a stern, old hag–like voice, "Watch it, young lady."

"Watch what? What else can I watch? I've lost everything. I have no father, no family, and now no Shane. So you tell me, what else can I possibly lose? You've taken it all. Do you want me, too? Do you want blood, is that what you want? Wasn't taking my father from me enough? Now you want more? Tell her, Aggie, tell her what you did! Tell her it was you on those visiting logs. Yeah, I know about them. And yeah, I know it was you who made sure he went to jail. You didn't give a shit about Shane or me, you only cared about *you*, locking him up all for yourself, you sick fuck. Don't worry, Aggie, you will pay for what you did. I visited him a couple days before you killed him and he told me everything."

My mother's whole body and face are twitching like a bomb ready to explode as I glance from her to Simone, trying to understand.

"Don't worry, Aggie, you will pay for what you did. My attorneys found out everything, so now tell us what you did!"

I'm hyperventilating, and my brain can't handle what's unfolding before me.

My mother slaps Simone across the face and walks away, unconcerned that she will retaliate. Simone screams the loudest roar I've ever heard from any woman. "You better tell her, Agnes. You've fucked us both up. Is money that important to you? Is it? I trusted you. I trusted you this whole time, only to learn that you were planning this all along. You've ruined her. You've ruined us all."

"Was getting back at my father that important? You've ruined her."

My mother spins her head like in *The Exorcist* and says in that same gravelly tone, "No, Simone, *you've* ruined her."

"Are you serious, Agnes? I cannot believe you're this sick. You fucking starved yourself almost to death just to get her here, you fucking crazy bitch. But guess what, Aggie. I've got news for you, he is not Shane's father. The attorneys will show you, so stop waiting for a paycheck that you are never going to get. Or maybe the money never mattered to you, did it? It was all about your sick obsessions and getting close to my father."

Simone kneels down, and her beautiful body shines like a living star on the filthy floor. She cups her face in her hands, crying into them. "Make it stop. Please make it stop."

I crouch down to hear her, but she lies down with her head against her arm, curling up into the carpet. Vivi approaches, but I shoo her away with my hand and ask her to keep coloring. Surprisingly, Rob realizes the severity of our family situation and calls Vivi into the kitchen. I whisper into her ear, "Simone, what is going on? I don't understand." She doesn't answer me. I shake her shoulder lightly, but she continues to sob. I turn to my mother, who has lit a cigarette and turned her attention to Vivi and Rob's snacks. "Mother?"

"Yes, sweetie?"

"What the hell is happening? Tell me what Simone means? What is everyone keeping from me? Please tell me. Someone needs to tell me. What is she talking about—is that how you got Rob to call me, because you stopped eating? That's how you *got* me here? For what? What is she talking about? Why would Bill Barron be my father? Did you orchestrate all of this to get me here? Why would you do that?"

"Ask Simone, honey. She needs to give you what's rightfully yours. I have been trying your whole life to get you what you deserve, but she is holding it back."

Simone rises like a newborn antelope and screams at the top of her lungs. "I've only been holding it back because of you!" She yells at my mother with extreme force and scratchiness in her voice. "You don't deserve it, Agnes, you aren't getting one fucking penny, or anything else. I've made sure of it. You are the most selfishly driven, deranged woman I have ever known and I hate you! Stop using your own daughter for revenge for an affair you had twenty-three years ago."

"Watch your mouth, Simone!"

"No, I won't. It's time. I'm sick of this shit. You were a townie, good enough to fuck but not to marry. You need to get over it, get over him. He fucking hated you! He would talk about you and your disgusting low-class manners. That's why we always had Shane with us, to keep her away from you. You were trash then and are trash now. The only thing you didn't count on is raising a daughter who isn't. She's not like you."

Simone looks at me and back at my mother and says, "Your sick fuck of a mother, if you could even call her that, came up with the idea to get you paid off and get my money sooner so I could keep him away from the baby, but it was all just for her to get closer to him. I was a stupid, trusting teenager and knew he would kill me when he found out about Vienne. She wasn't supposed to happen, but she did. I needed access to my trust fund to get away from him, so your mother thought we could use you without any harm. She took advantage of you, we both did. We used you. I am so sorry, I thought it would go a different way, but your mother made sure it didn't. She took him from me, and after he died she needed you here to get your DNA for the paternity claim she filed, and this whole time we've been waiting—" Simone's voice is hiccupping from loss of breath after what she's been holding in. "He wasn't supposed to die, Shane. He wasn't supposed to fucking die. He's all I had. I blamed you for taking him away, but when I saw my father, he confirmed it was your mother's obsessed plan. She visited him every day, did you know that? He must have told her I had been there and then she fucking killed him. She thought I had stayed away to protect Vienne, but I had to see him. I loved him. He was all I had, and I knew no matter what, he'd tell me the truth."

From the floor she faces Aggie and with a defeated look and swollen eyes says, "The lawyers showed me the logs. I didn't know what it meant or who she was until I saw the name. She used her old nickname, the one my dad told me about a long time ago. Belle. Fucking Belle. You aren't beautiful Aggie, you are dark and evil. You couldn't stand that he saw me and told me everything. Your cover was blown, you crazy fucking bitch. You know he told me he only agreed to see you because he was so bored and you fed his ego like sugar to the brain, bringing him gifts and treats and hand jobs under the table."

My mother's eyes light up. "He talked about me? What did he say? He told you what he used to call me?"

"You fucking killed him, Aggie. I know you did. Just admit it, you killed him. You must have poisoned him or something. Don't worry, I have all the money in the world to find out how. Was it your homemade desserts? Tell me, you fucking psycho!"

Simone collapses again with her face in her arms. "She took him from both of us," she sobs. "He's not your father, he's ours." She turns her head to Vivi, who is ignoring us, drinking a juice box in the kitchen.

I stare at my mother, who is throwing crumbs to the chicken. "Mother!" I scream at her.

"Yes, honey?"

"What did you do?"

"I needed you back here, Shane, so I could get you what was yours. When I saw you with Jake, I knew you weren't happy, and I made you that way. It was time to get you home and get you the inheritance you deserved. I tried for years, but he wouldn't talk to me. He had his big shot lawyers bury me in letters and threats. Finally, thanks to you, he was a caged bird and all mine. I don't believe he's not your father."

Simone lifts her head up and lets out a guttural cry before burying her face again.

"Girls, relax, you both waited long enough. So did I, and he wasn't budging. He wouldn't take responsibility for Shane, and I needed to make sure my daughter would finally be happy, that all of us would finally be happy and free. You too, Simone. I was beautiful, you know. He loved me when I was young. You don't know it, but Bill Barron and I were quite the couple."

"Oh my God, you're insane. It all makes sense, you really are batshit crazy!"

"Look and listen to me. I am a strong Lacy woman and I kept my mouth shut waiting for Bill to help us and accept his paternity. I begged, threatened, really tried everything to get his attention back to us, and every time I did, he would just send another team of attorneys after me. I didn't fit the kind of woman that he would have a child with. I wasn't from a wealthy family, I didn't play piano or go to prep schools. I was a girl from this town and he was a Barron, big deal. I did have one thing going, that I was fucking gorgeous, and he couldn't resist me. When I was eighteen and got pregnant he tried to claim it wasn't his and wanted you aborted exactly like he would have done to Vivi if I hadn't stepped in. You're welcome, Simone. Apparently, Lacy women are good enough to fuck but not have children with. He's the bastard, not me! I kept quiet, knowing someday I would get us what we deserve. I would get you the life Simone had. I wanted it all for you, Shane. We were supposed to have it all. He made me think he would give it to us, and I believed him. He took everything from me, my looks, my daughter, my life, and left us with nothing. I was always there for him, always and to the end. So when you were just old enough, I told Simone that I was afraid he was doing things to you like I knew he did to young girls, but that you'd never admit to it. But I knew you'd do anything for Simone, so we made up the Amanda story for you to go to the police with. I convinced her he'd never get put in jail, with all his money and power, even though I was going to make sure he was put away for life. She was so protective of you and also so jealous of his attention, and with her pregnant, I knew she'd believe it and go along, knowing it would release all financial power to her. She was like putty in my hands. It was so easy. I always wanted you girls to be together and be with me. Everything was always for the two of you, my Barron girls. You two just needed a little nudge, no big deal."

Simone rises up from her trance-like state, fuming, and stands tall, full of confidence. Her lips are quivering and her eyes squinted. She runs to her orange Birkin bag and shakily pulls out a paper, then walks over to my mother, shoving it in her face.

"She's not a fucking Barron, Aggie. Never was, never will be. You aren't and Shane definitely is not. Here's the fucking proof you've been waiting for, you crazy bitch. I've known for weeks that he wasn't her father and wanted you both to suffer. You took him from me, you both took him from me! You took Vivi from her father, he was ours. He loved being inside me, not you, Aggie, me! He wanted me! He always wanted to be with me, not you, not ever. But you knew that already and had to take him away. You wanted him for yourself, you fucking psycho." She drops to her knees, crying, and the paper drifts to the floor. I pick up the paternity results and it's clear that he isn't my dad—though I never thought he was.

"This is sick, Simone. He raped you. Vivi's grandfather is her father. It's immoral and disgusting and horrible."

She glares at me and my mother and with a deep voice says, "He kept it in the family and kept our name clean. The Barrons will never be tainted with outside blood, just as I would have done if Vivi was a boy, and every day I wish that she was. It's our legacy, no one else's. We are Barrons, and I love my father for what he did."

I gag on the vomit sliding up from my esophagus and in a zombie-like state walk down the hall to the dirty bathroom, where I glide down the web-covered wall and curl up in a ball. I view a troop of fungi growing alongside the tub, reliving all the lies I've grown up with and everything that's transpired until this very moment. I don't know what's true and who's real and who isn't. I want to grab Vivi, the only innocent being in this house, and run. The door opens and my mother enters with a glass of water and wet paper towels. I can't move from the fetal position. I don't want to see her, talk to her, or face another new reality—the truth. The only words to come are of regret and reflection. I ask her, "Mother, you caused all of this? I didn't have to leave? I didn't have to marry Jake? Why? Why?"

She rubs my back, and my skin cells retract from the touch of her bony, cold fingers. "I was trying to get you what you deserve. What kind of mother would that make me if I didn't? We were supposed to be Barrons, sweetie."

Tears fall from the corner of my eye and soak into the floor. My mind and body are numb. I lie there on the dirty floor and she sits down next to me, lamely trying to soothe my pain, but I have nothing left. I want to die here. All this suffering and filth as a child because of my mother's obsession over this man and her belief he was my father, all for money and the fantasy of living happily ever after as a Barron. My mother is the most manipulative woman I have ever known.

"I'm sorry, pumpkin pie. You can see now she was the puppet master. She orchestrated and controlled all of us, even the lawyers, and strung this along out of her own malfeasance."

"Don't call me that. Don't call me anything, because you did this. You both set me up, humiliated me, made me suffer. I cannot believe what happened to my life because of the plans you made. Your only job as a mother was to protect me, but instead you've gotten me to where we are right now—you destroyed lives."

She puts her head on her bony knees, speaking into them. "I know you're confused, honey. I did this for us. All this time, he had me so twisted in my head, making me believe different things, but seeing him helpless and desperate to see me each day . . . I can't believe that test. Stupid science isn't true. I'm sorry, Shaney, things just went a little crazy. I was so worried about what would happen and I wanted everyone to know I had a Barron child. I loved him. He loved me. I know he did. We made you together."

"Mother, leave, I can't—" A loud crash interrupts me. Something fell hard. It startles both of us upright and I'm snapped from my self-loathing trance. We both leave the bathroom, and as I turn the corner toward the bedroom, I see one of my turquoise tourmaline earrings shining bright on the linoleum floor. I bend to pick it up, scanning for the other one as I enter the bedroom, and accidentally kick my empty pill bottle, which bounces off the closet door and lands near a spilled bottle of Poland Springs water. I look over and see Simone lying on the ground. My mother gasps behind me, grabbing the doorframe, and my knees buckle beneath my body. I crawl toward Simone and yell and shake her, but she just stares blankly at me with her blueberry eyes. "Call the fucking ambulance!" I cradle her head in my lap and wipe the foam and froth from her red-glossed mouth. "What are you doing, Mother? Call them!" I gently lay Simone's head on the carpet and get up to do it myself, but my mother blocks the doorframe, holding me back with all her might. I'm screaming that I can't lose her but my mother covers my mouth and nose. Her frail frame shakes as she smothers me. Rob appears in the doorway. "I was outside with Vivi—" My mother lets go and theatrically screams as I gasp for air. "Oh, Simone, oh, you beautiful angel." But he can see she's already passed. My mother steps over her limp body and reaches for Vivi's hand. "C'mon, my sweet Barron child, you're all mine now." Vivi reaches to buzz my finger as my mother tears her away. She calmly turns to Rob and tells him to call for an ambulance.

I give a statement to the police and paramedics and have to explain that the pills are mine, which leads to a multitude of other questions. They ask why we didn't call sooner, saying overdoses take more than a few minutes. My mother answers with black in her soul. "I need to make Vivi some lunch. Goodbye, Shane. You can leave now."

I Think We're All Going to Be Good

I t took almost a year to make a deal and for everything to settle down. I gave the authorities and lawyers testimony that my pills caused Simone's overdose but that it was my mother's negligence and force that prevented me from calling for help, leading to her death. The autopsy revealed that Simone had also been taking Valium, which isn't surprising in retrospect, but it made for a deadly combination. The exhumation of William Barron's remains proved he was poisoned with a homemade cake on the day of my mother's last visit, and she was charged with homicide as well as obstruction of justice for using a fake ID when visiting. She was separately charged with negligent homicide for not allowing anyone to intervene and help stop Simone's suicide via overdose. Due to the persistence of Barron's lawyers, she was sentenced to seven consecutive life sentences for both crimes and will likely live out the rest of her life in the state hospital for the criminally insane. The hospital isn't far from the one she sent me to as a child—a vacation insurance would pay for, but this time the taxpayers are footing the bill.

She is under strict supervision at the hospital, but her manipulative nature couldn't help her from trying to contact the tabloids, telling people she was William Barron's estranged lover, and starting an etiquette class for the other criminally insane individuals. She appeared happy (and overweight) when they interviewed her about him, and she made it on to all the smut television shows.

The divorce between Jake and I was granted without his asking for anything except to never see me again. Sadly, I agreed to his wishes. I even saw Sebastian a few times and he tried to talk to me. Though there was a part of me that desired him deeply, I never allowed myself to succumb to those feelings, nor did I let him know the truth I came to find out about his past—that would stay between Sam, Professor Nutcase, and myself. Vivi and her mother were my only true loves. I realized I was prostituting myself long before I met Sebastian; it just took him exposing it for me to see it was true. Mr. Barron, pills, doctors, Jake, Simone, Sebastian—all of it to be something I was not.

Martin, Simone's companion, turned out to be a true grieving boyfriend who never paid her for sex or anything else and reached out to me several times to talk about her. I entertained the meetings a couple of times to keep the connection between Simone and I alive, but it was ultimately too painful to keep seeing him— and unconsciously associating him with Sebastian, whom I still secretly yearned for.

I spent a lot of time detoxifying my system of the pills that inevitably changed my fate. I made a promise to Vivi and to myself to never take another one again. During that time, I finally received my associate's degree and worked closely with Simone's team of lawyers, who granted me full guardianship and, eventually, adoption. Since Vivi was the sole remaining heir but too young to inherit, I worked with lawyers and multiple boards of the Barrons' companies to finalize their estate, eventually selling off the entire empire to start a new beginning and leave the treacherous past behind.

I quit working at the bar so I could concentrate on Vivi and school, but I visit often to say hi to the regulars and have lunch with Eddie, who always makes me some of his incredible (now vegetarian) soup. I kept the best form of normalcy I could for Vivi by also visiting our friends at the beach almost every day. For a while, spending time with Good was the only way I could reach her, and then she would slump back to sadness.

On one visit, we stopped for our usual lunch of chocolate-chip coconut pancakes and bacon for Good, but when we arrived we heard people screaming something about money. When we got closer, we saw some kids holding various bills in different denominations. When I asked to see them, one kid held up a bunch of hundreds, two of them with the words Sebastian had written.

The rest of the beach was littered with thousands of little brown paper bags and loose cash blowing in the wind, polluting the coastline where the waves met the sand. I dropped the food, and in my heart I knew he was gone. I looked to his shack and saw that it had been ransacked. The leather flap had been ripped off and papers were flying everywhere. I shouted to a kid coming out of his house emptyhanded, and he took off down the beach. I wondered to myself if this was a sinister attack or something else? Vivi held up a few of the scattered bags, putting the pieces together in her precious mind, and leaned into my knee, staring into the water. Tiny, quiet tears fell from her sad eyes, and I told her it was all going to be okay. She replied with one word: "Good."

A few seconds later I heard kids yelling and swearing in fear, and we turned around just before Vivi was tackled by her giant furry friend, who knocked her down and kissed her over and over.

"GOOD! It's YOU! That's my good boy. I've got you now." I finally heard her voice more clearly than ever as she whispered sweet words into his floppy ear. "I lost my mommy, and you lost your daddy, so I'm gonna take care of you. Okay, Good?" She hugged him tight, and he followed us to our new home on the beach.

IN EVERY SAM THERE'S A STORY

Submitted by Shane Lacy

Writing 201, Professor Melvin H. Louden

Someone once told me to never trust a man who doesn't eat red meat or has a first name for their last. Granted, that woman is living the rest of her life in a mental institution.

Samuel Clement Robert was born in Hawaii into a prominent military family whose authoritarian father was the first African American captain in the U.S. Navy. Samuel strongly believed in pacifism and fell knee-deep into the peace movement of the 1960s, refusing to join the Vietnam War. Despite his mother's hushed pleas, she and Sam's father both disowned their eldest child, focusing their militant efforts on his younger twin sisters, one who died serving in the war, and one who became a traveling surgeon in the Peace Corps.

The first time I saw Sam, he was being chased by a suit from a very fancy bank who handed him two brown paper bags, one with a sandwich that he immediately fed to his one-eared mongrel of a pit bull (now known as Good), and the other, I later learned, was filled with cash. I eventually discovered that this was part of a much larger conspiracy to cover up some of the wealthiest youths' indiscretions and how they make loyalty fall perfectly in place for them to walk away unscathed.

If you were fortunate enough to be allowed to call him Sam and were invited into his private life, you would find a homeless man with a gruff exterior living in a shack beneath the forgotten part of the city's historic boardwalk, inherited from another wayward woman who also once had a beautiful life but died collecting mice within her tinfoil-lined pockets. He liked to be called a veg-a-fish-a-chick-atarian and only believed in eating *dumb* animals, although he once professed to me that "...all animals are brilliant and people are fucking stupid."

I spent a lot of time trying to earn his trust, but always at a distance, first by bringing him food—which he didn't like and would give to the dog—then by sharing stories (but never too personal) and delicious homemade meals or by borrowing books from his library, finally becoming what I think, or hope, he'd describe as a friend. I don't believe he had any idea the impact he had on me or on the mute child who he allowed to visit at a distance, who would roll around in the sand talking only to his dog, who also harnessed secrets beneath his exterior scars. But that's what made both of them so "Good."

We stopped by often because I found Sam to be interesting and curious, like a puzzle that wants to be solved, but mostly because it was the only thing that brought a smile to that sweet little girl's face or a few words to her lips, whispered into a mangled furry ear. It all ended on the fateful day when she and I showed up unplanned for another visit and found hundreds, maybe thousands, of brown paper bags and cash strewn across the beach, beneath the boardwalk he lived under. Those brown bags from the bank had lined the interior of his home over the years, serving as insulation from the outside and, I believe, as a constant visual reminder of what he sacrificed to be there. The news did not care enough to cover the story—nor would Sam have wanted them to—but I learned from asking others within the homeless community that his drowned body was found washed up a mile or so from his shack.

In the following weeks, the little girl and I cleaned up as much of the mess as we could and began putting Sam's home back in order, setting it up for the next lovely human—a few of his comrades had already come around asking for permission to live there. I felt a special connection to his library, and as I carefully went through each of his books, putting them back where they belonged, I started to come across small slips of paper filled with handwriting. Sam had left behind a journal of sorts, fittingly hidden among the pages of his hundreds of books. I slowly began to piece together the story of his haunted past, most of the clues coming from the books he used as a nightstand next to his bed. I always knew Sam had secrets, but our serendipitous connections—and the heartache they had caused—ran deeper than I imagined.

AFTER THE HIPPY MOVEMENT OF the sixties had run its course, Sam, who was extraordinarily well-read but not formally educated past private high school, found a job working for an extremely wealthy shipping heir whom he coincidentally had attended prep school with. It worked wonderfully for a couple of decades, doing odd jobs and healthily supporting his loving wife and two children, whom he adored and lived for. But he was always having to choose between his own family and that of his employer. He was a dedicated and loyal employee who was always at the mansion to pick the children up and drive them to and from school or wherever they needed to go. He was around their children more than his own, and it began taking a toll on his marriage and family. As his employer's eldest son grew, so did Sam's responsibilities of driving him, his drunk friends, and whatever girls they picked up at parties safely back to their various mansions.

He hadn't taken one sick day in almost forty years, but it was his doting wife who insisted, when Sam was ill one day, that he stay home, and she tried to reach his employer, who was out of town. It was the son who finally agreed to the day off. Sam disagreed with his wife and readied himself anyway, heading out to work while still sick, unbeknownst to the son.

When Sam arrived and found no one home, he busied himself with his regular chores. What he didn't know was that earlier in the day, the son had taken Sam's usual livery, a large black Bentley, to another rich friend's mansion, drinking, snorting, and partying until the cops broke it up. He loaded as many people into the car as would fit, with plans to bring the festivities back home. Only a few streets away from his gated manor, he lost control of the car, slamming into the sidewalk and hitting a seven-year-old girl who was walking the puppy she had just gotten a week earlier on Christmas. Sam heard the crash and commotion and quickly got Sebastian and his friends back to the house and cleaned up the mess. He took the fall for everything in exchange for hush money that would take care of his family for the rest of their lives. There were rumors among the neighbors that it was the son, but they were too scared—or possibly paid off—and no one ever went against the powerful family.

Sam's wife never forgave him. Even if he hadn't killed an innocent child, in her eyes, accepting the blame was just as bad as the act itself. She didn't care about the money or their lawyers' contracts to silence him. What he did went against their family's ethics, and she refused to ever accept him again.

I should have heeded Sam's warning about "the son" who he helped escape responsibility—and likely prison—for his actions and who would later enter my life in the most sinister of ways. My friend was in that car. She held on to the son's secret for years, only to use it when the time was right, after her father had passed away and she was desperate for revenge.

Finding out about what Sam did and the sacrifices he made makes me appreciate even more who he was and what he meant to me. I know he tried to warn me and protect me from the ugly truth—that money and power can buy anything, even silence.

I assume Sam's death was a suicide, but I have no proof. I could let my mind wander and wonder if it was an attack on his life to make sure he stayed quiet. The ties between the powerful passenger who committed suicide, myself, and Sam were loosened. I chose to put the conspiracy theories aside to properly grieve and try to believe he died on his own terms. Like I saw with another old friend who took his own life, when sadness is a constant force in your life, you get to choose when you've had enough.

For a short but very special while, Sam and Good were exactly what that little girl and I needed, and I find comfort watching her smile and speak to that big ugly dog who we are honored to now permanently have in our home wreaking havoc and bringing laughter—and lots and lots of messy sand between the two of them. I never thought that the mysterious man who I grew to adore would influence us in such a divine way. He was the only "father" figure I ever knew. I will never forget the man who gave up everything because he, like me, was torn between two worlds.

ACKNOWLEDGMENTS

To the incredible people of Small Batch Books, whose attentiveness, thoughtfulness, kindness, and, most of all, belief in me have brought this little story to fruition. Thank you so much, Trisha Thompson, Allison Gillis, and Susan Turner! This truly took a village, and I could not have done it without the support of everyone at SBB.

Lily, I am in awe of you every single day, and I cannot wait to see who you become. I am proud of everything you do—even the stuff moms aren't supposed to be proud about, because you are constantly changing and evolving into one magnificently strong and beautiful lady. I love you so much. Remember, mistakes can be magnificent . . . if you learn from them, no regrets! Bold and brave! Oh, and you can't read this until you're at least forty. You'll never look at me the same!

Aggie, I mean Mom, you are truly the epitome of a strong woman, and I admire you more than you will ever know. I recognize and appreciate every single thing you do for Lily and me. You are the definition of a lady, but with a lot of humor, of course. . . . It's the Lacy way!

To all the lovely angels who've passed much too soon. You make me want to hug more, smile more, and tell the gorgeous living souls in my life how important they are for absolutely no reason. Dad, Grumpy, Grand'Mere, Grandma, Grandpa, Uncle Rich, and Cheri, I hope I made you proud.

Printed in the USA
CPSIA information can be obtained
at www.ICGtesting.com
LVHW072359270923
759264LV00001B/69

9 781951 568160